AMID CLOUDS AND BONES

USA TODAY BESTSELLING AUTHOR
ELLA FIELDS

Copyright © 2024 by Ella Fields

All rights reserved.

No part of this book may be reproduced, copied, resold or distributed in any form, or by any electronic or mechanical means, without permission in writing from the author, except for brief quotations within a review.

This book is a work of fiction.

Names, characters, businesses, organizations, places, events and incidents are either the product of the author's imagination or used in a fictitious manner. Any resemblance to actual persons, living or dead is entirely coincidental.

ISBN: 9798329912296

Editor: Jenny Sims, Editing4Indies
Formatting: Stacey Blake, Champagne Book Design
Cover design: Sarah Hansen, Okay Creations

For the villains in every story

PART ONE

WELCOME TO ETHERMORE

ONE

A RAT CRAWLED THROUGH A PILE OF BONES. Footsteps echoed down the stairs, and I hugged my bent knees tighter to my chest. My wet nose pressed against my silk skirts. The gold flowers among the pink and crimson pleats shimmered in the gloom. Bernie would be cross with me. It was my best gown.

Sharp, hurried steps grew closer.

Two cells away from mine, the rat squeaked and darted through the bars, headed for a small hole in the farthest wall of the dungeon.

As Bernie sighed upon finding me, I wished I could escape so easily. "A dungeon is no place for a princess."

"I don't want to be a princess anymore," I said.

It wasn't entirely true.

Being a princess hadn't always been so bad. I didn't have to do any of the things Bernie did. She often said I was lucky because I was allowed to play as much as I liked, as long as I remained out of sight from visitors and during important events. But if it meant escaping the Fae, then I would gladly surrender my title.

Surely, there was someone much better suited for a monster. Someone far braver and bolder. I didn't understand why it had to be me.

Bernie leaned against the bars of my cage, unaffected by the iron.

Her auburn hair had been combed into a tight bun. Ringlets sprouted free from the perfect nest, reaching for her heart-shaped face. Confident, refined, and unflinchingly dedicated to her duty as the future queen of Nephryn, my older sister was everything I wasn't.

But it was something else that caused a seed of resentment to bloom.

Princess Bernadette was human.

Therefore, the favored heir.

Her mother, Queen Agatha, liked to pretend I didn't exist, which suited me fine. When she deigned to acknowledge me, nothing good usually followed.

She was likely going to punish me for this.

Bernie's lips had been painted rose-red. They tilted affectionately as she offered her hand. "Come, butter."

I couldn't remember a time when she hadn't called me that. It made me loathe how my pale yellow hair set me apart from the rest of my family just a tiny bit less.

"I can't." My heart hadn't ceased racing since I woke. I was certain if I was wholly human, it would have failed me. "I don't want to leave you." I rasped, "Why are you making me?"

Her shoulders slumped. "You're not going anywhere today, Mildred," she said. "You won't wed the prince for a very long time."

Not nearly long enough.

My mind twirled. Darkness crawled from the corners of the dungeon toward me. I closed my eyes. "I think I might be sick. Tell Father and Stepmother that I'm unwell."

Bernie laughed, light and airy as if I were merely regaling her with one of my adventures in the woods. "Butter, you are ten years of age. You need not even look at Prince Atakan if you do not want to."

Just hearing his name made my stomach clench.

Having faerie hearing often provided immense entertainment—until I heard things I did not wish to. Murmurs from the staff had been circulating for days. They said the Seelie prince was a monster. That although he wasn't even full grown, he was known as Atakan the heartless.

"All you need to do is come outside and be present for a little while," Bernie said softly. "That's all."

Pondering that, I opened my eyes. "Two minutes?"

Another laugh fractured the darkness that dizzied. "Perhaps a bit longer than that, but I will do my best to make it brief."

I blinked up at her. "Truly?"

"Truly." She smiled and offered her hand again.

I stared at it, chewing my sore lip. I'd gnawed at it too much this morning. "But what if they try to hurt me?"

"No one means you harm, Mildred. Quite the opposite. This is the beginning of a powerful alliance. One that will help make this continent peaceful for centuries to come."

Peaceful.

Before this arrangement had been brought to my attention mere weeks ago, I hadn't known the faerie kingdoms were at war or that the continent of Elaysia was such a dangerous place. Then again, I'd rarely left the castle grounds.

Father and Bernie said I wasn't old enough to accompany them on their journeys. A nicer way of saying what Stepmother never had any issue telling me—that I wasn't to be seen or heard.

So while they were gone, I ventured through the woods, pretending our hounds were magical steeds and logs were bridges that hid dark wonders beneath.

Dark wonders were fun to imagine until they became all too real.

"How will I manage to accomplish that?" I asked, panicked by the mere thought of such ginormous responsibility.

"By simply being your magical, adventurous, and cunning self," Bernadette said, a brow rising. "Now, let us hurry before Mother decides to come searching for you."

Queen Agatha's fury would undoubtedly ensure embarrassment now and punishment later.

I winced and placed my hand in Bernadette's as she stepped forward to tug me from the ground. Atop the spiraling stone stairs of the dungeon, she stopped to fuss with my gown, brushing dust and cobwebs from the skirts.

"You've soiled it dreadfully," she admonished, then exhaled heavily. "There's no time to change, so we'll just hope no one notices."

I trailed her through the sunlit halls.

Beneath the melody of flutes, conversations grew in volume, a compass to our destination. Fresh wildflowers overflowed from vases upon every table and deep windowsill. Wreaths had been strung from doorways and even the terrace awning vines. The colors were all the same. A collection of luminous yellows and light blues.

Our kingdom's royal color was gold and the Seelie faerie kingdom of Ethermore blue.

I stopped to reach for the velvet petals above the door.

Bernie yanked my hand, and I stumbled to her side upon the stone terrace. The sudden warmth of so many bodies momentarily stalled my breathing.

"Just like I told you." Bernie leaned down to whisper in my ear, "Imagine they're all sheep, and you are a wolf cub, untouchable no matter how small."

It worked for only a minute.

These people were not sheep. I tried, but as we passed Stepmother's fancy friends and Father's guards and advisers, I couldn't envision it.

As rows upon rows of gray-and-blue uniforms blocked my view of my beloved gardens, I couldn't see a path forward for a wolf surrounded by immortal monsters.

There were so many of them on the grass. All of them were so big, so tall, I could scarcely see the treetops of the woods beyond their emblem-adorned shoulders.

Before the endless sea of rigid blue stood our father and a tall male whose face was blocked by the sun.

Hearing our approach, Father turned and smiled brightly, though the edges of his mouth appeared to flatten. "Bernadette." He placed a hand on her lower back and grasped my wrist to tug me to his other side. "Here she is." He released me, but his heavy hand fell upon my shoulder, a comfort and a warning to stay put. "My Mildred."

I didn't notice his arrival. Those perfect rows of blue-bedecked men squashing our emerald grass with their bulky boots were still all I could see. Except they were not men at all.

They were Fae.

And I wasn't sure I was breathing as I finally looked up at the tall boy who was not a boy but a faerie prince.

My future husband.

Atakan didn't look at me. Rather, he seemed more interested in a beetle crawling through the grass by his feet.

He squashed it so suddenly that I jumped.

My father's hand firmed on my shoulder. "This is King Garran."

Slowly, Atakan removed the pointed toe of his boot from the beetle's remains and looked up.

Before his eyes could meet mine, I gave them to the Seelie king. He had shoulder-length hair, the color reminiscent of sand, and a warm smile that didn't quite match his hazel eyes.

He nodded once. "How lovely it is to make your acquaintance, young princess."

My father chuckled jovially when I failed to speak. "And this is his son, Prince Atakan." Fingers tapping at my shoulder, he cleared his throat. "Don't be shy now." With a gentle push, he propelled me forward. "Say hello."

"Hello," I squeaked as a trembling exhale rushed from my chest, and I made sure to stop as far away from him as what might be deemed appropriate. I remembered what Bernie had instructed me to say over dinner last night and gripped my skirts with clammy hands. Curtsying, I forced a smile as I straightened. "I'm pleased to meet you, Your Highness."

A lie I hoped he couldn't detect.

My eyes met his—burning bronze with glowing flecks of green. "Pleasure," he drawled as if it were not a pleasure at all.

My nose crinkled.

He glowered at it, golden brows slashing over his fascinating eyes.

A rough bout of laughter dragged my gaze beyond the prince as King Garran clapped his shoulder. "You'll need to forgive my son's lack of manners. He was born upon a full moon, and I've been unable to rid the audacity from him ever since."

My father laughed once more. I wondered if I was the only one who could tell it was forced. "Let us feast, and let the young ones get to know one another."

Instantly, the stiff tension in the spring air snapped as people moved.

As whispers turned into chatter, and chatter into laughter, I ducked behind my father and waited for an opportunity to dash across the grass to the terrace unnoticed.

The faerie guards remained before the rose bushes. But they stiffly acknowledged our guards when they broke formation from the hedges lining the castle walls to greet them.

It was just what I needed.

But as soon as I reached the terrace, Agatha gripped my arm. "Where do you think you're going?" She knocked a russet curl from her plump cheek as she hissed, "You will walk with the Seelie prince, Mildred."

I blinked up at her, the sun's glow harshening the warning in her chocolate eyes. "But…"

"Go." She tossed my arm and ushered me toward the faerie guards.

Terror seized my bones when I looked back at the terrace. My father and King Garran headed inside, presumably to talk as kings did. Bernie chatted with her betrothed, a quiet nobleman named Royce, who went red in the cheeks at just the sight of her.

And Prince Atakan stood before a cluster of his guards, all of whom seemed disinclined to greet our own.

Hands tucked before him, the prince eyed everything with what could only be described as disgust. He didn't want to be here. I would wager my entire rare rock collection that he didn't want anything to do with this alliance.

At least we had one thing in common.

It emboldened me to continue across the grass. "I've been told to walk with you."

The breeze sent white-blond strands of hair over his sharp cheek. "Do you always do as you're told?" he asked without so much as glancing at me. "Truly an infant."

"I am not an infant," I said defiantly. "I am almost eleven years of age."

He scoffed.

Bernie had told me the prince was fifteen years of age, and that in time, our ages would not mean much of anything. Now, I wasn't sure I believed her.

As the prince sighed and muttered something about his goddess, I had a horrid feeling that no matter how old I was, he would still rather be anywhere that wasn't near me.

He fell in step beside me. His shadow swayed upon the grass as he swiped a hand through his long blond hair. Longer than his father's, it sat straight beneath his shoulders.

Never had I felt small. A nuisance, yes, but never small.

I'd always been a head taller than all the younglings at court. Yet I did feel like an infant next to him.

Atakan seemed as tall as my favorite climbing tree, and he smelled similarly, too. Most people smelled like bottled flowers and powders, or musky and unwashed. But his scent was an odd mixture of burning oak and peaches.

Knowing I had to say something, I admitted quietly, "I've never seen a faerie before today."

The prince said nothing. Each step he took seemed unworthy of his energy.

I blurted, "You smell different."

"As do you," he said. "Do all halflings smell like a mildewed corpse?"

It took me a moment to realize he wasn't merely picking on me but that he could scent the dungeon. A moment too long, for I spewed, "I'd rather smell like a corpse than act like one."

His rich laughter prickled my nape, and I froze in fear.

He walked to the maple tree, far enough to provide privacy from faerie ears but not so far that his guards couldn't see us. Knee-high black boots hugged his matching tight pants. Unlike his guards, his boots were not bulky but slim, and the thick leather agleam.

Hesitantly, I followed.

He leaned against the trunk. "It has claws." His arms crossed, crushing the gaping pale-blue sleeves of his airy and frothy tunic. "You'll need more than that for where you're headed."

I didn't dare stand too close, stopping as soon as my feet reached the shade of the tree. The breeze tossed my loose curls across my burning face. "Why?"

"Why?" he repeated, brows high.

I nodded and waited, gazing up at him though I wished desperately to look anywhere else. He was as handsome as the rumors claimed.

And just as cruel.

His smile was venomous, full lips curving to one side to reveal a devious dimple. He pressed a boot against the bark of the tree. "You'll see."

My stomach tightened. "My sister says a husband is supposed to protect their wife."

Bernie had promised that, no matter how forced a marriage, a husband was duty-bound to ensure their wife's contentment.

As if my fear and thoughts had conjured her, she called my name in the distance.

Prince Atakan's gaze flicked toward the faint sound, then fell upon me, glimmering with green shards. "Let me make myself crystal fucking clear, little thing." My eyes widened at the ease with which he'd cussed. "Out of all the dangers awaiting you in my court, I'm the one you'll need to be protected from."

Tears stung my eyes.

Before I could surrender to the urge to flee, he stalked past me, leaving me chilled in the shade of the maple tree.

TWO

Sparrow Hall resided at the heart of the continent, a barn-like structure nestled in a curve of the Ribbon River.

For years, I'd longed to see the river that fed the borders of all three realms. Now that I was staring at it, I failed to notice the way it curled into fluttering swirls when all I could see was Prince Atakan's white-blond hair and cruel smile.

Our carriage trundled over a large rock, and my stomach lurched with it.

For three years, I'd tried to rid my mind of the parting words from our first meeting. I'd been unsuccessful. Too many times, I'd woken with my bedsheets stuck to my sweaty limbs from nightmares.

Nightmares of clouds and mist, cloying as I tripped over bones and his laughter gave chase from the inescapable sky.

"Look at me, butter." Bernie grabbed my chin, taking my eyes away from the sparkling water beyond the carriage window. I scowled, but it melted as she brushed a tendril of hair that'd fallen over the band of braids along my hairline. "I'll stay with you."

"Don't make promises you cannot keep," I repeated what she'd always told me.

But she was married now. Soon, she would likely have a child of her own. One that was human and would take up all of her time. Besides, I was old enough to take care of myself. I'd learned to stop running from my rooms to hers whenever I woke from another bad dream.

Fear had kept me trapped and alone.

Bernadette couldn't change anything. I had to marry the faerie who'd warned me that he was just as monstrous as rumors claimed.

And now, it was time to see my betrothed again.

The war between the Unseelie and Seelie was no longer confined to the faerie kingdoms. This visit to the sacred place of peace was not merely a meeting between King Garran and my father, but a celebration.

An imperative show of support and solidarity, my father had said. The bloodthirsty Unseelie Fae would be brought to heel. Strategies to defeat them, constructed closely with the Seelie court over the past few years, were now being implemented.

When I was near, my father liked gentling his words, but I wished he'd just speak plainly.

The entire continent was now at war.

After the first war, the human realm of Nephryn had stayed away from faerie squabbles, and this ongoing feud between their two realms shouldn't have changed that. But pointing out the obvious was futile. That, and no one wanted my opinion on anything. Not only was I too young but my pointed ears, height, and oddly colored hair reminded them that I was also too inhuman.

Since my betrothal had been inked on parchment, I was tolerated more at court. Though Agatha still preferred that I remain out of sight. I preferred it, too. Especially now. I wanted nothing more than to stay in the carriage or hide in the trees filled with warriors.

Bernie offered me a troubled smile, then helped me out of the carriage despite knowing that, heavily gowned or barely clothed, I had long been able to manage it myself.

During our journey, she'd told me that the Unseelie Fae were now our enemies too, and to be cautious although Sparrow Hall was sacred ground. I'd glared at her before she could begin explaining why.

I might have only been fourteen years of age, but I was no longer blissfully ignorant. She knew I heard a great deal of things many wished I wouldn't. That I'd learned far more than she or my tutors deigned to teach me.

Such as King Garran being the reason his realm was in need of rescue.

The Seelie kingdom of Ethermore had been under constant attack for years, well before the Unseelie king had discovered his wife's death. When Queen Kalista fled from him, he'd sent his warriors, most of them beastly shifters, to hunt her down.

Hunts that left many villages and towns aflame or in disarray and many civilians dead. Even in their own kingdom, The Bonelands.

King Garran had supposedly harbored and loved the Unseelie queen. He'd also supposedly killed her when she'd tried to end King Vorx's wrath by returning to him. Garran kept it hidden for as long as he could, but when Kalista's fate was exposed, the Unseelie king's hunts became brutal and vengeful attacks.

As with all faerie tales, the truth sat somewhere within the elaborately twisted dramatics.

Regardless of who was more hideous, Ethermore couldn't withstand the might of The Bonelands. They needed our soldiers. In return, they would create a permanent alliance with the human kingdom by marrying me to their prince.

Although I now understood the reason for my perilous future, I still didn't like it. Mostly, I didn't like that I was powerless to change it. My muddled blood made me a crime my family had tucked out of sight, useless until they'd needed a pawn.

Of course, I wanted peace to reign throughout the continent. I was only half a monster. But I still wished upon every star that they'd find another way to end the Unseelie king's brutality.

The stench of horse dung and barreled wine stained the spring breeze. I fixed my shawl, clutching the apricot gossamer tight over my chest.

My gown was more fitted than any I'd worn before. As we'd readied ourselves at our last stop and I'd complained ceaselessly, Bernadette had hissed that I was becoming a woman, and the changes were, therefore, necessary.

I failed to see how making it nearly impossible to breathe was necessary. I'd also failed to remind her that I wasn't human. Not entirely. There was little point when she knew. When everyone knew.

When it was the reason I would one day leave all I'd ever known behind to live among faeries.

The stricken look on my face had made Bernadette laugh. She'd then given me the shawl she'd packed for herself to cover my cleavage.

Fae warriors and our soldiers surrounded the riverside clearing housing Sparrow Hall. In their gold-and-blue garb, they stood in unflinching formation along the tree line and winding dirt road.

Two Seelie warriors stood guard at the towering arched entrance to the hall. They took their time opening the mildewed doors, and I studied their emotionless features. The orange eyes of one and the scar slashing the cheek of the other.

Father had arrived ahead of us. As though he wasn't dealing with deadly beings, he slouched at the head of the giant banquet table, cheeks mottled from laughter and his crown hanging from a decanter of wine.

King Garran sat at the opposite end. The arched wood ceiling enabled their booming voices to carry easily over the courtiers and generals seated among them and the fiddle players perched upon a platform in the corner of the hall.

Mercifully, Prince Atakan was nowhere to be seen.

The feast drew to a close within minutes of our intentionally late arrival. After a nod from our father, Bernadette left me by the beverage table. "Stay right here. I'll return soon."

I didn't stay.

As more people of influence arrived and the fiddles were joined by pattering beats from small drums, I went outside before the celebrating began in earnest.

The hall stood a short distance from the river. A path of brown stones wended to it from the road choked with wagons and carriages. Tethered horses grazed by the water's edge.

I visited one of our own, Olive, who sniffed at my cheeks in search of the sweet tart I'd eaten in the hall.

My smile fell, and I loosened my hold on the mare's neck at the sound of feminine laughter floating downstream. The half-moon brightened as the final hues of dusk faded into night.

But I still saw them.

Two figures huddled together on the grass at the riverbend, concealed from Sparrow Hall beneath a weeping willow. The blond male came into better view when he rolled away from the female fixing her lemon skirts.

Prince Atakan.

More fascinated than scared, I watched across Olive's patched back as he combed his fingers through his long hair, then buttoned his shirt. His dress coat was tended to next, the night-sky blue brushed roughly to remove any debris collected from the ground.

I needn't have wondered what they'd been up to.

Though I'd never so much as been kissed, what I'd read and glimpsed in the seldom-used halls of our castle had taught me enough. Plenty enough that when Bernie had attempted to talk to me about sex shortly after I'd reached thirteen, I'd reminded her of all the books she'd let me steal from her chambers.

She'd laughed, tickling me under the chin as she'd said, "Should you find someone to your liking, do remember it's best to be cautious and keep such matters private, lest it affect your betrothal."

I hadn't found anyone to my liking. The boys at court were nothing but spoiled rodents who teased me whenever they could get away with it. The girls weren't much better, but at least they were somewhat civil to my face.

Even if I had taken an interest in someone, keeping such matters private would merely be to keep from embarrassing my father and earning more of Agatha's scorn. Faeries did not care for propriety and maintaining one's innocence for marriage.

To them, sex was as accepted as each new dawn. A way to honor their immortal lives and the twin goddesses who'd gifted them as such.

So Prince Atakan shamelessly fastened his pants as he rose.

He didn't offer his hand to the female he'd left upon the ground. He stalked toward the river, leaving her to contend with her abundant skirts and her loose bodice on her own.

Absently, I stroked Olive's neck, then decided to head back to the hall before I was seen, or Bernie came hunting for me.

I wasn't halfway up the pebbled path when his voice, even smoother now, sank into my back like talons that halted my feet.

"Attempting to sneak a look at what you'll never have, little thing?"

I shouldn't have said anything. I should have pretended I hadn't heard him and walked on.

Instead, I tugged my shawl over my chest and turned.

Eyeing him up and down with intentional slowness, I noted the damp stain on his black pants. "I missed the part where you soiled yourself, it seems." Smirking, I said, "Pity."

He didn't so much as glance down at his pants, though a muscle feathered in his clenched jaw.

He walked past me on the path and stopped.

Turning to him, I inclined my head, then shook it before walking around him. Something warm, perhaps a taste of victory, lightened each step.

Pebbles crunched beneath his boots as he trailed me.

His sweet and smoky oak scent, berried from the female he'd been with, engulfed as if his irritation and ire were flaring his energy. Perhaps it was, for he said with an apathy I remembered far too well, "Been sharpening those tiny claws, I see."

The reminder of his threat during our first meeting stilled my feet.

He took advantage and stepped before me again.

My stomach dipped.

He was far taller and broader than what I'd seen in my nightmares. And he would be. Three years had passed. Three years of trying to forget my fate. Three years of haunted sleep to remind me that forgetting was useless.

Unfortunately, he was also even more handsome.

His regal cheeks could carve hearts in half, after his lone dimple and pretty blond hair were done tricking them. But it was his eyes, a glowing bronze with crumbs of emerald, that truly ensnared.

Long lashes dipped, rising when his full mouth curved. "Time hasn't been kind to you, Princess."

I swallowed thickly. I'd been so unwilling to let him terrify me that it seemed I'd forgotten he could simply upset me.

As if wanting to be sure I'd received the insult, he stomped on my bleating heart. "You're still a halfling runt."

"And you're still an arrogant ass," I said before I could think better of it. "Who reeks of his own seed."

I walked around him, not breathing and fearing I wouldn't make it to the hall.

I did, but it was hardly a mercy.

The hours that followed stretched painfully—spent standing in the shadows while the prince and his faerie friends danced and laughed and continuously looked my way.

My only enjoyment came from watching Atakan attempt to scrub his pants with what looked to be wine.

I made my escape well before midnight and locked myself in the carriage to read while Bernie kept an eye on our outrageously intoxicated father.

But I'd been a fool to believe I'd survived my second encounter with the prince with some morsel of satisfaction.

Something thudded against the carriage floor. A hiss followed as I startled and dropped my book atop the creature.

A two-headed serpent.

I fumbled for the door, only to find it'd been locked from the outside.

Slowly, I pulled my feet up onto the seat while trying to think through the fear.

I'd spent so much time in the woods that my tutor had given me lessons on what to do if I encountered predators. She'd said they could smell fear. To steady my breathing and…

"Don't panic," I whispered. *Don't panic, don't panic, don't—*

The serpent lunged, and I screamed.

Two sets of fangs sank into my ankle.

I screamed and screamed and screamed, so loud that it drowned the laughter from outside the carriage I'd been trapped in.

I shook my leg, but the teeth wouldn't budge. Knowing the venom would spread dangerously fast if I worsened the wounds, I didn't try to pull the creature free. I gripped the bars of the window, rattling the steel as I continued to shake my leg and scream.

It was then I saw who'd tossed the serpent through the carriage window.

Hollering echoed, but I fell silent.

Prince Atakan stood next to Olive. He stroked her neck as he lifted a goblet of wine in my direction, then sipped.

Soldiers neared, and he smirked before disappearing into the dark.

I saw nothing more.

The carriage door burst open, and the two-headed serpent released my ankle to turn on the soldiers.

They retreated from the door, the female unsheathing her sword.

I closed my eyes as the venom burned a trail up my leg. As my chest filled with a similar poison—an ire that made me snatch the serpent around the neck and push past the useless soldiers.

I marched down to the water and tossed it.

The serpent writhed in the air before breaking the starlit surface of the river.

Bernadette gaped as she reached me and released her skirts. "Was that a two-headed serpent?" She inspected my face between her hands, then patted my arms. "Are you all right?"

I nodded, although I wasn't.

Anger and fear and pain drifted into one giant darkness. A darkness that sent me crashing into her, and we both fell to the grass.

Three

I stroked the slightly raised scars on my inner ankle. The ballroom had already filled to the point of overflowing, but I wasn't worried about arriving late. Once again, I'd wholly intended to. The less time I spent in the presence of faeries, the better.

My father hadn't been impressed when he'd found me sipping peppermint tea and reading earlier, nowhere near ready to join the arriving guests. He'd claimed these gatherings were just the thing to prepare me for my future.

I'd never told him the truth about the two-headed serpent.

It had taken a week, most of our journey home from Sparrow Hall, for the fever to break and the hallucinations to end. If I'd been entirely human, the bites might have killed me by the time we'd reached a healer. As it was, I remembered begging for death more vividly than anything else from the torturous journey.

I hadn't told Bernadette either.

I hadn't needed to. She'd noticed me touching the tiny scars more than once, and I'd surmised the soldiers she'd convinced Father to demote had confirmed what she'd pieced together. Concern had sweetened her scent and dulled her blue eyes in the days spent preparing for tonight's ball.

Another celebration.

After years of bloodshed and destruction, the Unseelie had been overwhelmed and forced to retreat to their realm in The Bonelands. The goal now was to maintain the upper hand by keeping them there. I'd heard the whispers from behind my father's study door.

Our unified strength would not be enough to stop the Unseelie forces from returning, so numerous witch covens were at work on a spell to confine them to The Bonelands.

Meanwhile, more souls perished as our armies continued to hold the ground they'd reclaimed—a victory Garran and my father were already celebrating.

Perhaps too soon.

I had no idea what the spell entailed, nor if such a thing was even possible, and I didn't much care. I cared only about carving the prince's pretty eyeballs from his obnoxiously evil head and stomping on them while he screamed.

Of course, I couldn't get away with something so overt and grotesque. Research stated it took weeks for faerie organs to fully regenerate. But I would get away with something else.

Letting my skirts fall back over my ankle, I rose from the armchair and left the darkened sitting room.

Guards lined the hall outside. Their chins remained high although I felt some of their eyes as I intentionally tugged at my bodice.

The ballroom was a gaudy explosion of sky blue and gold.

Flowers heaved from the architraves. Golden goblets of bloodred wine dotted every table rapidly filling with treats and meats. Globs of wax already weighted silk streamers fluttering from the wrought-iron-and-gold chandeliers.

I half hoped one would catch fire. Then we would all be forced to vacate the ballroom, and I could do anything other than this. Something that did not involve faeries.

Alas, I had a cold dish to serve.

A familiar tune from the piano welcomed me, and I smiled as I knocked a loose curl from my cheek.

Bernadette's husband, Royce, had been wary of me for some months after their wedding—the halfling little sister who stalked the halls in scheming and stewing silence. Over time, that wariness had turned into a dry humor I'd secretly grown to enjoy. He treated my sister like the queen she would one day become, so I didn't much mind how he felt about me.

But I loved listening to him play the piano.

Guests surrounded Royce, yet his smile was only for my sister when he looked up from the keys. Bernie's cheeks were rosy from rouge and happiness.

My father found me before I could join them and fracture their merry bubble.

"My Mildred." His arms spread as he neared. He placed a kiss on my cheek, then embraced me. "You look lovely."

Stepping back, I pressed my hand to his warm cheek.

Adorned in his preferred gold-and-black dress coat, his matching crown flattening his thinning gray-and-brown hair, he exuded unkempt authority. Although he'd ruined my life with this alliance, the thorns entangling my heart forever softened against my will.

Despite all he'd done to doom me, this king loved me.

Rejecting love when I'd had so little of it was nearly as impossible as accepting it. No matter how much it darkened with each passing year, my soul hungered for tastes of affection.

"That bodice is far too small." Agatha, gowned in maroon fringed with golden lace, hooked her arm through my father's. "You did something about that hair, at least." Eyeing my bell-shaped gown, she sipped her wine. "We should have Jacqueline's pay docked for the oversight."

It was no oversight.

I'd merely matured too much for the queen's liking. My breasts threatened to spill from the breath-snatching bindings, and my wide hips bruised more by the minute. It should have come as no shock, being that I'd surpassed sixteen years of age.

But I was not supposed to be appealing. In Agatha's eyes, I was to remain nothing but a consequence of her husband's failure, best tucked out of sight.

My father still had lovers, but when we were alone, he always reminded me that my mother, a faerie he'd had under his employ for many years, had been his true love. Listening to him talk about her used to fill me with aching bliss, and I would ask him incessant questions about the female I would never know.

In the years following my betrothal, I'd ceased asking about my dead mother.

Instead, I'd started listening.

I was a princess of Nephryn only because my Seelie mother had died giving birth to me in this castle. At least, that was what I'd been led to believe. Whispers said otherwise, and that if Agatha's plan hadn't been thwarted, then I too would have died alongside my mother.

The brittle disregard Julis Nephryn had for his wife spoke volumes about what had truly happened upon the night I was born. Once I'd matured enough to understand the whispers and her hatred of me, I never again called Queen Agatha my stepmother.

"With the exception of my late mother…" Tentatively, I touched the wild waves pinned into a pile atop my head. "Jacqueline is quite likely the finest tailor this kingdom has seen. Insulting someone held in such high esteem would not be wise." Royalty be damned, the woman would happily take her talents elsewhere.

Anger deepened the lines surrounding Agatha's pinched mouth.

But she knew I spoke true, so she merely huffed. "Come, Julis. The Seelie king and Lord Stone are waiting." Casting a dismissive glance at me, she said, "Do try not to stumble into anything venomous this evening."

Naturally, Agatha had insisted getting bitten by a two-headed serpent was nothing but a cry for attention. She'd crowed that all of my foolish wood-wandering had conveniently caught up with me at the most inconvenient of times.

My father was well aware that I lacked any desire for the future he'd forced upon me like a noose around my neck. He'd made no comment about the serpent, though I'd found him staring at me more than usual in the weeks after our return from Sparrow Hall.

He did so again now. Then he winked and allowed his wife to lead him into the crowd.

The Seelie Fae of Ethermore were easily spotted. Not merely because of their height, that eerie beauty and the revealing and dramatic ensembles, but because of their behavior.

They stood statue-still along the walls or walked with floating grace among the humans, regarding everything with what could only be described as a mixture of curiosity and revulsion.

None more than my dear prince.

Nestled within a gaggle of faerie females, Atakan slouched against the wall. The lone male with them, who seemed so bored he swayed on his feet, stilled when he noted that something had garnered his prince's attention.

Pale-blue eyes met mine as he peered over his shoulder. Delight twisted his mouth. Phineus Oldwood, rumored to be the prince's second cousin and lifelong friend.

Smirking, I took some wine from a passing server before retreating to the wall directly opposite the prince. I leaned against it.

And waited.

Shifting and dancing bodies hindered my view of the prince and his friends. But I kept my gaze fixed on where Phineus stood. A burly man moved, allowing me to see the scowl the prince handed his cousin.

I sipped my wine.

Across the room, King Garran put on a distracting display with his friend, Lord Stone. The latter's wife stepped back, shaking her head. Jewels glinted as the Seelie king tossed his crown toward the high ceiling using only his wind magic, and Stone hid it from view with a wave of his hand.

Mist, I surmised, as the slight cloud dissipated.

It was rumored that Atakan hadn't inherited his father's abilities, and that many believed resentment and shame were to blame for his ruthlessness.

Humans moved closer, too drawn to remember their fear of being burned. They laughed and clapped, encouraging the king and the lord to continue showing off.

Looking back at Phineus, I kept my curious eyes from my betrothed. I waited, sipped more wine, and forced my eyes to briefly wander around the room.

If I could lure Phineus, then I might just catch myself a prince.

But it was not Phineus who finally parted the crowd and strode toward me.

The evening was moving more in my favor than I could have dreamed.

Atakan stopped as he neared, the distance between us perhaps two of his long and gliding steps. He could convey distaste with that distance. He was far too close for my liking anyway, his scent no longer an oaky, sweet addition to all those in the room.

It was a cloud that formed around me, entrapping me.

He stated what he'd long known. "So you survived my venomous gift." His eyes raked over me, a slow perusal that made me fight a shiver. "Perhaps there's enough faerie in you to be worthy of a cage in my rooms."

"That sounds…" I pretended to mull it over. "Titillating."

"If your tastes stray that way, I could stick to my original plan."

Intrigued, I laughed dryly. "Dare I ask what that might be?"

Those pretty eyes lowered to my mouth. A moment later, they descended to my breasts. Despite loathing him, a smug, feline satisfaction purred within me.

"Leashed in one of the stable stalls." His gaze lifted to mine, solid bronze. "Naked."

I smiled. "Do tell me more."

His golden brows rose. "My…" Amusement wriggled his lips. "How you've changed, little thing."

"And you haven't at all," I lied and paused. "Still so confidently repugnant."

Five years my senior, Atakan was now twenty-one years of age. The tight fit of his ruffled white dress shirt over his muscular arms and shoulders certainly portrayed it. As did the harsher angle of his steep jaw when it clenched tight.

He'd wholly matured. Well, his body had.

Although aware that there was little he could do to me in my family's ballroom, and while surrounded by so many witnesses, I still braced ever so slightly.

But his jaw loosened. Just enough for that cruel mouth to curl as he murmured, "I look forward to showing you just how confidently repugnant I can be."

Peering at the filigreed ceiling, I sighed. "Life can be so dull here in this vast and beautiful castle." Then I fluttered my lashes and sipped my wine. "In time, you'll learn that threats only give me something to amuse myself with, Prince."

A server approached with a tray containing only one goblet of wine.

Atakan's eye twitched. The bronze brightened with flecks of emerald as he inched a half step closer. "You make a good attempt at bravery, but that's all it is…" He snatched the goblet without so much as glancing at the tray or server and sipped. He swallowed, then grinned wickedly. "Just an admirable attempt."

Tilting a shoulder, I boldly stepped forward to whisper, "I suppose time will tell."

I left him seething behind me and went in search of Bernadette.

Some might say such an effort for revenge was extreme, and I would assume those people hadn't an ounce of faerie blood running through their veins.

All I'd ever wanted was the comfort that came with love—with acceptance. What I was had only separated me from what I wanted most, and so I'd never wished to be anything like the pretty monsters visiting our ballroom.

Yet surrendering to the part of me I'd resented had given me a morsel of peace I hadn't felt in years—since before discovering my betrothal would mean my demise.

Revenge was a game the Fae refused to lose.

Finding a two-headed serpent this far east of the continent had been no easy feat. I'd journeyed deeper inland under the guise of meeting a seer as a gift for reaching sixteen years. Closer to the Nephryn and Ethermore border.

I hadn't met with a seer. I didn't wish to know the details of my future—the horrors awaiting me. I knew enough.

Instead, I'd paid the guards to await my instruction in town, and to inform anyone who asked about the delay in my travels that I'd met a boy I wished to toy with.

After three days of setting traps and camping by the Ribbon River, I finally captured a serpent. A babe. So although I had no love for the species after that week of terror and pain, I'd let it live.

Only after I was done with it, of course.

It had cost half a pouch of silver coins to have our potions maker secretly extract the serpent's venom into a vial. Another half to pay Jesper—the only kitchen boy I could somewhat trust—to deliver the wine at just the right moment.

Worth it.

Atakan's bulging eyes immediately found mine as he stumbled back into the shadows of the staff entrance.

I raised my goblet to him, then sipped.

And for the first time since I'd met him, true joy made me smile.

FOUR

SWALLOWED BY MIST AND SURROUNDED BY SNOW-KISSED and sloping woodland, Cloud Castle blended seamlessly into the Sky Mountains.

While hiding in my rooms or up high in a tree, I'd studied depictions of the forest-made fortress I would soon call home more often than I would ever admit.

My father happily sourced any books and illustrations I requested. His guilt required that he provide whatever I needed to acclimate to this forced marriage, and I took full advantage.

Sometimes I wondered what he'd do if he knew that what I needed could never be found on parchment. If he knew that such requests were not about easing my discomfort—but arming myself with the knowledge to better my chance of survival.

I wondered if he'd do anything.

The castle towers were gigantic ancient trees, their leafy branches almost touching, and the fortress between them crafted from wood and steel. A battlement built from branches stretched between the towers, dotted with patrolling guards.

More stood in stiff formation on either side of the steep mountainside drive.

By carriage, the journey across the continent would have taken three to four weeks, depending on the weather. This evening, it had taken all of ten minutes of preparation. King Garran had sent his most trusted to vanish us to Cloud Castle, esteemed warriors with the ability to move from one place to another at will.

Bernadette had almost vomited as soon as our feet met the dirt drive.

Quietly fascinated and only a little dizzied, I rubbed her back as she squeezed my arm, and the warrior made a face while quickly retreating.

Open wood and steel gates rose high behind us, allowing entrance to those ascending from the valley below in their glittering finery.

We'd been summoned to Ethermore to celebrate the demise of the Unseelie king.

The royal city of Cloudfall was a sparkling diamond in the distance, their celebrations illuminating the river beneath the mountain valleys.

King Vorx had joined his forces at The Boneland's borders, hunting the witches who'd worked tirelessly to guard the rest of the continent from his insatiable wrath. For months, covens had traveled under the protection of our armies to ward the Unseelie realm. Nearly half of them had perished, and one witch had been captured.

Bernie had told me that the witches were oath-sworn to take a potion if captured by the enemy. It would put them into a deep sleep. I needn't have asked if the captured witch would ever wake up.

Regardless, their spell had worked. King Vorx had been slain, and his son, Vane, now ruled over a kingdom trapped unto their own darkness.

My father and King Garran were more than pleased.

They were absurdly intoxicated. Wine sloshed from their goblets as they personally greeted every warrior and guest of importance who entered Cloud Castle.

Many warriors were dead. Others were gravely wounded, forever scarred, and many more understandably lacked interest in the festivities. Our own soldiers couldn't have traveled the distance even if they'd wanted to, as the worst of the bloodshed and the spell work had ceased only three days ago.

As we walked uphill to the kings, Bernie's grip on my arm tightened. "Stay close."

I frowned at her. "I'll be fine."

An uneasy look was cast at King Garran. Her whisper was so quiet, I barely heard it even with my better hearing. "Any oath is considered law to the Fae, and breaking it treason, but I still want you to remember that they've now gotten exactly what they wanted."

Our kingdom had aided the Seelie in their quest for safety against the Unseelie and their late king.

Now, I would wed their heartless prince.

They wouldn't break their oath. They couldn't. Yet they could find a way to bend it, and it would be no fault of their own.

Such as my untimely and unpreventable death.

I shivered, clutching my furred coat at my chest.

The wind blistered, so it was easily disguised as a reaction to the colder climate when Bernie glanced at me. I nodded, forcing a believable smile I'd practiced too many times. "I know the dangers." I knew far more than she would've liked. "And I tread carefully."

"So carefully," she whispered, "that the prince just so happened to fall ill after attending our ball two years ago?"

I pursed my lips. "He seemed perfectly fine when I saw him."

Bernie stopped me before we neared our father and Garran.

Grabbing my coat, she unbuttoned it to button it again, due to the watching guards astride the drive. "I don't know exactly what you did, nor if his sudden sickness had anything to do with you, but I do know that he torments you." Her eyes were damp when she stopped fussing and took my chin. "If you cannot find a way to make him soften to you, then you must make him leave you alone."

I almost laughed. "Say I do want him to leave me alone…" I spoke quietly. "How do you lose the attention of someone who hates you?"

"By being boring," she said. "So boring, he loses interest."

A spike of alarm and something else—something fluttery and warm—danced within my stomach. "He has no interest in me. He merely loathes me because of what I am and what he's being forced to do."

Bernie gave me a look that said I was being obtuse. "Just…" She sighed. "Be careful. I'll be royally pissed off if something happens to you."

"How pissed off?" I taunted.

She hushed me, admonishing with laughing eyes, "Language, butter."

I refrained from reminding her that I was over eighteen years of age, and we walked on to the kings.

Both of them engulfed us in hugs.

King Garran must have been under the influence of more than liquor to do more than greet us warmly. He reeked of wine and a citrusy soap, his arm too heavy around my shoulders as he mumbled about years of horror finally coming to a joyous end.

Guests approached behind us, and he forgot all about me. Relieved, I hurried inside with Bernie.

We paused in the foyer, our necks craning painfully as we gazed at the domed ceiling. Through the stained blue-and-pinkened glass, the moon was a gleaming scythe, and the stars patches of spilled blood.

I doubted Bernie saw them that way. She grinned and breathlessly admitted, "Simply magnificent."

Her awe remained as we meandered between two curling wooden staircases to the wood-paneled halls beyond. No fire flickered from the sconces. Glass orbs sat tucked within the copper leaves, and within the orbs, insects with glowing wings.

"What are they?" Bernie asked.

"I don't know. Bugs."

"What are all those books and portraits you've collected good for, then?"

Worried that someone might hear about my obsessive studies, I peered behind us down the empty hall, then hissed, "A handful of books doesn't make me an expert, Bernie."

We stopped at the entrance to another hall, lined with patterned blue-and-clear glass that gave a view of the Sky Mountains. My breath caught at the sight of a waterfall. We were too high up to see the river it fed far down below.

"They're glowflies."

Flushing at being overheard, I turned only because Bernadette tugged on my arm.

A lithe female in a slinky blue-gray gown stood in the hall, her hands folded primly before her. Her sharp chin rose. The edging of her gown and heeled slippers matched her silver eyes. "Cordenya." A feline smile accompanied a gentle incline of her head. "His Majesty's consort."

Though I wasn't sure we had to, I followed Bernie's lead when she dipped her head. She said, "Your home is magical."

"It is, isn't it?" I was given a careful appraisal that made her smile spread into something genuine. "Your betrothed should be along shortly. He's been…" Her bloodred lips pursed. "A very busy prince."

She then walked on, leaving us gaping in her honey-scented wake.

I frowned, saying when she'd disappeared at the end of the hall, "The king's consort?"

Bernie hushed me again, checking our surroundings before she whispered, "Cordenya's been a permanent fixture in this court for many years now. Garran refuses to take a wife after losing his great love."

A royal coupling was important for a myriad of reasons, my father had once told me when I was little and I'd asked why he'd married Agatha.

Insurance, primarily. Power not so easily bested.

As far as I knew, Garran's mother had been the last queen of Ethermore, and that had been some centuries ago. "The Unseelie queen?"

"Hush." Bernie looked around again. "I was quite young, so I don't remember well. But many believe it was Kalista, yes."

"Yet he killed her." I didn't even try to hide my disbelief. "How could she be his great love?"

Bernie patted my arm, her voice wistfully soft. "Love knows no bounds for mortals and has no end for faeries."

Those words plagued me as we followed the sound of revelry to a ballroom so full, I was eager to leave minutes after arriving.

King Garran swayed among a bevy of females. Beside them, Lord Stone, who'd recently lost his wife, observed the room blankly while twirling a clunky-looking ring. Bernadette was in conversation with our extremely unkempt father and two of his advisers by the balcony.

I made sure my presence was noted before I tapped Bernadette's hand twice, letting her know I needed some air.

Truthfully, I wanted to find a faerie who could vanish and ask them to take me home. I couldn't. Not yet. So I searched the halls to battle the fear that made me feel cowardly with a desperation to flee.

I'd need to grow accustomed to it. Living with fear and living within this tree-made castle of duplicitous and scheming creatures.

Only one staircase led to the third floor. Guards stood before it.

To my surprise, they stepped aside when I paused to stare up at the circular window atop the stairs. An orange sun framed in bright blue glass that resembled clouds—the Ethermore insignia.

I nodded my gratitude and climbed them, my steps unheard beneath the noise cascading from the ballroom.

I studied the moonlit glass, my fingers rising to the thorny rays of sunlight spearing through the blue. Before they could touch it, a familiar voice steeled my spine.

"Dreaded Mildred."

My hand dropped to my skirts. I clenched the velvet and silk as my stomach tightened.

"I find myself unable to decide whether I'm shocked or impressed by your attendance."

"Oh?" My heartbeat slowed, but I turned to where Atakan leaned against the wall, half hidden by shadow. I quickly absorbed his black ensemble. The slim leather boots, tight pants, and the way the high collar of his blue-lined coat brushed his divinely hewn jaw. "Well, you seem to be neither."

He regarded me in the same way, though his eyes took their time roaming over the bulbous skirts of my gold and yellow gown to the cream-filigreed bodice. They fastened to my chest before moving to my mouth.

His white-blond hair had been tied at his nape with black ribbon, making it hard for me to determine if he'd grown or trimmed it.

For two years, I'd shamefully recalled the heat of his attention.

Imagined what it might have felt like to have it in a much less sinister way.

"You poisoned me."

I widened my eyes and pressed my hand over my cleavage. It did as intended, drawing his gaze like a bird to the sky, as I breathed, "I do beg your pardon, Prince."

His teeth scraped his lower lip as he straightened from the wall. "The atrocious things I would do just to see you do that."

Unless I ran, there was little else to do but play along. "Do what?"

"Beg," he said, the word a forceful blow that wiped all trace of humor from his features. They turned to cold stone as he crooked a finger. "Walk with me, or I'll tell your precious father just how faerie you truly are."

He wouldn't dare. He would need to disclose his own cruelty if so.

Yet I crossed the landing into the hall aside the stairs, following as he stalked down it. Maybe it was fear of what he'd do if I disobeyed. Maybe it was plain stupidity.

Maybe I was just too curious for my own good.

We passed closed doors, portraits of sapphire-crowned ancestors, and beautiful paintings of Ethermore's mountainous landscape. The prince stopped when we met a new hall that overlooked the drive and slow-sloping valleys.

The open balcony doors allowed the biting breeze to drift into the hall, but it did nothing to stifle the anticipation warming my skin.

Atakan remained inside, hands tucked within his coat pockets as he gazed through the wooden doors. "I was sick for three days."

I kept a safe distance between us and scoffed. "I was sick for a week."

"So you admit it, then." He turned to me. "That you poisoned me with the same serpent venom."

A trick, the playful cadence of his milky-smooth voice. One I wouldn't fall for.

I blinked, then smiled. "Do I seem the type to poison anyone, Prince?"

"Princess Mildred." He clucked his tongue and took a single menacing step closer. "The time for coyness has long passed." He took another step. "What I want to know is how you did it."

He was far too close.

The flecks of green in his bronze eyes were too noticeable, his scent a weapon that hazed my senses. Every part of me turned both taut and liquid at once.

Yet I couldn't move. Moving would show weakness—would give away the fear thundering through my chest.

He could likely hear it. Scent it.

But my smile conveyed something I hoped would hide it—excitement. "I'm quite certain I have no idea what you're talking about."

He moved so fast that I couldn't have anticipated his actions. Between one bruising heartbeat and the next, my throat was seized, then squeezed.

His grip was unyielding, shocking.

Thrilling.

Breath escaped me with a touch of sound. My eyelashes drooped. My gaze fell to his perfectly shaped lips as he slowly backed me against the wall beside the balcony doors.

His hold loosened. His thumb stroked my jumping pulse. "You enrage me."

"The feeling is mutual," I crooned sweetly.

He was so tall, his mouth aligned with my forehead as he whispered, "You knew I wouldn't die. You knew I would retaliate." His lips brushed my skin like sliding silk, and my stomach dropped. "You did it anyway, thing." A burst of laughter roughened his words. "You fucking did it anyway."

All I could see was a glimpse of his chest and neck, revealed by the untied ribbon of his ruffled cream shirt. All I could feel was his hand at my throat, the continuous stroke of his thumb, and my erratic heart.

He swallowed as if trying to collect himself and failing. His throat dipped, and I was tempted to lean forward and lick it. Kiss it.

Bite it so hard I tasted his blood.

"Admit it," he growled low.

"Never."

He snarled, his head tilting for his eyes to meet mine.

Rage, true and terrifying, shone within them. But his restraint spoke of something else. Something he wanted hidden.

Something he probably loathed more than me.

Unable to resist, I prodded at the sore spot. "Don't you have females waiting for you to leave them to fix their finery and reputations all on their own?"

Atakan laughed quietly. "Sex does nothing to reputations here in my court. If anything, it only serves to elevate one's status." His gaze lowered to my mouth. "Besides, I find myself poisoned by thoughts of ruining only one dreadful little creature."

"I am no longer so little."

"I can see that." He glanced pointedly at my chest. Looking back at my mouth, he warned with breathiness, "But you'll be whatever I want you to be."

I didn't like that. Not one tiny bit. So why was I without words—my mouth drying the more he looked at it?

My question was rasped. "And what if I don't want that?"

"What you want will soon be irrelevant. You're a halfling who will breathe when I tell you to, eat when I say so, and pleasure my cock when you manage to make it hard."

"And here we all are, believing our united forces have herded the monsters into their spelled cage."

"They missed one." He inhaled deeply. Exhaling, he smirked. "Afraid, Princess?"

He knew I was. I refused to let it show and slipped my hand into his coat. I clasped his hip, enjoying his shock, the way he stiffened, and the granite feel of it. "Not in the slightest, Prince."

His brow arched. "You're lying."

"And you're a beast wearing the skin of a refined male."

Green embers sparked within that bronze gaze. "A beast who wants to kiss your pretty mouth until it bleeds."

"Why?" The question both betrayed and assisted me, a little breathless as it fled between my tingling lips.

Wrapped in silk and delivered with slowness, his answer wasn't what the foolish part of me longed to hear. "So I can lick it clean until you heal, only to kiss your lips raw again." A rumbled noise coated his harsh exhale. "And again."

Another part of me, the part that was just like him, relished the imagery.

I shouldn't have. But when his head lowered, I clung to his shirt at his hip and rose onto my toes.

His nose brushed my cheek, and he inhaled deeply once again. His exhale was groaned, and if blood could freeze, mine surely did. As exhilaration blinded, I became heated stone, a whisper of all I'd intended to be around this cruel creature.

"My Prince," a feminine voice said.

I was grateful that Atakan blocked me from view. Even so, my eyes closed. A growl, so low the intruder might not have heard it, preceded his clipped words. "Evidently, I am busy, Ruelle."

"So I can see," she said coolly. "But your father grows impatient for your appearance in the ballroom."

"Then he'll be mollified when you inform him that my betrothed is responsible for my absence." The tight words were more of a dismissal than an explanation.

The faint melody of flutes, violins, and laughter on the floor below muffled Ruelle's sigh. "You should also know that the princess's sister seeks her whereabouts." Princess was said as if she'd meant prey, her departing steps barely audible.

Atakan's fingers clenched.

Then left my throat.

My eyes opened to furious bronze, not a trace of emerald to be seen. "We are to marry now, and once we do, you won't have your mortal family to protect you."

Emboldened by the lust hooding his eyes, I glossed my knuckles across his cheek. It was shockingly smooth yet just as cold and sharp as it seemed. "I look forward to it."

His sneer drooped, and his brows furrowed.

I smiled and pushed off the wall, his attention a brand at my back.

Atakan never appeared in the ballroom.

Later, as we waited outside the castle to be vanished back to Nephryn, I tugged on my coat and made the fatal mistake of searching the cloud-dusted night sky.

The prince stood upon the balcony of the same floor I'd left him on.

Even with the distance, I could see it. The finger he rubbed over his lower lip and the bright flash of his teeth as he grinned.

As trepidation and exhilaration warred within me, certainty twined tight around my bones. Nothing else would work.

The only way to survive Atakan the heartless was to play this game of hunter versus prey—even if it drew blood.

FIVE

Jangling and clacking had me turning away from the driver waiting by the open carriage door.

"Are you half asleep?" With a small trunk in her hands, Bernadette hurried to the carriage. "You've forgotten almost all of your favorite belongings."

My heart sank.

She should've known—but of course she didn't. She should've known that anything soft would not survive in a castle of blades and thorns.

I'd packed clothing, a small collection of books, and a tiny velvet pouch my father gifted me last night. Taking more than I needed would only give the Ethermore royals more insight into my weaknesses.

It would only give me more to lose should any of them tamper with my belongings.

But I didn't tell Bernie that. I took the trunk from her and handed it to the drivers, then chewed my lip as they stored it in the carriage. I would need to pay them to return it home. Better that than explain to Bernadette and cause her to worry more than she already was.

"Now…" She clasped my hands. "You will write to me as soon as you get there, and I'll see you soon for your welcoming ball, then again for the wedding."

"I'll start writing before I even arrive."

Her eyes followed mine to our father's ivory tower. He'd already said his goodbyes to me. His guilt wouldn't allow for coddling.

"He worries for you," Bernie said.

Rather than say I understood, I just nodded. As much as I loved our father, he was sending me into a nest of vipers, and that fact wasn't newly discovered. He'd always known, and he'd traded me like a smudged jewel regardless.

I was nothing but assurance that the Seelie Fae would not move against my father now that their foes had been detained, and a guarantee that we had their support against any threats for years to come. Diluting the Ethermore line with our own was a transaction of peace via combined power.

Yet this journey had been postponed once already—Garran's excuse being that his kingdom needed to recuperate and grieve after years of violence.

I hadn't minded. But as the months had dwindled by, my father certainly had. He'd returned from a meeting just last week, stating the kingdom of Ethermore was now ready to welcome me.

I didn't believe they would ever be ready to welcome a halfling into their royal home. I believed they would have postponed again and again, if it weren't for whatever threats my father had dealt.

But I was postponing, too—by declining to be vanished and opting to travel.

I freed my hands from Bernie's and rubbed her growing stomach. "Remember," I said sternly, "drink more water than tea."

"Yes, yes." Her exasperation left as her mouth wobbled. She pinched her lips between her teeth, then threw her arms around me and whispered, "You remember the plan."

Her plan wasn't exactly a plan. But it made her feel better to think it was. To believe that all I had to do was send word, and she'd create a reason to be vanished to Cloud Castle to see me at once.

I returned her hug, tears burning. I refused to let her see them, so I held her tighter until the threat retreated.

"Most of all," she rasped, "don't let this make you forget you are loved."

Shadows crawled across the carriage floor.

I traced each one and watched them rise and meld into the black paint of the ceiling. Sleep came only during the hours spent trundling through the woods, across mountains, and wending along village roads speckled with curious citizens.

I could never sleep when the drivers did.

Instead, I wrote stories in the dirt by the fire as creatures bayed within trees that grew more barren the farther north we traveled. I made plans for scenarios that may never transpire while stroking the tiny scars on my inner ankle, a lifelong gift from a prince and a two-headed serpent.

Continuously, I recalled my father's farewell the evening before we'd departed.

"My Mildred," he'd sighed more than said, seated upon the lilac linen of my bed. "Your mother never wanted you to live among the Fae."

Most would call it a terrible betrayal, his long affair with a faerie tailor, if it weren't for the ever-spinning wheel of lovers my father entertained himself with.

"Your young life would have been miserable at best and deadly at worst. You know this."

I had known that. It had taken some years to wholly realize the nature of those we shared this magical continent with, but I'd understood even before meeting my rotten future husband.

"I believe Elorna knew what would befall her, as she made me promise to keep you." My father's hand had swallowed mine, large and smooth. He'd never wielded a weapon. Despite the Fae royals' high regard for combat, he'd always claimed mortal royalty had no need. "Even now that you're grown, she wouldn't want this. She wouldn't want me to give you to him, and it troubles me deeply to think of what she'd say." He'd squeezed my hand. "But as much as we both wish differently, you cannot spend your long life hiding in this castle."

At that moment, I'd recalled every one of Agatha's spiteful comments about our people never accepting a faerie, even a half faerie, as their princess, let alone their ruler. It might have been said to wound me, but she'd still spoken true.

Though knowing my father hadn't wanted me to leave, seeing the remorse ashine in his cloudy eyes… It would have been the perfect time to beg him to stop this. To give me more time.

To keep me safe.

But it would've been futile. The deal had been made a decade ago, the contract already withering with age.

Instead, I'd said, "It cannot be changed. Only survived."

The king had said nothing for the longest time. His hand had left mine, and I'd expected he'd leave.

He hadn't. From his pocket, he'd procured a small velvet bag. "Elorna wanted you to have this."

I frowned at it. "What is it?"

"A featherbone gifted to her by her mother. She never told me what it does, just that it's an heirloom." His ruddy cheeks had puffed as he'd sighed and placed the bag in my hand. "Evidently, it's time for you to have it."

With the exception of keeping it on my person as a weapon to stab the prince's pretty eyes, I wasn't sure what use a piece of bone had.

Even so, it hadn't left the pocket of my velvet coat. I'd chosen one of Bernadette's, an emerald green to match that of the bag. When I arrived at Cloud Castle, I would keep it there—safely hidden in the pocket.

My fingers rubbed the velvet bag and prodded carefully at the thin bone within.

I didn't dare remove it. I might not have trusted it was good for much, but I trusted the feeling that warned to leave it alone until I understood its importance.

During the nights that dawdled into sleepy days, it became a companion of sorts.

The drivers weren't too interested in talking to me. Our staff seldom had been, either. I used to fear it was because of what I was until Bernie had informed me it was because of *who* I was. I'd argued that they'd indulged me when I'd been small.

She'd given me a look that said I'd proven her point.

Faerie or human, I was now a grown princess. A princess promised to a court of beings far more frightful than my dour moods and haunting presence.

Often, it seemed as if the drivers had forgotten I was the reason for their journey. Sprawled across the leather seat of the carriage, I'd stare at the stars through the window, listening to their ramblings and inhaling the fruity smoke puffed from their pipes.

Heavy rainfall turned the last two days of the journey into three, as we were forced to shelter during a cluster of storms.

By the time the Sky Mountains came into view beneath the gray skies, I was almost relieved to see them.

It was here.

The moment I'd been dreading for ten years had arrived.

It was time to face it rather than fear it, and pray to both faerie goddesses that I could make it something more than a cage.

SIX

There was no fuss over my arrival.

In fact, no one greeted us at all.

Seeming perturbed, the drivers glanced warily at the two guards standing atop the rock-hewn steps of Cloud Castle's towering main entrance. I studied the etchings of arrows breaking through clouds upon the weathered oak until the doors groaned open.

Not arrows, I noted as my belongings were hurried inside to the foyer, but rays of sunshine.

A minute later, the drivers made haste downhill toward the open gates. The trunk Bernie had insisted I bring along headed back home with them.

Raindrops dried to the peeling paint of the statue in the center of the dirt drive. Hair of flowing rainbows draped over Etheria's breasts, and a cloud wrapped around her lower body. The goddess's upraised hand delivered water into a small pond containing tadpoles, moss encircling the chipped stone rim. The trickle grew louder as the carriage trundled farther downhill.

Behind me, a guard cleared his throat. The other laughed, failing to hide it behind a cough.

No one was coming.

Ignoring their sniggering, I lifted my chin and walked inside.

Only to find my belongings gone and a tall male with deep-blue hair that reached his waist in the middle of the foyer. "I've had it taken to the prince's rooms," he explained.

Stones piled into my stomach.

I'd known Atakan's threats hadn't been mere threats, yet I'd foolishly thought King Garran might have made other arrangements for me. Arrangements the prince would have ruined, but at least I would have had some ground to begin this battle with.

The male inclined his head. "My name is Elion, and I've been the Ethermore family's marvelous steward for far too many years." If I wasn't mistaken, a hint of glee brightened the male's near-black eyes when they surveyed me. "I trust your journey was horrid, so let's get you swept away and refreshed."

I hadn't much room to care about my appearance. Not when I was now attempting to envision a time when I might sleep again, let alone comfortably. I should've seized the opportunity to rest more during the past weeks of travel.

Elion took the staircase on the right, and I followed, tracing the notches and curves in the smoothed-branch railing.

On the second floor, I peered through the stained glass windows, catching a glimpse of the waterfall between the mountains. We walked down a hall that hadn't changed since I'd visited eighteen months ago and climbed the stairs to the third floor.

My heart pounded when Elion slowed upon reaching the entrance to one of the towers. Beside it, through the window at the end of the hall, I marveled at the mere hint of the tree-crafted tower's circumference.

"The prince is away." Elion plucked a key from a triangular pocket in his chestnut waistcoat. "Probably playing hunting games with the Unseelie."

I liked the way he easily supplied information. It made opening my mouth far less terrifying. "But the war has ended."

The arched door swung open without any noise, revealing a spiraling wooden stairwell. Atop it, only a small landing was visible where the tree tower appeared to widen.

Elion laughed, a rasped and dry sound that echoed into the space void of anything but stairs and cobwebs. He slipped the key onto a metal ring housing many others and returned it to his pocket.

"Princess, war never truly ends." The bell sleeve of his coat swayed as he brushed a hand over the white lapels. "Not when so many hunger for violence." His mouth twitched, and he gestured to the tree tower's wooden innards. "You'd do well to remember that."

I stepped through the door, then turned to ask him what he'd meant.

But there were only dust motes dancing in the orange glow of late afternoon.

Prince Atakan's bedchamber was a circular, lavish mess.

I wasn't sure why I'd envisioned something sterile to match his cold personality, but my incorrect assumption stilled my feet and filled my chest with ice. I'd wasted years clutching futile hope that this marriage would not move ahead while steeling myself for survival, overthinking the most minute details.

Something so trivial shouldn't have disappointed so much. It was more than disappointment, though. The surprise was a leak in the iron-clad armor I'd constructed.

A warning that I might need to tread far more carefully than I thought myself capable.

Silk scarves and a shirt hung from the posts and canopy of the giant bed. Black linen was piled on one side of the mattress, pillows and feathers strewn haphazardly across the silver sheet curling away from the corner. The frame, chipped in places and carved in others, sat on a brown-carpeted dais. Upon closer inspection, I discovered the posts didn't contain any etchings.

They were marks left by someone's nails.

I stroked them, as horrified as I was fascinated. What he must have done to someone for them to gouge the wood like that…

Or perhaps he'd made them.

Either way, I shivered and recoiled from the bed, nearly tripping over a large boot. It appeared to be crafted from reptile skin, the deep gray scales darkening to black at the pointed toes.

That was when I spied my belongings.

Through an arched doorway, in a small dark room containing hung garments, my trunk awaited. Whoever delivered it had placed it against the wall next to a chest of long and overflowing drawers that encircled half of the dressing chamber.

I left it there and went in search of the bathing chamber.

The wooden door creaked open. A claw-foot tub big enough for two grown males took up most of the curved room. Beside it was a washbasin and privy, a pile of clothing and a sword collecting dust between.

I stared at the tub, determining whether I had time to bathe before the prince returned. I wanted to be ready for whatever tricks he had up his pretty sleeves. But I had no idea when I might have the luxury of privacy again, and I desperately wanted to clean the journey from my body.

It had long been considered unwise for a royal to stop at inns without guards. So for weeks, I'd freshened up in rivers and creeks.

While the tub filled, I ran back through the bedchamber, jumping over a ripped floor cushion, and hurried into the dressing chamber to find something to wear.

My gowns would need to be hung, though the thought alone made me tense with dread.

The sword continuously lured my gaze as I scrubbed my skin raw with the lavender and mint soap. Rust speckled the blade as if it had dwelled in here for years, forgotten. I quickly washed my hair, wincing as my fingers caught on numerous tangles, then climbed free of the water.

Atakan's sweetened oak scent lingered heavily on the only towel on a hook behind the door. I tried not to think about it as I patted myself dry. I also tried not to think about what I was about to do. What I *had* to do.

I might have been afraid now, but I couldn't live in fear forever.

If the prince wanted me in his rooms, he should expect my clothing to hang alongside his. If he wanted to play venomous games, then he now knew that I wouldn't surrender and play dead.

Surrendering was where true danger lurked.

If faeries unchangeably loathed one thing, it was boredom.

By the time Atakan arrived, my gowns took up most of the remaining space in his dressing chamber. The boots, clothing, and bed had been tidied, and the days-old dishes placed on a silver tray by the door.

The prince paused there and peered down at it.

His hair had been cut. Sharp pieces now framed his forehead and lethal cheeks—until he pushed the thick white-blond strands back, and they stayed perfectly finger-combed over his head.

A scowl sank his brows as he glanced around his bedchamber, and I noticed those blond strands gradually shortened behind his pointed ears and toward his nape.

He then found where I sat in the well of the large, round window carved from a knot in the tree. A book I'd unpacked perched against my knees, but I hadn't been reading. "Hello, Prince."

The door slammed.

He didn't speak. He didn't need to. I could see everything he was thinking in the tic of his clenched jaw. In the fingers curling at his sides.

And in the steady rise of his broad chest before he exhaled harshly, flaring his nostrils.

Yet when he finally spoke, his words were as smooth as the silk scarves I'd rescued from his bed frame. I'd used them to secure the black velvet curtains against the four posts. "You've made yourself right at home."

"I would have preferred my own rooms, of course," I admitted and turned the page I hadn't read. "However, I was given no say."

"As it should be." He sniffed, then stalked to the bathing chamber. He pushed the door wide. "You've opened the window."

"I bathed. The steam needs to be released, lest you want more mildew growing on those lovely wooden walls."

He returned to the bedchamber. "Lest you want to be locked in there with the mildew, I would cease touching what does not belong to you."

Sighing, I set the book down on the cushioned seat beside me.

"You wanted me in here. What would you have me do?" I asked. "Sit among your filth and wither?"

"Precisely." He stopped before the bed, glaring at the tucked bedding and the fluffed pillows as if they contained a hidden threat.

I smiled as I recalled what he'd said when I'd last seen him. "Oh, that's right. I am to breathe when you say so."

"Precisely."

Containing a snort, I tilted my head, but I was unable to contain a real smile. "You are without words. Does my presence affect you that much?"

"It *bothers* me that much." He removed his long coat and tossed it. The black fabric landed beside the floor cushion in a whispering heap.

The scent of blood drifted from it.

As he crossed the room, I noticed the patches darkening his brown leather boots. Not wishing to lounge if he chose to loom above me, I twisted upon the seat to set my bare feet on the wood floor.

He halted with the toes of his boots intentionally touching the tips of my toes.

I looked down at them, then raised a brow. "Unnecessary, Prince."

"Your existence is unnecessary."

"As is our impending marriage," I said.

"That," Atakan said, "we can agree on." His attention was akin to the energy of a nearing storm until he ordered a tense moment later, "Look at me."

My gaze lifted from another patch of blood on his cream britches, as if tugged away by force.

Irritated, mostly with myself for obeying him, I searched his narrowed eyes. My fingers folded in my lap, tingling as my stiff body pleaded for some place to hide. For freedom from the scrutiny ashine in those bronze and green eyes.

"I suppose I will make this worth my while." His gaze dropped to my mouth. "Unfasten my pants."

I blinked, then blinked again. "You're serious."

His arched brow said he was deadly serious.

Trepidation danced throughout my chest. But I knew what this was. A test that made me wonder what he'd do if I actually did reach for his pants.

"Is this how you usually find your pleasure?" I asked, foolish yet I couldn't bring myself to test him in kind by doing as he'd said. "You demand it?" Perhaps it was true, though I couldn't help but think this was a game invented solely for me.

And I was far from flattered.

"What I usually do is none of your concern, dreaded Mildred."

"No more little thing?"

"Certainly not with tits that huge."

I gaped.

He smirked.

I laughed, disbelieving. Then I rose, uncaring that it brought my eyes level with his broad shoulder, nor that it meant half of him brushed against me—as he refused to move. "If you wish to touch them so badly, all you need to do is ask."

Shock rose his chest sharply. I used it to my advantage and rounded him. His laughter was cold. "As if anyone would want to touch your half-human tits."

"Humans don't seem to mind them," I lied, unwilling to make him aware of my innocence.

Atakan's response was delayed. "They wouldn't." But the blow failed to strike as he'd intended. Maybe I'd imagined it—the delay, and the way his voice had roughened.

Regardless, I was unable to believe his lack of interest. Not entirely. So I continued to taunt him. "The way you look at them certainly implies that you wouldn't mind touching them either." As my bravado threatened to heat my cheeks, I made my way to the bed to put more space between us.

A flare of energy further chilled the room.

"Your audacity might have been adorable among mortals." He warned, "But it won't last here. Not with me." With that, he left.

He just... *vanished.*

Plumes of nearly imperceptible mist swirled in his absence. The energy hadn't been a gathering of tension.

It had simply been his.

All of our encounters had led me to believe the rumors about Atakan having no magical abilities were true. But he was royalty, and those with so much as a drop of noble lineage often harbored gifts that set them apart from the rest of their ilk.

I told myself it was good to know his strengths.

Even as I quietly despaired over what else he might be capable of and all the ways he could use vanishing to make my life worse than it already was.

SEVEN

I DIDN'T SLEEP UNTIL DAWN LICKED THE SKY.
I made a fire and curled before it on the floor cushion, studying the silver whorls in the caged hearth while awaiting the return of my ghastly betrothed.

But Atakan never returned to his rooms.

As the flames died and bright birds flew by the doors to the slim balcony, I finally closed my eyes.

"What a well-behaved pet, sleeping on the floor without instruction."

Startled awake, I yelped and lifted my head, unaware the prince stood on strands of my hair. I made sure the rest were safe before sitting up, and rubbed my smarting scalp.

Long and curving yellowed strands lay trapped beneath the toe of his brown leather boot.

Atakan feigned a gasp. "Oh, look at what I've done. My apologies." Yet his devastating grin said he was anything but sorry. The way he kicked the strands toward the fireplace further proved it. "Your presence is required downstairs in the dining room for breakfast." He headed to the bathing room. "Etheria knows why. Just imagining it has ruined my appetite."

He slammed the door.

I scrubbed my eyes, then inspected the apricot sleeves of my gown. Deciding it would do, I fluffed the floral skirts and didn't wait for Atakan to return. It sounded like the bathing tub was filling, so I stepped into my satin slippers and quietly made my escape down the tower stairs.

Elion stood beneath the staircase on the second floor.

Sunlight gilded the wood, revealing critters and vines within the worn steps. My thumb traced the bends in the branch railing as I descended, my skirts in my other hand.

The steward ceased fussing with the gold rope binding the heavy sky-gray drapes, and tutted. "Your hair." He shook his head. "Follow me, Princess."

I didn't think it mattered what my hair looked like. Certainly not after the prince had shown such an evident lack of care for it. And trusting this steward could be a mistake. I supposed now was as good a time as any to find out. So I trailed him into a sitting room and sat on the wooden stool he plucked from an ornate writing desk.

A comb was procured from an interior pocket of his lavender coat.

He turned my chin forward, explaining, "Do you think my hair stays this fantastic all day long?"

I laughed despite being in no mood to. "You do have lovely hair. Lots of body."

"The trick is to bunch it while you sleep."

"I'll keep that in mind." I smiled at the painting of the goddess upon the wall. Within the bronze frame, Etheria had been depicted similarly to the statue atop Cloud Castle's drive but in vivid color.

No one truly knew what the twin goddesses looked like. Fable stuck to repetitions of rainbow hair, delicately cloudy wings, and gold eyes for Etheria. In contrast, Asherlin was rumored to have dark hair, even darker feathery wings, and starlight in her night-blue eyes.

Supposedly, the goddesses—day and night or sky and earth, depending on beliefs and territories—were fond of the chaos in our world. It distracted from their heartbreak. Their shared love for a daring mortal had caused the Fae's creation. A love that had ended with them tearing him in two.

Quite literally, many stories had said.

Etheria and Asherlin had been fooled by their pet human. For years, he'd taken advantage of their adoration. Unless speared through the heart, decapitated, or drained of blood, faeries were immortal, and he'd intended to breed an army of them to conquer the continent.

For the most part, it had worked.

By the time the twins had discovered his treachery and tore him in two, hundreds of faeries had already been created from their mystical wombs. Fae with abilities that would begin to shape each realm and their royal bloodlines.

Many claimed he'd died laughing—victorious even in defeat—as the only mortal to ever gain the love of the divine.

Others warned that to utter his name would invoke a swift death and damnation in the dark pocket of everlasting nothing. Where it was said the same male now ruled—immortal and gleeful in his gruesome attempts to gain the attention of the goddesses.

My family and the realm of mortals worshipped a god named Errow, who had not forgiven the mistakes made by his twin sisters. Song and story shared that he'd retreated deep into his beloved seas to keep his hatred for all they'd done leashed.

I'd never known which deity to give my faith to, on account of lacking much faith at all.

But I'd wondered if the Fae's devotion might be less about true worship and more about placating the twins. A way of ensuring their powerful existence would continue. For no matter how much the goddesses might love their children, they were a constant reminder of their heartbreak.

The steward's gentle combing lulled, and I fought to remain awake as he braided strands into a thick band along my hairline.

Lifting my chin, he inspected his work, then my features with inky yet soft eyes. "Beautiful."

For some reason, I believed he was sincere. That, or I was too tired to guess at his reasons for helping me. "Thank you."

"I heard you were mortal, and it was only rumored that you had a faerie mother." He stepped back. "But with hair that yellow and eyes a green so dark…" He pocketed his wooden comb. "Well, the prince will loathe you all the more for the way others will soon admire you."

"Better be careful with those sneaky compliments. If I start to believe that not everyone has sinister intentions, I won't last long here at all."

Elion chuckled, a lovely deep-chested sound. "Your fingers are rather short," he said. "Very human-like, and your ears aren't nearly pointed enough."

At that, I laughed, too.

But the lightness he'd gifted my steps was soon weighted by the many eyes in the dining room.

Elion bowed, then gently pushed me into the room before closing the doors.

Though daylight poured in through the blue-stained windows backing the overflowing buffet, flame flickered from the chandelier's black branches over the expansive table.

I curtsied toward King Garran, whose hazel eyes gleamed as he chewed and nodded.

From the corner of my eye, I caught a brunette female slithering onto the prince's lap. Chatter resumed, but gazes still pressed upon me as I straightened and took an empty seat closest to the doors.

"Mildred." Garran grinned. "We've waited so long for this day."

Unlike most other times I'd seen him, he wore no crown. Maybe he was similar to my father in that he preferred not to if he didn't need to.

The longing for home grew teeth at the thought, and I desperately cast it aside.

Beside the king, Cordenya lifted her crystal goblet. But she failed to hide the curl of her pink-painted lips. Her long wine-red hair had been pinned behind one pointed ear, revealing a row of glinting rubies.

Garran asked, "How was your first night in my son's chambers?"

The female seated atop the aforementioned prince laughed.

"Traumatizing, no doubt," said another female with sleek brown hair that fell over her shoulders like a silk curtain.

The faerie on Atakan's lap buried her head in his neck and snorted. "It might have been," she said, and pressed her lips to his jaw. "If he'd not been in my room all night."

A tiny pit of flames burned low in my stomach.

Garran gave his son and the female a disapproving look that was ruined by the slight twitching of his lips. "Perhaps he was not aware of your arrival, Princess Mildred."

"Come now." Atakan nudged the female's arms out of the way and reached for a strip of pork. "I most certainly was."

The desire to flee was almost impossible to fight.

Doing so would give them too much satisfaction. So I tried my best to seem unaffected by fixing myself some peppermint tea, a small bowl of fruit, and some buttered bread. All the while, prying eyes became needles pricking at my skin.

"I do believe the king asked you a question, Princess," said the female on Atakan's lap.

"It's quite all right, Ruelle." Garran leaned back as Cordenya refilled his goblet of wine. "Let Mildred eat."

Although I was no longer very hungry, I nodded once at the king, then nibbled at the bread while the faeries surrounding me resumed their meals and low conversation. Fixated on eating and keeping my heartbeat under control, I failed to give any thought to the male beside me.

Phineus.

"Welcome, Princess." His mouth curved mischievously when I turned to him. "Might I just say that you are far more alluring than the rumors suggest?"

"Dare I ask what they suggest?"

He pursed his lips, pale-blue eyes dancing. "Well, to put it kindly, they say you are so plainly human that your faerie ancestry must be a lie."

Atakan snorted.

I'd wager he took part in sharing such rumors.

I wasn't bothered, as I wasn't surprised. "I do love a good rumor," I whispered conspiratorially. "Excuse my half-mortal ignorance, but what is your name?" Of course, I knew his name, but I wouldn't reveal my attempts to study this court during my encounters with them over the years.

Atakan muttered something that sounded like, "Pest."

The male beside me paid him no mind. "Phineus. Your betrothed's cousin."

Atakan informed, "Second cousin."

Phineus smiled. "He's fond of semantics."

"I'm also fond of stabbing things that irritate me."

I placed a grape in my mouth, chewing slowly as I chanced a look at my betrothed. He was glaring at me as if I were the one he wished to stab.

The female with the shiny, straight hair said without looking up from the parchment she wrote on, "You're both intensely irritating."

As her hand moved, I realized she wasn't writing but drawing.

Atakan pushed Ruelle from his lap and snatched a pastry from a silver dish. "No one is forcing you to dine with us, Pholly."

Ruelle pouted as she plonked onto the seat beside him.

Pholly set down her bone-crafted quill. "I'll remember that next time I'm ordered to attend breakfast by order of the king."

"We're all here to welcome the princess," Cordenya said, pushing her hair over her shoulder before sipping her wine. "Can we not act civil for five minutes?"

"It's not in our nature, I'm afraid," Phineus informed. "Certainly not Atakan's."

Atakan forced a dramatic gasp. "I'm the portrait of civility."

"When you're sleeping, I'm sure," I couldn't resist saying.

A mistake.

As everyone laughed, the prince stabbed a piece of melon with his knife, his eyes hard upon me. "I don't sleep, *dread*. You'd do well to remember that."

Even as my blood cooled, the new moniker made me raise a brow in question.

"Oh, Great Mother," Cordenya groaned. "I warned you, Atakan."

"Dread?" Pholly asked.

Ruelle said through a laugh, "Rather close to the word dead, isn't it?"

Atakan chewed as he grinned.

Phineus chuckled. "How many times have you threatened Princess Mildred since her arrival?" Intrigue dripped from the question. "I'd wager at least five."

"I'd wager you should've stayed trapped in your mother's womb to rot with her corpse."

From somewhere beneath the table, Pholly seized a dagger and leaned over Ruelle to point it at Atakan. Her gray-blue eyes glinted with rage. "Speak of our mother again, I dare you."

When my gaze bounced from her to Phineus, he explained, "We're twins. Pholly came first, and I got stuck." He shrugged and stole a grape from my bowl. His forefinger and thumb squeezed it, juice drenching his hand as he said, "She bled out before I was forcibly removed from her—"

Pholly's dagger landed right between the elegant fingers on his other hand, the gilded hilt swaying slightly from the impact.

Every inch of me tensed.

Pholly rose, snatching her parchment and quill. "You all disgust me."

Atakan chuckled. "Even my betrothed?"

I balked at hearing the genuine sound—the rough interruption of his silken sharp tone.

Pholly swept through the dining room doors, her sheer pink skirts floating behind her. "That remains to be seen."

In the quaking silence, Atakan raised his brows at me in unmistakable challenge.

"Shouldn't you be seeing to your upset friend?" Phineus drawled to Ruelle, then whispered to me, though everyone could hear, "After all, Pholly is the only reason she's tolerated here."

Ruelle's peach-stained lips peeled back over her teeth. "I was invited to take part in the upcoming *events*."

I bit my lips to keep from smiling at her refusal to properly acknowledge the prince's impending nuptials.

Phineus pried the dagger from the table and scratched at the slim crevice in the polished wood.

"Well…" Atakan stood, fluid and brushing crumbs from his belle-sleeved tunic. "I'm quite done tolerating the lot of you." He exited the dining room, and Ruelle followed.

Cordenya sighed.

King Garran huffed, then raised his crystal goblet to me. "Welcome to Ethermore, dear Mildred."

EIGHT

GARDENS CLIMBED THE HILLSIDES BESIDE THE TOWERS and met behind the castle in a lush bowl that overlooked countless forest-filled slopes.

I admired them through the windows while writing to Bernie to inform her of my safety. Snow fell, dusting terraces and filming the blue and pink tulips. Idly, I wondered what magic was needed to keep them thriving during the colder months.

Guards stood under awnings. Others patrolled the cloud-shaped hedges and flower beds. Now and then, a glimmer of armor sparked just beyond the tree line of the woods.

I could only guess what Garran might fear now that the Unseelie had been locked in their realm. I hadn't lived long enough to know what life had been like for these royals prior to the war. Perhaps such precautions had always been necessary.

Yet murmurs within the castle halls ceaselessly interrupted my attempts to write. As did Elion's warning and the memory of Atakan's blood-spattered boots and clothing.

Distracted, I decided to keep the letter precise but long enough to comfort my sister. I gave it to Elion, who promised to ensure an owl would depart as soon as night fell.

The murmurs became clearer as I floated through the halls and drifted toward the soft voices. Staff spoke of skirmishes near Ethermore's royal city of Cloudfall and whispered excitedly about the impending ball.

Evidently, danger still lurked beyond the spelled borders of the Unseelie kingdom. Although intrigued, I failed to feel much else when my own safety was but a long-ago wish.

The staff merely paused in conversation to dip their heads when I passed, seeming unconcerned to be caught gossiping while on duty. Agatha would've had them tossed from the castle grounds—disgraced—unless my father caught wind of it. Then they would simply have their payments docked for a time.

I missed lunch. Intentionally.

Taking advantage of whatever the prince was doing—likely torturing unfortunate souls or entertaining Ruelle—I curled upon the floor cushion to nap.

I woke before the door opened, blearily watching the flames in the hearth. So when it slammed, I sat up before my hair could be trodden on again.

Atakan set a tray of delicious-smelling stew on the nightstand. "You will not be joining us for dinner."

If he expected me to be offended, then he hadn't even half a brain. "Merciful Mothers." Loud and close to laughing, I sighed in relief. "Perhaps your sour persona is hiding something a little sweet."

He tensed, and his immediate irritation almost caused me to do the same.

Before he could spill his vitriol, I gestured to the meal. "Am I to believe you haven't poisoned it?"

"If you're truly half faerie…" He walked to the door, a smirk thrown over his shoulder. "Then use your lacking senses to find out."

The stew cooled in the frosted air barely touched by the fire.

After long deliberation, I did as he'd said and sniffed the bowl, cutlery, and even the bread. I was no expert at detecting poisons, but I'd sensed enough oddities in my twenty years to know when something was off and when something was simply wrong.

I devoured every drop of stew, dragging the bread through the remnants and leaving no crumb behind. Pleasantly full, I foolishly took more time bathing than I should have.

The door swung wide open.

Atakan leaned against the frame. "Still breathing, then," he said.

"Disappointed?" My arms itched to cover my breasts. The water hid them, though not quite enough. If I moved, he'd see all of them. If I left the tub, he'd see all of me.

Damned idiot, I inwardly scolded.

"I've yet to decide." He tilted his head, blond strands falling over a thick brow. "Perhaps you should get out so I can properly ascertain how I feel."

His voice had dropped—deepened.

Maybe there was simply water in my ears. "You know I won't hide from you."

His teeth scraped his lower lip. "Do I, though?"

The steamed air chilled.

He was challenging me. Hide or play. Fight or surrender. He knew I loathed cowering from him.

He also knew I wouldn't.

My toes curled against the porcelain as I grappled for a way out of this. "Why don't you go and bother Ruelle with your cruel charm?"

He hummed and scratched at his clean-shaven jaw. "If I thought that might bother you, then I would. Alas…" He straightened and unhooked the towel from behind the door. "I suspect you'd rather I spend the night in her bed than in my own." As he offered the towel to me, his mouth curled. "And I do hate to give you what you want."

"Prince, I've already told you…" My eyes narrowed on the towel as if it were a hidden trap in the woods. "If you wish to touch me, all you need to do is ask."

"I don't like asking, and I don't like you."

My laughter was genuine. "You've made that abundantly clear."

"I never said anything about touching, either." He shook the towel. "Make your choice, dread."

"Call me something else, and maybe I'll make my choice quicker."

"I think you've already made it, and you're just enjoying making me wait."

He wasn't wrong. I was making him wait. But I wasn't enjoying it.

At least, I wasn't until I gripped the side of the tub and stood.

Water cascaded down my body. The prince's eyes widened ever so slightly. Impressively quick, he steeled his expression. His features turned to stone, save for that muscle feathering in his bladed jaw.

With my eyes on his and his own on my breasts, I took the towel.

That glowing gaze drifted to my soft stomach, fastened upon my wide hips, then dared to roam even lower. Before it could settle between my thighs, I draped the towel around me and stepped out of the tub.

Then I left him in the bathing room to sit in front of the fire.

Atakan entered his bedchamber a moment later. Stroking the scars upon my ankle, I listened as he removed his coat. His boots thudded against the wood floor. His bare feet would have made his approach nearly imperceptible if I hadn't been wound so tight—so hyperaware of his presence.

He stood behind me.

In an effort to stop fear from increasing my heartbeat, I asked, "So what have you decided?" At his silence, I reminded him, "Are you disappointed that I still breathe?"

"Yes and no."

Then my hair was gathered—so unexpectedly and so gently that I stilled.

He didn't let me stay surprised for long.

He wrapped it around his hand, tight and stinging my scalp as he stepped closer and pulled. My head was forced back until I stared up into those menacing yet beautiful eyes. "Drop the towel."

Satisfaction slithered through my cold veins, warming them instantly. "Why?"

His eyes narrowed. His hand tugged. "Then don't." But he didn't release my hair, and he didn't move.

He was so close, his knees brushed my shoulders. I wanted to drop it. Goddesses knew why, but I wanted to unwrap the towel. I wanted him to see me again, and I should've felt ashamed.

He was more than despicable. He was a monster.

Yet the towel fell to my lap with one nudge of my fingers.

I held his gaze, and he held mine. I understood then that this wasn't about embarrassing or shaming me. He'd long learned that he couldn't force those things so easily.

This was what I'd suspected when I'd left this very castle a year and a half ago—a game of hunter versus prey.

One neither of us wished to lose.

His grip on my hair gentled as he inhaled sharply and allowed his eyes to move to my breasts. My nipples had already hardened. *From the cool air*, I told myself. But the air couldn't make them ache.

It was his attention that awakened my body. That made it betray me by hungering for the one thing I should never crave.

I didn't want him.

I just… *wanted*. Victory, mainly, but I would settle for the smallest of prizes to use as stepping stones along this perilous journey.

Judging by the way he shifted, he tried to stop it.

He failed. His throat bobbed as he swallowed, and more flecks of emerald darkened his gaze. He was lusting after the creature he loathed.

His order was ragged. "Stand up."

I did so without thought.

"Good." He released my hair and stepped back.

I collected the damp strands over my shoulder, combing them to appear unbothered as he studied me.

His nostrils flared, and his eyes met my mound. A slow blink, almost drowsy, and then his gaze jumped to mine. "You're aroused."

Tilting my head, I frowned and feigned confusion.

"I can smell it." His voice was rough, crinkled brows further confirming his perplexed state. "You know I can."

"What would you like me to say?" My burst of laughter was breathy yet genuine. "That I'm sorry?" Shaking my head, I moved for the dressing chamber.

"You will sleep in the bed."

Stunned, I turned back to face him. I hadn't thought this far ahead. It likely showed as I stood frozen. "Naked," I said, to be certain that was indeed what he'd meant.

In answer, he loosened the already loose ties at the neck of his tunic, then lifted it over his head.

"You truly are a monster." I refused to look at his chest. It would only give him more tallies on the scoreboard.

He kept his britches on, and I caught a glimpse of the violent definition of his hips when he leaped onto his bed.

"You have no idea." He stretched over the side farthest from me, his elbow bent and his head in his hand. "Are you not dreadfully tired after barely sleeping last night?"

How he'd known such a thing when he hadn't returned to his rooms was something I'd need to ponder another time. When I wasn't wholly focused on his every breath, word, and minuscule movement.

I confessed, "I am, actually."

His brows rose as I traipsed to the bed.

Gingerly, I lowered over it. Surprisingly comfortable despite the atrocities he'd likely committed on the mattress, I turned on my side, too, and curled my arms over my chest.

He glared. "Remove them."

I smiled. "But—"

"Remove them, or I'll tie them to the headboard."

I shivered, feigning delight at the thought. But although it would terrify me to be at his mercy in such a way, I couldn't ignore the jolt of excitement within my chest.

"I thought you were simply being a bold fool, but perhaps I was wrong," he murmured, seeming utterly sincere as his eyes left my exposed breasts and met mine. "You do enjoy this."

"Enjoy what?" I whispered, not meaning to but suddenly without enough breath.

His answer was a wide smile that revealed his dimple and tightened my stomach with anticipation and alarm.

Perhaps Etheria, the goddess of this realm, was as cunning as her children. Monsters shouldn't look like him. Shouldn't be granted the beauty to disarm their prey with a simple, half-dimpled, portrait-worthy smile. Every inch of Atakan Ethermore was a trap designed to entice and torture and kill.

The fire crackled. The air in the room stifled, thickened from tension.

Feathers rustled, crushed as the prince dropped his head to the pillow and placed his hand in the space between us.

Painstakingly slow, his last two fingers curled with his thumb, leaving the index and middle finger standing straight toward the curtained canopy of the bed. "Sit on them."

My heart roared in my ears.

Hearing its fast dance, Atakan smirked.

Useless excuses spun through my mind as I remained silent and stared at that cruelly divine mouth. Excuses I didn't want to voice. I shouldn't have even been tempted to rise to this challenge. It might have been another game, but he was completely serious.

I could surrender, as I was sure he expected, or I could chase the feelings warming my body and win.

A bargain cannot be broken. It went against the spiritual laws of these creatures. One cannot be cunning and trustworthy at the same time—so deals were essential to maintain relationships and a semblance of order.

I stated my terms. "If I sit on them, then you will sleep on the floor."

Long lashes nearly met his thick brows. "My, my…" He dragged his tongue over his teeth. "You are bold indeed."

Reaching over the mattress, I stroked those two fingers. "The choice is now yours."

He didn't move them, and he didn't remove his eyes from mine. I'd gained the upper hand. So of course, he said, "Fine, but only if you come."

I wasn't sure I could.

But I was shamelessly sure I wanted to try.

My finger traced the long length of the two digits he wished to place inside my body, pausing at the callus upon his knuckle. I would've preferred only one finger, but saying so could give away my innocence.

The last thing I needed was for Atakan to learn about that.

Just as his fingers began to curl around my own, I exhaled, "Fine."

His chest rose, then fell in a heavy heave when I sat up.

Slowly, I inched toward his hand on my knees. Not since I was so young that I needed assistance bathing had I been this exposed. I'd been so fixated on the future I'd now met and ruminating on how I might survive it that I hadn't thought I wanted to be.

I'd never realized how much I wanted to be.

As soon as his fingers brushed my core, I gasped. I stared down at his hand, waiting for it to move.

It didn't. Wouldn't.

This was my decision. This would be my doing.

I took his fingers and, with care that likely hinted at my inexperience, slid them through me until they encountered my opening.

Then I lowered onto them.

Atakan hissed. Veins bulged in his forearm as it clenched. He wanted to do it himself, and realizing the restraint he battled gifted me the bravery to ignore the burn and spread my knees wider.

I pushed down.

I made sure to stop before his fingers met the barrier I'd yet to break, and while I breathed through the discomfort, I dug my own fingers through my hair. My eyes closed. My breasts felt heavier as I shifted the long strands over my shoulders.

I bit my lip and glanced down at the prince.

His mouth had parted—gone slack. His eyes fastened to his hand between my thighs, almost completely emerald.

Allowing my own to roam over his pectorals to his abdominals, I traced the deep grooves between them and imagined what it might feel like to touch them. Scrape my nails over them. My earlier arousal returned, and I rocked my hips to chase the growing heat.

Faster. Harsher.

"Dreaded Mildred." Atakan slid his teeth over his lip, and swallowed. "You're dripping all over my hand."

Those husked words only ignited more flames. But it wasn't

enough. I needed more, but I couldn't bear down. If I did, I would break. I also couldn't touch myself. I knew he wouldn't allow it.

"Touch me," I rasped.

As if he'd been waiting, he accepted the challenge instantly.

I thought he'd touch my breasts, as he'd seemed somewhat fascinated by them. Instead, he licked his thumb.

Then brushed it over my clit.

My thighs shook, and I moaned.

The sound shocked us both. His eyes climbed to mine, then returned to the fingers I rode with desperate juts of my hips. He brushed me again, then waited and watched. On the third touch, he applied more pressure, and I moaned louder.

I had no space in my hazed mind to feel embarrassed about the guttural sound. Pleasure swam through me, bittersweet.

Atakan crooned, "There we are." He took his thumb away, waited for suspended seconds, then circled my clit. "Give in, defiant creature." Softly, he flicked it.

Rapture stole me. So swift, I became nothing but feeling. Nothing but pulsing and mindless warmth. My body took over as I surrendered to it.

A mistake.

Pain chilled me to my quaking bones.

A near-silent scream fled me as I fell forward onto my hands. My arms and breath trembled.

I hadn't realized how close the prince was. Not until he moved my hair aside to study me as I breathed through gnashed teeth.

Lust glazed his eyes, but shock rounded them. He sniffed, then sniffed again as he reared back. "No…" His laughter was hoarse with disbelief and unmistakable delight. "What have you done?" He wriggled his fingers inside me.

I flinched and growled.

He chuckled. "Darkest fucking skies, dread."

The burn was so intense, so complete, it was all I could do to keep from whimpering.

"You saved yourself for me." With unexpected gentleness, he removed his fingers from my stinging body. "How unfortunate," he said, thick with dry amusement.

His throaty groan lured my eyes.

He dragged his tongue over his fingers, then placed them into his mouth. The pain faded the longer I watched him lay there, lazily and thoroughly cleaning my pleasure and destroyed innocence from his hand.

My body rewarmed.

Before I could manage thought, let alone tell him I hadn't saved anything for him, he left the bed. A burgundy scarf I'd used to secure the drapes to the bedpost unraveled with a yank. The mattress dipped as he moved in behind me on his knees.

To drag the silk through my wet core.

Again, I flinched and tried to crawl away. My hair was seized.

He tutted and gathered the strands around his hand, tilting my head back. His gaze crashed into mine. The words were a caustic whisper in my ear. "You really shouldn't have given me that." He nipped my earlobe. "Never will I let you forget it."

Then I was released.

I collapsed over the pillows, too exhausted to so much as think about cleaning myself. I pulled the twisted bedding over half of me, uncaring after all he'd seen.

The prince opened the nightstand drawer, then closed it three seconds later. He'd placed the scarf in there. I knew it in my weary bones.

Sleep had almost taken me when he snatched a pillow from behind me.

He muttered a myriad of wonderful curses as he settled upon the floor. "Don't think it's escaped my notice that you won twice just now."

I smiled into the pillow covered in his scent, feeling safe enough to close my eyes. At least for tonight.

NINE

"Waiting for someone to save you?"

I turned from the blue window to find Pholly, my gown whispering over the wood floor.

The revealing number had been delivered and hung in the doorway of Atakan's dressing chamber while I'd slept, a note pinned to the lace to explain its existence.

The ball to celebrate my arrival at Ethermore had come sooner than I'd expected. Too soon to allow for last-minute invitations to my family, apparently. Intentional, no doubt, though I couldn't decipher why.

Who had written the note, I didn't know. The prince certainly wouldn't have. I'd woken alone and grateful for it, yet annoyingly curious of his whereabouts.

"I don't need saving," I said, and far too harshly. I swiped my clammy hands over my hips. If it weren't for the cream-laced clouds covering the sky-blue silk, I would have assumed the dress was a nightgown, due to it molding to every curve of my body. "I just..." I gestured to the ballroom entrance. "I don't really want this ball."

A pointless thing to say.

What I wanted didn't matter. It never had.

"This evening is not about you, halfling." Pholly studied the faeries saturating the expansive room—seemed to steel herself with a lift of her pointed chin. "This is but another excuse to overindulge and get up to no good."

With that, she walked on to the open oak doors.

Her beaded silver gown revealed her arms, shoulders, much of her breasts, and one of her defined legs. Silver ribbons climbed her ankle from her heeled slipper. The glimmering beads threw sparks at the shadows in the hall.

They seemed to retreat, flinching back toward the deeper dark behind me.

I wished I could have done the same.

My betrothed was nowhere to be seen when I entered the room. Standing near the doors, I feigned checking the ribbon I'd weaved into my loosely braided hair. Curving tendrils lined my cheeks and tickled my neck. The ribbon matched the silk beneath the cream lace of my gown. I'd been relieved to find it tied to the same hanger, as I hadn't had time to search for Elion for assistance.

After waking late and eating lunch alone in the dining room, I'd returned to Atakan's bed. I'd intended to distract myself from this ball by reading one of the books I'd brought from home. I'd woken hours later on the end of the bed, the castle alive with merriment from arriving guests.

Perhaps Atakan wouldn't be attending. I hadn't seen him since last night, and surely, he would have needed to return to his chambers to prepare.

No such luck, I soon discovered.

A tendril of hair stirred at my cheek as sudden energy warmed from behind. I knew before he spoke that such energy could only be his.

"Dread."

I didn't turn. I kept watching the fiddle players twirl throughout the ballroom. Some guests clapped and danced as they neared them. Some ignored them. Others sneered.

Mercifully, my tone was as crisp as I'd intended. "I wasn't sure you'd make it."

He stood beside me, adjusting the cuff of his sleeve beneath his coat as if loathing the tight fit. "I'll never forfeit an opportunity to torture you, halfling. You should know that by now."

I glanced at him. Just briefly.

His hair was damp. It seemed he'd only managed a quick wash, too. Curiosity over what had kept him away all day climbed from a simmer to a boil as he dragged a long finger over his bladed jawline.

He appeared to check it, then exhaled and shook out his arms. Sky-blue silk lined his dark blue coat. He tugged it closed over the cream shirt beneath but left it unbuttoned.

Unable to resist, I said as I returned my gaze to the colorful collection of guests, "I was beginning to wonder if such a loss was making it difficult for you to face me."

Faeries now glanced our way. Some outright stared while smiling and smirking and whispering to one another.

I kept my features still, not wishing to react to their murmured insults. It was better they thought I lacked the ability to hear them due to being half-human.

"I've been thinking about that too, actually." His smile was evident in his dry tone. "And I do believe the blood drawn makes me the victor."

Irritated—by his undeserved smugness and by the fluttering in my stomach from knowing that he'd been thinking about me—I gave him a new challenge. "Then maybe we should dance."

He laughed, deeply and so genuine, I almost flinched. Gazing down at me, he slowly closed his mouth. His jaw firmed.

A brow raised, I waited.

His jaw ticked, the only indication of some internal struggle.

Then he smirked as the crowd parted for Ruelle, and he left without a backward glance.

Her dark pink gown matched the tint on her lips. The pleated skirts swished as Ruelle reached Atakan and took his arm. She led him to a server bearing a tray of crystal goblets.

Moments later, they were swallowed within the crowd.

A monstrosity of a cake perched atop the banquet table in the center of the room. To fix my uneven breathing, I studied each line of cloudy-blue icing over the white fondant and identified each gleaming glob of fruit.

The king's boisterous laughter drew my gaze, and I caught the roll of Cordenya's eyes behind him. She drained her goblet as Garran lifted two females over his shoulders. He turned them in circles, their kicking feet nearly catching his consort in the face.

Scowling, Cordenya stepped back, then headed toward a server for more wine.

Phineus arrived.

He grinned when I snagged his attention. His attire seemed almost casual. "He's an enigma."

Knowing he'd meant the king, I eyed his frothy olive green shirt and brown leather pants, asking, "How so?"

"Everyone's friend one second, the next he could be beheading someone or taking their wife as a lover for weeks as punishment." He offered me his goblet of wine. I declined, and he shrugged. "The two extremes can often make for an interesting event."

"Seems he gifted only one extreme to his son."

My betrothed was being fed wine by Ruelle. Another female, white-haired and willowy, danced before them next to a smaller banquet table along the wall.

Phineus soaked them in with a hum. All the while, I pretended to observe the lace-covered table. The array of cream-topped strawberries, cloud-shaped cheeses, and bowls of brightly shelled chocolates.

"It has been said that he truly was born without a heart."

Unable to trap it, I laughed. "I cannot imagine anything more true than that."

As if hearing the sound above the others in the room, Atakan glanced our way. His eyes sparked. The vivid bronze morphed into green, tugging forward the memory of his fingers and his unwavering gaze on my sex.

Fighting a silent battle against the heat rushing through me, I didn't notice Phineus's extended hand until he chuckled.

I looked at it, then at him.

He said, "Atakan might be heartless, but he is still a faerie male. Trust me."

"You'll need to forgive my inability to trust anyone in this castle."

He wasn't offended. "Then take a chance. Just for a few minutes."

Before I could deny him once more, he drained his goblet and handed it to a passing guest.

The near-bald male balked at it, then at Phineus with outraged amber eyes. But we were wading into the crowd of dancers before he could find words to join his glower.

Phineus placed my hand at his shoulder and kept the other in his as he tugged me against him. "Lord Hillings," he explained. "Not too long ago, he made the mistake of trying to touch my sister."

Taller than me by only a few inches, I could see the guests over his shoulder. A small comfort, with skies only knew who floated behind my half-exposed back as we swayed.

"So you are defending her honor by disrespecting him," I surmised and tried not to trip over the small lace train of my gown as it tangled around our feet.

"She doesn't need me to do that. He wears the evidence of her ire in his permanently crooked finger. I merely enjoy irritating him."

Impressed, I admitted, "Pholly grows more and more admirable each day."

"She's a viper, but her heart is pudding." He paused, true fear entering his voice. "Don't tell her I said that."

I smiled, failing to find his twin sister in the shimmering dim of the ballroom.

Orbs strung from the rafters threw splashes of sun-shaped shadows over the muraled walls. As I watched them flicker, tension ceased stiffening my movements.

That is, until Phineus whispered so quietly I almost missed it, "Sniff me."

"What?" I nearly shouted.

"Lower your nose to my neck…" He pressed his mouth to my ear, breathing the words into it. "Just for three seconds, and make a show of scenting me."

After another stunned moment, I did—forgetting how foolish I felt when I inhaled deeply. Against his sun-kissed skin, I asked, "Apple?"

"My favorite soap."

Slowly, I lifted my head.

Over Phineus's shoulder, Elion's gaze caught mine. But it wasn't me who seemed to have his attention.

Phineus noticed when we turned, and I could've sworn he held me closer, tighter as flutes and light percussion joined the floating notes from the fiddles.

My assumption was bold, certainly, yet no more than what I was already doing. "You're attempting to make someone jealous."

Phineus didn't even try to deny it. His smile was rueful, and his voice whisperingly low. "Do you think it's working?"

"Well…" I waited until the steward came into view again. "He's still watching."

"I know."

Confusion had me asking, "Surely, Atakan knows you prefer males, then?"

"He knows I love everything." He spun me, and I laughed. Bringing me back to his chest, he whispered to my cheek, "And here he comes."

A thrill spiraled down my spine, straightening it.

His presence was a flare of heat at my back, and his voice low and scathing. "Remove your hands, or I'll remove them from your body and make you eat them."

Phineus grinned, his eyes brightening to the same blue of the muraled ballroom as he released me. Stepping back, he made an amusing show of bowing.

Atakan took my hand before he'd even straightened.

Tentatively, I placed the other over his broad shoulder. Tension screamed from his taut frame and in his bruising grip. My fingers protested the squeeze, but I moved my feet in time with his.

His scent flooded, awakening the defiance in me. "I thought you didn't want to be seen with me."

"And I thought you valued your insignificant life." He spun me away from him, then hauled me back to his chest with force that dizzied. His hand slid to my lower back, his fingers digging into my exposed skin—too firm to be possessive.

Punishing.

I asked, though I already knew, "What gives you the impression I don't?"

"You've publicly insulted me."

"By dancing with your cousin?" I pressed. When he didn't answer, I laughed. "Because I sniffed him."

Still, Atakan said nothing. He didn't need to when a strange noise, not a growl but not a grunt, rumbled from his chest.

A morsel of concern had me confessing, "You've embarrassed me, too."

He glared down at me, his gaze fire-shrouded emerald. "Why should I care about that?"

For a moment, I was struck still by the loss of so much bronze—by the predatory glow. Then one of his eyes narrowed. Not because I hadn't answered, but almost as if he couldn't quite figure something out.

I needed to look away from those eyes but refused to show fear. "I'm not saying you should. But if you don't, then you also shouldn't care if I dance with someone."

"I don't care."

"Then why are you dancing with me?"

"I want to fuck you." The gritted words burst between his teeth as though he'd been biting them since he'd arrived.

A shocked laugh fled me, my head shaking like I'd been slapped.

Eyes fell upon us, piercing and curious and prying. I forgot about them, and about where we were entirely as I read Atakan's earnest expression. The utter stillness of his skull-sharp cheeks and features. "You mean that."

He just blinked slowly.

"You truly do want to, and I think you hate it."

His smile was serpentine before his mouth neared my temple, his lethal words for only me to hear. "I've ruined your innocence with my fingers. Now I want to stretch and stuff you with my cock until tears leave your eyes and your defiant mouth can't form words."

My stomach hollowed, then filled with heat.

"You can't scare me," I whispered, even as fear hitched my breath. "Not with games I am happy to play."

His inhale hissed. "Prove it."

I pulled free of him, weighing the steady glow of his gaze.

Then I walked through the watching guests toward the nearest exit.

Atakan wouldn't follow. He wouldn't dare be seen leaving with the halfling he was being forced to marry. So I knew I would be made to wait like the desperate creature he wished me to be.

Yet I hadn't thought I would be waiting all night.

I tossed and turned, the bedding torture over my naked body. Not as torturous as the want I shouldn't feel. I shouldn't have wanted this. Not with him.

But I did.

I wanted him enamored. I wanted the safety that would come with his obsession. I wanted the freedom to live without the constraints of fear and uncertainty.

Most of all, I wanted the challenge of him.

An unfortunate side effect of this game of survival—the addicting high of victory, no matter how small.

This time, victory was undeniably his.

The cunning creature had made me leave my own welcoming ball.

He remained downstairs, drinking wine and perhaps even entertaining Ruelle or some other female, all the while knowing that I was in his bed. That I was waiting and willing.

As night crawled into the early hours of a new day, I began to wonder less about who he'd chosen to entertain himself with and more about who I might have been without this game. Without this fate I'd never wanted.

Without a prince that made even defeat taste victorious.

TEN

I WOKE NAKED BUT NOT ALONE.

On his side, head perched on his hand, Atakan watched me. For hazy moments, I wondered if I was dreaming or falling into another nightmare. It unnerved me. The way he stared as if he were trying to ascertain what to do with me.

He proved my assumption true when he murmured, "I can't decide if looking at your body makes me happier than the thought of watching you die."

"Good morning to you, too."

"I searched the ballroom for someone with hair like yours, eyes and hips like yours." His gaze narrowed on my mouth. "Lips like yours."

"Foolish." Sleep thickened my voice. "I was right here."

"Oh, I know."

Realization soured my stomach. "Did you succeed?"

He didn't answer. But he smirked.

It faded as his bronze eyes drifted over my body again. When they returned to my face, emerald peppered them. They halted on my mouth once more. "Put your lips on mine."

I wanted to.

I might have wanted to more than I wanted to flee from him and this kingdom.

Instead, I kicked the tangled bedding from my legs and threw them over the side of the bed. I drained the water from the goblet on the nightstand, but it did nothing to douse the bitter taste of jealousy and the sweetness of relief.

As soon as I set the goblet down, an arm hooked around my waist, and I fell back over the mattress.

The prince, on his hands and knees, loomed above me. "You won't play with me."

"I'm not in the mood."

He frowned, and how quick it happened made it sort of endearing.

Until he lowered his head and the tip of his nose touched mine. Strands of his blond hair tickled my chin and lips, and the scent of peppermint tea lingered on his breath. "I don't like this."

"I don't like you."

"You liked me enough to wait naked in my bed."

"Oh," I laughed out. "You thought I did that for *you?*"

Fury darkened his bronze eyes.

The growing flecks of emerald hypnotized, his lashes touching his heavy brows as he scowled. "If you so much as think about playing with anyone but me, I will tie you to this bed with their entrails and paint you in their blood while I fuck you."

Breath burned past my lips at the mere thought.

But I refused to let him distract me from winning after such a fatal loss. "Yet you can play with whoever you like?" I laughed again. This time, without humor. "That is hardly fair."

"What isn't fair is your existence," Atakan seethed, his mouth leaving my forehead and moving closer to mine. "The way you make me crave and loathe you in equal measure."

I pressed my thighs together, and he groaned—sounding almost pained.

Then his mouth descended.

He brushed his lips over my own. So softly, I thought I truly was still asleep.

I waited, scarcely breathing, for the violence he'd once vowed to bestow. My heart failed to beat. My body didn't move. I just lay there, my face upside down beneath his, knowing what I wanted yet so unsure of what to do. Not sure if I should reach up and touch his hair.

And take what I wanted.

An immortal lifetime passed in a moment of indecision. Then my heart rattled in my chest. My lips rubbed over his. My breath whispered between them, carrying a slight moan.

Snarling low, he shifted closer. Pressed harder. His hand framed my cheek, fingers digging underneath my jaw. Then he opened my mouth with his tongue.

Instinctively, my teeth snatched it and dragged over the soft flesh.

An animalistic noise climbed his throat. He licked my bottom teeth, my lower lip, peeling it back before reaching my chin.

He bit it, then whispered, "I want to do this while your tight little cunt struggles to adjust to my cock." And the way he'd said it not only made me shiver, but it made me believe he hadn't done it before.

Made me want to be the first he gave such attentiveness to with his mouth.

But no amount of wanting could rid the thought of him finding another to bed while I'd waited for him like a besotted and desperate fool.

So I smiled and rolled off the bed, swinging my hips as I traipsed into the bathing room and closed the door.

Almost everyone was absent at dinner.

Those in attendance, Phineus and Ruelle, appeared interested only in eating. The clank of cutlery and serving utensils joined the crackling fire in the silence.

I'd had no desire to eat in the dining room. But I hadn't wanted to wait until everyone was done to make a plate to eat alone in Atakan's rooms. After losing sleep last night, I'd chosen a nap over lunch, and I'd woken starving.

"Garran is probably still sleeping," Phineus eventually informed as he dumped another potato onto his plate. "Rumor has it he didn't return to his tower until dawn."

Ruelle glared when I reached for the bread at the same time as her. Even as my fingers curled into my palms, I smiled with sweetness that likely looked as forced as it was and gestured for her to pick first.

She took her time, so I helped myself to some vegetables and tried to ignore imaginings of her and my betrothed.

As if my barely tamed jealousy had summoned the monster, Atakan arrived a minute later.

Wearing fresh brown britches and a floating ivory shirt that was far too thin for early spring, he stalked into the dining room. He took the seat opposite me. His eyes swung from me to his cousin and thinned in warning.

Phineus poured a mint-scented cream onto his meal, ignoring him.

The scent of it brought forth the ever-present memory of Atakan's carnal kiss.

It scattered instantly when Ruelle moved to the empty seat beside the prince, her dinner dragged with her.

Candlelight from the chandelier swayed the shadows behind her chair. They seemed to meld into her gauzy black gown as she fussed with the skirts.

Paying her no mind, Atakan piled beef onto his plate.

I discovered he wasn't even paying attention to what he was doing when I looked up from the mess he was making and found his focus solely on me. He filled his crystal goblet with but a glance, then sipped from it, his unreadable eyes still stuck to me.

I carved into my meal, feeling that gaze as if it were another hard press of his mouth on my own. Another lick at my teeth and lips.

Ceaselessly, I'd tried not to think about it. I'd tried to think of anything else. He'd broken my innocence with his fingers, yet not even that could take up space the way that stupid kiss did.

Perhaps it had poisoned him in the same way, and that was why he continued to watch me. Perhaps he was merely thinking of new ways to torture me when we left this room, and he issued me a new challenge.

Halfway through my meal, Ruelle broke the silence by climbing onto the prince's lap.

The clang of Atakan's fork against his plate jarred.

I forced my eyes back to my food, even as I straightened in my chair.

"Mildred," Ruelle said. When she failed to earn my gaze, her tone sharpened. "You left your own ball when it had only just begun."

It irritated that she would wait until she had the prince's presence to attempt goading me.

"I was feeling…" I peered at Atakan, who stabbed a hunk of meat with his knife before tearing it in two with his teeth. Coyly, I touched my mouth. "So very overwhelmed."

Atakan stilled.

Then he flashed those teeth in a feral half smile as he chewed.

Ruelle huffed. "But do you not think that's disrespectful?"

That earned my whole attention. "No. Do you know what is disrespectful?"

She blinked, then raised a daring and slender brow.

"You." I smiled brightly. "Sitting on my betrothed's lap."

Phineus coughed, thumping his chest as he gave in and laughed.

Ruelle glowered. "Unlike you, halfling, I am wanted here."

"But you're not," Atakan said, then promptly picked her up and dropped her into the seat beside him.

Mortification painted Ruelle's cheeks crimson. Her eyes glossed, and guilt nibbled when she whispered to Atakan, "You cannot mean that."

Brightest skies, perhaps she desired more than a place in this court. Perhaps she was in love with the prince.

Atakan said nothing.

Ruelle followed his eyes to me, then pushed to her feet. "If you think he'll actually marry you, halfling, you're as delusional as the rest of your mortal kin." With that, she snatched her plate and left the room.

Phineus cursed and reached for the decanter of wine.

Atakan continued to eat, though with his eyes now on his food.

Minutes of tense quiet stifled before I found the courage to poke at what Ruelle had said. "How are the wedding preparations coming along?" I asked. "It's a mere week away, and I've yet to see so much as a sample of fabric or cake toppings."

"We're not to be bothered with the tedious chores of it all," Atakan said.

His answer and curt tone wouldn't deter me. This wedding was nearly a decade in the making. It was not just another ball for the influential to attend. It was a history-making event for this entire continent.

I opened my mouth to demand more information, then looked at the open doors when Atakan did.

Rushed steps echoed from outside, slowing as they neared the dining room. Two guards appeared, dressed in a mixture of leather and plated armor.

One pushed the cover of his helmet up, revealing flushed cheeks as he tapped on one of the doors. "Please excuse us, my prince." He bobbed his head toward me. "Princess."

Surprised he'd addressed me when many hadn't since my arrival, I was too slow to smile nor ask about their presence.

Atakan was already on his feet and marching to the door. "Where?"

The guard whispered, "The eastern woods."

I heard nothing more before they left, their quick footsteps rapidly dissipating.

Phineus rose, still chewing his food.

Curiosity got the better of me. "What were they talking about?"

His wink was betrayed by the tension in his jaw. "Better you don't know, Princess."

The door creaked open well after midnight.

Stumbled steps and the ringing thud of steel against the wood floor followed.

Between the half-drawn drapes, the full moon leaked into the bedchamber just enough to see the stains marring the prince's shirt. But I hadn't needed to see them. Not when I could smell it.

Blood.

Not merely his own, I realized, rolling over as he dropped onto the side of his bed. His boots were kicked off. A slight groan joined the thump of them meeting the floor as he gripped the hem of his once lovely shirt.

"Tell me something, dread." His voice was tight—pinched. "Do you only sleep after you've found pleasure?"

I smiled despite not wanting to. It wavered when he attempted to lift his shirt and hissed.

Instinctively, I sat up and moved toward his back. "What happened?"

He gave no response. He tossed something onto his nightstand. A dagger that hit the wood with a knock that nearly made me jump.

"You're injured," I said.

"Answer my question." The gruffness of his tone only further confirmed that he was wounded.

"Of course I can sleep without it. I merely struggle to rest when I don't know if someone will plunge a knife into my heart."

His low laughter broke, and he cursed.

Shuffling closer, I asked, "Can you lift your arms?"

"Can you run away from this castle already?"

I sighed and rose to my knees behind him. He didn't so much as tense when I gripped the neck of his shirt in both hands and then tugged. As it tore cleanly down his back, he did.

The fabric was stuck to his wounds.

Many wounds, I discovered, gasping as I peeled the shirt away from his wet skin. "What in the skies happened?" I made to touch them—the dark and bloodied holes speckling the expanse of his broad back and tapered torso.

"Iron splinters happened."

My fingers paused, floating as my eyes widened. "What type of weapon is capable of such a thing?"

"Wind magic." He huffed. "And considerable luck."

"But that is Seelie magic." And such power was nearly always inherited from noble blood.

His silence was telling.

I asked nothing more. He swayed, and I pushed him up by his biceps, then reached over him for the blade on his nightstand.

Maybe I imagined it, but I could have sworn he sniffed my hair before I settled back behind him.

I should have let the wounds fester, let the iron weaken him, and hope the splinters moved toward his rotten heart. But if I didn't help him, someone else would, and being the one to do so could very well help me.

Countless times, I'd lain awake over the years, wondering what would happen to me if Atakan Ethermore died. When I'd dared to ask Bernie, she'd said to pray to every deity that he lived a long life. For the faeries of this court would find worse ways to use me—or simply get rid of me.

Besides, that he'd come to his rooms upon returning from wherever he'd been was alarming and informative.

That he didn't move an inch when I carefully pried the splinters from his smooth skin confirmed that he'd come to me for a reason. He didn't want anyone to know he was wounded. Perhaps he didn't even want them to know where he'd been.

But I only said, "How sweet you are to disturb my slumber when there are healers far more adept at this."

"Like I told you," he said, gritted when a particularly large shard left his skin. It fell to the bed, then clacked to the floor when I used the dagger to flick it away. "You will sleep when I say so."

Though he spoke true, it had also proven to be somewhat of a lie. "And how did you know I was awake, monster?"

"Your heartbeat," he said.

I pondered that as I picked three splinters from between his shoulder blades, my fingers slippery with blood. I wiped them on the soiled bedding, as well as the stone hilt of the blade, then continued.

He'd been paying attention—learning my tells.

The satisfaction that delivered birthed a smile I was glad he couldn't see. "What is happening in those woods, Atakan?"

"The usual," he said, apathetic. "Leftovers and sympathizers dooming themselves with bold attempts to undo what cannot be undone."

"The Unseelie," I whispered, wincing as I dug at a larger piece of iron right next to his spine. "They're attacking to reach the castle and have you remove the wards caging The Bonelands?"

He tensed, breath sailing from him when I freed the shard from his skin. "They attack because there is nothing else to be done. The wards cannot be removed."

That gave me pause.

However finite, there was always a way to break through such spells. Always a loophole for any curse. Although plucking a thread that would unravel something of that magnitude would inevitably invite severe consequences.

I didn't say what I thought. I didn't dare put voice to what this prince already knew. He and all those who'd played a role in caging the Unseelie knew they would free themselves from what our kingdoms had done to them one day and seek retribution.

The likes of which this continent had probably never seen.

I shivered and hoped that time came only after a few centuries of living, and I was long dead. Though what that living might entail, I could still only guess at. Perhaps that was why The Boneland's curse bothered me now, when I'd never given it much thought before.

I knew what it was to crave freedom. To wish to unleash every ugly feeling born from my captivity on those who'd forced it upon me so mercilessly.

The prince swayed again.

My hands enjoyed the feel of his skin too much as I steadied him before I set the dagger down and left the bed in search of more light.

"What of these Seelie sympathizers?" I took the candle from his nightstand. He didn't answer, and I supposed he didn't need to. The Unseelie likely had numerous allies in this realm.

Lighting the candle on the dying flames in the hearth, I asked, "How many Unseelie warriors remain in Ethermore?"

"Too many," he grunted. "Next time you disobey me, perhaps I'll toss you into the woods to play with them."

I smirked. "You said I wasn't allowed to play with anyone else."

"And I meant it." Pain edged the lethal whisper.

"Then perhaps you should think of a different threat." When I crawled back onto the bed, my nightgown tangled beneath my knees as I raised the candle over his back. "Besides, I would enjoy the change of scenery."

I used his ruined shirt to wipe his back, the flame bouncing as I made sure every gouge in his skin was closing. Only one continued to weep, so I snuffed the candle and grabbed the blade.

As I did, he said, "You're not to leave the grounds, dread," and so seriously that I stilled.

He seemed perturbed. Truly concerned about these enemies intent on reaching this castle. If not to free The Bonelands, then for revenge.

I itched to ask more. To inform him that I'd had some defense training—enough to surely help to some degree. But he tilted as soon as I removed the last splinter, as if certain that no more remained, and collapsed over the bed.

For mere moments or too many minutes, I watched his breathing settle before washing my hands in the bathing room.

Upon the window seat, I curled over the cushion underneath my sister's emerald coat and studied the sleeping monster. The unjust beauty of his lax features. The blood on his clothing and blades.

When I woke, only small patches of dried blood remained where the prince had lain.

'ELEVEN

The prince didn't return for a week. Our wedding date came and went.

Bernie's concern was evident in her most recent letter.

Perhaps I should've been concerned, too. Yet for the first time in years, I wasn't.

Of course, I wasn't comfortable. I doubted I would ever feel wholly comfortable in this castle of trees and tyrants. But I was enjoying it—certainly the quiet that came with the absence of the king and prince.

The lack of fear.

The trepidation caused by my betrothed had settled into a low simmer. So much so that I almost missed the heat of it boiling. Almost missed him.

The company, at least, however perilous or ghastly.

Pholly wasn't interested in making a friend. Maybe I would have been offended, if I weren't looking for more of an ally and hadn't noticed that she had no interest in being social with anyone. Not even Ruelle, who sullenly stalked the halls for any word of Atakan's return.

Phineus had joined the prince, Pholly had said when I'd asked over breakfast some mornings ago. She'd seemed annoyed that I'd interrupted her drawing, so I'd let her be after she'd curtly informed me that they were out hunting.

We both knew what they were hunting. Pholly likely knew far more than me, but I understood enough.

Over the days that passed in a blur of dwindling snow and wet wind, I'd taken to leaving the castle between gaps in the weather to wander the gardens. Each time, I walked closer to the woods, drawn to the darkness between the trees. Patrolling guards kept me from venturing any farther.

Hidden villages winked within heavy woodland across the mountains on either side of the castle.

Smoke rose near one in the east. Too much to be considered chimney or factory made. After lunch, I went to the balcony of the prince's rooms to find it had spread like a fast-moving fog.

Fire.

The halls were absent of souls. Only murmurs traveled from the staff quarters beneath the ground floor. No guards were stationed in the rear courtyard, where overgrown vegetation crawled across mossy pavers in dying and muddied chunks.

I lifted my skirts and held them as I met the grass.

Wildflowers intent on defying the harsh climate shivered in the breeze. In the distance, water could be heard falling into the river wending between the mountains. Birds soared overhead, arcing down the sharp-sloping hills beyond the bowl of gardens.

Hedges and quaking tulips were all that remained, new life unable to bloom until the remnants of winter relented. Ethermore wouldn't warm as the other kingdoms did. Regardless, a glimmer of excitement unfurled at the thought of witnessing the unveiling of spring.

A shrieked-growl drew my eyes to the woods.

Guards no longer patrolled the tree line. I discovered why when I gazed up, shielding my eyes against the glare of the cloud-covered sun. The fire had spread uphill. That, or there were now more blazes burning near—or even within—the mountain village.

But it was the creature moving through the sky that succeeded in chilling my blood.

My breathing quickened as I hurried closer to the trees.

A felynx.

The monstrous mixture of feline and canine flew toward the smoke, the shadow upon the felynx's back barely visible between its wings.

I'd never seen one outside of books and paintings. Bernie claimed she had when she was young and passing through towns bordering

The Bonelands. I wondered how many of them roamed the continent, unable to fly beyond the wards entrapping their kin.

Wards made to keep them in, not out.

What Atakan had said about leftovers returned. I'd surmised there'd be plenty, as had my father in all his dealings, but I'd never expected to see them. To have them venture so boldly close to Cloud Castle in their desperation.

If they refused to accept their fate, the Unseelie were to be captured, imprisoned, and interrogated. Yet the patrols had been called hunts for good reason.

I'd assumed they'd hide in order to survive.

Many probably did, I thought as I continued toward the tree line. Many more probably weren't like them—*like me*—and were not content to play games in order to remain breathing.

Disdain clawed sharply at my chest when another felynx soared over the treetops. I didn't know whether it was for myself or the Unseelie faeries intent on causing destruction even after they'd been defeated.

I had no idea what I was even doing. It wasn't as if I could get too close. It would take hours to reach those fires on foot. I should have been inside, taking advantage of the quieter castle by bathing as long as I wished and lounging around.

But now confronted by this different form of danger, the luxury of safety no longer seemed so appealing.

I'd heard of skirmishes, but not once in my two weeks at Cloud Castle had I heard rumors of this type of violence—battles with armies and beasts and fire. Perhaps the castle staff hadn't known.

They surely would now.

Branches snapped under my flat boots, the leather too fine and thin for such terrain. I didn't care. I tugged my gown higher and followed the sound of another ferocious roar. A wolf shifter, perhaps.

Rushing steps crashed through the brush uphill, and I paused mere feet within the tree line.

"It's southbound." The male warrior's shout carried through the trees, as if delivered by the mild breeze. Heavier smoke now traveled upon it.

More hurried steps echoed. Armor glinted distantly.

Before I could decide whether to cease exploring, another roar sent birds flapping from treetops into the skies.

Body heat met my back.

A hand clapped over my mouth, and a familiar scent liquefied my limbs. "Just where do you think you're going?"

I whirled, my heart pounding so fast that I shoved the prince. "You scared me."

My meager strength didn't move him an inch.

His brow rose. Blood crusted it and browned thick strands of his near-white hair. "Me?" He gestured past me to the woods. "I am nothing but a thorn compared to where you were headed."

Though the warning intrigued, I said, "I wasn't going anywhere."

"Liar," Atakan crooned.

The sound of his voice, the sight of his lean and seemingly unharmed physique, and the emerald sparks in those mischievous bronze eyes…

There was no calling the warmth that spiraled through me anything but pure relief.

Eyeing the blood splatter on his burgundy tunic and the drops on his leather-lined pants, I smiled. "Are you injured again?"

He wasn't. But the barb did as intended.

His slight sneer brought forth a feeling of comfort that shouldn't be, cold tendrils that ridded my body of that misguided warmth.

"You're out of luck today, dread, but if you tell me what you're doing out here, maybe I'll let you touch me anyway." He closed the space between us, his dimple catching my gaze. "Playing pretend might be fun."

"If you need to pretend to hide the fact that you want me to touch you, then be my guest." I shrugged. "Regardless, I'm not interested."

"That's why you waited all night for me in my bed." His grin was as beastly as the creatures growling in the distance. "Naked." Then he looked over my shoulder to the woods. "You're interested in the bloodshed."

The reminder of that night almost made me bristle. "I'm merely curious about what's happening," I admitted. "And why it's happening so close to the castle."

Another roar fractured the silence trailing my words.

Atakan glanced at the skies. Then my hand was snatched, and I was dragged back across the grounds.

Before we reached the castle, he stopped at a small garden shed astride the courtyard's pebbled path. He opened the wooden door and tugged me inside, then released me into the dark.

He closed the door. Alarm prodded when he slid a rake through the rusted handle to keep anyone from entering.

Light filtered in through slits between the rotting slats, illuminating Atakan's rigid shoulders and the tic in his jaw when he finally turned to me.

I retreated a step and collided with a pile of sacks. Old grain, I realized, pressing my hand to the hessian and squeezing to better keep my heart from racing.

I didn't want him to hear it. I didn't want him to mistake my nervousness and excitement for fear. I didn't even know how to differentiate between the three to decide how I felt.

And I had no time.

In two strides, he stood before me. Over me. His hand swept into my hair to the back of my head. The strands tangled in his fingers were given a harsh tug, effectively tilting my head until my eyes met his, just as he desired.

He searched them, my face, then my chest.

The latter heaved with my shortened breaths, though I tried to control them.

He made that impossible when he kicked my feet apart and pressed so close, his groin encountered my stomach. "I'm going to ask you one more time," he whispered. "What were you doing in the woods?"

"I was hardly *in* the woods."

He simply waited, those cruel features void of expression.

I sighed. "I've already told you."

He hummed. His other hand settled at the curve of my hip, then squeezed it. Heat flooded my body. A devastating grin sent it straight to my core when he asked, "Do you like that?"

I needn't have answered, let alone lied. If he hadn't already, then any second now, he'd be able to scent the truth. Still, I smirked. "Like what?"

His gaze narrowed, and his smile drooped. "I see."

That gaze stayed on mine as he ever so slowly inched my skirts up my legs, allowing time to answer his question and to tell him to stop. To prove him wrong.

I couldn't when I didn't want to.

Cold air coated my skin. I barely felt it—felt nothing but the whoosh of my heart and the graze of his fingers and knuckles as he gathered my skirts to my waist. Keeping his eyes on mine, he released my hair to lift me onto the sacks. He tucked the cotton layers behind me, beneath me, and I bit my lip when his fingers slid underneath my ass.

He was so close, I could snatch his head and kiss his luscious mouth.

But he laid a hand on my thigh and waited. When I merely glared, impatient, he moved it higher. His eyes flared. "You're not wearing undergarments."

"The few I brought with me are being washed," I lied.

He saw through it, yet I doubted he cared. His thumb brushed my mound, and I shivered. "The woods." His voice thickened, throat dipping as he said, "Tell me."

I heard the unspoken command within—*play with me.*

And I wanted to. By the darkest skies, for once, I wanted to so badly I might have questioned why, had I the chance. "I saw fire," I said truthfully. "And I've been bored, so I've taken to roaming the grounds in your absence."

He rewarded me by parting me with a lone finger.

I gasped, gripping his arm.

Muscle clenched beneath my hand. He peered at my flushing cheeks and my heaving chest. When his head rose, the tip of his nose skimmed mine, those long lashes bobbing. "There's more."

Not wanting him to stop, to cease touching me, I happily rambled on. "Guards normally patrol the tree line. I suppose they were called elsewhere. Perhaps to assist in the mountains. So I crept closer out of curiosity."

A glide of his finger through me made my teeth join and my legs spread wider.

"How far would you have gone?" he asked.

I had the distinct feeling he was not merely referring to a walk in the woods but to the night I'd left my own ball to wait for him in his bed.

Exhilaration coursed through me when I clasped his cheek and he didn't pull away. "I suppose we'll never know."

Then I kissed him.

His finger entered my body, and as I flinched and moaned, his tongue entered my mouth.

For moments that stole then returned my breath in a hitched flutter, he just held his finger still and as deep as it would go. His tongue stroked mine before retreating.

He sucked in a ragged inhale, his exhale heating my lips. "You're so warm," he groaned out. "So fucking soft."

Even if I could have spoken, I had no response to that.

"I need to feel you with my cock." When I said nothing and only blinked in a daze, he wriggled his finger. I whimpered, and he grinned. "Do you want it inside you?"

"I'm not playing this game again."

"But you're such a good little player," he crooned, kissing the corner of my mouth. "Fine." He withdrew his finger. His hooded eyes soaked in my slackening features as he slowly pushed it back into my body. "Give me those venomous lips."

I did, and luxuriated in his throaty groan when my teeth took his plush lower lip. I sucked it, then nipped as I released it, only for him to take my own. He bit it so hard, pain clanged against the chorus of pleasure swimming through my bloodstream.

As copper dampened a sweet caress from his mouth, I found I didn't hate it. I gripped his face, urging him to do it again. To do more.

To make me feel so much more.

He obliged and curled his finger inside me, stroking as his mouth battled mine. He did so again after withdrawing, stroking over and over until I was tugging at his hair and his mouth was at my throat. His teeth marked my collarbone, and his broad shoulder quaked beneath the clawed grip of my hand.

Pleasure dizzied.

My heart thundered in my ears alongside his hoarse curse when I began to shake—when I began to fracture. I braced for it. Breath halted, I braced for the same euphoria and pain I'd experienced last time.

But a low laugh cracked the haze. Cold washed in as his finger and mouth left me trembling.

I should have touched myself to carry me over the edge. Instead, I glared in disbelief. Though such wickedness shouldn't have surprised me at all.

Atakan stepped back, his finger in his mouth. He sucked, eyes aglow in the dark of the garden shed. His mouth curved as he surveyed me, as he watched me shove down my skirts. "Something the matter, dread?"

I wanted to hurl obscenities at him. I wanted to leap at him and glue my mouth to his and push any part of him into my body to alleviate the ache he'd given me.

But only one answer would suffice.

So I smiled while smoothing my hair back from my face. "Nothing I cannot fix myself."

His amusement died.

I sauntered past him to the door.

At the last moment, I thought better of it and pretended to trip and teeter. He cursed, stumbling back against a tower of pails. They hit the damp stone with a racket that would be heard by anyone nearby as I fell against him.

"Oh, my skies." My hands grappled for purchase, one brushing his erection. My eyes bulged, a genuine reaction that ridded his anger and earned me a deep laugh far too lovely for a creature so hideous. I cleared my throat, my voice flatter than I'd intended. "I suppose my inferior half-human senses are to blame."

His expression sobered as we stared at one another in the gloom.

It was strange to simply look without worry nor interruption. So strange that I hadn't allowed myself to acknowledge just how enjoyable it was to study him this intently.

I stepped back to leave when a flash of light through the wood slats unveiled a bruise along his sharp jawline.

Without thinking, I touched it.

He let me.

"How bad was it?" I breathed, gently tracing the purple smudge.

His brows were furrowed when I glanced up at his eyes. Emerald had nearly swallowed the bronze whole. "None of your business."

My lips twitched. "Of course." I leaned in, my mouth skimming the bruise, and whispered, "But whether we like it or not, you are my business, and I asked you a question."

His fingers stole my chin, his glower so severe, I half feared he'd shove me away and storm out into the gardens.

But it softened the longer he looked down at me, and disappeared entirely when he murmured, "Enough to make me miss the creature I loathe the most."

Then his mouth captured and consumed mine.

He walked me backward to the sacks again, my hands lifting my skirts before his could leave my cheeks.

One tangled in my hair, his hold tight, and his rough words exhaled into my mouth like much-needed air. "I want you. I want you as much as I loathe you—so much, it feels like I can't breathe." His parted lips dragged across my cheek, his whisper scathing near my ear. "Give me back my fucking breath."

Though this war between us was far from over, I smiled against his cheek.

"What would you do for it, monster?" I dared to ask, even as I unfastened the leather ties of his pants.

"Murder, maim, and…" He groaned when my hand wrapped around his cock.

Thick and long, the silken weight in my hand concerned. It also delighted. I had him, quite literally, in the palm of my halfling hand. "And?" I prompted with a gentle squeeze and a kiss to that sinister dimple.

"Bleed," he confessed through gnashed teeth.

Victory sang through my veins. A song so sweet, I released him and pushed up onto the sacks of grain. I bunched my skirts and opened my legs. "Show me just how much you loathe me, my prince."

He took himself in his hand, eyes fixed on my sex as he rubbed the head of his cock over it. "Say that again."

"Say what?" I fluttered my lashes, feigning confusion.

Our eyes locked, and he smirked. It widened into a menacing grin as he stepped against the piled sacks—effectively pushing himself inside me.

My body bucked.

He gripped my thighs, forcing them to remain open as he filled me in one slow yet determined thrust. His nostrils flared when he seated himself, and his chest heaved as he exhaled a ragged, "*Fuck.*"

I concurred but for a different reason.

Pain scalded. It spread from my core to tighten each limb and steal the beat of my heart. My pulse screamed. My eyes burned. I closed them, swallowing thickly.

Atakan squeezed my thighs. "Look at me."

I wouldn't. Not until I was certain the tears had abated.

"Mildred."

It might have been the first time he'd ever solely used my name. The guttural tone was so shocking, so deliciously telling, I obeyed.

My lashes lifted. The bronze in his eyes had been reduced to flecks swimming among an emerald sea. He frowned at the sheen coating my own.

A quiet snarl made me tense until he gently parted my lips with his.

I exhaled a sigh as my eyes closed again. He licked beneath my upper lip, then kissed my lower lip so softly, I shouldn't have felt it everywhere.

As though he was deciding which part of my mouth he enjoyed most, he licked lazily at my teeth, tongue, and lips before snatching the latter in a prolonged and bruising kiss. Over and over, he repeated the same explorations until I eventually wrapped my legs around him and fought back.

Only then did he slowly begin to move.

And with each blistering thrust, the burn gradually extinguished.

I wished the same could have been said for the organ in my chest. My eyes opened. My stuttered exhale made my lips leave his. His gaze refused to relinquish mine, and my heart danced, drunk on feeling that riddled me with fear and confusion.

As if hearing the wild beat, Atakan increased the pace.

My stunted breaths became moans I failed to quiet, my teeth sinking into my lip.

He withdrew and glanced between us. "So gloriously wet." He hissed as he eased back in. "One might think you loathe me as much as I loathe you."

"I'll wager I loathe you more," I said, all breath.

"You'll wager, huh?" His exhale of laughter dried when my thighs began to shake, and his harsh swallow deepened his voice. "Prove it," he said. "Come on my cock before I fill your pretty cunt and leave you dripping on these sacks."

Those hideous words sank into my skin, my very bones, awakening and emboldening.

I grabbed the chest of his tunic and brought his mouth to mine. "Make me." My teeth nipped his upper lip.

His thrusts sharpened. "Fine," he gritted, and his hand swept over my cheek into my hair.

A yank tilted my head back, his mouth ravaging mine far too briefly before roaming to my jaw and throat. All the while, his thrusts slowed and grew more precise as he listened to each moan and felt every contraction.

I grasped his neck. Stubble lining his typically clean-shaven face prickled my other hand as I clutched his cheek.

Sensation delivered a delirium that made it all too easy to forget who he was. Just how wretched he was.

It made his groaned approval believable. "Skies, you feel so fucking good, too good…" He growled when I unraveled, then continued to deliver me to heights I'd never thought to reach for.

Not with him.

It should have been impossible for a creature intent on giving me pain to gift me pleasure beyond words.

And as every part of me tensed and shook, bliss falling through me from my scalp to the tips of my curling toes, I wondered if maybe—just maybe—I could do more than survive this rotten prince.

As he stilled and jerked, I wondered if I could enjoy him, claim him, and perhaps even ruin him the same way he was ruining me.

His head dropped to my shoulder, breaths leaving him as fast as my own.

For minutes that felt both never-ending and far too fleeting, we didn't move. Neither of us seemed able to.

So when he finally freed his cock from my body, his hooded eyes clasped to the mess he'd made between my thighs, I failed to believe his cruel words. "Well, that scratched an itch." He tucked himself into his pants. On his way to the door, he tied them and threw me a smirk. "Now I can cease wondering."

TWELVE

"You know," Elion said, joining me on the third-floor balcony, "there are better ways to spy."

"I'm not spying," I lied.

He huffed, tugging at the lapels of his stiff silver coat. He glanced up at the clouds stained by the pink of sunset and sighed. "You aren't worried about the wedding being postponed?"

I didn't much care about the wedding. My interests stalked elsewhere. But they did include the prince who'd fucked me in a crusty garden shed.

Although I'd ignored what I'd been doing over the past two days, it didn't make it any less true.

I'd waited for him before each meal but ate alone or with silent and scribbling Pholly. I'd anticipated his rich voice, smoothed and deepened by apathy, whenever nearing conversation in the halls.

I'd looked for him endlessly, only to find his absence.

It certainly didn't escape me that something I should have been grateful for had now become something I quietly lamented.

Admitting to any of that would be woefully unwise, yet I couldn't bring myself to feign concern over the wedding to better hide what haunted me. "No," I said. "I know it's not safe."

Elion studied the procession of warriors marching toward the guarded castle gates.

Blue flags bearing the sun insignia flapped in the early spring breeze. The king rode at the front, covered in black and silver armor. No hint of the prince nearby.

Elion and I both knew why the wedding had been postponed. That it wasn't because of the attacks—the Unseelie warriors gaining ground toward the castle.

They were simply the perfect excuse.

The king and his son would prolong the union until it could be prolonged no longer. Wedding a halfling into their pure-blooded line was never something they wished to do. My father had known that. He might have had some lofty goals, but he was no fool. He'd made the deal regardless.

An agreement he expected would be upheld.

I wondered how long he would humor their avoidance before he threatened them. Maybe he'd take me home. Maybe he'd do something far worse.

I shifted, suddenly freezing.

The steward kept his voice barely above a whisper. "You were supposed to marry when you reached nineteen years, were you not?"

I hummed in confirmation.

"The war's end got in the way," he said casually. Too casually. "Of course."

I smiled. He was good at this. "Of course."

"And now, war may well intervene again."

"It may well," I agreed.

We watched the warriors and king file through the gates until wagons carrying the fallen came into view at the end of the procession.

Only then did Elion speak once more. "If it's any comfort, I don't believe there's much to gain from your death."

Containing a snort, I nodded. His attempt to comfort me wasn't necessary, but that he wished to was a comfort in itself. "Thank you, Elion."

He gave me a grave sort of smile, then hurried inside to greet his king.

A sea of armor and horses flooded the drive and the hillsides on either side of it. I waited on the balcony until warriors began to disassemble with their steeds, leaving the castle grounds for the barracks and stables down the mountain.

He wasn't there.

A hollowing weight sank within me. It stopped the sluggish beat of my heart as I searched the two wagons of the deceased for white-blond hair.

My nails dug into the wood of the vine-wrapped railing, close to breaking, my lungs too tight and—

A hand covered my mouth and the scream that tried to leave it as I was pulled back into the dim hall of the third floor.

Atakan pushed me against the wall and removed his hand. "I do believe we've been in this exact spot before, dread."

I scowled. "You need to stop sneaking up on me."

"But I live to keep your heart galloping because of me."

He *lived*.

His eye was cut and slightly swollen. Without thought, I took his chin and rose onto my toes, turning it side to side to inspect his face. Then I shoved him back, feigning disgust when really, I just wanted to assess the rest of him.

Unscathed, seemingly.

He saw right through it. Brows furrowed, he stared down at me. As though my display of concern might have ruined his horrid intentions, he appeared unsure how to proceed.

I gave him a taunting smile.

It did the trick. He closed the small space between us and seized my face. His fingertips dug into my jaw. His gaze searched mine. His features creased.

Then he kissed me.

Hungry and bruising, he claimed my mouth with a firm press and a graze of his teeth. Our tongues met, and his hand dropped to my chest to fold over my breast. He squeezed it hard, ensuring I felt it through the layers of velvet and cotton. My fractured exhale earned me a groan that washed over my lips.

Nearing steps clacked.

He ignored them, so I did, too.

"When you're quite done tainting yourself with the halfling you would rather murder than wed…" Ruelle said crisply. "General Kern is asking for you."

Amusement was the last thing Atakan's smile conveyed when he released me and stepped back. His teeth flashed at Ruelle, a look in his eyes that typically promised punishment.

Glancing back at me, he vowed, "We'll play later, dread."

After the way he'd left me before his return to the mountains to hunt the Unseelie, I wasn't sure that was wise.

But I was sure I didn't care.

Dinner was spent alone in the dining room.

I couldn't determine why I didn't eat in Atakan's chambers instead. The cluster of tangled feelings might have been to blame as I hoped for a glimpse of the heartless prince. Perhaps it was the longing to feel secure.

To keep carving space for myself until I might fit.

Regardless, there was something odd and gratifying about sitting alone at the grand dining table in this castle that had played a role in many of my nightmares.

As I made to leave, distant steps pricked at my senses, and I halted in the doorway.

"Kern is right. Mark my words." Disappointment lowered my shoulders at the growing sound of Garran's voice. "He's vanishing in and out of the wards."

"We need more proof," Atakan said, and those tangled feelings exploded into terrifying sparks.

"The influx of his warriors is all the proof we need. You cannot possibly believe they've all been hiding within our lands since the wards were created." Their steps stopped. "Despite our victories, their numbers only climb higher."

Atakan said nothing.

"The witches even said there was a possibility the king could vanish beyond the cursed borders."

Atakan drawled, "I did warn you that keeping one of them alive would be beneficial."

My breathing stalled. They'd killed the witches who'd survived spelling The Bonelands?

"Find him, Atakan," Garran ordered, voice little more than a seethed whisper. "Kill him, and their antics come to an end. All of this ends."

My thoughts fell free of confusion. For there was only one king they could have been talking about—the Unseelie king.

Atakan took his time responding. When he did, it was not about King Vane but my father. "What of Julis?"

Irritation sharpened Garran's tone. "What about him?"

Silence.

Then, "Don't be obtuse. He's made two requests for a meeting since we postponed the wedding." Atakan hissed his next words. "*Again*. He's more than displeased."

"So we let him calm down. Few things are more grating than dealing with mortals and their undeserved entitlement." Rustling sounded, followed by their continued footsteps. "A couple more weeks will give us time to fix this mess and assemble solid reason."

If I wasn't mistaken, something akin to impatience tightened Atakan's response. "You are aware that no amount of excuses, no matter how reasonable, will be accepted."

Garran groaned as if tired of the conversation. "Then perhaps it's time we make Julis accept that his daughter's life is meaningless to us, and he should be grateful we've humored him thus far."

Believing the conversation had ended, I slunk back toward the dining table in case they approached.

But Garran laughed, a boisterous bark. "Don't tell me you've begun to grow a heart after all these years." He continued to laugh, even as he said with eye-widening seriousness, "Not when we are reliant on its lack of existence, my cold son."

"You disgust me." Garran's rising laughter muffled Atakan's venomous tone. "Almost as much as the halfling."

I waited until they'd moved on down the hall before returning to Atakan's tower.

His words didn't bother me.

It wasn't because I thought them a ruse to hide his growing affections for me. Such contempt had become a blade dulled by too much time.

It was the conversation itself that unnerved me. The confirmation my suspicions needed.

This betrothal was nothing more than a game. Another war that would drag out over years. Potentially lifetimes. It wasn't supposed to be a squabble that would reach a bloodied climax any time soon.

But as my skirts dragged upon the stairs I slowly climbed, I feared my father would not stand to be further insulted.

That neither kingdom would stand for it.

Cold air blistered when I opened the balcony doors in Atakan's chambers. I welcomed the chilled caress until I felt my frayed nerves calm, then I turned inside for Bernie's coat.

Tucking my hands into the velvet pockets, I returned to the balcony.

My fingers brushed against more velvet inside the pocket before I remembered the hidden featherbone. I stroked the little bag, eyeing the dark and wooded expanse of the mountains.

There was no more smoke. The fires had been extinguished before the king and his warriors had returned. Guards once again lined the perimeter of the castle grounds and patrolled the trees beyond. Now and then, glints of armor, the swords at their backs, winked beneath the watery moonlight.

The sharp point of the bone poked through the velvet bag, snagging gently on the skin of my thumb.

A beastly snarl startled birds from trees. They screeched as they flapped toward the sky. Envy filled my heart at the sight, immediately followed by a bolt of shame.

I'd never wanted this. This treacherous life. This betrothal. The heartless prince.

Yet I couldn't deny that a part of me now did.

I should want nothing more than to have this wedding postponed again and again and again. I should wish only for what I needed—the power to escape this fate.

But I'd learned long ago that wishing was futile. That survival was found in careful steps and the outrunning of fear.

Though even if I could seduce Atakan, play his games until he wanted nothing but me, I would never be free. Never be loved. A partial cage for a pet was still the best I could hope for.

Decade-old rage rattled the steel I'd spent years forging around my heart. Tears filmed my vision. For the first time in years, I didn't care about survival.

For the first time in weeks, all I wanted was to go home.

Unaware I'd been squeezing the tiny bag, my breath caught as it cooled within my fist. Pulling it from my pocket, I opened the velvet and peered into the pouch lit by the creamy featherbone.

Curious, I walked inside and carefully pried it from the bag.

The bedchamber darkened.

My scream was lost—swallowed within a void of twisting, thunderous night.

Part Two

THE BONELANDS

Thirteen

Sound and sight returned slowly, but I remained unbalanced where I'd arrived upon the unfamiliar stone floor.

I braced my trembling hands against it and looked up through the tangled mess of my hair when a man spoke.

"Well…" He leaned forward in his chair and rubbed a hand over his thickly bristled jaw. "I'll be fucking damned."

Not a man, I realized as I moved back onto my ass and breathed in his scent. A spiced and smoky musk.

Another faerie.

Dizziness dissipated, and I assessed what appeared to be a bedchamber. The marble fireplace was empty, the portrait above ruined by slashes. I frowned at the carvings in the headboard of a bed large enough for a family of four. Silk sheets rippled, aglow from sconces hung above tall nightstands.

Looking back at the stone beneath me, I breathed, "What happened? I must have…" I swallowed. "Did I vanish?"

There was no such thing as a half faerie with magical abilities. After years of researching, I knew it was true.

I was dreaming, surely.

The male just made a strange noise, a grumble of sorts, and kicked at something.

The featherbone.

It clacked against the floor in front of him. *She never told me what it does*, my father had said what felt like eons ago.

Well, apparently, it took people places. Places they shouldn't be. Despair howled through my mind. For I knew. I knew exactly where I was before I said, "Tell me who you are."

"Vane," he grunted. He needn't have said anything more.

King Vane. The Unseelie king.

My eyes closed. I was so perilously doomed.

They opened at the sound of a rustling swish and widened as the king rose from the large armchair. A book might have been set down on the round table beside it. I wasn't sure because I couldn't remove my eyes from his settling wings.

Black feathers lined the sharply curved apexes, morphing into a steel gray beyond broad shoulders. So broad, I glanced at his body and questioned how any wings could transport a creature of his size. Muscle twitched in arms the size of small tree trunks as he clapped his hands together and walked toward me.

I made to stand until he said, "Do not run. I will only frighten you more by hunting you."

Fear and anger got the better of me when I should have kept my mouth firmly shut. "You're threatening me? I'm not even supposed to be—"

"Informing you," he supplied.

His voice was thick and rough, like the mud puddings I'd made in the woods when I was young.

I stared at his bulky leather boots, similar to what I'd seen in our military, and pinched my wrist. Nothing happened, so I bit my tongue. Blood filled my mouth, the coppery tang too real for this to be a dream.

The room grew dark.

His intimidating form blocked the meager light as he crouched before me. I refrained from flinching away, even as my fingers itched to reach for the featherbone so that I might stab him with it and run.

His nostrils flared as he sniffed.

Blue eyes as bright as the midmorning sky searched my features with a nearly comical scrutiny. A small crease appeared between his furrowed brows, and a soft rumble climbed his throat as he exhaled.

Then he snatched my hand.

His grip was tight, his own hand so large that mine looked like an infant's. He brought it to his face, and I thought maybe he intended to kiss it.

But he held it against his long nose and scented me. My palm was given the same treatment. His warm exhale tickled, and I blinked rapidly. He grumbled again, frowning at my hand, then at my face. "Merciful Mother."

He dropped my hand. It fell to my lap as he grabbed a lock of my hair and leaned closer.

And I was no longer so shocked that I would further indulge whatever this strangeness might be.

I pulled away, scowling. "What are you *doing*?"

Confusion lowered his harsh brows. "That is obvious."

"If it was, I wouldn't have asked."

He stilled, jaw tensing. After glaring at me for a moment, his rugged features eased. "I'm trying to determine whether you are the one."

"The one?" I asked.

"The one we need."

"For what?"

"To break the curse," he said far too simply. Then he straightened to his full and imposing height.

"Curse?" I stood, too, regretting it when I wobbled. Stars danced, blurring my vision.

He caught my forearm. "You are not used to vanishing."

"Whatever that was…" I swallowed thickly. "It was not vanishing."

This king was more than a head taller than me. I had to crane my neck to meet his eyes, which roamed over me. He blinked when I stepped free of his hold, his long lashes a shade darker than his deep red hair.

"You didn't mean to use the featherbone," he determined. "To come to my realm."

I laughed, perplexed and astonished. "Why would I mean to do that?" I didn't dare say where I'd disappeared from, nor who I was.

I feared he already knew.

He glanced at the featherbone. "Long ago, an elder prophesied that a curse would befall these lands." He looked back at me. "Many years dawdled by, and although tensions grew between kingdoms, her ramblings were almost forgotten."

So the featherbone had been spelled. Only, what that spell was, and why it had answered to me… I wasn't sure I wanted to know.

"And then it happened," I needlessly said.

The king nodded once, arms folding over his wide chest. The bulk of him creaked the stitching of his gray tunic. "You hail from a family of schemers."

Thoughtless words flew from me. "Don't even try to pretend you know me, King. I'm not sure what I'm doing here, but I can assure you…" I gestured to the arched windows on either side of the fireplace. "The one you need is still somewhere out there."

"That featherbone and your scent say otherwise." His plump lips rolled between his teeth, then he confirmed that he did, in fact, know me. "The heartless prince is all over you, Princess Mildred."

Dread cinched my stomach.

I whirled in a circle, not wanting to give him my back but too desperate to care. I marched to the bone, picked it up, and squeezed it just as I had on Atakan's balcony.

Nothing happened.

A low and vibrating chuckle prickled my skin and stiffened my spine. "It has served its purpose. Might as well throw it in the hearth."

I turned back, wanting to unleash every inch of my panic and confusion upon him. Perhaps the featherbone was at least good for gouging out one of those pretty eyes.

Alas, he was not Atakan. This Vane was a monster in his own right, certainly, but he was also a king. A different beast.

A foe I'd yet to study enough to survive.

Irritated and unsure how in the darkness I would fix this, I shucked off my coat and tossed it to the floor.

The king looked at it, then at me when I began to pace the length of a deep brown rug at the foot of the bed. Denial and pleading were useless. As was defiance. "Did this elder happen to say how the wards might be broken?"

His answer came instantly. "She said to remember that a curse ends for the same reason it was made. A captured witch who aided in erecting the wards confirmed as much."

I didn't ask what had become of the witch. If the information this king needed had been provided, then they were dead. "I'm going to need you to speak plainly. It's been quite a night."

He huffed. "Our enemy stole my father's heart, so now we must steal our enemy's." There was a pause before he said, "Prince Atakan's heart, to be precise."

"I'm assuming you don't mean that in the literal sense." Now was not the time to inform such a monstrous creature that his enemy had no heart to steal.

King Vane knew. He'd even said it himself.

Which meant I was seriously doomed.

I needed a plan. I needed to escape this realm before he realized I wasn't capable of doing anything. Yet again, I needed a strategy for survival.

Even if it meant playing another game.

Fear clipped the question Vane waited for. "And how might you accomplish that?"

The Unseelie king cocked his head. A slow smile rendered his features less severe and more alluring. "You must fall in love with me."

'FOURTEEN

Those words turned my addled mind into mush as I sat in a chair in the chambers of a king.

You must fall in love with me.

Even if I did, his plan was impossible. So wildly inconceivable that, for the first time in years, I truly wanted to cry. If this king thought he could free his kingdom with something as elusive as love, then he deserved the disappointment headed his way.

I just needed to make sure I was long gone before it arrived.

Minutes after the king's abrupt departure, the doors were nudged open.

A silver tray rattled in his hands, tea spilling from the spout of a floral teapot. I frowned as he approached and set it upon the table beside me. "I do not need refreshments. I need to leave."

"It's peppermint," he informed as if that mattered.

But it did. It had been my preferred choice for years. Before I could ask him how he knew, he cursed, attempting to fit his large fingers through the teapot's handle.

I bit my lip when he gave in and grasped the entire pot. It was undoubtedly terribly hot.

"I can do it."

He ignored me, filled the white teacup, and then put the teapot down without so much as a wince. I would commend him if it hadn't been unnecessary. As it was, a thank you sat tight behind my teeth, unwilling to budge.

I wasn't thankful. I was stuck yet again, and with yet another royal who intended to use me for their own gain.

Gratitude was something I'd forgotten how to feel.

I was no longer even angry. What I felt had crawled beyond the threshold of rage into numb and reckless stupidity.

No matter what I did now, nothing good would come from it,

and of course, whatever happened would be my fault, although I'd wanted none of this in the first rotting place.

"You're anxious," the king said, stepping closer when he was already closer than I was comfortable with.

"I've been taken from one castle to another without any say in the matter. Anxious barely scratches the surface."

"Two castles."

At that, I tore my eyes from the steaming tea and gave them to him.

He dragged a hand through his crimson hair. The wavy strands fell over his shoulders, reaching for his pectorals. "You were forced to leave your home."

My chest tightened further. In need of space, I rose from the chair. "You've done some research."

King Vane's chambers were both refined and bland. Filigreed molding curled from the corners of the room like cobwebs to meet the rocky ceiling. A brass chandelier with real cobwebs tilted precariously over his bed, candles burned to nothing within.

I assumed he only used the brass sconces. Two were aflame between the windows I walked alongside and one above the entrance to the bathing room. Those above the nightstands gave a better view of the dust sprinkling the books beneath, piled beside a half-rolled map.

Save for the one atop the fireplace mantel, there were no portraits. I stopped and pointed at it. "Who wrecked this?" I asked, though I already knew.

And I knew who the painted female was. Queen Kalista's hair was the same shade as her son's, and her eyes an autumn-touched green.

"My father. These were his rooms, and that's my mother."

"She did more than wound his pride, then," I surmised.

"We all know that by now," he said gravely. "But it's the only portrait of her that I have, so it stays."

Intrigue arose. I snuffed it. Whatever he'd endured was no concern of mine. As I turned away from the slashed face, I squeaked in surprise.

King Vane grinned, more beastly than charming. "May I have your hand?"

"What for?"

"I'd like to touch it."

The earnestness of his quick response had my hand extending before I could find my brain.

Carefully, he took it.

Then he tugged me to him and seized my face in his paw-like hand. He released my own to touch my back. Slowly, his head lowered until his mouth was scant inches from mine.

My brain returned. Panic stole my voice.

I swatted at his mountainous chest and shoved my hand over his face. My finger met his nostril, his arm a band of steel at my back.

He grunted, gruffly saying, "Remove your tiny claws from my face."

"Then remove your bulbous arm and hand from my body."

"Bulbous?" he repeated, chuckling as he released me.

"What in the skies are you thinking?" I stumbled back, my legs meeting the divan by the window.

"I'm thinking I need to free my kingdom."

"You cannot just grab me," I hissed. "And try to *kiss* me."

He studied me, my heaving chest and undoubtedly wild eyes, and his features twisted. "How am I supposed to win your heart if I cannot touch you?"

"I don't know." And I didn't particularly care. I walked backward to the table, half fearing he'd strike again. Taking a seat, I pulled the teacup toward me while keeping an eye on him. "But not like that, I can assure you."

"You enjoy kissing, though," he stated. "Sex." After a shake of his head, he gave me a strange and almost worried look. "Do you not?"

Withholding a shocked laugh, I nearly spilled the tea. I sipped it. "You're not off to a great start with this heart-stealing thing."

His forehead creased. "You speak as if you do not want me to even try to steal it."

I thought it best not to give that a response.

He scrubbed at his heavily whiskered jaw. "I'll give you whatever you want." His wings lifted, splaying slightly as he turned and paced toward the doors he'd left ajar. "Good food, good literature, good housing, and good sex…" He spread his hands. "I will give you everything a female wants. All you need to do is let me."

I sipped more tea to be sure this was truly happening. Out of all the outrageous things I'd heard and seen and even felt, this situation won by far.

For some moments, I had no words. I wasn't sure I could find even one. After all, what he'd said did sound humorously appealing, and yet…

"Love isn't found in pleasures, King."

Undeniable desperation gritted his question. "Then where is it found, Princess?"

"If I knew, maybe I would tell you," I quipped, not entirely sure I would, but certain it mattered little right now.

He turned to me and glared. "*Maybe?*"

"Actually…" I traced the rim of the teacup, unable to control a flare of temper as this new reality settled like stones tied to my ankles in deep water. "I likely wouldn't, being that I have no desire to be here, let alone enable you to seek retribution by breaking those wards." Foolish, *utterly moronic* words.

But it was too late to gentle or regret them.

The flames in the sconces flickered. One extinguished. Shadows danced from the tips of his wings, seemingly birthed from the black feathers. And his eyes…

They were a blazing blue, aglow with fury.

"You're no remedy," he growled. "You're but another punishment from the dark mother."

"And you're but another tyrant who doesn't need freedom from a curse you've brought upon yourself."

Silence.

So much silence, fear chomped at my chest.

After years of worrying over my survival, I'd known better than to react in such a way. I knew when to stomp and when to tread carefully. Yet, for some reason, I hadn't any energy to care.

Perhaps this was true defeat. No way out. No way forward.

Irrefutably fucked.

"I'm a tyrant," the king finally said. "Is that right?"

Though this was a hopeless situation, I still refused to cower. "I believe that's what I said."

"That's what you've been taught." His jaw worked as he eyed me, harshening the violently square angle. "Which means this will be even more difficult than getting you here."

"Then…" I sipped more tea and gave away a morsel of my knowledge by saying, "Why not vanish me beyond the wards, and I'll return to Cloud Castle?"

There was still time to make it look like I'd merely wandered throughout the castle, or even the grounds. I hadn't been gone so long that my absence couldn't be explained.

"To your beloved prince?"

I flashed my teeth. "Please."

He huffed, quiet as he watched me, that fury still burning bright in his gaze. "How did it feel, Princess?"

"How did what feel, King?"

"Taking the cock of a male who'd rather die than admit he cares for you."

With that, King Vane vanished—as if to punctuate that he could indeed get beyond the wards trapping his realm. He could take me back to Ethermore.

And that he wouldn't.

The remainder of the night was spent upon the divan beneath the window, staring at the stars. Clouds passed over the scythe moon, luring my thoughts to Atakan.

There was little point in wondering if he worried for me. More likely, he and King Garran were worried about the alliance with my father. I pondered how long they might hide my disappearance, as they certainly would, and what my father might do once he learned of it.

There'd been too much war. With the Unseelie attacks increasing despite the wards trapping their realm, I doubted they'd encourage other tensions to escalate.

But that was the way of kings. Bloodshed and brutality. Displays of dominance to soothe their bruised pride and need for total control.

So although I wasn't anything worth killing for, an example would still need to be made. I was a halfling, but I was also a princess. A tool made for trade.

And my father, as gentle as he'd often been, did not take kindly to disrespect of his belongings.

My disappearance could create a lack of trust our kingdoms might not recover from. Certainly not when trust between humans and faeries was already an impossible feat to begin with.

Alas, that was the best-case scenario. At worst, my father might believe the Seelie had murdered me and gotten rid of all evidence. In which case, retribution must be sought.

Come what may, I still couldn't find it within myself to care.

I'd had no say or hand in any of this. Though it had been unknowingly, my father had even provided me the key to leave one cage for another.

My father and Garran had done this.

Let them squabble and cause a ruckus over a problem they'd given themselves—while I once again tried to survive another bloodthirsty male.

And his sneaky spies.

The king hadn't returned to his chambers, but his shadows hadn't left. Whenever they neared, I flicked at them, and they retreated with a haste that resembled flinching. I might have stopped. I might have felt bad.

But their stalking darkness and the Unseelie king's parting words revealed a truth that bit at my bones.

Vane had been watching me via the shadows that marked him as a ruler of The Bonelands.

Perhaps the battles nearing Cloud Castle had been an effort to capture me. Perhaps he'd been waiting for me to seek the bait my father had handed me.

I had no idea how he would have known I was in possession of the featherbone or if he even did. I didn't know much of anything and loathed it almost as much as my new predicament.

The castle was quiet, any occupants slumbering.

Sleep finally took me as the stars faded beneath the brightening blue, but it wouldn't stay as dawn arrived. A hum of energy seeped from below—through the cracks in the mortar and stone.

The leather divan creaked as I pushed up from the headrest to better see through the window.

Outlined by violet willow trees, the dirt drive resembled a serpent curving toward the dense woodland separating the castle from what lay beyond. That, coupled with the view of awnings and rusted pipes from floors beneath, suggested the king's rooms resided on the highest floor of Ashbone Castle.

The doors opened.

I straightened, blinking blearily at King Vane.

He kicked the doors closed with one of those same clunky boots he'd worn last night. A fresh burst of his scent and the different clothing told me he'd bathed and perhaps rested elsewhere.

Another tray in hand, he crossed the room, and I shamelessly noted how his olive pants hugged his thick thighs. The tight fit of his black tunic.

My stomach mercifully gurgled before I was caught, my attention stolen by the food he uncovered on the tray.

"You didn't sleep."

"You and your little spies would know," I said, voice groggy.

He released an amused breath, then untucked one of the two armchairs before gesturing to it. "Don't tell me you will also refuse to eat."

Hunger sent me to my feet with unexpected ease. I smiled

venomously. "I didn't refuse to sleep. I simply struggle to feel comfortable doing so in the lair of a beast."

Stepping back, the king nodded once. "You believe a den of serpents is a safe place to lay one's head each night?"

I plopped onto the chair. "Better the enemy you know."

It seemed he had no response for that. At least, none he was willing to share. A muscle feathered in his hairy jaw, those luminous eyes riddled with things I didn't wish to hear. Perhaps he knew that, and that was why he remained quiet and left for the bathing room.

My mouth dried as I looked at the bowls spread before me and hesitated. But he couldn't make me fall in love with him if he poisoned me.

So I ate. First, I demolished the raisin-speckled oats, and then I picked at the bowl of glowing fruit while leisurely drinking some peppermint tea.

All the while, the king leaned against the doorframe of the bathing room, arms folded over his chest. His wings twitched when his mouth did. Attempting to hide his smirk, he ducked his head.

"Dare I ask what is so amusing, King?"

He dragged a finger over his plump lower lip, and his eyes rose to mine. "You."

I waved a piece of sliced apple. "Care to elaborate?" Easing back in the chair, I made a show of exposing my crossing legs. "After all, I've nothing but time while kingdoms wonder over my whereabouts and how they might retrieve me."

"If my people cannot leave, then yours cannot get in."

I half rolled my eyes, flashing more of my teeth than necessary as I bit into the apple.

He slid his own over that lower lip, eyes dropping to my legs with a slowness that seemed intentional. "You're not what I expected."

"And that amuses you?"

"I find your defiance and feline attitude amusing."

My eyes narrowed to slits upon his growing and perfect smile before I forced them back to the breakfast tray.

For a moment, I couldn't resist thinking it was a dreadful waste—a shame that he was who he was. Even with that long mane of hair and his clear aversion to shaving, he was more than intriguing to look at.

Vane Ashbone held an allure that didn't request attention but commanded it. He exuded a primal energy that tugged at some mystical and deeply feminine part of me. I didn't doubt he had the same effect on many females.

The muscles and wings certainly didn't help.

Suddenly uncomfortable, although this entire situation was anything but comfortable, I asked the most pressing question I had. "If the only way to break the wards is to steal your enemy's heart, why can't it be King Garran's?"

"His blood wasn't used to bind the wards," he said. "Atakan's was. A safer bet, we assume, given his ruthless reputation." His tone became edged. "Any curse must have a thread to unravel it, no matter how small, and we all know Garran murdered the only creature he's ever truly loved."

"The wards required the king's blood?"

Vane grunted. "Or a direct descendant's."

Due to Garran stealing Vane's mother's heart and thus beginning the war in earnest.

I assumed Atakan's death wouldn't break the wards, or he wouldn't be gallivanting through the mountains and risking his life to hunt the Unseelie.

The mere thought made me instantly wish to think of something else.

"You look troubled."

I wanted to laugh. "Because none of this is troubling at all."

Vane didn't appreciate my sarcasm, apparently. Eyes narrowing, he just watched me intently.

It was akin to being silently ridiculed.

It shouldn't have bothered me. I had far bigger things bothering me. Yet I quickly reached for something to fill the quiet. "Is it true there are bones crushed within the mortar of this castle?"

He stared at me for a knowing moment longer.

Then he relented with a nod. "Nobility and distinguished warriors who fell in the first war were honored by having their remains included in the restoration of this fortress."

At that, I paused. "It was destroyed in the first war?"

"A good portion of it." He looked at my food. "Most of these upper floors have been rebuilt."

Without meaning to, I said, "With the bones of those souls trapped in the mortar forevermore."

"Again, it is considered an honor unlike any other for their sacrifice and service." He licked his teeth behind closed lips, then revealed them in a half smile. "Are you afraid of ghosts?"

"I've yet to meet one, so it's hard to say."

As if trying not to laugh, Vane's smile broadened. "They are not known for conversation, Princess. At least, not the ones I've seen. They merely act as silent sentinels."

"The remains serve as wards, then."

He nodded once more.

It prompted me to say, "Your shadows crept beyond Cloud Castle's wards."

He huffed. "If that were possible, perhaps my father would have been better prepared to keep our people from entrapment."

I still wasn't sure I believed him. "Then how do you know anything about my relationship with the prince?"

"People talk," he said with a gravity that sagged my shoulders. "And you weren't always in the castle, Princess."

My entire body stiffened. I tried to hide my reaction by eating.

A handful of unhelpful minutes passed. My skin began to itch from his words and what they'd implied. I finished my tea and quietly reassured myself that his shadows hadn't seen me with Atakan in that garden shed. That my gown and the warmer climate were to blame for my discomfort.

Which then led to a mild panic over not having any of my belongings. Nothing more to wear.

"If I am stuck here, then I need clothing." I set the teacup down. "A hairbrush and that good literature you spoke of."

"You will be cared for," Vane vowed. "You have my word. If you desire books, I will show you to the library on the second floor." He seemed to choose his words carefully before asking, "What else do you desire?"

The stilling of his rugged features made it clear he was no longer talking about material items. Even so, I sought clarity. "What do you mean?"

"Show me how to win your heart, Princess Mildred, and not only will I give you whatever you need…" He straightened from the doorframe, sincerity deepening his voice. "Whatever you ask for, no matter the magnitude, will be yours."

I shook my head. "*Show* you?" Incredulity sharpened my tone. When he merely nodded, I laughed. "I'm afraid I'm tired of teaching males how to treat me."

"I don't intend to treat you poorly. I'm simply…" He once again appeared to search for the right words. As if unaccustomed to needing to, he exhaled roughly. "Trying to hasten the process."

His frustration, the hint of desperation, gentled my reaction without my permission. "But how can we fall in love if I've forced you to be someone you're not?"

Rain arrived in a downpour. Pattering against the windows and steel awnings, it drowned the loud and telling silence.

"I see," I finally murmured.

"You will also have my protection," he added, a softening of what he perceived to be a blow. "Forevermore."

And it was somewhat of a blow.

Not because I wanted this Unseelie king to love me in return. That was the last thing I desired—right beneath wanting to love him. It was because this would be another game.

Yet again, I was a means to an end for a king. This time, if Vane's asinine plan proved successful, the cost wouldn't only be my life.

It would be my heart.

Fortunately for most, heartbreak was a survivable curse. And if there was one skill I had, it was making sure I lived.

My spine steeled, even as my stomach quaked. "Whatever protection that might be means little. My father's kingdom is at stake." Though he was well aware, I reminded him, "We have an alliance with Ethermore."

"Your father met his end of the agreement."

He was right. Regardless, the repercussions of escaping this mess would be vast. "Yet his daughter would be the reason the wards fall and your beastly warriors terrorize the continent again. I refuse to be the reason you're able to seek retribution."

And what was sure to be unmerciful, blood-bathed destruction at that.

For weighted seconds, the king just smirked.

Finally, he simply said, "The offer will stand, so you needn't decide what you want right now. Just tell me when you're ready." With that, he stalked to the doors, those giant wings tucked to keep from brushing the frame. "And you'll find clothing in the dressing chamber."

'FIFTEEN

Nestled between two rows of the king's clothing, beautiful garments lined the far wall of the dim dressing chamber.

A candle in hand, I admired the array of browns, oranges, creams, and greens. Amid the flowing skirts and blouses that would be frowned upon at home in Nephryn was my emerald coat. I stared at it, then checked the empty pockets. After selecting a cream gown with short gossamer sleeves, a cinched satin bust, and pleated mustard skirts, I exited the narrow room.

The king's gigantic-sized clothing—tunics, coats, cloaks, and pants that ranged from britches to fitted to loose—danced through my mind as I set the candle in a holder at the edge of the bathing pool.

So deep that half of it sank some feet below the gray-tiled floor, the pool contained steps to sit upon or use to climb out. A dish of colored soaps awaited at the wash basin. To my delight, someone had crafted a bar of lavender and mint. The memories accompanying the scent scattered imaginings of the king wearing loose linen pants.

Scrubbing viciously at my skin with a flower-embroidered cloth, I surmised such a brutish male seldom made time to lounge around anyway.

The rain remained, tapping at the three slim windows standing tall beside the pool. The one in the middle contained a stained depiction of a white crown, wings on either side with steep tips that branched into the mist. A replica of the Ashbone insignia—a crown of bones and emeralds between monstrous wings and spiraling shadows.

Momentarily, I sat stunned, unable to believe what I was staring at. Unable to fathom where I was.

With a sudsy hand, I pushed the nearest window open to let the steam out. The hinges squeaked, then humid air and the grumble of distant thunder crawled into the dark bathing room.

I peered around but found no sign of moving shadows. A small mercy in this unmerciful turn of events.

A bird, or at least I'd thought it was, soon flapped by the castle. A ghastly shriek followed, and I pulled the window closed and vacated the pool.

A wooden hairbrush and steel comb waited in the drawer beneath the wash basin. I inspected both, finding a bloodred strand in the brush. I plucked it free, studied it for a second longer than necessary, and then attempted to rid my hair of tangles before getting dressed.

I had no desire to leave these rooms. I also had no desire to be in this realm. So after searching for my featherbone, I went in search of the king who'd stolen it.

The hall outside his rooms was empty of souls but filled with portraits. Brass sconces between them made it easy to take a surreptitious peek at the mountains veiled in mist beyond a drab depiction of this castle. As well as the shrewd blue and emerald gazes of Ashbone ancestors.

At either end of the hall loomed darkened doorways to watch towers. In the center was a marble-and-stone staircase that widened at each landing. As I descended to the first, flickers of firelight revealed a glimpse of the foyer on the ground floor.

Beneath the stairs, before the doors I couldn't see in all their giant oak glory, the Ashbone insignia spread in colored tiles toward stone halls on either side of the foyer.

My skirts swished.

Believing it was one of the ghosts the king mentioned, I tensed until a black cat meowed.

My heart calmed. Still, I glowered at the creature, my hand on my chest. It purred and brushed against my leg again before leaping up onto the stair railing.

I hadn't realized Vane kept pets. Then again, there was little I actually knew about the king who hadn't been king for more than a handful of years.

The library was easily found.

That could have been due to it swallowing nearly half of the second floor. Overflowing shelves lined every inch of wall space between arched and vine-shrouded windows. Crooked stacks of books collected dust atop the marble fireplace mantel, beside armchairs, and upon the small and large glass tables.

A cobweb dangled from the rungs of a wooden ladder resting against the largest block of shelving, which met the ceiling.

Flame swayed in a sconce by the doorway and in a stained blue lantern upon the glass table between the two leather armchairs. There wasn't space for more lighting, I surmised. Though the library seemed thrice the size of the king's considerable bedchamber, there wasn't even enough room for all of the books.

Energy prickled my nape a moment before the stranger behind me spoke. "The king often visits this musty place."

Though I couldn't disagree, it was indeed a little musty, I was too shocked to do more than gape as a tall male sauntered past me into the room.

He stopped upon reaching the round emerald carpet before the armchairs and turned to face me with his hands in his pant pockets. "His father, Vorx, practically lived in here." His brown gaze moved from the shelves to me. "Before he was slain for attempting to stop the madness created by your father and that of your betrothed."

King Vorx had been slain for far more than that, but I refrained from saying as much. "If you're trying to intimidate me, you'll need to try harder." Smiling sweetly, I folded my hands before me. "I've spent years dealing with creatures far more direct and duplicitous than the likes of you."

The faerie nodded twice. A pretty grin revealed a dimple in each clean-shaven cheek. "Atakan the heartless."

I walked deeper into the room. Though I had no idea who this male was nor what he wanted from me, I assumed he knew why I was here and, therefore, didn't intend to harm me. Not physically, at least.

"Rumor states he warms for no one." An intentional silence preceded words I'd anticipated. "Not even you."

There was no sting.

I was more aware than anyone of the prince's feelings for me. Feelings which, over time, had softened due to my careful tactics. Not as much as I'd needed, but one day, they could have.

All for nothing now.

The misery evoked by the gloomy thought annoyed.

Forcing another smile, I leaned against one of six leather chairs tucked beneath the large glass table. I surveyed this stranger with hair the color of freshly turned soil and eyes just as dark. "Who are you?"

"Cerwin." He folded into a bow that was nothing short of mocking, hand flourish and all. "His Majesty's royal right hand and longtime friend."

"Of course."

As he straightened, a dark brow arched in question.

I shrugged. "Who else would gift me such a lovely welcome?"

He chuckled but quickly sobered. "You are not as meek as they say."

"Never underestimate the quiet ones." Then I asked, "And where is your king?"

"Away," he said.

"Right." I headed for one of the many shelves when the cat pranced into the library.

"Took your time," Cerwin drawled, yet his mouth curved.

My next breath caught as the cat leaped into the air toward Vane's royal right hand.

And disappeared beneath an explosion of shadows.

They dissipated as a short female patted her shoulder-length orange curls, then tossed her arms around Cerwin.

After a kiss that sent heat to my cheeks and my face to the shelves to hide it, the female said, "You'll need to forgive my rude mate. He's extra prickly before lunch."

Mate.

Such bonds between souls were rare. Almost fable. Intrigued, I eyed her velvet, tunic-style dress and matching blue slippers. The latter clicked over the stone as she walked toward me.

"I'm extra prickly before knowing people's true intentions, you mean."

The cat-shifter glared at Cerwin. "Stop it."

He smirked but had the good sense to keep his mouth shut.

"Daylia," she said, her pink lips rising to reveal slightly pointed canines. Tiny fangs. "Steward, though not by choice." Cerwin snorted. She ignored him. "But because this place falls apart without me. Here…" She snatched a book without so much as glancing at it and shoved it at me.

Collecting it from my chest, I frowned down at the faded gold whorls on the cover, then tried to keep up as she moved along the shelves and plucked more books, seemingly at random.

After ten or maybe eleven threatened to send me teetering, she thankfully stopped. "Just a few of my favorites."

"Just a few," I repeated, scarcely able to see her over the stack precariously balanced within my arms.

Another chuckle came from Cerwin.

"They're all very steamy," Daylia whispered. "If you know what I mean."

"She's winking," her mate informed dryly. "Just in case you can't see past the pile of damsels in distress in your arms."

"Good to know," I returned just as dryly.

"They don't all feature damsels in distress," she protested, though not to me, her slippers clacking toward Cerwin.

"They all feature plenty of sex."

"Keep talking, and none will feature in your near future, you fun-sucking grump."

He grumbled something about sucking I didn't quite catch on account of trying to find my way safely out of the library and back to the stairs.

As I neared them, Daylia hissed, "You frightened her away."

"She hardly looked frightened." A pause. "Struggling, maybe." He laughed, then groaned. "What? A good introduction can reveal a lot about someone, such as their motives." Another pause. "The way she managed to get here shouldn't be ignored."

Their voices grew distant as I slowly climbed the stairs.

"If Vane believed she'd hurt any of us, she wouldn't be roaming the halls, let alone sleeping in his chambers."

"Vane cannot afford to be cruel to the halfling," Cerwin stated. "That's why he has me."

"Your logic is so flawed, it almost makes sense."

"Day, that makes no sense."

Despite the strangeness of what I'd just experienced, I fought a smile, then cursed viciously as books toppled from the tower in my arms mere steps away from the king's chambers.

The days following my abrupt arrival in the enemy's lair were spent lounging upon the divan before deciding the king's bed was far superior.

I'd read two of the books forcefully recommended by Daylia, reluctantly admitting when she'd delivered my meals that they were indeed worthy of being dubbed favorites. I was halfway through the third when the rain ceased, and murmurs gathered volume in the castle halls.

After three days, it seemed the king who would only grant me my freedom in exchange for my love had returned from darkness only knew where.

I'd taken to leaving the doors of his rooms cracked in case I heard anything of interest, but also to hear someone's approach. Seldom had I left to explore the castle. I hadn't much need with my meals being delivered and entertainment available at the turn of a page.

I might have been a captive, but I certainly wasn't being treated like a prisoner.

I'd been given the finest cuts of meat and the sweetest fruits and treats. Even wine accompanied dinner. Daylia lingered every other visit, attempting to rouse me into conversation about books before veering toward the subject of Vane. How funny he could be. How brave and loyal he was. How even his dour moods were but a short storm.

I'd always ignore her, remaining silent until she'd sigh and bid me a good day or good night.

Maybe King Vane and his loyal subjects thought me defiant. Petulant. Even cruel.

It suited me just fine. As I refused to admit that I was enjoying myself far more than I ought to be. I failed to recall when I'd last truly relaxed, and any guilt or shame for doing so was snuffed by reminding myself that it might be the last time I did.

After this insanity met whatever end it would, the odds were high that I'd be dead or trying very hard not to be yet again.

Something akin to nervousness—perhaps trepidation over all I'd never wanted to be a part of—filled me at the thought of seeing the king after his absence. So much so, the book I'd been devouring now failed to keep my attention.

I left it face down upon the rumpled sheets of the king's bed, called toward the sunshine and bustle of activity.

Heading down the stairs, I gathered the cotton skirts of my gown. The simple number had roses embroidered in the low neckline and along the flared hem of the elbow-length sleeves. I veered left in the foyer into a long hall that cut through the center of the castle.

It spat me out into a puddle of light. Conversing staff quieted when they heard me enter the adjoining hall. Two of them bowed, a male and female, while the smaller one, perhaps one of their offspring, blinked and gaped.

I nodded in greeting. "Which way to the gardens?"

The blond female pointed beyond me. "Go right at the end of this hall and then continue." Her mothlike wings joined behind her head. "There are big glass doors that give entrance to the courtyard. You won't miss them, Princess."

I smiled my gratitude. Their whispering stalked as I followed the instructions. A mention of the wards tensed my shoulders.

These people would have been better off searching for other

impossible ways to end their curse. Though the sooner they realized that, the sooner I would be in grave danger. I had to find a way to escape these lands before that happened.

Vane could have been lying about the featherbone. Leading me to believe it was useless certainly was in his best interest. Regardless, I wanted it back.

Indeed, the doors weren't easily missed.

Light grew glaringly bright as the hall widened toward them. The glass doors lined half the protruding wall, two open in the center. Vines crawled over the others, which I surmised were seldom used.

The courtyard presented similarly.

Moss carpeted the legs of a cracked stone bench and covered most of the pavers. Vines birthing violet flowers strangled the wooden posts and hung from the awning in sagging curtains. I ducked to avoid them and stepped onto emerald grass.

My slippers sank into the blades softened by the rainfall, the satin immediately soaked. I shielded my eyes from the sun, stunned by the vast greenery and color spread before me. From one end of the castle to the other, flora flourished. Many plants I'd never seen before.

In the distance, wood and stone buildings stood large against the bright sky. Stables, I assumed, noting the paddocks to the west. The rest might have been staff housing. Maybe guard barracks.

Carved between the acres of lush life were grass pathways. More stone benches hid beneath vines and strange flowers reminiscent of bluebells.

As I walked deeper into the gardens, I regretted not choosing something lighter to wear.

Spring certainly favored this western realm. A light sweat misted my skin from the humidity. Beads of water clung to leaves larger than my hands. Bird-like critters with sword-sharp beaks fluttered stumpy wings, hovering atop gleaming flowers.

Some of the plants swayed away as I neared, while others lurched closer, causing me to gather my skirts.

Too late, apparently.

A giant purple flower snatched my gown, halting me.

I turned toward it, trying to yank my skirts free. But the thorns tugged as the thick stem curled. Mystified and irrationally frightened, I hissed at it, "Release me right this instant."

A deep chuckle straightened my spine and cooled my clammy skin.

The flower let go, retreating into the bed among its colorful brethren. As the king leisurely strolled down the path, everything appeared to still. Even the chirping and buzzing of critters and insects ceased.

In scuffed black pants crafted from thick leather and a matching long-sleeved tunic with an armored chest, Vane hardly resembled a king.

He resembled a bloodthirsty warrior in one of his gruesome armies.

His hair was tangled and unbound, a creature in his arms pawing at the crimson strands. Soil, blood, and sweat joined his smoky scent, igniting my curiosity all the more.

He stopped a respectable distance from me. "They want your attention." He nodded toward the now-still flowers. "If you don't acknowledge them, they will try to force your hand."

"Yet I see that they'll leave you alone."

"I am the king." The statement wasn't smug but matter of fact. "When I was young, they tried their nasty tricks on me, too."

But I'd lost interest in the flowers.

I moved a step closer to inspect the pile of gray fur and leathery wings in his arms. A wolverine snout and glowing eyes turned my way. Tiny tufts of fur sprouted from the tips of tall and pointed ears.

I did my best to keep my mouth from falling open. "Is that a felynx?"

He nodded again. "Lone survivor from a litter of four."

"What happened to the rest?"

"Found dead near the border. The young often fail to sense the danger of the wards."

Dismay dug into my heart as the cub released a weak growl. It looked so tiny in the bulk of Vane's arms. But when I stole it from him, I was shocked by the heft and size—nearly double that of a cat.

Vibrant gold eyes blinked up at me as I hushed the cub's protests and stroked its velvet nose. "That's where you've been, then?" I asked Vane. "Visiting the borders."

The king didn't answer.

He headed back down the path, his giant boots crushing sodden leaves. "She will need to be fed twice daily if you want her to survive."

"She?" I questioned. "Wait." I blinked. "Excuse me, King." I hurried after him. "*Me?*"

A groundskeeper pretended to rake as we marched by him to the courtyard. Vane ducked his head to avoid the sagging vines. "You eased her suffering. She's now yours."

Panicked, I came close to running. "I touched its damned nose." The beast in my arms curled against my shoulder, gripping it as if worried I'd drop her.

"That's all it took."

"You soothed her first."

"I've already bonded with a felynx. He was shot down by numerous iron-tipped arrows during our attempts to find the witches warding our lands."

That shouldn't have saddened me, and it absolutely didn't. Yet my arms tightened around the felynx cub.

Staff gasped as I burst through the glass doors after their king. "Then you can bond with another."

"I'm not willing."

"And you believe I am?" The question was almost shouted down the hall. But this was ridiculous. "I don't want a pet. I don't even want to be *here*."

Vane climbed the stairs with grace unsuited for his formidable form. "A felynx is not a pet, Princess, and the way you've been lounging around for the past three days hardly screams misery."

Taken aback, as I hadn't glimpsed his slithering shadows since his departure, I asked, "You've been spying on me again?"

He just grunted.

Surmising sour Cerwin had kept him informed, or even Daylia, I returned to the issue at hand. "I'm serious, King." Trailing him up the stairs, I adjusted the felynx in my arms. "What will become of it when I leave these lands?"

"She will simply follow. The wards will be down."

He had a damned answer for everything, it seemed. I refused to let it sway me. None of this was right, yet somehow, *this* pushed me toward losing my addled mind. "You cannot just force a cub upon me."

He reached his rooms. "I didn't."

I was so incensed that I almost missed how he held the doors open for me before closing them after I'd stormed into his chambers. "This is doing the opposite for your cursed realm, you know." I set the beastly babe on the floor and my hands on my hips. "If you want to help make me love you, then you'd best find this poor thing someone else to care for it."

He groaned, scrubbing his cheek. The scratch of his skin meeting coarse hair distracted. "I have no desire to repeat words I've already spoken."

"Well," I said, venom coating my tone. "I still have no desire for the likes of you. So you may as well vanish me back to Cloud Castle."

I had to go back. Not only was my fate unavoidable but I also didn't want to be here. Though something curdled within me at the mere thought of facing familiar foes.

"You do not wish to return."

What I wanted didn't matter. Not to anyone. Including this monstrous king. "Presumptuous of you."

He kicked off his boots, leaving them by the door. For cleaning, I guessed, my nose crinkling at their cruddy state. "Spies, remember?" he said. "I know your time there was uncomfortable at best."

My blood chilled.

He'd already made it abundantly clear that he'd been watching me. That his shadows had been reporting back to him. And if he'd been spying on me for however long, he'd been prying into whatever else transpired in Ethermore.

His smirk was knowing as he walked barefoot into his dressing chamber. "You might not want to love me, but you are loving the freedom from a particular prince's dark obsession with you."

The sight of his giant feet stayed and rankled. He wasn't entirely wrong, but he also wasn't entirely right.

Scratching sounded at the doors. The felynx turned to me, her gold eyes reminiscent of the bronze belonging to the aforementioned prince. "You will wait a minute," I told her without thought. "I'm not done…" I threw out my hands, settling on, "Arguing."

A grunted laugh left the dressing chamber with the king. "I am." He slung a pair of those linen pants over his broad shoulder. "Your pent-up rage can wait until I've bathed the past three days from my bulbous body." He entered the bathing room.

I was glad he couldn't see the heat staining my cheeks. He couldn't have known I'd thought about those exact pants on him. His shadows and friends couldn't read my stupidly adventurous thoughts.

To my surprise, the cub was sitting, the tufted black tip of her tail swishing as she waited.

I sighed, then glared toward the bathing room when I heard the pool filling. "You haven't closed the door."

"My rooms. Didn't know I had to."

Bristling, I took the cub I didn't want back outside.

SIXTEEN

It was evident this king brought out the worst in me. Maybe it was paranoia, but I couldn't help but think that was part of his ludicrous plan.

To climb under my skin and irritate.

After years of perfecting the art of biting my tongue and learning how to hone my words to a precise and sharpened edge, I should have been able to keep from constantly reacting.

It more than unsettled me. It made me feel like a failure. Like someone who'd lost the skills to survive.

It made me fear I couldn't control my emotions.

The felynx hissed before we'd even rounded the stairs into the foyer, scenting the black cat perched atop the banister.

Lime green eyes disappeared behind gathering darkness that burst as Daylia morphed into her faerie form. "Oh, my great goddess." Hurrying toward the cub, she pulled at her high-waisted lacy skirts, then crouched. Her question was pitched. "Aren't you just the most precious thing?"

"It has fangs the size of my little finger. I'd hardly call that precious."

Satisfied Daylia wasn't a threat, the felynx brushed her head against the steward's hand.

"She doesn't mean it, darling," she crooned to the cub. "She secretly adores you, doesn't she?"

I snorted, then walked past them to the stairs. I made it halfway up them before the cub joined me, and Daylia asked, "What have you named her?"

At the landing, I frowned and turned back to her. "I don't intend to name her."

"But you have to." She pushed a thick orange ringlet from her cheek, her eyes agleam. "She's likely waiting for it."

I peered down at the felynx, who waited patiently beneath the next set of stairs. It wasn't that I didn't think she deserved a name. I supposed it was that I believed she deserved more than me. More than someone who would take her into an uncertain and perilous future, if any at all.

"I don't think forming much of an attachment is wise."

"It's far too late to worry about that," the steward said.

Exhaling heavily, I continued to the king's rooms, pleased to find he'd finished bathing and had vacated them in my brief absence.

As much as I loathed it, Daylia was right. The cub needed to be called something. So I rummaged through the king's nightstand drawer for the parchment and ink I'd glimpsed when I'd searched for my featherbone some days ago.

A ruse, really. I needed that featherbone, but I'd also delighted in foraging through his simple belongings.

I'd known he'd discover my nosiness. If not from his shadowy spies, then from my scent. I hadn't cared. Save for small blades, a well-loved book about war and peace, and more maps, I hadn't found much of interest.

After a late lunch, I stretched over the king's bed and continued to scribble names upon the parchment. I'd narrowed it down to two possibilities by the time the sun sank toward the horizon. Deciding to mull it over in the bathing pool, I left the door ajar in case the cub didn't appreciate being locked out.

The felynx yawned when I returned, then curled into a furry ball upon the divan, a leathery wing covering her like a blanket. "Just like that, huh?" I couldn't help but laugh. "Taken from all you know, and you sleep as if nothing happened at all."

"It's because of the bond she's formed with you," the king said, seated at the table.

Tensing, I clutched the silk robe tight over my chest.

I hadn't heard him enter nor any sound of dishes being prepared. It was too late to care about putting something proper on, his gaze an ember that drifted over my bare legs.

It returned to the table—to the list of names I'd curated. He poked it. "Stripes," he scoffed. "An insult."

"She has black stripes in her fur."

"And you have the darkest green eyes I've ever seen, but I don't call you seaweed."

Stunned momentarily, I laughed. I searched but found nothing to say to that. So I muttered, "Stormy it is," as I padded over to the table and took the seat opposite him.

"Just as bad, if not worse."

"Apologies," I crooned dryly. "But I don't remember asking for your input."

Ignoring me, he pushed half a potato into his mouth. It bulged in his cheek as he mumbled, "Found her in a meadow. Call her that."

Reaching for the decanter of wine, I discovered my goblet had been filled. I stabbed at the green beans, about to refute his suggestion. I couldn't, but I still refused to admit I liked it.

"When will she learn how to fly?"

"She already knows how." He sipped his wine, gesturing to the window he must have opened. "She'll leave when she trusts she'll be let back in."

I looked over at the felynx watching me with one half-open, glowing eye. Being wanted in such a way would take some getting used to. Being needed for nothing more than company and refuge.

While eating a few mouthfuls of lamb, I peered at the king's wings, which sat carefully tucked behind and beneath him. "And when did you learn to fly?"

He paused in gathering the remnants of his meal and seemed to ponder it. "I think I was five or so years." His smile was a brief tilt of his lips. "My father pushed me off the ballroom balcony."

I blinked.

"Vorx was far from a warm soul, as I'm sure you've heard, yet he should have forced the matter much earlier." The king shrugged. "A necessary cruelty when one is afraid of heights."

Still mildly shocked, I ate slowly before asking, "Are you scared of heights now?"

"Petrified." A gruff and quick confession. "I rarely fly unless I have to."

It shouldn't have, but such vulnerability failed to settle right. That a male of his status, with such power and brawn, could be scared of anything.

Resisting the desire to prod at him was impossible. "You've revealed a weakness, beast king."

"If you believe you can push me from any great height, I encourage you to try." His feral grin was an invitation. "Princess."

Fighting a smile, I resumed eating, unsure the information he'd provided was useful. But it was wise to gather what I could nonetheless—for when the inevitable came and I'd be forced to play more games to keep my life.

The king collected our dishes and set the tray outside of his rooms.

I watched him, savoring the dregs of my wine, as he removed his loose tunic and tossed it to the floor beside the bed. Within grabbing distance, I noted, attempting not to explore the maze of his abdominals with my eyes.

Some of the rumors were too true. He was indeed a monster.

His broad chest tapered slowly into large hips so sharp, they could injure. Dark auburn hair dusted his chest, a thick smattering leading toward the waistband of his pants. His pectorals were small mountains, shifting as he fluffed the pillows.

It was then I woke from my trance. "What are you doing?"

He dug out his favored book from the nightstand and sat on the bed. The wooden frame squeaked. "I do believe that's obvious." His wings stretched, the grand span and gradient darkness stealing my attention and irritation.

"But…" I set the goblet down with a thud. "Where will I sleep, then?"

His wings folded as he reclined on his side. "These are my rooms,

Mildred, and I've been away from them long enough. If you don't wish to share the bed, you may sleep on the divan." He opened the book, setting a strip of leather that had marked the page next to his stomach.

I shook my eyes free from his abdominals once again. "*You* sleep on the divan."

"Again, my rooms." He huffed. "And I'd have trouble fitting."

My bones tightened. I rubbed my neck as I glanced away from him. "Then kindly find me other accommodations."

"Not going to happen."

"Why?" I'd discovered plenty of empty guest rooms. One with a small balcony overlooking the wild gardens had piqued my interest.

He turned the page. "That is obvious."

"Stop saying that."

"Then stop asking redundant questions."

My teeth clenched. Colorful cusses formed over my tongue. I didn't set them free. I couldn't because I needed to stop reacting and because how dare he desire to sleep in his own bed, in his own rooms, in his own castle…

I'd grown comfortable in here during his absence. Far too comfortable, it seemed.

Sighing, I tipped the remaining wine from the decanter into my goblet. But I only needed a gulp before remembering what I did best.

This was another challenge, and I'd be damned if he was going to win.

Vane's gaze remained on his book as I crossed the bedchamber. Even so, he was wholly aware of every step I took. Likely every breath I drew. Changing out of the robe would only show more hesitation and fear. So I tightened the silk ties and crawled onto the bed.

The felynx joined me.

She settled between us, perhaps knowing I desired a buffer from the king who'd found her. Grateful, I stroked her soft fur. As she purred, I pondered naming her meadow in an effort to ignore the flood of Vane's scent and the heat he expelled. It was akin to lying next to a dying fire.

His voice was a rough grumble. "Do you always sleep in a robe?"

I'd wager he knew I didn't. "I'm not exactly going to sleep naked, am I?" An intentional prod, but I couldn't help myself.

"You certainly could, and I certainly wouldn't mind."

I did my best to ignore that. I failed, rubbing my hot cheek into my palm as I curled onto my side. "Comforting, thank you."

He chuckled, turning the page again.

I wasn't sure he was truly reading. I was sure he'd read that book many times already, so maybe it didn't matter if he wasn't absorbing the words properly. I shouldn't even care. I should be ignoring him—dragging this ordeal out until I found a way out.

For some reason, his presence alone made that impossible.

"You're a king, accustomed to having females fall at your feet." Referring to how I'd arrived here, I smirked. "Quite literally." I scratched the cub's cheek, which appeared chunky until my finger sank, and I discovered it was all fur. "Is that why you assumed I'd want to kiss you upon first meeting you?"

As if he had been reading and wanted to finish a sentence, a few moments passed before he answered. "I don't know how to do this. I haven't…" He stalled. "I've little experience when it comes to romancing females."

"Beyond fucking them."

He released an amused breath. "Yes."

Quiet settled.

My tone softened against my will. "That's why you asked me to show you how to make me fall in love with you."

"That," he said, "and you also made it clear quite quickly that taming you would be no easy feat."

"I'm not in need of taming."

His response was so delayed, I thought there wouldn't be one. "I'm beginning to see that."

I smiled at the felynx when she attempted to nip my finger for being too rough. My hand fell beside me, and she nudged it with her velvet snout. "Well, I'm beginning to like Meadow."

A comfortable silence blanketed.

Perhaps a minute later, pages fluttered. The book lay on the bed, Vane's fingers stilling over the cover.

Gently, I pulled it free of his hand and found the last page he'd read by the stronger trace of his scent. I tucked the leather strip in place, then set the book on the nightstand.

His snoring soon rumbled through the bedchamber.

I should have been offended that he thought me no threat—this king who trusted I wouldn't or couldn't kill him. Rather, I wondered when he'd last slept and why he hadn't.

Seventeen

A week later, the Unseelie king returned from yet another journey.

Cerwin grudgingly informed me that he'd been seeing to important matters by the eastern warded border and tending to those in need.

I believed he'd spoken true. His stiff stance and the reluctance to tell me anything else confirmed as much. But I also knew there'd been far more to it than that, especially since Vane had left before dawn without a word.

I'd woken to find Meadow curled around my feet and the king's book gone. He'd put it back in his nightstand. I hadn't expected to be notified, but I certainly hadn't expected him to leave right after he'd just returned.

So naturally, when I caught wind of his arrival, I floated throughout the halls until I heard his voice from a room I'd learned was his study.

Meadow found me moments after I'd found the king, greeting me with a purr I feared would be heard through the thick wood of the door. I made to leave, not entirely sure why I cared to lay eyes on him anyway.

But Vane wasn't alone.

A feminine voice neared the door, and I caught her frustrated words. "They're now hunting for information. If we don't move the mountain units, they'll succeed in more captures."

"Let them," Vane said.

"Neerin hasn't been seen since the last push. If you think they'll let him or anyone else live, then—"

"I don't," Vane growled. "We wouldn't either. But we *must* keep them chasing their tails while we finish preparations."

Silence dripped before whoever it was moved away from the door, and their voices lowered to murmurs.

Meadow twined around my legs, tangling in my skirts. She flopped to her back, pawing at them and tearing a strip of lace at the hem.

I crouched to free her, and ignored the growled hiss of disapproval as I nudged her down the hall.

Straightening, I caught the end of a different female's words, assuming she must have been pacing or moving throughout the study. "… Lord's update to finalize preparations."

"Tell him I wish to see him," Vane said. "Tomorrow evening."

Then the door opened.

I froze, blinking as if momentarily blinded.

An incredibly tall and willowy female grinned. The type of grin I'd glimpsed upon my father's face when he heard pleasing news. "Princess Mildred." She lowered her head.

The female behind her stepped forward and did the same. She was shorter, her apricot hair curling around high cheeks like wet leaves. Eyes as blue as the deeper depths of the sea widened during an appraisal that caused me to tense. "You are not as human as I thought you'd be."

My stiff shoulders dropped as my eyes threatened to roll. "Not the first time I've heard that."

She laughed, a crisp burst of breathy sound that made me feel at ease. That is, until she said, "Felinka, commander of His Majesty's royal armies." Glancing at her tall companion, she seized her hand. "And this is my wife, Nia."

Nia's apple-green gaze narrowed as she added, "High general."

Felinka smirked. "If you desire a visit with the king, Princess, I must advise waiting."

Her wife glanced over her shoulder into the study, then whispered, "At least until he's fucked something or slept."

Before I could ask why, they both laughed and left me facing the open study door.

Darkness awaited within, the drapes closed. I frowned at the outline of an armchair, unable to see Vane, then at the departing females. Sunlight gilded their brown-and-black leather uniforms, their quiet laughter fluttering down the hall.

Vane now stood in the doorway. His energy made his presence known before his bland question did. "Is there something you need, Mildred?"

Blood muddied his scent. My eyes journeyed from his dirt-caked boots over his fitted leather pants and long-sleeved tunic, inspecting carefully. No sign of injury. I frowned, searching his features. Except for the shadows beneath his eyes, brightening their sky-blue hue, there was nothing.

Nothing, yet his displeasure was detected in the lowering of his brows and in the clenched state of his ticking jaw.

Realizing I'd been staring for far too long, I dredged up a question to which I already knew the answer. "I've been hoping to write to my sister," I said. "Bernadette is likely fretting."

"If she's heard of your disappearance from Cloud Castle."

My stomach sank.

"They've hidden it for this long?" It hadn't been terribly long, but nearly two weeks had passed since that bone brought me here. Plenty of time for word to begin to spread, no matter how tightly contained they tried to keep it.

"Our sources say so, yes."

"By sources, you mean your shadows."

A twitch of his lips failed to soften the severity of his ruggedly hewn features. "Believe it or not, my shadows cannot be everywhere." He scrubbed his jaw, eyes darkening like a cloud moving over the sun. "Or anywhere right now."

That would explain why I hadn't seen much of them during his absences. It would drain him of considerable strength to have his shadows vanishing to places to gather intel, and judging by his worn appearance, strength was something he currently lacked.

The urge to ask him what had happened during this longer journey—why he was so drained—knocked at my teeth.

Maybe I imagined it, but I could have sworn his features gentled as he studied me. First, my half-braided hair, then my lavender blouse and matching ruffled skirts, and finally, my bare feet. "You look…" He cleared his throat. "Nice."

"Nice?" I repeated, feigning mild offense from the simple choice of word, when really, a patter in my stomach had my toes scrunching over the stone.

His eyes narrowed, then seemed to lighten upon my chest.

He wasn't admiring the swell of my breasts above the gathered neckline of my blouse. No, he could hear my heartbeat. How it raced the longer he watched me.

I looked at the ground, fighting the impulse to flee as an odd feeling of elation and fear quickened each breath. "So…" I lifted my gaze when I was certain my cheeks hadn't stained. "May I write to Bernadette?"

Vane blinked as if he'd forgotten what I'd asked him mere minutes ago. "Not yet."

Then he stepped back and closed his study door.

Defiance glimmered within the deep-blue gaze of the male in the largest cage in the dungeon.

A network of cells encircled his, all of them empty.

Something dripped. Something scuttled.

The male seemed eager for me to reach him, the clip of each step spreading his arrogant smile. I took one last whiff of my favorite scarf, then tucked it back in my coat pocket.

In the other pocket, my finger stroked the sharp edge of the small blade.

Just for annoying me, I'd take those eyes first.

I stopped before his cell. "Bring in the lover."

That defiance leaked from his eyes, rendering them a dull blue as he failed to keep his features from paling. Fear, true and so fucking sweet, emanated from him.

Finally. I loathed dawdling.

As scuffed steps neared, and the female growled at the guards who struggled to contain her, I grinned. "Despite my stellar reputation, I am a male who can be reasoned with." I snatched the female from the guards and sank the dagger from my pocket into her stomach, stilling her. "To a certain extent."

Her scream escaped her gritted teeth.

The once-stubborn prisoner dropped to his knees and clung to the bars, uncaring of the iron's burn. "Karis."

"I'm fine," she panted.

I withdrew the dagger, and she fell to the ground with a groan, clutching her stomach.

"Love," I said, dragging my finger over the bloodied blade. I left the heaving female with the guards and walked closer to my prisoner. "Such a cumbersome curse, is it not?"

"We won't speak," the female hissed.

"Oh, well…" I smirked down at her caged lover. "Good thing I haven't asked you to."

My prisoner swallowed thickly, then tore his gaze from the female and his hands from the iron bars. A quick nod, likely missed by his love, and I turned to the guards. "Take her to the eastern woods and await my signal before releasing her."

Her anguish echoed through the dungeon long after she'd been dragged up the stairs. She knew she wouldn't see the wolf shifter trapped in my cage again.

But he would make sure she lived by tell—

A groan and a splash woke me.

Dotted in sweat and breathing too fast, I clenched the bedding for something tangible.

Just a dream, I told myself.

Just another nightmare that would soon fade into unrecognizable patches.

It had to be nearing midnight, and it seemed the king had finally visited his chambers. Although I'd shared it with him before he'd left, I turned onto my side and scooted closer to the edge of the bed.

But sleep wouldn't return.

It remained like a stain, glaring in the dark. The dungeon. *His* voice. All of it so clear as if I'd been a witness to Atakan's cruelty.

Yet through his own eyes.

It made no sense. It had to be another dream. Except none of my dreams had ever felt quite that real. Never had one stayed with me like a vivid memory rather than haunting pieces.

Meadow mewled when I threw myself onto my back. The felynx crawled from underneath my leg, eyes aglow with unmistakable displeasure for being disturbed.

Another groan slipped through the bathing room door, which King Vane had left ajar.

It was none of my business, whatever he was doing in there. But it wasn't a groan of pleasure. It was a tight sound, as if he'd wanted to keep it trapped behind clenched teeth.

Again, I tried to ignore him and sleep.

Time crawled by, and I failed. Meadow's purred snores filled the bedchamber. The longer I lay there, staring up at the chandelier in desperate need of repair, the more certain I became that the blood I'd scented outside of Vane's study had been his.

Before I could think better of it, I padded across the bedchamber and tapped on the bathing room door. "Are you coming out any time soon?"

No response.

Leaning closer to the candlelit gap, I heard it—snoring.

"Vane," I called, knocking on the door again.

Still nothing but the sound of his rumbled breaths.

Exhaling heavily, I headed back to bed. It wasn't my problem. If he wanted to sleep in the bathing pool, then so be it. A relief, really. I'd get the bed all to myself, just as I'd prefer.

But sleep never came. The king never woke, and his snoring soon overpowered Meadow's. The water was likely freezing.

Not my problem.

A lie.

Whether I liked it or not, this king had made himself my problem. I might not be able to escape a land locked unto itself, but that didn't mean I wished to stay here forever. Leaving him to wrinkle in a cold body of water wouldn't exactly endear me to him.

Maybe he'd assume I never woke. Maybe he would think nothing of such callousness. Maybe he'd even expect it due to his opinion of the kingdom I hailed from.

Maybe I was giving it too much thought when it shouldn't have mattered.

For some reason I couldn't find, it did matter.

I tossed off the bedding and stomped to the bathing room, the door swinging open with a creak that failed to rouse him.

A candle burned low at the corner ledge of the bathing pool that had been fashioned with his royal ilk and those wings in mind. His formidable form came close to filling the space that could fit four of me. The water covered his manhood, gently wavering against his torso.

Still, I kept my eyes averted as I whispered harshly, "King, wake up."

He didn't so much as stir.

I growled, walking two steps closer to the sunken tub. His dark lashes twitched, but his eyes didn't open.

Then I scented a peppered and milky aroma. Healing salts.

For just a moment, I took the opportunity to stare at those fierce features without him knowing. The strong nose, the tiny scar beneath his right eye, and the perfect arches of his thinner upper lip. His mouth was slightly parted, and for another moment, I wondered if his lower lip was as cushiony as it looked.

I wondered what it might feel like to run my nails over the heavier scruff beneath his regal cheeks while I sampled those lips with my own.

His next snore broke. His eyes opened.

I stepped back, my heart immediately in a panic.

He blinked. His thick brows drooped over cloudy and bloodshot blue eyes. "Mildred?" My name was rasped, confusion soaking it. He looked around the bathing room and groaned, "Fuck."

"You've been in here for a long time. I thought you might be cold."

He made to straighten and hissed. Pain creased his features.

"You didn't look injured when I saw you earlier, but I could smell it," I whispered, unsure why. "The blood."

"Wing," he grunted. Bracing both forearms on the pool's edge, he pushed himself up to sit properly. The tiles creaked, and the water sloshed around his stomach.

But my attention was stolen by a section of ruined feathers in his left wing, close to his back. The blood had been washed away, revealing severed flesh and muscle.

That explained why he'd been in such a mood.

"You've been across the borders. Over the wards." I remembered the fires near Cloud Castle. The hunts and battles. I dared to voice my next assumption. "You've been leading the attacks to provoke the Seelie?"

He didn't answer. I wasn't sure he needed to.

"Provoke," he eventually said, and huffed. Then his teeth gnashed. "Fuck these fucking things."

I peered at his wing once more. Sinew re-stitched. It was both fascinating and utterly disgusting.

And evidently unmercifully painful. The slowest form of torture.

Breath left him in quiet pants between his teeth. Muscle corded in his neck beneath slick strands of his hair and flexed in his arms.

Though I shouldn't, I lowered beside the bathing pool. I'd woken him, so I should have returned to bed with a clear conscience. But he wasn't leaving the bathing room until he was in less pain.

His eyes had squeezed shut.

They flashed open when I touched his fingers. Gently, I pried them from the tiled edge and turned his hand over.

He said nothing. A long exhale left him when I laid my hand over his palm. The tips of my fingers reached halfway up his. Marveling at the size difference, I nearly forgot what I was doing until his fingers curled to touch mine.

They retreated a moment later, and I couldn't look at him. I kept my eyes on his hand and traced the callouses in his palm, the lifelines spreading in large and deep arches.

"How were you going to do it?" The pain-thickened question stilled my fingers. "Survive a court who would rather not have you among them."

The nicer way of putting how the Seelie Fae felt about me made my lips wriggle. There was little need to withhold an answer or honesty. Although I'd feared for my life since the contract was signed a decade ago, I shrugged. "Whatever it takes."

"You speak in present tense."

"My future hasn't changed, King."

A low grumble drew my gaze from his hand to his face. His eyes were still murky from the torment of his healing wing but no longer bloodshot. They held mine, almost gently, however that was possible, as he said, "You know that isn't true, Princess."

I failed to find a response.

He was right. Regardless of the absurdity of what Vane needed from me, everything would be much different when I left his realm. I would need a new strategy. But strategy required research, and it unnerved me—not having the means to assess much of anything.

After that dream I'd just had, it more than unnerved me. It terrified me so much that I knew in my bones I'd be better off hiding in a ship and sailing across the Moss Sea than learning a new dance with the Ethermore royals.

When the time came, I feared Atakan would no longer wish to duel.

He would only strike.

But maybe I wasn't entirely without the ability to study my heartless opponent. "Have you heard word of what transpires there?"

As if knowing why I'd asked, Vane's brows hovered low over his cobalt eyes. "They've got their hands full putting out our fires."

"Indeed," I said. "I saw some within the mountains."

My smile fell the more I thought about that.

The more I thought about what this king was doing and what he might hope to achieve. "You want more than freedom from the wards." A statement rather than a question.

"Even if I didn't, retribution is required to ensure such malevolence doesn't happen again."

As his deep words reverberated in the dark chambers of my heart, I glared at him. After a minute, I stared at the candlelit royal crest in the window. It would be my fault when his warriors, armies of shifters, once again spread across Elaysia.

It would be my fault when other beasts fled the bounds of their habitats to terrorize the continent among those armies and their king.

I couldn't not say it. "You are freeing a land of monsters."

"Since their creation, all beasts have flown and prowled freely throughout Elaysia." He groaned and shifted slightly with a twitch of his wings. "It's important we remember why that changed."

His father and mother had been the reason it changed. But putting voice to a truth he already knew was pointless.

The faucet dripped in the stale silence.

He knew what I'd been thinking. "I will admit that I never wholly agreed with my father's methods. He was obsessive and ruthless. He never deserved my mother, nor did he treat her well. But that doesn't mean he wasn't right to seek vengeance for her death." He let out a rattled exhale. "And it doesn't mean that revenge isn't even more necessary now."

I'd spent most of my life focused on one creature's battles and well-being—my own. It now seemed such selfishness had delivered me straight into the bloodied hands of this long war.

A war that hadn't ended at all.

Strange discomfort weighted my limbs. I was rescued from the sickening sensation of spiraling deep down into dark spaces by a touch at my jaw.

Vane traced it with his forefinger, his eyes trailing. Then the shape of my lips. My breathing turned shallow when that finger grazed the curve of my neck. He brushed the dip of my collarbone and sniffed.

My heart faltered. He could scent it.

The advancing heat of arousal.

Glancing away, I placed my hand beneath me to rise. To flee and pretend this never happened.

Heavy warmth folded over my other hand, still beside the bathing pool. "Stay." A soft command I was about to ignore until the water drained, and he leaned back in the giant tub. His eyes closed—an invitation to escape what had just happened.

One I took, relieved and quietly confused. Wholly aware he could feel my gaze on his features, I stared anyway.

I watched his throat bob as he swallowed. The way his jaw slowly loosened as his wing further healed. I frowned at his lashes, the breadth of his cheekbones. I absorbed his strange and rugged beauty until my head lay against my arm upon the tiled ledge of the pool.

As dawn kissed the sky and my back met softness, my eyes fluttered open. The bed, I realized, Vane's arms releasing me a moment later.

'EIGHTEEN

The arrival of breakfast opened my eyes, Daylia's sugary scent lingering after she'd quietly closed the doors.

I rolled over to stare at the king's pillows, his own scent fading but fresh enough to suggest he'd lain in his bed beside me. Then I rose and stared at the bathing room, wondering if I'd dreamed of the king in there, wounded and wanting my company.

Meadow returned to the king's chambers after lunch. She nudged open the door I'd left cracked, and pranced toward me with a dead rodent between her teeth. Plopping it before my feet, she then sat, tufted tail swishing as she gazed up at me with rounded gold eyes.

I peered over the book I'd been reading. "Would you like a reward?"

She blinked.

Before I said something withering, for I'd discovered she could tell how I felt from the tone of my voice, I sighed and set the book down. I didn't feel like being glared at for the rest of the day or having my feet played with while I slept.

"Though it's comforting to know you're learning to fend for yourself…" I gestured toward the doors. "Kindly consume it elsewhere."

"You'll need to show her." The king straightened from the doorframe I hadn't realized he'd been leaning against.

I made a face at what might have been a giant rat. The mere thought of touching the bloodied thing made me lose all interest in finishing my lunch.

He chuckled, then proceeded to the dressing chamber and left me alone with the vermin. His wing looked completely healed, sunlight catching on the dark array of soft-looking feathers tucked close to his back.

"Could you do it?" I called.

"No."

I huffed and returned to my meal. "So much for earning my love."

Vane gave that no response.

Minutes later, he exited the dressing chamber in a long-sleeved charcoal dress shirt. The collar sat high. Onyx buttons gleamed, matching his fitted pants. Also his polished pointed boots. He secured his hair with a sliver of black ribbon at his nape while walking to the doors.

And the result of removing the bloodred strands that usually curtained his face…

My stomach lurched.

I blinked down at my vegetable and herb stew. Still, all I saw was the cliffs of his cheeks, the severe arches of his dark brows over impossibly blue eyes, and his finely-wrapped bulky form.

Evidently, he had important matters to tend to. Matters that required ridding his typical attire of tunics and boots that could squash someone's head. He left his rooms without another word, and I again pondered if sitting with him beside the bathing pool had been another odd dream.

Meadow poked at her kill with a paw that was rapidly nearing the size of my own hand. She looked at me, then at the rat.

"Fine." I leaned down to offer my hand. She leaped toward it, purring when I scratched behind her tall ears. Then I stood and pinched the rat's tail between my fingers. "Now we take it outside." I gave the felynx a pointed look over my shoulder on my way to the doors. "Where anything you kill must stay."

The reason for the king's change of clothing was a gathering of sorts taking place in the throne room.

Before dinner, I'd passed the open doors with Meadow, spying a full table before the throne crafted from bone, steel, and emeralds.

The king had been seated at the head of the long table. Cerwin and Daylia dined with him. A female with a voluptuous figure and short black hair had been at the king's side. Beside her had been a male I couldn't place at a glance but who'd looked vaguely familiar.

As their merriment grew, so did my irritation.

Laughter climbed through the halls, poking at my skin until I set my cutlery down. Perhaps it wasn't so much their dinner but rather, my seclusion. For although I'd been enjoying days of idleness, I couldn't choose this forever.

I couldn't stay here forever, awaiting a safe way out.

And although they were clearly having a grand time, they were gathering for a reason.

A reason I needed to know about.

Firelight illuminated the carvings of winged serpentine beasts upon the dark oak doors. They remained open, so I walked into the throne room, pausing briefly to clutch my taffeta skirts and lower my head in formal greeting.

Conversation crashed to a halt.

Daylia grinned, bright and beautiful, her orange curls pinned back from her rouge-dusted cheeks. Beside her, Cerwin frowned.

Vane stared, his goblet poised before his mouth. He lowered it to the table, the crease between his brows hinting at shock or confusion. Perhaps both.

The chestnut-haired male covered his smile with his ring-bedecked hand, and a startling memory of the stuffy ballroom at Cloud Castle infiltrated.

Lord Stone.

The Seelie faerie had been present at many celebrations over the years, including that of the Unseelie's defeat. My heart thundered in my ears. I made no comment, even as our eyes locked long enough to convey that we recognized one another.

It wasn't uncommon for the two faerie realms of Elaysia to intermingle. But it was uncommon for nobility, who thought too highly of themselves to sully their time and bloodlines.

Daylia sighed. "My king, I believe this is where you ask your guest to join us."

Said king blinked, then shot his steward a slight glare before rising.

"It's quite all right." I opted for the empty seat at the end of the table, directly opposite the king but nearest the doors. "I can seat myself."

Cerwin chuckled, stabbing a slice of roasted duck. "I'm afraid Vane is rather lacking when it comes to courting females."

The king sat. "You might find yourself lacking something in a minute," he grumbled, fixated on his meal although I sensed it hadn't any of his attention.

Everyone laughed.

Daylia gestured to the lord. "This is Lord Stone." Her eyes twinkled. "You might know him."

The lord gave me a nod. Far too much knowledge of where I'd come from and what I'd experienced shone in his eyes. "Call me Stone."

I forced a smile. It wavered when silence settled, and I found the raven-haired female beside the king eyeing me curiously.

The only dish within reach was baked potatoes nestled in a bowl of rich cream. I pulled it toward me and used the serving spoon to gesture to the female. "You've yet to be introduced."

Someone, maybe Cerwin, cleared their throat.

I carved into a potato, dabbed the spoon into the cream, and ate while awaiting an answer I assumed would come from Daylia. Surprisingly, the steward remained quiet.

The female had orange eyes that matched wings reminiscent of a butterfly. They shifted with her evident unease. Black dust drifted toward the empty hearth behind her, as she said in a silken voice, "Perhaps because that might be a tad inappropriate."

She didn't expect me to pry. So it pleased me to say, "How so?"

An amused glance was given to Vane, her hand falling upon his forearm.

And staying there.

My eyes stuck to it. Meadow made her presence known with a strange noise. Not quite a growl but more of a whine. She padded beneath my chair, then rose onto her hind legs to poke at my knee.

I shook my gaze free of the female and Vane, saying quietly, "The cream will upset your stomach."

The felynx sat, her annoyance portrayed in her flicking tail.

Vane released a rough exhale.

He patted the female's hand, then removed it. Gently, he set it back by her plate as the silence began to break with shifting and sipping and chewing. "Morona is a friend."

At that, Morona served him a look that was not quite a glower. Hurt, maybe, shone in her orange eyes.

I might not have been exceptionally knowledgeable when it came to matters of the heart—unless it pertained to how I might keep it beating—but I understood that friends did not look dejected when called as such.

My tone softened. "How long have you been friends?"

Morona answered, "A few decades."

I nodded, chewing a mouthful of potato, and decided to cease making it look like I cared when Daylia smiled up at the chandelier.

It too had been fashioned from bones. At least two dozen candles illuminated the differing shapes and sizes upon each tier. Real bones. I glanced at the sconce-lined walls, but save for two tapestries either side of the throne behind the king, the glinting rock was bare of decor.

One of the tapestries was black, a white design of another winged beast within. The serpentine body curled around the tip of a shadowed mountain, the long maw exhaling fire.

A pytherion.

A dying breed of dragon who submitted only to the king of this dark realm. Their rarity was a mercy, considering the devastation they'd caused during the first war. Remaining pytherions resided in the mountains blocking this castle from the rest of the Unseelie kingdom.

A mountain range that supposedly harbored the biggest military facility in The Bonelands.

The other tapestry was a brown-backed royal crest of wings and shadows, and the bone crown I hadn't seen Vane wear.

Deciding to kill the tense silence and learn what I could of Lord

Stone's presence, I smiled as warmly as possible. "I've interrupted important chatter, I'm sure."

"You do not seem the least bit remorseful," Cerwin drawled.

"Because I'm not." The large spoon hit the bowl with a clank, and I reached for the decanter of wine. I tapped my fingers over the glass, eyeing everyone. "Merely curious."

Vane was the only one looking at me. His gaze dropped to the decanter, then returned to mine. His mouth twitched. "Would you like a goblet, Princess?"

"I'd hate to trouble you with the effort." I lifted the decanter and sipped carefully so as not to spill wine on my flower-speckled bodice.

Out of all the gowns I'd grown fond of in the dressing chamber, this one was my favorite. Slowly, I brushed my hand over the dried orange and dusky pink flowers sewn into the delicate black silk at my chest.

Amusement danced in Vane's eyes. He motioned Daylia to sit when she rose, likely to get me a goblet. "Is this about the rat?"

"I'm surprised you care to remember."

"I forget nothing." Those rough words brought forth the memory of a dimly lit bathing room and his fingers at my chin, mouth, and collarbone.

Ignoring the squirming in my stomach, I grinned, my gaze moving to the lord. "I fear I have the same affliction."

Lord Stone regarded me with his shaven chin perched on a sparkling fist. "You're wondering what I'm doing here," he said, eyes flashing wide. "Dining with the enemy."

Decorum long done away with, I reached across the table for a green bean, then lowered back to my seat and dangled it beneath my chair. "I'm all ears if you'd like to share, even if they aren't as pointed as yours."

Meadow snatched the bean, her sharp teeth just shy of my fingertips.

Stone huffed, chin rising from his hand. "That's how you did it." I frowned, but only after sipping wine and dabbing at his thin mouth with a white cloth did he explain. "Your calculated boldness is the reason you gained Prince Atakan's attention." He placed the cloth down and handed me a look that quaked my bones before he said the words. "And his heart."

Vane's stare was an uncomfortable weight.

I refrained from shifting. From letting my own heart gallop at the asinine thought. "Everyone knows Atakan has no heart."

"Yet here you are," Cerwin interjected, bringing his goblet to his mouth. "Perhaps the only thing he cares about and, therefore, the only way to ruin those wards."

Daylia nudged him.

He cursed as his sip of wine spilled over his chin. She giggled, turning his glacial glare to a warm warning of punishment.

Whatever I'd hoped to glean from this dinner no longer seemed worth it.

I didn't want to think about Atakan. Not until I had to. Not after he'd invaded my dreams. Not when I'd spent a decade with him consuming my thoughts in the worst of ways.

Mercifully, Vane got rid of the chilled silence. "Stone has been an ally of ours for some years. Garran has never known, and he never will."

It wasn't a threat. Rather, a statement drenched in firm confidence. By the time King Garran became aware that his friend wasn't who he'd thought, it would be too late.

Nodding once, I sensed it was safe to ask Stone, "What made you betray your own ilk?"

"What made your own ilk betray you?" he asked, finger circling the rim of his goblet. "Opportunity, I'm sure."

It was true. He knew it just as well as everyone in this room—including myself. So I didn't argue. Instead, I pushed a little more. "What opportunity are you seeking?"

His answer was swift. "Retribution." He sat back in his chair, revealing a thick scar beneath his jaw. "What else?"

What else indeed.

No longer feeling the need to pry, I waited to see if he'd provide more information, perhaps about what had befallen his late wife. I'd learned that it took very little to offend faeries. And the easily slighted were rarely ever forgiving.

Not for one second would I allow myself to believe that those in this throne room were any different, no matter how different they'd seemed thus far.

Morona remained quiet as Daylia attempted to rouse the table into merriment once more.

Assuming she wouldn't succeed until I left, I made to stand when the lord gestured from the king to me. "You are not yet falling in love, I take it."

That didn't need answering.

Cerwin laughed. "At this rate, I fear many of us won't see the rest of the continent in this immortal lifetime."

Daylia shot him a glower.

"What?" He shrugged. "She cannot stand him."

That piqued Morona's interest. Her eyes sharpened on me, as though she were attempting to figure out what was wrong with me.

I hated that I needed to say something. I *didn't* need to. But I refused to stay quiet and evidently bothered. "I never said I cannot stand him."

"Then, please." Cerwin spread his arms. "Cease dawdling and climb into his bed."

My eyes met Daylia's, and something warm filled my chest. She hadn't told anyone I'd been sleeping in Vane's bed. Not even her mate.

Morona asked, "Is your lack of affection because of the prince?" Her thin brows jumped high as she scoffed. "He is but a pretty portrait to veil the evil lurking within."

I smiled, and the words left me before I could stop them. "You're not wrong about that."

Silence rang like a bell.

Then everyone laughed. Everyone, I noted, except for the king.

Vane carved into his roasted duck. Our eyes locked when he delivered a forkful to his mouth.

I watched him chew as he watched me. I smirked.

His eyes thinned slightly. Then he swallowed, and my gaze dipped to his throat.

I forced it to Daylia when she spoke as she refilled her goblet. "Males are all the same. Unaware that love means more than an obsession with humping someone."

Unable to help it, I laughed.

Cerwin licked his lips. "I'm sensing I should keep my mouth shut."

"Should you wish to hump me any time soon, then that would be wise." Daylia set the decanter down.

I remembered the one before me and took a quick sip as Meadow's snoring was interrupted by more laughter. Peering beneath my chair, I smiled. She'd curled into a ball, head tucked beneath a leathery wing.

Wood scraped over stone. "If you'll excuse me." Morona rose, tugging at the maroon chiffon tightly wrapped around her curved form. "I have that meeting to prepare for in the city."

Vane immediately stood.

Morona smiled warmly at everyone, including me, before being escorted out by the king.

Watching them go, his hand upon the small of her back might as well have been an ant continuously biting my skin. I tried to ignore the odd sting. Glaring at the glass decanter, I waited for it to pass as Daylia and Lord Stone chatted about an upcoming gathering the lord was hosting.

The feeling won.

Meadow released a yawned growl when I carefully climbed out of the chair to avoid hitting her with one of the legs. She trailed me into the hall, a furry shadow I was growing too attached to, though it sometimes still grated.

Especially now, when I wanted to catch a glimpse of Vane and Morona. He led her through the formidable castle doors to an awaiting black carriage.

Before he could disappear down the blocks of stone steps into the night, I decided spying wasn't what I needed. For some reason, I needed him to come back inside where I could see him. So I made my presence known by clipping my heeled slippers over the tiled foyer, then leaned against the curled end of the stair railing.

Meadow did a better job of giving us away. She darted through the open doors, vanishing into the dark.

Seven seconds later, Vane returned, leaving a door ajar for the felynx although she could find another way in.

"Say I do fall in love with you and free your kingdom," I said. "Will you truly give me anything I want?"

Vane halted in the middle of the foyer, head cocked.

He studied me as if attempting to determine what I was thinking—perhaps what had caused me to interrupt his dinner.

Before I could worry that he knew, he procured a dagger from behind his back. As he crossed the foyer, eyes still tight on mine, he dragged the blade over his palm.

He didn't so much as rustle a feather. He tucked the dagger away, then extended his hand. "A deal forged in blood is a promise unbreakable, Princess."

Knowing what he intended to do, I offered my hand.

He ran his finger over his cut lifeline, then traced my own in his blood. "When you break the wards trapping my realm, Mildred Nephryn, I solemnly swear to give you something of your choosing."

My cheeks warmed as his roughened finger tickled.

"Now…" Low and thick, he asked as though he had his own ideas in mind, "Any ideas on how we can move this along?"

Unable to meet his gaze, I took my hand back and stared down at his blood on my palm. "A picnic," I said, not really thinking it through.

Not wanting to. Not even certain I wanted to do something as mundane as eating food from a basket outside with this beastly king.

But I'd never been able to forget the way Bernie had looked upon returning from one during her betrothal to Royce. Her eyes had glimmered like jewels, happiness coloring her cheeks. More than that, when she'd spoken of it over dinner, she'd seemed different.

Like she'd crossed a mystical line between desire and love.

Vane's eyes narrowed. "Picnic?" he asked as if he wasn't entirely sure what it was.

That was fine. He could find out.

"Yes, you will take me on one." I smiled, turning to climb the stairs. "Tomorrow morning."

NINETEEN

Daylia flitted around the kitchens, wearing a smile that seemed permanent.

The cooks made themselves scarce as soon as she'd entered the stuffy rooms nestled in the rear corner of the ground floor. I couldn't say I blamed them, as the steward left a trail of mess in her wake and nearly overturned a pot of gurgling stew upon the stove.

"Sandwiches," she muttered, a finger pointed in the air. "It's not a picnic without sandwiches."

The more mayhem she created, the more undeniable it became that I would need to commandeer this task. Searching the wooden benches lining every edge of the room and the two in the center, I collected a jar of almonds and leftover diced fruit from breakfast.

Atop wooden crates by the door was a basket of fresh herbs.

I set it on one of the island benches, put the herbs in a clean bowl by the sink, then placed the nuts and fruit in the basket. All the while, Daylia smeared far too much butter upon mounds of bread and hacked at a block of cheese.

"You've little skill with a knife."

She didn't seem offended. I wondered if much could offend her as she shrugged. "Never needed it. Now, Morona..." Casting me a knowing look, she said, "Vane has known her for quite some years."

It took a stupid amount of effort not to roll my eyes. "So she said."

"She's still rather enamored with him." Curls bobbed with her head. "But Vane never wanted to make such a commitment."

I snorted. "It would indeed be such a chore to spend an immortal lifetime with just *one* female."

Daylia ignored my sarcasm. "He believes it a waste to invest all of his heart in someone when he might one day be forced to sever ties." She almost sang, "You never know who the goddess might put in your path."

Momentarily perplexed, my mouth parted. It promptly snapped closed when what she'd said settled properly.

Great. So not only was I being forced to fall in love with this king and then deal with the repercussions, but I had to fall in love with someone awaiting a divinely gifted mate.

Ridiculous. All of it.

"But mates are a dying phenomenon."

A smile entered her voice as she hinted at her own bond with Cerwin. "Are they, though?"

I stepped away before my frustrations, and something akin to resentment, freed more bitter words from my mouth.

In the hall outside, I found clean cloths in the long row of serving drawers. I used one to cover the fruit dish as Daylia went on about the king and how she couldn't believe he'd agreed to go on this outing.

"Even before the war, all he did was hunt and fuck and fight and read things, so I cannot explain how momentous this is. A picnic!" She exhaled a breathy laugh. "By the dark mother, I wish I could have seen his reaction." She bit into a jagged slice of cheese. "Was he shocked? Disgusted? Wait…" She hummed another laugh as she swallowed. "Does he even know what a picnic is?"

I spread two more cloths over the benchtop. "I'm sure he's asked around." Then I stole the sandwiches and wrapped them before she made them inedible.

Unusually quiet for a moment, Daylia cut into the cheese although there was no longer any need to torture it. "You've not asked much yourself, you know."

"About Vane?"

"Some think you don't care to even try to break this curse."

Her bluntness worked. My spine stiffened, and a curt response formed over my tongue. I withheld it because she was sadly right. "Truth be told, I don't care," I admitted. "Not enough."

Her mouth pinched. I'd officially offended her.

Before she unleashed the ire dampening her eyes, I set the sandwiches in the basket and whispered, "All I've ever done is what others have forced upon me." I met her gaze, weariness flattening my rising voice. "My life has never been my own."

Daylia said nothing. She just watched me fill two canteens with water.

As I placed them in the basket, she released a loud breath. "The life of a royal is never their own. It's another curse disguised as a blessing. That still doesn't exempt you from responsibility."

Decade-old anger soaked my question in venom. "And what responsibility does a lowly halfling have?"

"What you are doesn't matter, Princess. You have a title, and those with titles were given them to do more than drink fine wines and play games of power. You are to protect the balance, which has been grossly destroyed." Setting down the knife, she smiled faintly. "Use your heart, Mildred. You'll find that if you do, freedom often follows."

"And what about Ethermore's freedom from more torment?" I asked. "After years of enduring unspeakable brutality bestowed by your late king and his armies of ruthless warriors?"

Both Fae realms were as rotten as each other, but what I'd said was still undeniably true.

"You cannot make an entire kingdom pay for one king's callousness and expect to get away with it." With that, she left the kitchens.

I glowered at the basket, feeling his energy before I saw him.

Tempted to ask how long he'd been standing there—how much he'd overheard—I took my time to acknowledge him. Snatching the basket, I decided to darkness with it. "I suppose you agree with your steward."

Vane straightened from the wall, a toothpick between his teeth. He didn't answer.

He eyed my layered lavender lace and tulle skirts, then my sleeveless cream blouse. I'd intended to dress simply. Perhaps I'd failed. His teeth flashed, blue eyes ashine with amusement and something that looked alarmingly close to approval.

In head-to-toe black, save for another pair of bulky brown boots, he'd dressed far more simply than me. Taking advantage of having his back, I admired the tight fit of his pants, the way they hugged his backside, as I trailed him through the halls.

A black carriage awaited beneath the castle steps, the royal crest painted in smoky silver upon the door.

Vane opened it and flicked his toothpick, but rather than take his offered hand, I gave him the basket. He frowned at the contents, and I smiled as I climbed into the carriage's mahogany and leather interior.

We jostled forward as soon as he settled on the seat opposite me.

The basket he'd placed beside him still had his attention. He poked at the cloth covering the sandwiches. "I smell so much cheese."

"Blame Daylia." I pulled the velvet curtain aside to peer out the window.

A river curled through the trees lining the drive we ambled down. There were no gates to open, so the drivers didn't stop. "Where are your royal guards?"

"They're shifters who patrol the grounds and woodland, so you'll seldom see them. We've no need for many."

That made me look at him. Dryly, I asked, "Because your might is so formidable, no one would dare attack your fortress?"

He folded his hands in his lap, thumbs brushing together. "Such sourness from such a sweet mouth." His eyes gleamed. "I look forward to tasting it."

Blinking, I blurted, "What makes you so sure you'll get to?"

"The look in your eyes right now."

The large cabin suddenly felt far too small. Too warm. "I believe what you're referring to is more commonly known as contempt."

He chuckled, hearty and rasped.

If I could have climbed free of my uncomfortable skin, I would have. Alas, there was no escape. Not from this carriage. Not from this realm.

Not from this king.

White flashed in my peripheral, and my eyes returned to the world beyond the window. A temple hid within the trees, the stone open and empty and swallowed by vegetation. The road became bumpier. Trees tried to claim it with roots that lurched and arching branches filled with squawking birds and buzzing insects.

I'd merely intended to ignore the king and the oppressive warmth of his gaze.

But as we left the road to the castle and veered around a bend onto another, I found myself transfixed. This land of monsters was a lush sight. Color splashed the never-ending greenery in breath-catching bursts that made me long for parchment and ink so that I could describe them to Bernie.

So that I could remember.

At the creek we traveled alongside, a fawn-like creature munched on leaves as big as its head. The water wasn't red or brown with blood, as rumor and myth often told, but a clear blue that reflected the sky peeking between the canopy of ancient and thickly trunked trees.

The carriage soon slowed. A clearing came into view as we trundled to a halt.

Vane exited before the driver could reach the door, a silver-haired male with a missing eye. He smiled briefly, then stepped back as Vane offered me his hand.

Again, I merely gave him the basket. Then I jumped down onto the grass-speckled road that ended right where we'd stopped.

I saw why when I walked into the clearing that sloped toward a cliff.

Beneath it, in the distance beyond more woodland and the infamous River of Serpents, the royal city was a glinting cluster of darkness. But the rocky and tree-dense sentinels curling around it stunted the beat of my heart.

Skeleton Mountains.

Vane neared as the carriage ambled back down the road. "The view is even better over here."

I followed him downhill. Upon the emerald grass, he set the basket down a safe distance from the sharp rocks lining the cliff's edge. Soft yellow wildflowers tickled my arm as I sat and placed my skirts over and under my legs to keep the breeze from stealing them.

Vane dumped himself upon the ground and snatched the jar of almonds. A safer choice than the sandwiches. Even so, I unwrapped one and removed the cheese before biting into the heavily buttered bread.

When I found him watching me intently, I frowned. Then I offered him the sandwich.

He huffed. "You keep it."

"Then what is it?"

"Your hair," he said, plucking a wildflower. "It's the same shade of yellow as these petals." The breeze knocked his own hair toward his tucked wings, a thick strand blowing over his cheek. He looped it behind his pointed ear, then passed me the flower.

Rather than tell him hundreds surrounded me and that I could pick my own if I wanted to, I gently took the stem from between his fingers.

A screech in the distance drew my eyes from the petals and curdled my blood. Against the fluffy puffs of white clouds flew a dark figure, its long body curling with each sweep of its large wings.

A pytherion.

We both watched it soar toward the mountains, then disappear. Another screech announced its arrival.

Recalling what Vane had said in the carriage about the lack of royal guards, I couldn't keep from smiling. "These mountains are the reason you don't fear ambush."

"Partly," he confessed, chewing an almond. "Those who dare attempt journeying through them do rarely live to tell the tale."

"What about your military facility?"

He wasn't surprised that I knew. He couldn't be when the stronghold had existed there for eons. "The pytherions are accustomed to their presence. And though they're extremely ill-tempered, unless ordered otherwise, they seldom attack those who respect them and present no threat."

"Ordered otherwise?"

He seemed to ponder his response for a moment. "A long time ago, they were used for battle. Due to their bond with the Ashbone bloodline, they tolerated riders so long as the king or queen commanded the legion."

I'd read that Unseelie rulers had once been gifted the ability to shift into a pytherion—granting them the power to better control the monsters who had the power to destroy too much.

Over the years, many speculating that a secret pairing with a Seelie faerie was to blame, the ability skipped generations and eventually died out. Some texts called it a consequence of a dying species. Now, the only evidence of their connection to the Ashbone family loomed upon King Vane's back—his wings.

I shivered at the mere thought of such creatures blocking out the sky as they delivered doom, and diverted my attention to the water astride the mountains.

On one side, the River of Serpents, and on the other, the Moss Sea. The only way inland was via heavily guarded river bridges. "But what about threats from sea?"

Chomping on another almond, Vane snorted. After swallowing, he drawled, "Taking inventory of potential weaknesses, Princess?"

Rather than deny it, I asked with a sidelong glance, "Are you admitting there are more?"

He just laughed.

The deep and throaty sound had me dropping the bread into the basket and drinking some water to distract myself from the bubbling in my stomach. I tried to stay on topic but ended up asking what I truly wanted to know. "Where do you go when you disappear for days at a time?"

"Wherever I am needed."

"Vague, King." I placed the flower in the basket. He wouldn't see my next question coming. If I was being honest with myself, I didn't either. "Did you intend to fuck your friend during her visit?"

The look he hurled at me was soaked in shock.

As his features relaxed, a hint of mild offense darkened his gaze. Then a hummed laugh left him. "That's what this…" He threw his hand at the basket. "This picnic is all about?" His brows furrowed. "Morona?"

I couldn't deny it. Not entirely. But I would certainly try. "No."

"No?" he repeated, disbelieving.

Conceding just a little, I confessed, "I mostly wanted to poke you for information about where you've been going. What you're intending." If it meant hiding my jealousy, I would admit whatever I had to. "I heard you talking about preparations." Tentatively, I peered up at him. "Don't suppose I'll find out now."

A long silence accompanied a hard stare that gradually softened.

His broad shoulders dropped a fraction as he sighed. "Morona is not only an old friend, but a spy with deep connections due to her ability to shapeshift into insects." He took the canteen from my fingers, sipping before he went on. "We're ensuring we're ready for when the wards fall. Ready to make sure no one tries anything so bold again."

I sat with all that could mean for a heavy minute.

The more knowledge I gained of this Unseelie realm, the more I began to understand why the Seelie loathed them. With many faeries able to shapeshift, their power was vast. So vast, that if they so desired, they could have this entire continent eating out of the palms of their goddess-blessed hands.

And they might have succeeded if Garran hadn't garnered military support from my father.

Vane pointed toward the city. "See the sea to the left?" At my nod, he said, "Miles down the coastline is Jade Cove."

"The trading port."

He grunted. "Half resides here in The Bonelands, the other in your family's realm." He lowered his hand. "As it should be to keep things fair. To maintain order and balance among the humans and the Fae. Now, no ships can reach our port."

"How are you receiving goods?"

"Some of our people stuck beyond the wards deliver what they can obtain to the border for me to collect."

"Because you're the only one who can vanish beyond the wards," I stated pointedly.

His smirk was confirmation I didn't need. "But to trade with us means risking execution. Some crews still do, but it's discreet. Otherwise, we are forced to ambush the warriors who patrol the docks and take what is rightfully ours."

"You kill them."

"They kill us, too." He capped the canteen and tossed it into the basket. "The war never ended with those wards. Just because you can't see it doesn't mean it's not happening."

Elion's words returned again. *War never truly ends.*

"We need this curse removed. Not only because it's not right to exert that type of control over a realm that is not your own but because there are families who've been forced apart. Younglings without parents here and in Ethermore. Creatures perishing without the ability to return to their natural habitats. Businesses suffering and failing because of a lack of resources and customers. The list, unfortunately…" He rubbed his chin. "Goes on and on."

I tried to make sense of it. Not of what he'd said—which made perfect sense—but of Ethermore's desire to entrap this realm. All this time, it had been said that they merely wished to stop the bloodshed. "Does Ethermore want to control trade?" For that would mean having control over the entire continent. "And to weaken the power this kingdom possesses?"

"Might seem like it, but we know that's not what sparked this blaze. The blame falls on the root of all good and evil." His eyes met mine. "Love."

"Your father truly did love your mother, then."

Vane's teeth slid over his lower lip. He released it and looked toward the mountains. "As a noble's son, my father was born entitled. Yet he always claimed he couldn't believe he'd been blessed with a marriage to my mother. Although arranged, he loved her instantly. Madly." He smiled, but it appeared sad. "So madly, I suspect he couldn't handle her milder affection for him."

Wanting to dig into why Queen Kalista had fled, I asked around it, "Did you worry for her when she left him?"

He admitted easily, "I was too furious. She'd been gone for many months before Daylia finally told me what my father had done to her." He swallowed. "She overheard it. But my mother made her vow not to tell another soul, as she was the only one who knew."

"Your father would have hurt Daylia?"

A huff pushed at his cheeks. "He would've killed her, and if she'd been lucky, he'd have made it quick. So I pretended not to know."

I frowned at his profile, the wind throwing his hair over his distant eyes.

He didn't bother removing it as he went on. "Though it soon became apparent that although Daylia was the only one to witness his cruelty toward my mother, many had their suspicions. Many knew. They just kept quiet about it until he was killed."

I wasn't sure it mattered, yet when he said nothing else, I couldn't help but question aloud, "What happened when Vorx died?"

"I wasn't there, but reports claim he fell from the skies due to an injured wing." His tone hinted at disbelief. "That he landed on fallen arrows, and they punctured his heart. But when I inspected his corpse, his heart was missing. A gaping hole in his chest had been packed with someone's innards."

"You suspect foul play," I surmised.

He tipped a shoulder. "His heart was never found. I assume it was eaten or fed to something else." Then he turned to me. His crimson hair fluttered over his broad shoulders. "Is that enough intel for one day, Princess?"

No, I didn't say. "I've yet to decide," I said instead.

His mouth curved.

More questions sat on the tip of my tongue, trapped behind my teeth, for that look in his burning blue eyes… I'd seen it before.

Hunger. Want.

A dare.

I'd seen it upon another male more times than I cared to recall.

For whenever I did, the thorns he'd entwined around my heart had sharpened and pressed until I couldn't draw breath.

I didn't miss him. I couldn't. I could never yearn for someone as vile as the Ethermore prince.

But I couldn't forget him. The memory of him was a shadow, stalking so close it may as well have been my own. He was a nightmare who visited my dreams.

I refused to let him haunt me in broad daylight.

As the king's taunting gaze morphed into one of contemplation, I looked toward the waves of green, sun-gilded darkness on the horizon. "I want to see it. This military within the Skeleton Mountains." Vane could very well see my desire to learn what I could as intent to harm him.

But maybe he didn't.

Perhaps he simply saw it for what it was—a way to arm myself with the knowledge to navigate and survive my perilously uncertain future.

I was inclined to believe it was the latter when he said firmly, "Then I will take you."

Peering at him, I tilted my head. "When?"

"Whenever you'd like."

"Tomorrow."

His jaw fixed, hesitation creasing the corners of his eyes.

"You have plans," I assumed.

His lips curved again as he watched me closely. So closely, he likely knew I was testing him. "None that I cannot postpone."

"I can wait," I said with scathing softness.

His smile broadened into a blinding grin. "I will never keep you waiting, Princess."

He'd said it in jest, yet those words still seeped beneath my skin to caress my flesh. Legs curling under me, I leaned closer. Not only did I want to know more but I also wanted to listen to him. "Tell me more of this evil love—I want to understand all that happened."

"I think I've said enough for now."

"You just said you will never make me wait."

He placed the basket on his other side, then shifted closer. "There is a difference between waiting and timing."

I laughed. "Faeries and their riddle-like words that make no sense."

"You speak as if you are not a faerie yourself." Before I could refute that, he said, "It does make sense. You need only think about it." He winked. "The right timing is a kindness."

Even more curious, I said, "I don't know that I agree."

"You don't have to, Princess." His wing brushed my shoulder as he took a thick lock of my hair, and I could've sworn he shivered. He rubbed it between his fingers. "Hair of pure sunshine and eyes of emerald." His own eyes lifted from the strands to mine. "I desperately want to kiss you."

If it weren't for the heat clouding his eyes and drenching his voice, I wasn't sure I would have believed him.

Still, I asked, "Because of your curse?"

"Because I want to."

"Fine," I whispered. "Then you may kiss me."

His grin vanished every reservation from my head and turned my heartbeat into a giddy dancer. Warm and roughened, his fingers pinched my chin. He tilted it, his head lowering.

My eyes closed, then opened when all I felt was the graze of his nose on my cheek and the warmth of his breath on my mouth. The clashing of our eyes as I awaited his lips on mine was a cruelty.

I felt exposed, nothing but bones, beneath the weight of anticipation.

Right as I went to pull away, his mouth touched mine. Just touched when I'd expected to be devoured. The droop of his long lashes and the rumble that climbed his throat told me it was something else entirely.

A hunter enjoying the slow demise of his prey.

It was nothing but a press. Yet it touched far more than my mouth. Awakened far more than hunger.

My eyes closed when his did.

And fear, different from any I'd felt before, stole my breath as his hands stole my face. He held me there, trapped yet willing, as his mouth molded to mine with an unbearable gentleness that revealed his lips were indeed as soft as I'd wondered.

The wind swayed our hair across one another's cheeks, and he breathed me in. His exhale was a groan that caused every tense part of me to liquefy.

The way he parted my lips with nothing but the parting of his flooded my body with need.

He'd claimed he had no experience with seducing females, but you didn't kiss someone like this without intention—without knowing what you would do to them.

The thought sliced through me, a bolt of rage.

I broke free and climbed onto his lap, seizing his cheek and tunic in my hands. "You said you wanted to kiss me."

He frowned, eyes glazed with lust. "I thought I was." Then something cleared his confusion. He folded his lips between his teeth, and his hand settled at my hip. It should have warned that I wouldn't like what he'd say. "He didn't treat you tenderly."

My stomach churned.

I didn't need him to clarify who *he* was. I was far too interested in getting more from this king, in the erection pressing into my skirts, to care about minding my words. "An understatement."

Vane didn't find that amusing.

The hand at my hip gently squeezed. He glanced at the view behind me. "How did he kiss you?"

"Like he hated that he wanted to." My mouth dried, and my grip on his tunic loosened. "Like he was trying to find out why he wanted to."

His wings flared slightly, as did his nostrils. Those beautiful eyes darkened a shade when they returned to my face. "You liked it." It wasn't a question.

"I don't want to discuss Atakan." Just saying his name tightened my bones. I lowered my mouth over Vane's. "I just want you to kiss me properly."

As soon as my lips met his, he grasped my cheek in his other hand, halting me. He stared up at me for seconds that ticked in my ears alongside my heartbeat. He searched my face as if looking for clues to a puzzle.

Then he gave me what I wanted.

His hand slid into my hair. His mouth opened mine instantly. Our tongues touched before his retreated to skim my upper lip. He denied my efforts to fight back with nips of his teeth, one of his canines breaking the skin.

Copper welled and dampened.

He groaned, taking both sides of my face to hold me still as he licked the blood from my lips.

It was more than what I'd expected.

It was exactly what I needed—sweetness veiled in brutality. Every graze of his teeth was chased by a caress of his lips or tongue. Caresses that coaxed, luring me to seek more before he punished me for doing so. A punishment I relished, rocking over him as want fired through me.

Want for him. Want for more. Want for this wondrous distraction to never end.

A breath carrying sound escaped me, earning me an approving groan as I pulled my mouth free from his.

Needy and transfixed, my eyes refused to move from his kiss-reddened lips. "That was…" I swallowed. "Not quite what I had in mind."

A lie. That kiss had been reminiscent of what I'd grown used to. What I wanted, even if I hadn't thought I would.

My gaze jumped to his with his rough question. "Did you think of him?"

I didn't want to admit it. To give him the satisfaction. I also didn't want to wound him. "No." The conflicting feelings rasped my voice. "Not at all."

His hooded eyes searched mine. He brought my face to his. He kissed me once, and whispered, "Then I kissed you properly, Princess."

I glowered, and he chuckled.

The sound of wheels rolling over rock and dirt quietened the birdsong.

"If you're still not convinced…" His mouth glossed my cheek as I looked over his shoulder to the returning carriage. "I can kiss you more on the way back."

I smiled, unable to hide it when he tipped my chin and brushed his thumb over my bottom lip. His gaze lowered to my chest, and his throat bobbed. "You're almost too lovely to look at."

Never had I been handed such a compliment. But I'd been given enough insults to know those quiet words hadn't been one.

I still questioned it, a brow lifting. "Too lovely?"

"Indeed." He grinned. "The awful things I would do to look at you forevermore."

He helped me to my feet when I sat there, torn between the desire to kiss him and cuss at him. In the end, I waited until we were seated in the carriage before saying to the window, "Cheating with pretty words won't do you any favors."

"I don't need favors." I looked at him as he vowed, "This is war, and I intend to win."

Twenty

The king retired after I'd fallen asleep. A relief, I realized as he pulled my body unnecessarily tight against his the following morning to vanish us to Skeleton Mountains. That stupid picnic had corroded something vital in my brain, and I wasn't sure I would have denied any further efforts he made to sway me.

My breakfast threatened to leave me as the void of shadowed wind spun us to a knee-jarring stop upon a stone ledge overlooking the innards of a mountain. Rope fencing surrounded the small lookout.

A pit loomed below.

I thought the lookout was a landing point for vanishing until I heard a faint growl and scratching. The echo climbed the dirt and rock walls of the cavernous mountain.

I wasn't given time to glimpse what lurked deep down in the darkness. Vane clasped my hand, to steady me, it seemed, and led me through a tunnel carved into the earth and stone.

Fire flickered from torches in the steel beams, illuminating figures behind a window up ahead. The king knocked once upon the glass door to a room built into the mountainside. Some type of command center, I surmised, as we entered, and uniformed faeries looked up from long rows of desks.

They all rose, bowing and then returning to the maps and reports spread before them. All except one muscular male with blond hair shorn close to his tattooed scalp.

"Commander Kreyts," Vane said.

The commander bowed to me, and I nodded in greeting. Though the display of respect didn't match the look in his storm-gray eyes, nor the thin press of his beard-lined lips.

Vane didn't miss it either, his hand squeezing mine ever so

slightly. "I thought it pertinent to show Princess Mildred the power we've accrued since my father's demise." That gave me pause before he asked, "Any updates?"

The commander glanced at me. He was uncomfortable sharing anything in my presence. I understood, yet I was glad when he did. "Most of last season's hatchlings will be ready to join the fleet before the next moon."

Fleet.

As ice-cold dread spiraled through my veins, true joy morphed the king's features into something alluringly distracting. He ran his free hand over his hair, which he'd bound in a low ponytail at his nape. "May we see?"

Again, the commander hesitated. "They might not take kindly to a stranger, even with you there."

"Then they are not ready."

With that, Vane led me through a door at the end of the room. It opened onto a bridge made of rock, steel, and wood built into the side of the mountain.

As soon as the door closed behind us, a screeched roar stilled my feet.

Between the twin mountains, a ravine yawned. It widened in places and narrowed perilously in others. Two advancing pytherions navigated it expertly, turning and twisting their long, serpentine bodies. Water sprayed from a touch of claws. Wind whipped at my unbound hair as they soared past hooting and hollering faeries below.

Warriors, I realized, training upon a large expanse of flat rock. Their laughter and grunts and curses traveled through the ravine. Gazing up, I found more perched upon the cliffsides surrounding us and watching from bridges and windowed rooms above.

Perhaps I should have expected it. I'd known these mountains were home to The Boneland's military. But as the king pointed out another pytherion advancing from the sky, I wondered if Garran and my father were aware of just how advanced this military had become.

Even if the wards upon this realm didn't fall for centuries, these beasts would outlive the magic that had made them. If I couldn't break the curse, another loophole would be found long before then.

The pytherions would only multiply.

With an army of them, vengeance wouldn't just be had. Defeat, bloody and brutal, was guaranteed. Their might could allow the Unseelie to conquer and control this entire continent.

The pytherion drew closer. Sunlight brightened dark green scales. I wasn't sure I breathed as it twirled into a spiral toward the ravine floor.

Then its wings spread, and warriors hollered as the beast soared back up the mountainside.

Straight toward us.

I shouldn't have cared about kingdoms who saw me as nothing but a coin for payment and insurance. Yet as the pytherion darkened the bridge—as rock crumbled from its grip on a stone ledge right above us—fear unlike any I'd encountered before turned every inch of me stiff with the desire to flee.

As if sensing it, Vane squeezed my hand. "Surella won't hurt you."

"Surella?" I rasped, though it was evidently the pytherion's name.

More rock crumbled. I squeezed his hand hard when a spiked tail swung against the mountainside.

He merely pointed up.

A head angled down at us from a long and curled neck. My stomach roiled, the mixture of monster and serpent utterly horrifying. Slit pupils spread within giant bronze eyes. A forked tongue flicked toward me.

"She's scenting you. Keep still."

The soft information wasn't necessary. Even so, I was grateful for the sound of his voice as day turned to absolute night. Rock dust sprayed toward the ravine below, the beast shifting over the cliffside to better see us. That long and thick tail blocked all sunlight, gold spikes glinting. A foot braced upon the railing before us, claws curling, bowing the steel.

The king stopped me from surrendering to the instinct to move back. To retreat and hide. "Stand still and tall and look only at her."

I didn't need to ask why. I knew better than anyone not to present as prey, but by the twin goddesses…

This wasn't a beast.

It was a nightmare with a maw the size of a cave.

Half of the pytherion's head now in view, I marveled at the scales. Armor but also weapons—the sharp sides flared as the serpentine dragon continued to assess me with flicks of her black tongue. Her tucked wing appeared scaled atop and leathery beneath, lined in the same silvery-gray feathers behind her scaled cheek.

Finally, her eyes left me.

As soon as they met the king, he stepped forward. Mercifully, he released my hand so I wasn't forced to join him as he bowed to Surella and extended his fist. I would have thought him merely showing off and reckless, but then I remembered.

The bond between beast and the king of beasts.

The pytherion closed her maw. She released an eerie clicking sound and exhaled through slit nostrils.

The heat of it misted my skin in sweat.

I refrained from moving and found I didn't want to as the creature finally touched her long snout to the king's fist.

Submission, however reluctant she was to give it.

That she had didn't comfort as she then flung herself from the mountainside. Stones and dust rained, and Surella disappeared into the shaded portions of the ravine.

A chilling roar ridded the damp from my skin.

Vane tugged me along more bridges, talking about numbers and eggs and pointing at a nest upon a ledge above an indoor training room, but I couldn't say much.

I couldn't shake the cold kiss of dread.

Even when we'd vanished back to the castle, it coiled tighter and tighter around my bones. "That was…" I failed to find words and ceased trying.

Vane took his time releasing me from the bulk of his arms. As he did, he smirked. "I never grow tired of visiting them."

A burning sensation constricted my throat. I shook my head, unable to voice just how much the visit to the mountains had troubled me. Unable to understand exactly why it did. Trying to express it likely wouldn't be wise. Vane had taken me to Skull Mountains for a reason, and not just because I'd asked.

He watched me too closely. "You look pale."

I stared down at the colored tiles in the foyer. Tried to remind myself that all those warriors and pytherions couldn't seek this king's vengeance right now.

"Did you show them to me as a gesture of trust?" Trust that would be broken in a very dangerous way when he realized that even if I fell in love with him, the wards wouldn't break.

I was no longer sure how to navigate this—how to survive something so beyond my control. Something so much bigger than me.

When I peered up at the king, I found him studying me with unreadable features. He then scrubbed his bristled chin and sighed. "Mostly, yes, but also because I'm beyond proud of what we've accomplished. We've lost many in our mission to breed such a rare species. I wanted to show you that it's been worth it," he said, gruffer now. "How incredible they are."

I should have kept my mouth shut. But I'd already told him before, and he hadn't listened. So it wasn't as if I'd been keeping it from him. "Trust requires honesty. So believe me when I say you are breeding an army of monsters for no reason, Vane."

The use of his name earned me a curious tilt of his head. He seemed to see my attempt to ensure my safety once again. He dragged his thumb beneath his lower lip, scraping the coarse hair. "Your heart races."

I didn't let his more playful tone deter me. "I do not have Atakan's heart. It's true what they say…" I swallowed thickly. "He is heartless."

Which made me utterly useless to this Unseelie king.

For endless yet suspended moments, my heartbeat went wild though I didn't breathe. He stared down at me, and I pondered what he might do. Yet, no matter what horror I imagined, I failed to believe he'd harm me.

Then he grinned. "Fear not, Princess." His fingers bumped beneath my chin. "My sources have told a very different story."

My heart ceased racing.

It stopped beating entirely before pounding at my sternum. "I don't believe you."

I couldn't believe him. Not only did it seem impossible for Atakan Ethermore to love anything, but it would mean what I'd just seen might be unleashed upon the continent of Elaysia all too soon.

And though I'd asked for none of this insanity, it would still be my fault. I would live with that forevermore, and that was *if* I lived.

But only if I fell for this king of monsters.

Vane stepped so close, the tips of his boots kissed the pointed tips of my own. Gently, he clasped my chin and tilted it to search my eyes. "Then I'll just have to prove it to you."

My foolish heart kicked when his head lowered, and his lips descended toward mine.

Hurried steps clapped down the marble stairs. "Vane."

We separated to find Cerwin three strides from us. His expression gave away nothing, but an odd look—almost pitiful—was cast at me before he said, "Word has arrived."

Vane didn't look at me. He trailed his right hand from the foyer into the far hall. Unsure why, I decided to wait rather than return to the king's chambers.

Hushed murmurs were all I could hear beyond the quiet screech of my pulse in my ears.

Meadow rumbled a purred greeting, paws padding whisper-soft over the stairs. She leaped down the last row into the foyer and rubbed against my legs.

I scratched behind her tufted ear when she rose onto her hind legs to tap my hip, lost to thoughts of pytherions, the king's mouth, and a prince in a faraway land.

Vane returned before I could uncloud my mind and unglue my feet. "We've just received the report." The grim set of his harsh features should have been a warning.

But nothing could have prepared me for the words that left his mouth. "I'm sorry, Mildred." He exhaled roughly and took my hand, thumb brushing. "Your father and stepmother have been murdered."

***

No one knew specifics, and I wasn't sure I was ready to know them.

I'd been forced into realizing that grief had yet to touch me before now. Forced to learn the difference between sorrow and hurt.

My father had never been a good man. He'd also never been a bad man. I didn't know if who he'd been nor what he'd done mattered. Not when staring at what would never be.

What once was had become an endless never.

Never would I see his eyes crinkle when he laughed. Never would I catch him looking at me with that soft smile before he looked away. Never would I get to ask him all of the many questions I'd been too stubborn and angry to ask about my mother.

Never would I get to lie to him by telling him that I forgave him for selling me to a doomed fate.

And Agatha…

Love wasn't needed to feel saddened by someone's passing.

The report claimed that my father and stepmother had been traveling to meet with King Garran about my disappearance. They and their companions were found in a bloody heap in the middle of the road just an hour shy of their destination.

A sword bearing Ethermore's royal crest had been embedded in the roof of my father's carriage. A message, Vane had said, in the bleary hours that had followed our visit to Skull Mountains.

More details weren't necessary when that sword said everything.

For three days, the pytherions, Atakan, and the Unseelie king's motive to make me love him disappeared beneath a numbness that wouldn't abate.

I half hoped I'd cry so I could feel something else. Something more than the shocking permanence of death.

As the sun crested the trees once again, Daylia made her presence known in the corner of the bedchamber by setting the breakfast tray on the table. She then stood there, watching me although I didn't remove my gaze from the sunrise.

She'd brought me every meal, as per usual, save for dinner. The king had taken to delivering that himself. But he hadn't said anything more since delivering me a blow that might not heal.

He'd sit quietly in an armchair at the table or half reclined over the bed, reading while I stared through the same window or soaked too long in the bathing pool.

Though I could hardly taste anything, I ate bits and pieces. Just enough to keep from being ordered to. I feared that if anything were demanded of me right now, all of my carefully secured furies might explode into uncatchable fragments.

"You look so tired, Mildred."

I feathered my fingers over the scars adorning my inner ankle and said nothing.

The steward lingered. Her peering eyes pressed upon me while she fussed with dishes.

A shadow flitted from behind the divan.

Vane entered, the scent of blood worsening the empty ache in my chest. "Day," he said, the greeting gruff.

A look passed between them. One I didn't see but could feel in the silence.

Daylia sighed. "How is it looking?"

"Good," the king said, and the bathing room door closed.

Daylia finally left the king's chambers.

I drifted into sleep, the gentle fingers glossing my cheek startling. My forehead peeled from the cool glass of the window, and I blinked up at Vane.

He'd left last evening after he'd delivered my dinner, muttering something about returning shortly. I'd wished I'd wanted to ask why and where and if I could write to my sister.

But I did the same thing now that I had then. Nothing.

It seemed he wasn't going to let me get away with that for much longer. After eating breakfast, he turned in the chair and crossed one leg over the other.

He wore linen pants and no shirt, and I tried to will some semblance of feeling into my body at the sight of all that bare skin and muscle.

I failed.

As I was about to return my head to the window, he spoke. "I need to visit Lord Stone this evening." He paused, perhaps awaiting interest. "Would you like to accompany me?"

That earned him a rasped, "No, thank you."

He finished chewing a piece of fruit, then rose from the chair and walked barefoot to the divan.

I stared at his large feet with eyes so dry, I wanted nothing more than to close them again. The divan creaked as he sat by my own bare feet. His clean scent enveloped, luring my weary gaze to his.

His mouth quirked, a tremulous tilt, as those blue eyes clouded with something that might have been concern. His hand slowly rose to rest upon my knee. My silk robe slid over my skin when he curled his fingers. "Cerwin and Daylia will be attending. I cannot leave you alone in this state, Mildred."

"You can."

"I won't be able to focus on anything." Strands of damp red hair escaped from behind his pointed ear. "Nothing but you."

A twinge in my chest made warmth drop into that emptiness with a splash. But although his words were sweet, I still said, "What difference does it make if I'm miserable there or here?"

His response was instant. "You won't be alone. You'll be right where I can see you."

Another twinge became a violent pinch when he leaned closer to brush my tangled hair from my cheek. "Come with me, Princess. Return to life," he whispered. The plea brightened his eyes. "Just for a few hours."

Twenty-One

Boneyard City was as bustling and cramped as every story depicted.

Faeries filled shop stoops and the cobbled streets hours after the sun had set. I caught a glimpse of wings and even claws and hooves. Muggy air carried the scent of charred beef from a cart at the end of the tight street. Smoke crawled from the chimneys of most buildings. Something luminescent and foul trickled past the cracked stone of the stoop we stood on.

Due to the wards guarding our destination, we couldn't vanish inside. So we'd avoided notice by vanishing straight to the doorstep.

Lord Stone's hideout was a bookstore so slim, it was a good thing it no longer functioned as a business. Few would see the building between the giant clothing and shoe stores on either side of it, let alone the faded replica of an open book on the mildew-spotted window.

Vane removed the hood of his cloak as he entered. He waited until I'd followed, then closed and locked the door.

To my surprise, shelves of books still drowned the first floor. Yet I couldn't find a shred of interest for the dusty tomes piled haphazardly on broken shelving and beside a ripped armchair.

The king led the way through the candlelit dim to a skinny staircase.

As the cream lace of my long sleeves threatened to brush against the marked walls, I looked up to find he'd turned partially to his side, wings standing high. My lips wriggled, but I sighed as the smile failed to bloom. A step near the top had a hole filled with cobwebs, Vane murmuring to be mindful as he skipped it entirely.

I did the same, then released my floaty lavender skirts.

The room above the forgotten shop was just as narrow but far less cluttered. A small kitchen hugged the back corner, and beside it, a bed dressed in plain brown linens. To my right, a tiny washroom lay beyond a half-open door.

To the left stood a long table with peeling red paint; plates and goblets and cutlery awaiting.

Cerwin sat in one of the wooden chairs upholstered in dark floral patterns. He thumped a tankard onto the table, but his grin waned as he noticed me behind the king.

I understood why when he nodded to me. "I'm sorry for what befell your parents."

My gut churned as I took the seat offered by Vane. "Are you truly, though?"

Vane removed his cloak. He draped it over a chair, then sat in the one beside me, directly opposite Cerwin. The wood groaned as he leaned back, his wings trapped behind him and their tips resting against the floor.

Cerwin looked at his king—his friend—then back at me. He tapped his knuckles upon the table, smiling slightly. "They were indeed our enemies, but that does not mean I don't sympathize with your grief."

I had no harsh rebuttal. He spoke as if keenly aware of what that grief felt like.

He confirmed as much. "During the final battles to stop the wards, I lost many people I cared about. Worst of all, I lost my eldest sister."

Vane pounded his fist on his chest. "A fierce warrior."

I asked, "What was her name?"

The king's royal right hand gave him a brief tilt of his lips, then he said to me, "Methina."

I nodded once. As a somber quiet descended, I frowned at the empty seats at the table. "Where's Daylia?"

"She couldn't make it," was all Cerwin supplied.

Lord Stone's booming laughter accompanied the slamming of the door downstairs.

Cerwin muttered, "Thank Goddess," and reached for something on the chair beside him. "I'm starved."

A fiddle.

He plucked a fast melody, then set it against his chair as Stone reached the top of the stairs. The Seelie lord wasn't alone.

Morona joined him in bowing to the king.

The pretty faerie wore a slinky, shimmering, and thin-strapped gown. Those butterfly-like wings flicked when her eyes met Vane's.

Lord Stone slid a paper-lined basket of slow-roasted beef and vegetables onto the table, then untucked the chair beside Cerwin. Morona gave him a thankful, rouge-red smile. Unlike Vane, she took care with her wings, and I couldn't help but assume the light and dusty texture made them extra sensitive.

She smiled at me. As Stone fetched decanters of wine and a jug of mead from the kitchen, I could only nod.

The lord took a seat at the head of the table. I sat back and watched as everyone helped themselves to beverages and the steaming food. I assumed it had come from the end of the street, but I didn't care to ask.

Vane stabbed a hunk of beef. It dripped over the table as he delivered it to my plate. He knocked it from his knife with his thumb, then licked it.

The sound drew my eyes to his mouth.

Morona's as well, I noted as he reached for some carrot and a sweet potato. She looked away, carving carefully at her meal. For a moment, I studied her and wondered if she was in pain, too.

A different kind, but pain all the same.

As conversation about the pytherions dwindled into a discussion about the attacks in the mountains surrounding Cloud Castle, interest finally awakened.

I picked and poked at my food, keeping my eyes on my plate as they had been for some minutes. I wasn't sure what hiding them would achieve. My mere presence at this seemingly casual meeting meant they were not afraid to speak in front of me.

It also suggested that they did not expect me to ever leave this realm.

"The eggs you dispatched are safe," Lord Stone informed

smoothly. "No one suspected a single thing, courtesy of the new fires in the east."

"Getting Surella to forgive me might prove more difficult than taking them," Vane said. "She fucking snapped at me when I returned empty-handed." He rolled his black sleeve to reveal the healing punctures in his forearm.

I blinked and couldn't resist remarking, "I'm surprised you still have an arm."

As if stunned I'd spoken, I felt all eyes find me. But I stared only at Vane's scabbing skin. That explained why he'd been bleeding at dawn.

Cerwin sounded perplexed. "But they're Crosia's and Myrtle's eggs."

"Doesn't matter," said Vane. "Goes against their instincts to endanger the young." He huffed, saying with a glance at me. "Hatchlings are just about the only creatures they'll protect."

I frowned.

As we'd walked those mountainside bridges, he'd told me they'd bred nearly thirty pytherions, and that a female laying one egg per season was a rare feat. "What exactly are you doing with the eggs?"

Silence settled, as if they were all suddenly pondering how much to say.

Ridiculous. They'd already said too much.

It was Morona who finally spoke, a glint in her orange eyes. "They're part of the plan."

Vane reached for a decanter of wine. "I've been vanishing to Sky Mountains to personally see to the safe placement of eggs." He filled the goblet before me, then his own. "We want to use them, yes, but not risk them."

"Placement?" I questioned. I shook my head, my eyes widening as it dawned. "You're putting pytherion eggs near the castle?"

"And one in the middle of Cloudfall City." Morona squashed her carrot beneath her fork. "Pytherions breathe fire when enraged, Princess."

"You're using them as bait," I said.

"She's so clever," Cerwin said dryly.

I didn't care about their teasing. A wave of horrified awe stole my barely-there appetite at the thought of those mighty beasts descending upon the city of Cloudfall and Cloud Castle.

A castle made mostly from trees.

"They'll burn it down," I stated the obvious, blinking at each one of the faeries at the table.

"And we'll take what's left," Stone said, easing back in his chair and swiping his fingers over his mouth.

"Now, Duhn." Morona gave him a feline grin. "We've spoken about this."

"I know." Stone raised his hands and feigned a sigh. "The jewel troves only." His wolfish grin cracked the tension.

Vane's laughter was a warming and deep rumble. "You've got enough jewels to bathe in, asshole."

Indeed. They glimmered upon his hand as he grabbed his goblet of wine. Retribution, I remembered. That was this sneaky lord's motive.

The motive of everyone in this cramped dwelling, and likely the desire of many throughout this entire realm.

It was understandable. Still, I couldn't lose the feeling of discomfort. No matter how right their anguish and anger made all of this seem. "Is Garran aware of your pytherion army?"

Cerwin arched a brow. "The king who gave the order to have your father and stepmother killed?"

I held his gaze, even as those words burrowed into the bleeding core of me.

He relented. "He's probably heard rumblings about it by now. It's impossible to keep the growing numbers of such beasts secret forever." A cruel smile curved his mouth. "But due to those wards, there's nothing he can do about it."

Vane gathered an impressive amount of beef and sweet potato onto his fork, seemingly done with this conversation.

Cerwin sipped his mead, then snatched the fiddle.

He struck the strings with mischievous delight that failed to dull even as he handed the king a wide-eyed look. A look so swift, I would have missed it had I not been staring beyond the right hand in a daze.

A warning, perhaps. That despite what my fate would be, they'd all said quite enough in my presence.

Vane pushed his chair back, confirming as much when he offered me his hand.

I'd yet to regain any interest in eating, so I let him lead me downstairs into the bookstore.

I hadn't known what he'd intended, but I certainly hadn't expected he'd stop in the center of the crowded room and pull me into his arms. Maybe he simply wished to talk without being overheard.

But he began to rock side to side, so at odds with Cerwin's lively melody that I couldn't help but laugh. "What are you doing?"

"There it is," he said softly. Leaning away just enough to better see me, he splayed his fingers over my lower back. "That beautiful smile."

I pursed my lips, and he chuckled. Then he gathered me against him once more. A heavy shadow bobbed by his ear as his fingers wove between mine.

I didn't hear anything, and as he stiffened slightly, I assumed only Vane could hear what his shadows said.

The murky patch of darkness slimmed into a tiny tendril, melding into his wings. Where the black edges typically morphed into a gradual gray had become more slate.

"Your feathers are darker when your shadows are with you," I said. "They're not out hunting?"

"Except for one keeping watch from the roof of this hovel, they're now all with me."

Being so close to him caused his smoky musk scent to overpower the mustiness of the room. His embrace, the tickling fingers at my back, soothed in a way I hadn't known I needed.

After a minute, Cerwin's fiddle-playing slowed, matching our steps.

Vane kept his voice whisper-quiet. "Are you concerned about the Ethermore's royal tree house?"

Although he wasn't jesting, I smiled again. It was faint, falling as I whispered, "It's magical, I cannot lie, but they killed my father." Just saying the words out loud aroused a sickness I feared might evict the small amount of food I'd eaten.

Vane hummed. "Vengeance will be had."

"Good," I said, glad he couldn't see the quivering of my mouth.

It meant nothing if Atakan truly cared for me in the way these Unseelie faeries were relying on. The Seelie prince was as ruthless as his father. Worse, really.

Maybe Atakan didn't lack a heart. He simply lacked a soul.

The sobering thought made room for another, and the realization sank into my bones.

If King Garran could so easily kill my father, then killing me—the bride he didn't want for his precious prince—would be even easier.

As if sensing my dismay, the fear I'd long lived with unraveling within me, Vane murmured to my temple, "You will never have to see them again, Mildred."

Relief tried to heat my chilled blood, but it only traveled so far. "I hope not."

"I don't make vows lightly."

I believed him, and nestled even closer to show my gratitude. But as the fiddle's pace increased, Vane said, "Enough worrying. I want to see that smile again."

Before I understood his intent, I was swung away from him.

I gasped, my hand tugged, and my body hauled back to his. My free hand slapped against his hard chest, fingers gripping his tunic in vain. He spun me across the rotting wood floor again and again.

And each time we collided, some of the heaviness I'd carried into this old shop dissipated.

The Unseelie king grinned, bright and more dizzying than the twirling circles he spun me into around him.

My laughter came rasped at first, set free against my will, but it melted quickly into its typical melody. Too quickly, I feared, the ice blue of his eyes ensnaring.

Only when I'd circled him entirely did he keep me gathered against his chest.

This time, his hand roamed up my back into my hair, scrunching gently as he whispered into my ear, "When you laugh, I remember what joy feels like."

I couldn't speak but let my hand move from his chest to his shoulder. I toyed with his soft hair, my heart and eyes aflame. Closing them, I laid my head against his chest, his strong heartbeat another melody in my ears.

Maybe it was the exhilaration still burning through me, but the question escaped unexpectedly. "Wards aside, do you want to be loved, Vane?"

He didn't answer right away.

He pondered it, which should have been a bad sign. But I needed truth. A rarity in this world of careful lies. "I want you," he said, all rough breath, barely heard beneath the strain of the fiddle. "I didn't think I would, but I do. That's all I know for certain."

I peered up at him—searched his stern features. He let me, but only for a moment.

He kissed the corner of my mouth, a gentle press that closed my eyes. Then he met my seeking lips as I rose onto my toes. He groaned, fingers curling tighter into my hair. He was warmth and safety, his embrace a fortress I knew I could happily live within.

My mouth parted when his did, and he captured my lower lip so softly, heat gathered in my stomach.

The fiddle slowed again, and Lord Stone called, "Dessert is served, lovebirds."

Cerwin chuckled, silencing the fiddle abruptly.

Vane's mouth left mine, and he sighed. He kissed my forehead and led me back upstairs.

But gone was the tension that had been present during dinner.

As strawberries slid down the melting frosting of the leftover cake, the wine and mead began to run dry. Military strategy was discussed, most of it too vague for me to understand.

But I ceased playing with the frosting on my plate at the graphic description of a fallen unit within the Sky Mountains surrounding Cloud Castle.

Morona noticed, giving me a smirk when I glanced up.

I went back to drawing a poor depiction of Meadow's face on the porcelain.

"If that doesn't further prove them responsible for the deaths of the human royals, then I don't know what can." Cerwin came close to slurring his emphatic words, his tankard hitting the table a touch too hard. "Limbs every-fucking-where."

"It is his signature, I've heard," Stone said. "Carving at things until the only way to identify them is by piecing them back together via their scent."

"It is indeed," Morona confirmed. She ran a lithe finger around the base of her goblet. "I'm surprised you escaped him in one piece, Princess Mildred."

I straightened and reached for my wine. It was empty, so I poured more while they all waited for a response. I didn't feel like saying anything. But after taking a long sip, I humored them. "I'm surprised, too."

Mostly, I was surprised to discover that the creature in their gruesome tale was Atakan. Though I shouldn't have been.

It prompted me to free a stunted laugh and say more. "Perhaps I was saved by the many times he went out hunting your ilk."

"Our ilk?" Cerwin drawled.

My brows furrowed.

Vane said, "He enjoys catching bigger prey, then."

Morona tucked strands of silky hair behind her ruby-studded ear. She smiled faintly across the table at the king before looking at me. "Did Atakan force you to fuck him?"

As Lord Stone released an almost shrieked burst of laughter, I drank more wine.

Vane shifted, as did his wings, feathers rustling against the wood floor. "Morona," he gently warned.

"What?" Her eyes widened playfully. Behind her hand, she whispered loudly to me, "I hear he's a positively beastly lover." Eyeing me closely as her fingers wrapped around her goblet, she laughed. "And you certainly look spooked."

Spooked wasn't quite the right word to describe the roiling sensation in my gut.

"Merely perturbed," I lied, making it seem as if Atakan hadn't touched me in that way at all, let alone fucked me.

And just as she'd described.

I dug deep within for my decade-old practice at playing games and drank some more wine as they all laughed at my expense.

"If he didn't try to fuck you, then what did he do to you?" Morona asked.

Vane cursed.

I placed my hand over his on the table, letting him know it was fine. I was fine.

I was so far from fine that I could hardly remember what it felt like, but I caught the quick dip of Morona's gaze to our hands and smiled as genuinely as I could. "He taunted me, mostly."

Stone hummed. "I do believe you poisoned him at one point." He clicked his fingers. "Yes, it was some years before you were whisked away to Cloud Castle."

"No," Morona gasped, delight ashine in her eyes.

I nodded. "He locked me in a carriage with a two-headed serpent at Sparrow Hall, so I retaliated."

"The heartless isn't so heartless after all." Stone belched very un-noble-like and pointed at me. "He would have killed anyone else the moment he discovered such treachery."

Vane's gaze pressed into my profile.

I refused to look at him as heat climbed my neck, and I confessed, "I think the reason I survived him is purely because I kept entertaining him."

"Makes strange sense, actually." Cerwin nodded and rubbed at his clean-shaven chin. "Such evil expects submission, and it sounds like you gave him nothing but defiance."

"Which should have seen her killed," Vane said gruffly, as if struggling to comprehend.

"Ah, but the reason she wasn't is due to her audacity to seek revenge while he *couldn't* kill her." Stone thumped the table. "Her lack of fear."

"Oh, there was plenty of that," I admitted.

"But you didn't let it control you. You controlled it by prodding at him until you earned more than his infamous ire." Stone grinned fiendishly. "You earned his fascination."

I looked from the Seelie lord to the others, and found them all smiling similarly at me.

Morona broke the silence. "You're no halfling." She raised her goblet to me, then said before she sipped, "You are far more faerie than mortal, darling."

Everyone drank to that, including myself. Though it was for a lack of knowing what to do with such naked approval.

Never had I experienced it before now. Never from anyone other than the prince it seemed I'd bested.

You feel so fucking good.

And with the exception of Bernie, never had I felt even a morsel of such acceptance.

Don't let this make you forget you are loved.

The sudden invasion of memories propelled me to my feet. I swayed slightly.

Vane's fingers curled around my wrist. "What is it?"

"Nothing. I just…" I shook my head, then forced a yawn. "I think I just need a minute."

Understanding softened Morona's shrewd gaze.

I waded downstairs on heavy feet. A lone candle still burned, the flame faint and scarcely touching the dark. But my shambled mind found relief in the dim bookstore.

"What did he do to you, Princess?"

So rattled by thoughts of Bernie, of the life I'd lived for so long that it was hard to accept it was now just memories, I hadn't sensed his approach behind me. I hadn't even heard his boots on the stairs.

I turned to Vane, who stood with his arms crossed and his feet braced. The defensive stance confused until I saw his clenched jaw. The way he studied me as if hunting for answers before he could be shocked by them.

The storm within me calmed.

I closed the space between us and placed my hand on his forearm. "I'm more worried about Bernadette."

His thick brows gathered. "Your sister."

I nodded. "I worry about how she might be coping. Not just with her grief but with her pregnancy and the responsibility of being crowned queen."

His arms unfolded, and he took my hand. For a moment, he just stared down at it. "One day, I hope that you can see her again."

Hope wasn't good enough, but I would push for something else if it were all the promise he could give me right now. "Let me at least write to her, King."

His eyes met mine, the blue bright in the darkness. He didn't answer. He released me and strode to the back of the store.

I watched the shadows welcome him and fought for breath as anger and hurt swam through my chest and stung my eyes.

Then I stalked after him.

Perhaps it was the wine. Perhaps it was the way each inhale sliced my throat. But he couldn't do this. He couldn't force me into wanting him and then refuse to give me something so small—

He turned from an overflowing desk, a pot of ink in hand. "I can't seem to find parchment that hasn't mildewed—"

The ink fell from his thick fingers and clacked against the floor when I threw myself at him.

He caught me with a grunt and chuckled.

I stole the vibrating sound with my mouth. He cursed. Hands smoothing around my ass, he delivered me to the desk.

Books toppled to the floor. Parchment and quills were trapped beneath me. I failed to care, taking his face and allowing him to take control of the kiss.

He parted my lips and inhaled a ragged breath, as if tasting me. Lifting my chin, he stroked it while his other hand clenched my thigh. Our tongues dueled. He won, rendering me pliant as he lapped and bit at my lips. Heady—so domineering yet sweet.

And it wasn't enough.

My legs climbed his hips. His wings rustled, lifting as my feet dug into his lower back. I tugged myself forward with a hand at his shoulder and moaned against his mouth as my core met his erection through our clothing. I wanted that clothing gone. I wanted to grind against him until I forgot everything but this. Everything but the heat he elicited and stoked until all I felt was hollow with desperate need.

He groaned, hips jerking. His cock pressed into me, and I gasped.

His fingers tangled in my hair at my neck and shoulder. He lavished my jaw and throat in kisses that had my head tilting back and our bodies pressing harder.

Something thudded upstairs. Stone's laughter followed.

We remembered how much company we had, no matter how tucked away we were. If we went too far, they would hear. I wasn't sure I cared. The desire to chase these feelings, to let this king devour me whole, seemed as crucial as breathing.

Mercifully, Vane had enough sense for us both.

He straightened and clasped my face.

The fingers beneath my jaw tipped my head back. His thumb rubbed the crest of my cheek, and the way he gazed down at me with those hooded blue eyes made me wonder what he saw. Made me wonder if that was indeed adoration in that stare, in his touch, or if I was so lost that I merely imagined it.

That I needed to imagine it.

He kissed my forehead. "Write to your sister," he whispered against my skin. "And we will finish this later."

He was striding from the small room before I could ask how much later that might be.

I looked down at the scrunched parchment beneath me, bleary-eyed and unsure whether to follow him.

Instead, I did as he said.

I snatched a quill, the half-spilled ink, and took a pile of the aged parchment into the store—where I stared at the spots of dripping ink and wrote nothing at all.

Cordenya stepped into the wood-paneled hall. "Atakan, talk to me." Concern stilled her lovely features.

I continued past her down the hall, fighting the urge to rush to the windows and slam through the glass into the open air as rage pounded viciously at my skull. My fucking chest. "I knew you weren't taking that sleeping tonic."

She trailed me. "How can I sleep with so much chaos?" I had no answer. But I stopped when she said, "The human king, what happened?"

I unclenched my teeth but didn't turn to face her. I glared at the moon through the windows ahead and whispered, "Just as the reports say."

I didn't need to look at her to know her fingers fluttered over her mouth. "He was in pieces, Atakan." She touched my back, and muscle tightened. "They were all mutilated in the same way you like to—"

I scoffed, but then laughter echoed. Mostly male. A tinkle of female. Faraway yet so close.

I turned, my heartbeat quieting as every sense awoke. I stared at the ceiling, then down at Cordenya's stricken face. To confirm what I suspected, I asked, "Can you hear that?"

I woke with a hitched breath, chilled to the bone and curled across an armchair.

Parchment lay crumpled against my chest. Ink had dripped from the quill in my loose fingers, staining the tattered chair. I blinked at the books around me as confusion cleared, too stiff to move.

And it was best I didn't—as it might have interrupted the conversation drifting down the stairs.

"No suspicions," Vane murmured.

Cerwin asked, "No one is tracing it back?"

"They're trying, but I doubt they'll succeed. Your assassins were too clean," Lord Stone said. "They wanted their military strengthened, not the marriage, and Garran's stalling made everyone aware of that. Which makes it even more impossible to prove that Julis's death wasn't their doing."

Each breath I remembered to take seared.

Stone then huffed a quick laugh and added, "They're so busy looking for proof to salvage their alliance with Nephryn that they've yet to realize the wards have fractured."

"It won't be long now," Cerwin said grimly.

Fractured.

In the silence that reigned, I glared at the cobwebs in the cornice through tear-flooded eyes. I tried to keep my breathing steady, praying to both goddesses that the faeries upstairs wouldn't hear my untamable heart.

They'd killed my father and stepmother. Murdered their associates.

Vane had slain my father.

And he'd made it look like Ethermore's doing to ruin the alliance I'd been sold to obtain. Now, the Seelie no longer had my father's kingdom to aid them against the Unseelie.

When Vane unleashed his monsters and warriors upon the continent, it would be an easy victory at best.

A war of three kingdoms at worst.

Why Vane had chosen to recently deliver the pytherion eggs beyond the wards made more sense. They weren't wasting the young by keeping them from incubation. Their plan was about to be executed.

The time for vengeance had come.

"How long do you think it will take for the wards to fall completely?" Morona asked.

Vane answered instantly. "Any day now, I'd say."

Such fucking confidence.

"Thank the darkness." Morona seemed to exhale the words. "I like her tenacity and unfitting innocence, but this has taken too long."

Rage heated the tears pooling in my eyes.

Cerwin and Stone laughed, the former saying, "You've done far better than most would have."

"Regardless," Vane said cold and quickly. "It's in our best interest to find more gaps to use."

A moment later, the fiddle came alive. I might have thought it sweet that Cerwin played softly, so as not to disturb my slumber, had it not been for all I'd overheard.

I stayed so perilously still that I feared I would never unfreeze.

Tears persistently tried to push free of my eyes. I closed them and breathed shallowly through my nose. I needed a plan. A way to escape this.

But there was no escape.

Footsteps, light and booted, more than startled me.

Instinct forced me to my feet, though I should have continued to feign sleep. Too rattled for proper thought, I gripped the quill in my fist as if it might be a useful weapon against a creature who needed none.

But it wasn't King Vane.

Lord Stone halted at the bottom of the stairs. His violet-blue eyes gleamed as they widened upon me.

My hand shook around the quill.

He glanced up the stairs, then slipped in front of the bookshelves next to them and pressed a finger to his mouth.

I frowned, not breathing, not moving…

He looked back toward the stairs, appearing to listen to any talk beneath the fiddle, and then he walked straight to me.

I stepped back, the floor creaking like a crack of thunder.

He winced like he thought so too. He gestured to the armchair.

"Sit," he said so faintly that when he spoke again, I had to read his lips. "Sit back down."

But I couldn't trust him.

He'd betrayed his own king for Vane. For vengeance.

As if knowing everything I was thinking, his shoulders slumped. He waited, his hard gaze gentling.

I couldn't understand why, but I trusted the feeling. A nudge in my gut that sent my feet quietly padding back to the chair.

Even so, I refused to lie down. Refused to relinquish my tight hold on the quill I wouldn't hesitate to stab into his jugular if he continued to lean too far over me—

"If you wish to survive, you need to never so much as think about what you've evidently heard."

My voice didn't work. A blessing as the fiddle's melody slowed. Each rasped word lacked sound. "They killed my—"

"And they could very well do the same to you once the wards finish falling." He leaned back and eyed my distressed state. "Or when they realize those fractures are likely all they'll get from you."

That sank beneath my flesh with talons and teeth.

My fingers relaxed around the quill, but I squeezed the ripped arm of the chair and whispered, "You're not a spy." His raised brow made me realize aloud, "Not for Vane."

Lord Duhn Stone was a spy for the Ethermore family.

Again, he pressed a jeweled finger to his lips. Then he returned to the enemy he'd been duping upstairs. "Still sleeping," he told them. "But it looks like she was writing something. I tried to read it, but it's too crumpled."

"A letter to her sister," Vane said.

"Cruel." Morona clucked her tongue. "Letting her think you'll allow such a thing to be sent."

"Just like you told me," he grumbled. "Whatever it takes."

Twenty-Two

Vane woke me by lifting me into his arms to vanish back to Ashbone Castle.

Except I hadn't been sleeping. I was certain I'd never sleep again. Not in this realm with this king or any of his companions near me.

I feigned confusion and drowsiness and even curled into him—looped my arm around his neck. The scent I'd come to find comforting now made my stomach gurgle with sickness.

A game.

This was nothing but another challenge. I thrived within the bounds of uncertainty. I came alive under the scrutiny of those who anticipated my weakness. I found freedom while trapped.

So why did this feel so different? Almost… impossible.

As soon as Vane reached the open doors to his chambers, I wriggled, wanting to leave the arms I'd thought would provide safety. Wanting to whirl upon him and slam my fists into his face and scream obscenities at him.

Never had I lamented not being full-faerie and gifted with magic. Not carrying so much as a trace of noble faerie blood.

Not until now.

Instead of submitting to the beast within me howling for retribution, I mumbled something about needing to relieve myself and walked to the bathing room. I made sure to stumble, then laugh for good measure.

When the door closed, I breathed. I inhaled deep and exhaled slowly—let the burn rise to my eyes as I slid down the door to the tiles and covered my mouth.

I thought I'd been quiet enough.

I'd thought wrong. A gentle tapping on the door made me scramble forward.

"Mildred?" Vane called softly. "Are you well?"

I sniffed and did so loudly because I was at a loss for what else to do. There was no hiding my fear and heartbreak as he opened the door.

"I'm…" I coughed. "I'm fine."

He was a darkness blocking the meager light from the bedchamber. His wings rustled as he stood in the doorway and stared down at me.

I didn't look at him. Not until I could force a shaky smile and rasp, "I just needed another minute, I suppose. Sleep makes me forget, and then I wake up…"

I needn't have said more.

Understanding, he took two of his large steps to crouch before me. Carefully, as if I were a tiny doll that might break, he swept his knuckles over my damp cheek. "It pains me to see your pain."

I almost laughed. Mercifully, the sound that left me was more of a choked sob.

Vane groaned as if he'd spoken true, and it did pain him. "Come," he said, holding out his hand. "Let's get you to bed."

I nodded and tried to rise. Tried to look at those eyes.

I wasn't ready. So I pretended to be weak, although rage and sorrow threatened to make me leap to my feet and reach for a bar of soap to bludgeon his handsome face.

He did as predicted, collecting me into his arms with ease. But he didn't release me. He sat upon his bed, leaned back against the headboard, and turned me into him until I had no choice but to look at him.

I couldn't.

Instead, I tucked my face into his neck, where his scent was most overwhelming, and I let myself grieve. I let myself fall into sharp pieces in the arms of the monster who'd broken me.

And I let him believe I didn't know.

I reinforced it by wrapping my arm around his shoulders and pressing a wet kiss against his thick neck. Perhaps I should have shuddered and felt repulsed. All I felt was a sadness so deep, it blistered my bones.

He'd almost had me. This king had nearly reshaped me into the remedy he needed.

"Goddess," I whispered to his skin. "I've had too much wine."

He smoothed his hand over my back, then toyed with strands of my hair. "I shouldn't have forced you to come with me." His voice lowered to a throaty rumble. "You needed more time."

"No," I said and found I meant it. "I have to start living with it." *Living with what you've done,* I didn't say.

Panic twisted my innards into a knot more painful than his betrayal. Somehow, some way, I had to escape this lair of hunters masquerading as trapped prey.

"But living with it's just…" I sighed, rubbing my forehead into the crook of his neck.

"I know," he murmured. He cupped the back of my head, turning his own to lay his lips on my cheek. "I will kill them for all they've done, Princess." He kissed my wet skin. "I promise you."

Indeed, promise dripped from those words.

Suddenly stifled, I pressed against his chest and pushed up. I swiped beneath my eyes, ready to roll from his body when his hand banded tight at my hip. I made the mistake of looking down. A mistake that filled my eyes anew.

I met his gaze.

And I felt my entire face crumple at the gentle concern in his blue eyes. How he could possibly care when he hadn't cared enough to keep from breaking my heart…

"What do you need?"

"Nothing." I swallowed thickly. "I just loathe them so much."

His features hardened. He demanded an answer to the question he'd asked hours ago. "Tell me what Atakan did to you, Mildred."

I didn't want to tell him anything. These faeries already knew too much. But when I tried to climb from his lap, he stopped me. And that he would force me to talk about that right now only made my fury burn hotter.

"He played with me like I was an unwilling pet," I said through gritted teeth. "One he didn't want." It wasn't a lie, but it was all I wished to say.

Vane waited for more.

Fine.

I leaned back, feeling his erection beneath my ass and wondering if my anguish aroused him or if it was simply a result of our touching bodies.

Feigning insecurity, I tucked a tear-dampened lock of hair behind my ear and stared at my hands on his hard chest. "I hate him, but I think I hate myself more because some part of me…" I made my breath hitch and closed my eyes. "Some part of me wanted him. Despite his cruel nature, I…" I opened my eyes but kept them away from his to appear shamed. "I couldn't help it."

Vane seemed to absorb that for crackling seconds. Absorb me.

He ran his finger over mine on his chest. "The thrill of surviving against all odds gives an addictive high."

Survival hadn't been the reason I'd wanted to kiss the prince nor take his cock inside my body. Still, I portrayed being grateful for his attempt to comfort me and smiled.

It fell as my eyes lifted to his. "I can't go back." I looked at his mouth and whispered pleadingly, "Please don't make me go back."

"I told you…" Vane tugged me over him until my hands reached his shoulders. One slipped on his tunic, nearly touching his wing. "You have my protection."

I wasn't sure why I believed him. I certainly didn't want to. "Protection isn't what I'm asking for out of this."

"You have it regardless."

He pushed my face toward his. His gaze hooded upon my mouth. Unable to think of a way to avoid it, I closed my eyes so tight as he kissed me so softly.

My heart bleated in my ears. My stomach churned. Yet my body melted over his as if forgetting what had been discovered.

When his lips parted, I retreated before he could take it farther than I thought I could go. "My stomach feels a little…" I failed to find the right word for too many things. "Off," I settled on.

"Then let me help you feel better," he said, gruff against my mouth.

He reclaimed it, and I moaned in protest as he immediately separated my lips with his tongue. He mistook it for a moan of pleasure, rolling until I was splayed beneath him.

He might have been a murderer, but he sure knew how to make me forget that important fact. His hand swept down my side, gathering my skirts. Slowly, as he lavished my mouth in gentle adoration, he lifted the material over my legs, fingers grazing my skin.

"You're so soft," he whispered, mouth slipping over my chin to my neck. It tilted, giving him better access. "I need to know if you feel like silk everywhere, Princess."

My eyes fell upon the carvings of pytherions in the headboard and widened as those calloused and calculated fingers crawled over my thigh. Only one male had touched me so intimately, and although Atakan was anything but caring, I'd still wanted it.

I wasn't certain I could say the same now.

But my legs couldn't close. Not with Vane's bulk between them.

Not when one caress of his fingers over my core caused my eyes to shut. Bile climbed my throat, even as heat gathered low in my quaking stomach.

Does that feel good, dread?

My eyes flashed open. His crooning voice was another evil. One I feared would never cease tormenting.

Or does it only feel good when you think of me?

Maybe it had finally happened—I truly had been broken. For I thought defiantly, *I'm not thinking of you.*

A sinister laugh sounded so real. So close, as if Atakan were tucked within the stalking shadows of the room. *I wouldn't be here if you weren't.*

I gasped too loudly. Vane reared back and tilted my chin, his gaze searching. "Did I hurt you?"

So fucking much, I thought but didn't say. I closed my eyes and laid my arm over them. "I really do think I've had too much wine. I'm rather dizzy."

And hearing things.

And doing things I didn't wholly want to do.

I expected he'd try to sway me, but a moment later, I felt my skirts lower over my legs, and then the embrace of cool night air in his absence. "Get some rest, Princess." His boots thudded one by one against the stone.

I peeked beneath my arm as he settled on the bed, fully clothed. "Will I upset your stomach more by holding you?"

Yes, I wanted to scream. *Of course you will.*

But I rolled over to keep from looking at him and said, "I want you to, anyway."

Twenty-Three

After barely sleeping, I listened to Vane bathe and get ready for the day.

I made it known I was awake by stretching as he headed for the doors. He halted, then asked, "How are you feeling?"

I smacked my lips together. "A little ordinary."

An understatement.

But he chuckled and gestured to the water he'd placed upon the nightstand while I'd pretended to sleep. "I have a breakfast meeting, but I'll return before I head out."

"You're leaving again?"

I needn't have asked where he was going. After overhearing his intent to find more fractures in the wards, I knew they'd be scouting the borders for them.

"There's much to do." He seemed to hesitate, then promised, "I'll see you before I leave," before closing the doors behind him.

I had no desire to see him at all. I also had no desire to lay in his bed and hope for a miracle to save me from him.

The wildflower he'd given me on our picnic peeked out from the pages of the book I hadn't finished reading. Endless what-ifs seared as I opened it and gently touched the butter-yellow petals.

Then I slammed the book shut and dumped it back onto the nightstand.

I dressed in a gown far too fancy for breakfast. The black chiffon skirts were pleated, the gathered bust putting my cleavage and the globes of my breasts on full display.

As I finished weaving my hair into a loose braid over my shoulder and tying it with one of Vane's black ribbons, I pondered when he might have wished for me to wear such a gown.

Upon hearing his deep laughter, I lost the thought and all others. The sound squeezed the heart he'd nearly claimed so tight, it ached. Meadow skipped stairs to the foyer, rubbing against the doors to be let out. I cracked one open, longing to bound after her and away from this castle.

Vane looked just about done with breakfast, as did Cerwin and Daylia, when I entered the throne room and walked barefoot to the same seat I'd taken before. That night seemed a dream now that I'd found myself in another nightmare.

Daylia smiled brightly, her orange hair pinned back in a messy pile of curls and egg yolk staining her cream blouse.

But Vane and Cerwin didn't cease discussing the merits of depositing one last pytherion egg near Cloud Castle.

"If it's going to burn, better make sure it can't grow back until we want it to," Cerwin said.

I crossed my legs, placed my elbow on the table and my chin in my hand. "I want to come with you," I said by way of greeting.

Vane finally looked at me and blinked.

I refrained from bristling as his gaze fastened to my breasts for much too long. "No," he said to them. Then he met my eyes, smirking as if knowing what he'd just done and not caring. "After last night, it's evident you need more time to recuperate from all you've endured."

Dismay had me straightening in the chair and clenching my hands underneath the table.

He would never vanish me back home. But if he was leaving to do as I'd assumed, then I stood a far better chance of escaping at the borders than here.

Daylia looked at Cerwin, who sipped his water and shrugged.

Then she looked at me. "What happened?" She glared at the king. "You told me all went well."

"It did," I said for him, tracing a gnarled curl in the wooden table. "But I've discovered that wine and heartbreak don't mix very well."

Daylia gave me a sympathetic look.

She knew. Surely, Vane's steward knew exactly what they'd done. Yet she sat there, appearing to care when she hadn't cared to keep my father from being assassinated.

"You're right about the egg," Vane said to Cerwin, vigorously chewing a strip of pork. "But right now, we need to stick with the plan and search for gaps."

"Gaps?" I questioned.

"In the wards," Daylia said, excitement sparkling in her eyes.

I blinked at Vane, my mouth falling open.

He stared as if seeing right through my feigned shock. As if he saw through me to the rage that steadied my flayed heart.

Of course, he couldn't. He assumed I was a crushed fool torn between two royal evils.

And he believed it so easily because I was.

"You didn't tell me that." I licked my teeth and lowered my gaze, my eyes beginning to burn.

This king had almost succeeded in breaking his curse. He'd really had me believing that not only might it be safe to fall as he'd needed me to, but that he might fall too.

But of course Vane wouldn't love me. There was no point when he only needed me to love him.

"I'd intended to, Princess, but the night took a turn," he said, not unkindly.

Only when I was certain my eyes were clear of his betrayal did I look up at him. After a moment of holding his softening gaze, I nodded once. I pretended to understand.

Then, mere minutes later, I followed him out into the hall.

Cerwin and Daylia walked ahead, the latter giggling as the king's right hand pulled her to his side and whispered something to her temple.

Vane took my hand, stopping me beside the stairs. "This journey will be brief. I hope to return with the new dawn."

I stepped into him and smoothed my hands over the thick black tunic covering his chest. "Are you sure you don't want company?" I smiled down at his bulky boots. "I might be miserable, but I can still be useful."

He tipped up my chin, smirking. Then he lowered his head to

skim his lips over mine. "Show me just how useful you are when I get back, and I'll consider taking you next time."

Inwardly, I bristled.

Exhaling a breathy laugh, I pressed my mouth to his, then my teeth into his lip until I drew blood.

He snarled, but I drew back before I could taste his essence, smiling in a way that suggested he'd be sorry for leaving me behind. Smiling in a way that felt all too real when our eyes met, and anger melded with heartache.

For although there were plenty of monsters who seemed far worse, none were as monstrous as Vane Ashbone.

The castle was quietest in the afternoon, which made my search efforts loud.

As pointless as my searching could be, I couldn't sit idle when every part of me itched to claw free of this cell I'd accidentally vanished into.

Cerwin must have accompanied Vane, as I hadn't seen him since interrupting their breakfast meeting. Which left Daylia, floating members of staff, and Meadow to contend with.

But it wasn't out of character for me to roam the halls. It certainly wasn't out of character for me to hunt for new reading material. After digging through drawers and shelving in various sitting and guest rooms, I'd eaten a few mouthfuls of soup-soaked bread for lunch before moving on to the library.

The wards might be ruined enough for me to flee through the gaps, but to do that, I needed to know where they were. I needed to find a way to them, and any useful borders of this kingdom were hundreds of miles from this damned castle.

I needed the featherbone. If it brought me here, then surely Vane had been lying and it could take me back. Though where I'd go…

I couldn't think of that. One risky decision at a time.

I continued hunting, plucking books forward from shelves and peering behind them. If I were a lying and murderous king, where would I hide something important?

It could be anywhere. It could even be kept on his person.

I looked regardless. All the while, my mind raced in circles. I worried about Bernie and if she believed Ethermore was responsible for our father's death. I pondered how I might warn her in a letter without giving myself away and if I could sneak said letter to an owl without Vane knowing.

Then I froze.

My chest caught aflame. The burn spread when I realized I would miss the funerals. My father's funeral. Bernie's coronation. The birth of her babe.

A slight mewl alerted me to Daylia's presence in the doorway.

Her tail swished, feline curiosity aglow in her lime green eyes even as she morphed into her faerie form. "I could sense your anxiety from down the hall."

"My father is dead. The wards on this kingdom are falling." Looking back at the shelves, I pretended to search for something to read. "Any day now, war will ravage this continent again." I glared at her over my shoulder. "How are you *not* anxious?"

She leaned against the large table, looping one of her curls around her finger. "Because we've been eagerly awaiting this moment for too long."

I turned my glare to the shelves, hoping she'd leave, yet knowing she'd found me for a reason. One that had little to do with how I felt. "So you're excited, then."

Her laughter was brief and tight. "I suppose. But right now, I'm mostly wondering how your visit to Lord Stone's hovel went?"

"You already know."

"Apparently not all of it," she said, referring to what had been divulged at breakfast.

I slid my finger down the spine of a worn, leather-bound book of poetry. "What exactly would you like to know, Daylia?"

"You don't wish to speak of it."

Facing her, I leaned against the shelves to better steel myself. "It's just rather…" I scratched at my cheek, then ducked my head for good measure. "Mortifying."

After a long moment of silence, I met her studious gaze. She nodded. "Well, if you would like someone to talk to, I know misery quite well."

I didn't doubt that. I also didn't doubt her offer was genuine, although she'd evidently found me to pry.

Not about me, it seemed.

"What is the Seelie lord like in his home realm?"

Taken aback, I shrugged. "I've only ever seen Stone at events. He always seemed charming but arrogant, just as he is here." Relief pooled warmly in my stomach at the change of subject, but it grew cold when I suspected why she'd asked. "Why do you wish to know?"

Her lips pursed before she sighed. "I didn't trust him. Not at first. He earned the king's favor after being captured a few years ago. He spent all of a month in one of our camps before weaseling his way out and into a meeting with the general and then the king."

Curiosity got the better of me. "How was he captured?"

"His manor resides near the northern border, and it was destroyed during the warding of our realm."

"That's when his wife died," I surmised.

Daylia nodded. "He's kept very quiet about her death, but he told us it was the Seelie king's doing. That he'd defied him by refusing to offer his land to their warriors and your father's soldiers."

It hung there—her disbelief of what happened at the lord's estate. Perhaps she'd heard differently about who'd ruined his home and murdered his wife.

Perhaps their own forces were responsible. I didn't dare seek confirmation. Not when I recalled what Stone had done for me and what he could still do.

He was nobility. He could vanish, and now that the wards were damaged, he could do so without Vane.

He could be my only guaranteed way of escape.

So I said, "Losing love changes people."

Daylia agreed with a sad smile. "It alters values, and sometimes, who we are entirely. For who are we without our inner compass to guide us?" Her head shook. "Powerful, love. Perhaps the most powerful magic of all."

This is war, and I intend to win.

Casting aside my fury, I forced my shoulders to slump. "I didn't notice anything unusual at the hideout if that's what you're asking." Attempting to sway her more could arouse suspicion, so I went on. "But I've never really known Stone." My laughter was surprisingly genuine as I admitted, "There are very few creatures I know well, including myself."

"I disagree with that last one." She straightened from the table, amusement ashine in her eyes. "You're a survivor, Mildred Nephryn. A wolf too accustomed to hunting alone to trust in any pack."

Then she left me gazing at puddles of sunlight beneath the windows.

Daylia's words lingered as I trekked through the brush along the drive in search of Meadow.

It grew dark, and I wanted her near in case Lord Stone appeared and agreed to vanish me home to Nephryn. To Bernie. I refused to leave the felynx behind, lest she be used to lure me back for another attempt to make me fall in love with a king who'd eradicated his chances.

I wouldn't return, and she would likely be killed.

My skirts snagged on a thorn. I paused to free them and scented blood. I trailed it deeper into the brush to a dead hare. Fresh, I determined, nudging it with the toe of my boot.

Then I caught a whiff of a different scent.

A smoldering, oaky sweetness that shouldn't exist. Not here.

I was imagining it. Just like I'd imagined that crooned voice the previous night. Perhaps I was sleeping, and he'd invaded another dream.

But the wards had fractured. And if Vane and his most trusted were already seeking more of the gaps, then...

I whirled to the dancing willow tree behind me.

He stood beyond reach of the scythe moon, leaning against the thick trunk.

Cold warmth turned my bones to stone. "Atakan."

His teeth flashed bright in the falling night. "Hello, dread."

Meadow dangled from his fingers, hissing at the prince who held her by the scruff of her neck. His features were void of emotion. Iced apathy dripped from each word as he said without care for his volume, "Time to go."

Part Three

The Root of All Good and Evil

Twenty-Four

A SILVER SPIDER CRAWLED ACROSS A WOODEN RAFTER IN the soil ceiling.

I'd never dared to look at the dungeon during the weeks I'd spent at Cloud Castle. Now, it was all I'd seen for hours. Perhaps days. Time was absent here. Souls, too.

The six cells surrounding me were empty. Just like the dream I'd had of Atakan and his prisoner, the seventh stood in the center of the underground tomb. Reserved for prized prisoners like me, it seemed.

Three torches between the other cells lit a walkway encircling it.

Aged footsteps imprinted the soil. Some bare feet, most boots. I'd attempted to use an incessant drip coming from the shadowed corner of the dungeon to mark time in the dirt.

After counting two hours, I'd given up.

Atakan had vanished again right after delivering me. Not a word more had been said as he'd snatched my hand, nor when the dark void had spat us out onto the hard-packed earth of the dungeon. I could only assume he'd taken Meadow with him, and I hoped he knew that harming her would be extremely unwise.

Though gaining any sort of advantage while locked within a cage of iron would be difficult.

I stepped close to the bars, trying to peer into the slim hall between the two cells across from me. Stairs leading to the castle above would undoubtedly be found through there. No one lurked in that darkness. No guards. No sinister princes.

Some dungeon, I inwardly scoffed.

Eventually, I stopped caring about protecting the black gown I'd been wearing since Vane's breakfast meeting. I sat on the hard dirt, wondering if he'd been made aware of my disappearance and what he'd make of it.

I'd yet to decide what to make of it myself. Only that I would make something of it.

Maybe the Seelie kingdom was far more dangerous for me than that of the Unseelie. But I'd escaped the king who'd manipulated my heart while plotting my father's demise, so I welcomed the danger.

Something within me awakened and uncoiled, as if finally free, although I was very much trapped.

The iron bars didn't burn my skin from my flesh as they would a full-blooded faerie. It still burned as if boiled water splashed my fingertips when they tapped the bars.

Reclined across the ground, I touched them again to remain awake. The jolt of pain did the trick. As did footsteps, measured and crunching, approaching from that dark hall.

I returned to drawing in the dirt. "Finally."

"Have you missed me, dread?"

Lazily, I drawled, "So much that torture won't be necessary, monster."

Atakan's steps ceased. "Pity. I was looking forward to hearing you moan again."

That earned him a slight smile. But I continued creating patterns in the dirt, unsure I was ready to look at him. To meet those luminously cruel eyes. "Where's Meadow?"

"The felynx he forced upon you?" That crisp amusement had left his voice. "I'll tell you when I know."

It worked just as he'd intended. I sat up, pushing hair from my face and glaring.

He tucked his hands into the pockets of his long black coat, the collar standing high at his bladed jaw. His lips parted, curving into a devious half smile that hitched my heartbeat.

But those emerald-flecked bronze eyes…

They were almost completely green by the time he spoke. "Aren't you a riveting sight." His near-white hair had been combed back, unable to soften the displeasure hardening his menacing features. "Did you wear that dress for him?" His head tilted. "Or for me?"

"Had I known you'd come to collect me to liven up this dank place…" I gestured to the cells around me and grinned. "I'd have worn something far brighter." I added, "And warmer."

"For him, then," he determined. "And after you'd discovered his treachery."

I said nothing. Not only because I didn't want to speak about Vane, but because there was no need.

Atakan had already figured it out. "Still so bold." He began to walk the perimeter of my cage. "So daring." His hands clasped behind his back. "Did you think you could seduce him into taking you back home to dear Bernadette?"

My teeth gritted.

He hummed a laugh. "Your cooperation is required if you wish to leave this dank place."

"I don't see how these questions are of any use to you."

He continued circling. "They are more useful than you could possibly know."

It became difficult to hold his gaze, and I found I couldn't when I whispered, "I tried to convince him to take me on a scouting journey. I couldn't just do nothing. I had to try to leave."

"Then how fortunate you are that I came to your rescue."

I made a show of peering around. "I'm afraid I've yet to see anything fortunate about it."

He ignored that. "I would have vanished into that ghastly castle, of course, were it not for the wards seeping from the stone." He feigned a shiver. "Alas, I spent hours hiding in a fucking tree with your felynx until you finally came to find her."

"Why?" I asked. "Why bring me back here?"

"Many reasons," he said. "The primary one being that you are my betrothed, and your disappearance has created some rather nasty consequences."

"The alliance between our kingdoms is broken, Atakan."

"Maybe."

My eyes narrowed, seeking his.

He smirked. "Now…" Crouching in front of me, he hissed as he dragged a finger down an iron bar. "Tell me how the Unseelie king managed to snatch you."

I looked at his melted flesh, the skin stuck to the iron bar. Then I met his eyes. "A featherbone."

He blinked. Bronze darkened his gaze, and his lips parted ever so slightly before he asked, "And just how did you come across an item so rare?"

"It belonged to my mother," I supplied easily. "My father gave it to me when I left Nephryn."

He stared for seconds that slowed my heartbeat, as if weighing the truth of my words.

But I had nothing to hide. I didn't care about anything except surviving what had happened and what would come. To do that, I needed to get out of this dungeon.

I needed him to trust me—as much as a creature like Atakan was willing to trust anyone.

He seemed to take great pleasure in saying, "Your mother was Unseelie."

"No." I frowned. "My father told me she was Seelie."

He tutted, rising to stand. "Likely because it suited his endeavors. Seelie cannot use featherbones, dread. They're heirlooms of a sort."

My heart sank.

Though it didn't matter which kingdom my mother hailed from, it mattered now. It mattered because I'd been given to the Seelie royals as a half-Seelie faerie to wed their prince.

"Oh no." Atakan exhaled heavily. "It seems I've unearthed a little secret."

I hissed, "I didn't know."

"Evidently," he drawled. Again, he walked around my cell. "Secrets are dangerous things, Princess. Luckily for you, I like to collect and tuck them away for safekeeping."

I didn't doubt that, and I loathed to think of all the secrets he'd collected to use against people.

"So the featherbone took you to the mighty King Vane."

"Yes." Just hearing his name made my chest constrict. "Which is why he instantly believed I was who he needed. It delivered me straight to him." I fought against the invasion of the memory. "Straight to his chambers."

At that, Atakan laughed.

A delicious yet chilling cadence that transformed his ethereal features into something deceptively captivating. "You ended up in that castle because featherbones harbor ancient and powerful magic, but due to the wards, even it had its limits. Without his aid, no one could vanish in and out of Vane's lands, so the featherbone appeased the magic of the wards it bested by taking you to him."

My chest hollowed.

Now, courtesy of the gaps in the wards, anyone could vanish to and beyond The Bonelands.

Anger pushed the bubble of guilt until it popped, and searing resentment surged through me.

"Yet he sold it to you as some great feat of fate." Atakan sighed, smiling up at the cobweb-dusted rafters as he walked, slow and almost merrily. "And you bought it."

I gave that no attention and said, "Then the wards would have ruined the featherbone."

"Just as they destroyed those who tried to use their magic to break through them," he confirmed silkily. "The featherbone collects morsels of soul from each generation it's passed on to, strengthening its magic, and those fragments protected you."

He'd known. Vane had known why the featherbone had been rendered useless.

"It's another way of vanishing, if you will." Atakan lifted a long finger before him. "Except it will take you to one place only."

I stared at that finger and failed to ignore the memories of it touching intimate places.

"Home." He stopped walking. "Why did you seek to go home,

dreaded Mildred?" His next question grazed like a sharpened blade. "Did you finally grow tired of sparring with me?"

I tried to recall how I'd felt at that moment. On the night I'd donned my sister's coat and discovered the forgotten featherbone within the pocket. A coat I'd left behind in Ashbone Castle. "Honestly, I cannot really say."

Perhaps Atakan believed me. Perhaps he was merely waiting for me to further indulge him.

Frowning at his knee-high boots, I gathered my ruined braid over my shoulder. "I'd just overheard a conversation you'd had with your father about the wedding, and I put on a coat in your rooms to stand on the balcony. The featherbone was in the pocket, where I'd kept it since leaving home."

"You were sulking and didn't know what it could do," he surmised.

Though he was right, I glared up at him. "What use is keeping me down here when I'm willing to talk?"

"Maybe I simply enjoy seeing you caged." His smile was wolfish. "Wholly at my mercy." But then emerald reclaimed his eyes, that smile fell, and his jaw clenched. "You fractured the wards, dread."

That constant dripping became the only sound. The weight of what that meant seemed to snuff all the air from the damp dungeon. It became hard to breathe.

But I wasn't in love.

I could have been. It was undeniable that Vane had indeed stolen some part of my heart. Just enough to ruin the wards. Not enough to get rid of them.

Regardless, love wasn't anywhere near what I felt now.

All I felt was patient fury.

So Atakan could stare at me with something shockingly close to condemnation and betrayal. He could even loathe me more. I had no qualms about sparring with him. In fact, doing so forced me to realize how much I relished it.

I tipped my head back and smiled. "They might be damaged, but they haven't fallen, Prince."

He didn't return my smile.

He slipped his hands into his coat pockets, and continued to stare down at me. A stare so bright yet so dark. His clenched jaw shifted, the only fracture in his veneer.

Then he stalked back to the shadowed hall, his long coat sailing behind him.

Twenty-Five

"You must be tired indeed." A feminine voice opened my eyes. "To sleep in the dirt of your enemy's lair."

I blinked at the black ribbon I'd removed from my hair, then squinted at sandaled feet, the leather straps tied in a bow over slim ankles. Groaning, I rolled from my numb arm that I'd used as a cushion to my back.

Lilac tulle puffed beneath Pholly's knees, tightening at her waist and melding into a satin bust. Her sleek brown hair sat sharply over the tulle clouds at her shoulders.

Her nude lips tilted, and I blinked some more. "Are you smiling?"

"I can do that from time to time." Crouching before my cage, she cocked her head. "And watching you sleep is rather comical."

"Not sure I want to know why."

She felt inclined to tell me anyway. "You mumble a lot."

"About?"

"Beasts, it seems."

I narrowed my eyes. "That could mean anything."

"Or anyone."

At that, I sat up, but a yawn ruined my glower. I tried to smother it with my hand until I sniffed dirt and winced. "Any chance you've got some breakfast hidden beneath that big skirt of yours?"

"It's nearing dinnertime."

I frowned. That meant I'd been here for one whole day. My bladder screamed, though I'd had nothing to drink. "What's for dinner, then?" I tried instead.

Pholly smiled again, but this one was more of a warning. "You have a pet felynx."

"Where is she?"

"She's fine."

I licked my teeth, unsure what I wanted more—something to freshen my dry mouth or a fucking direct answer for once.

"Then why speak of Meadow?"

Her gray-blue eyes brightened. "That's her name?"

If I'd known the way to Pholly's dark heart was a wolf-cat, perhaps I'd have found a king to force one upon me sooner. "Yes," I said, ignoring the twinge in my chest when I remembered who had named her.

"You broke the wards."

"A little, apparently."

She tucked her silky hair behind her pointed ear. "Just enough to know that it's awful?"

I frowned.

She explained, "Love, of course."

Oh.

Intrigue made me forget the awfulness she'd referred to, and my hunger and bladder. "Who broke your heart?"

"A mortal man who is long dead." Quick, lethal words.

Words that enlightened. "You killed him."

Pholly waved her hand, then procured a small pad of parchment from her skirts, as well as a piece of charcoal. "Enough about that. Tell me about the castle."

"Ashbone Castle?"

She rolled her eyes. "Unless there's another Unseelie castle."

I didn't want to think about it. But if she wanted information in exchange for food, or even a pail to relieve myself in, I'd start singing about all of it. "Dreary," I said. "But colorful outside."

She gave me a bland look. "That's it?" Then she twirled her hand. "I've seen your letters to your sister. You can be more descriptive than that."

"You've seen my letters?"

"Someone had to check them."

I should have known Elion couldn't stop certain people from snooping.

Knowing it wouldn't help me right now, I withheld a scathing response and combed my fingers through my hair. They snagged on a knot, so I crossed my legs and folded my hands in my lap.

I started with the long drive that led to the cracked blocks of steps, the trellises sagging around the grand oak doors giving entry to the stone fortress. By the time I'd gotten to the stained glass of the king's bathing room window, I was certain I might cry from the need to urinate.

"Go back to the library." Fascination had turned her typically intimidating features into something breathtaking. "Books are everywhere?"

Pholly didn't want information, I realized far too late. She simply wanted to draw Ashbone Castle.

I nodded. "Every table and shelf, and even in piles beside chairs and before the overflowing shelves." An idea struck me. "I'll describe you something better if you let me out."

She wrote down those details before saying, "Such as?"

"A pytherion."

She smiled at her pad, then closed it and stood. "No need." Just when I'd thought she'd leave me pleading for her to help me, she stopped in that slim, dark hall.

A large ring of rusted keys in hand, she returned. I could scarcely believe she was freeing me, and I kept quiet as it took her a moment to find the key to my cell, lest I say something that changed her mind.

Only when she'd opened it and walked back to the hall did I speak. "Where am I to go?"

Her eyes gleamed over her shoulder in the dim. "Wherever you dare." Then she led the way through the shadows to the stairs.

Atakan's rooms hadn't changed since I'd vanished to The Bonelands.

The only exception was more clothing littering the bed and floor. I ignored the itch to tidy them for collection and went straight to his nightstand drawer for the dagger he kept there.

Relieved that he hadn't better hidden it—as he probably hadn't thought I'd leave the dungeon—I snatched the worn hilt. It nearly slipped from my soiled fingers when I spied the burgundy scarf.

The one he'd swiped through my core, the silk stained in dark patches by my innocence.

My stomach hollowed. My body tensed from the phantom touch of his fingers breaking me as I'd lost control with my climax.

I slammed the drawer shut, effectively pushing the memory away, and hurried to the bathing room.

Perhaps a bath shouldn't have been high on my list of priorities. Finding Meadow should have been. But although I shouldn't trust anyone in this castle, I trusted Pholly had meant it when she'd claimed Meadow was fine.

And I couldn't think clearly with the gown I'd worn to seduce Vane clinging to my filthy skin.

The tub filled as I finally relieved myself. While I sat there, I tore the gown over my head. It ripped, the sound satisfying. I bundled and lobbed it at the floor. It landed in a soft heap, and I closed my eyes before they could well.

Tears were useless when I wasn't sure I would survive this court again, or that any of us would survive what Vane was about to do.

I climbed into the tub, and for minutes that dazed, I stared at the rust-marked faucet.

The drizzle outside turned into a deluge, further hindering my senses as I focused on scrubbing the dungeon from my body—and the king who'd fooled me into thinking that he might be different from every other faerie I'd met.

The prince made his presence known with a soft murmur. "So Pholly managed to smuggle you out of your cage."

Although stunned, I pretended otherwise and didn't look at him.

I finished washing the soap from my skin. "I won't go back without a fight." I held up my hand. "It took too long to clean the dirt from my nails."

He didn't respond for tightening moments, so I expected he

wouldn't. That he'd either haul me from the water to return me to the dungeon or simply leave.

Instead, he came close to purring, "I believe we've been here before, dread."

After squeezing droplets from my hair, I retrieved the blade from the edge of the tub and stood, sudsy water falling from my body.

Atakan didn't fetch me a towel. But he watched as I carefully crossed the tiles to unhook his from behind the door he leaned against.

He'd discarded his coat. His rather plain cream tunic sat loosely over his broad chest and tightened at his tapered torso due to half of it being tucked into his fitted black pants.

I quickly patted myself dry, then wrapped the towel soaked in his heady scent around my body, securing it as I walked past him.

He extended his arm across the doorway, halting me.

Then he lowered his head to my neck and inhaled so deep, a throaty rumble caused gooseflesh to pebble my skin. His head lifted, eyes riddled with green. "Smelling much better."

I squinted at him, ready to remind him that it hadn't been my fault I'd been trapped in a cell, but he stalked into his bedchamber ahead of me. "Less like something you're not."

I frowned at his back. "Dirty? Compliments aren't your usual—"

"His."

I blinked.

Turning, he surveyed me slowly. "Don't tell me you're puzzled, dread." He tossed himself backward upon the bed. "Seems your time away from me hasn't served that clever halfling brain of yours well."

I clenched the dagger as I tried to assess what he was up to. Tried to pick at his words as I padded into the dressing chamber, surprised to find my belongings right where I'd left them.

"No serpents?" I called.

"Rather than find out, perhaps you should remain naked."

Biting back an irritating smile, I decided on a blue gown with cream flowers embroidered in the belle sleeves. But I didn't put it on in the dressing chamber.

I dropped the towel when I entered the bedchamber and tugged the gown on. It proved difficult, as I didn't wish to relinquish the dagger.

The prince tsked. "Do you ever wear undergarments?" He turned onto his side to watch me pull the heavy skirts free of my stomach and down over my legs. "Or might you be playing at something?"

I was, of course.

But his own tactics and one look at those eyes told me he was also playing at something—and that even if I planned it well, I wouldn't get what I wanted unless he wished for me to.

We'll see, I thought, challenge sparking my cold blood.

Amusement glinted like true gold in his gaze as he said, "You look different." He relaxed against the mess of pillows, rumpling the bedding more beneath his boots. "Dare I say…" Those perfect lips pursed. "Angry. Did the not-so-sweet Unseelie king hurt your half-mortal heart?" He smiled, cruel and bloodthirsty. "I'm curious, did you happen to meet his—"

I snarled and leaped atop him, straddling his thighs. "Where's Meadow?" The edge of the blade pressed against the seam of his pants, bulged by his erection. "Tell me."

Atakan laughed, free and deep and distracting. "You won't do it." His gaze darkened to emerald right before my eyes. He snapped his teeth at me. "You like it too much."

Smiling, I sliced across his thigh.

He hissed between his teeth, then groaned when I moved down his legs to lick the blood seeping from the tear in his pants.

Such a venomous creature had no right tasting so sweet.

"I can play this game for as long as you want." I licked my lips as I rose, readying the dagger to strike at his chest next. "Tell me where—"

Breath whooshed from me.

I blinked up at the canopy of the bed.

Atakan grinned while smoothing his hands up my arms until they were above my head, my hands trapped in one of his.

Gently, and without taking his menacing gaze from mine, he plucked the dagger with mortifying ease from my slack fingers. "So you want to retrieve your felynx and flee from me." His hair flopped forward, kissing his temples.

I squirmed. Futile. I wasn't going anywhere.

And I didn't intend to.

Even so, I ignored the part of me that didn't want to move for other reasons—that enjoyed the way his legs trapped mine between them and the thrill slithering through my veins.

"Yet…" He turned his head, eyes roaming all over my face. "If you truly wished to leave, you'd have tried to without your little pet, knowing full well that although she is embarrassingly lazy, she has wings and would inevitably find you." His attention dropped to my heaving chest, eyes dancing as they returned to mine. "No. You don't wish to leave at all."

"Meadow is not lazy," I lied, then inwardly scolded myself for letting him distract me. "You would kill her if I left her here."

"Perhaps." I stilled as he dragged the tip of the blade, wet with his blood, over my jaw. "You want something, my dreaded Mildred." He tapped the tip against my lips, his own curving. "Something more than my cock returning to your lovely cunt and my mouth feasting on yours."

Heat exploded within me.

I swallowed, and though he could scent it, I still attempted to hide it by kissing the blade. Atakan's smirk became a grin so feral, the part of me that was more creature than human awoke with a soft purr.

I fought the instinct to lift my hips and rasped, "I want to make a deal, monster."

"Oh?" He tossed the dagger to the nightstand. "You're hardly in a position to barter."

"I'll tell you what I know. Everything I've learned." I waited a moment before adding, "And in return, you'll give me safety."

"Safety?" He chuckled. "You do know who you're speaking to, don't you?"

I ignored that. "Fix the alliance, Atakan." The words were whispered, yet I felt not an ounce of fear as I said, "Make me your wife."

Twenty-Six

My breathing settled as I waited, staring up at the prince who wouldn't cease fucking smiling.

"Say that again," he finally seethed between his teeth. "I'm not entirely sure I heard you."

He'd heard me just fine. So I merely smiled and writhed beneath him. His gaze dipped to my wriggling body, returning to mine when I said, "You don't need me to. But you do need my sister's kingdom for what's to come."

A light brow arched. "And you're rather…" He lowered to croon against my mouth, "Intimate with such knowledge?"

I didn't cower, nor falter. I pressed the tip of my nose to his and whispered, *"Extremely."*

He snarled, then shocked me by biting my lower lip. Hard. His teeth scraped when he released it and used the hand braced beside my head to push himself up.

I didn't need to question it, and I wouldn't mention it. It didn't need pointing out when it glowed in his eyes.

Atakan the heartless was jealous. In fact, he was more than jealous. He was enraged.

His nostrils flared as he stared down at me, and if I had to guess, I'd say he was attempting to soothe his pride. Attempting to forget that someone else had touched his pet halfling.

But he failed.

Though his shoulders gradually loosened, his jaw remained tight. As were his confirming words. "Did he fuck you?"

"That's hardly relevant."

"Perhaps not, but it is imperative that I know."

"Why?" I taunted.

"So I know which part of him to mutilate first."

Iced water dripped into my chest. He was utterly serious.

I couldn't let the trickle of fear keep me from playing. "I would start with his lips."

He growled. "Mildred."

"Then his tongue."

He pressed his nose against mine. "You're doing a *very* poor job of bartering."

"Maybe his hands."

His glower suddenly turned into a grin, and he straightened. "You can stop now."

"I'm not done."

"You are."

I frowned. "You don't know that."

"You said maybe." He left to lay beside me. "He kissed you, and for that he will pay. But no matter…" He bit into his wrist as though it were fruit and not his own flesh. "You'll soon forget you cared enough to let him."

Too distracted by the blood pooling upon his wrist, the bulging veins in his forearm, I hardly heard what he'd last said. "What are you doing?"

"You want to make a deal," he drawled, extending his arm between us on the bed. "You must drink to seal it." When I just stared at the blood, unsure what trap I was about to land in, he sighed. "Really, dread, do you not know anything?"

I scowled at him.

I was well aware that the Fae always used blood to bind deals. The memory of Vane's promise flashed through my mind like lightning.

But that hadn't required drinking.

"Hurry now." Atakan shifted closer, his blood dripping onto the bedding. "You have until it dries."

I rolled to my side to face him. "You haven't asked me about what I might know."

He just waited.

Carefully, as if his arm were another two-headed serpent, I picked up his hand and leaned over his wrist. I didn't know why, but I closed my eyes.

Maybe I knew this was not merely a deal, and I didn't want to see any of my stupidity.

First, I licked the blood cooling upon his smooth skin, intending for that to be enough. But then I lapped at the punctures he'd made and sucked, falling victim to a hunger I hadn't known I could feel.

A hunger so demanding, I bit into his flesh, seeking more—seeking all that he was—and swallowing only when his blood filled my entire mouth.

Vaguely, I felt his fingers upon my inner wrist. Felt his mouth caress the sensitive skin before the sharp sting of his piercing teeth rendered me still.

Heat blazed an instant trail through my limbs.

They quaked with my moaned breathing. My very bones seemed to hum as I licked and sucked and swallowed. As I feasted with desperation that should have shamed.

There was no room for that. Not even when Atakan ceased drinking from my wrist, and I didn't want to stop. I wanted more. So much more.

Need, powerful and painful, bloomed in my core.

I panted from the brutality of it as he pushed me onto my back and moved atop me. For dizzying moments, he just gazed down at me.

"What have you done to me?" I croaked.

Through the haze of desire—a hunger so sharp it hurt—I saw his emerald eyes. I heard him swallow thickly. Then he murmured, "You must be famished." Challenge soaked each lethally soft word. "And it's dinnertime." With that, he left the bed.

And then his rooms.

Atakan was already seated when I entered the dining room.

Ruelle was nowhere to be seen. At his side, Pholly lowered her goblet of wine. Her eyes narrowed on me, then widened as she looked at the prince. "You didn't."

Walking from Atakan's tower had been torture, but making it across the room when I caught a whiff of his scent seemed impossible.

I tripped on nothing and halted just beyond the doors, his pheromones causing the heat within me to boil. I hadn't eaten since returning to Cloud Castle, and I was indeed starving.

But not for food.

Whatever Atakan had done to me felt incurable. I knew I needed him. He needed to fix it. After lying upon his bed and fighting the urge to touch myself, I'd come to demand he find me the remedy for what had possessed me—castle full of foes be damned.

Phineus cursed and failed to smother a coughed laugh.

Garran was absent. Cordenya smiled from his seat at the head of the table, petting my felynx. Sitting beside the king's consort, Meadow flicked her tail impatiently while eyeing the food on the table.

Her smile might have been serpentine, but Cordenya's silver eyes appeared pleased. "Mildred." Her mouth drooped as she noticed my flushed state. "Skies, you look awful." Setting her wine down, she then gestured to the table. "Join us and eat something."

I couldn't resist. It was as if his presence alone commanded me to look at him. To seek him out.

Atakan, seeming wholly unaffected by the exchange of our blood, watched me. One look at those bright eyes, the teeth he sank into a chicken leg, made my thighs clench and my mind burn.

Cordenya tossed my felynx a chicken breast. "Relax, Princess. No one here means you any harm."

The gleam in Atakan's eyes said otherwise.

Meadow collected the chicken and hurried from the dining room, paying me no mind at all. *Some bond*, I thought, though I hadn't the energy to care.

I wanted to believe Cordenya, especially since I was in no state to sense a threat or defend myself. But these faeries had every reason to wish me ill or even dead.

Believing they were unbothered by the consequences of my time in the Unseelie realm would be a foolish mistake.

Atakan's gaze narrowed as I looked at the empty chair next to him, and then opted to take the one beside his cousin.

"I would say you look well," Phineus said. "But you certainly do not." He feigned thinking about why. "Was the Unseelie king as beastly as they say?"

I couldn't spare a thought for Vane. For anything but the hollow ache within me. "More so," I said flatly, staring straight at Atakan.

His clenched jaw rotated.

Cordenya tsked. "You must be positively traumatized, darling."

"I think I must be," I said, still looking only at Atakan.

My peripheral caught Cordenya leaning over the table. She needlessly whispered, "Did he ever turn into an actual beast?"

I almost laughed. "No."

"Not once?" Pholly asked.

Participating in conversation seemed absurd.

I drew in a breath through my nose, and forced coherent words to form. "He doesn't shift. But his steward does." I waited for the sadness to come at the thought of Daylia, but the heat engulfing me permitted only a morsel. "She turns into a cat."

At that, Atakan looked at Pholly, brows rising a little. But he said nothing, and Pholly hummed. "Is she clothed when she leaves her cat form?"

I nodded.

"Then the steward isn't a shifter. She's what you call a mirage."

"A mirage?" I asked.

"Faeries who can present as their soul animal."

Unable to care about shifters and mirages, I reached for the water. My hand shook.

Phineus said, "Allow me."

The test proved Atakan wasn't as unaffected as he seemed.

He leaned forward to pour me some water himself. He set the

goblet in front of me with a thud, and took his time dragging his fingers free of the crystal before leaning back in his chair.

My mouth dried.

Though it physically hurt, I met his gaze as I sipped. Pure promise shone within. The rigorous chewing and the way he shifted in his chair the longer I stared at him made it clear I wasn't the only one suffering.

And that this was but another game.

Cordenya cleared her throat delicately. Pholly snorted while continuing to eat.

Amused, Phineus said, "The scents in here are…"

"Overpowering, yes," Cordenya intervened. "They did such a lovely job with the chicken. I'll be sure to pass on the compliment to Herwen and his new apprentice."

"Indeed." Phineus carved into his meal. "So warm and…" He said around a mouthful, "Moist."

Pholly spat wine back into her goblet, her laughter choked.

Atakan ignored them. He stabbed at pieces of corn on his plate one by one, as if doing so needed all of his attention.

I selected a chicken breast and focused on slicing it open. Watching the steam rise, I pondered if the heat in my body was worse than that of the dead bird.

My thighs clenched with my core when Atakan rose from his chair to put creamy sauce over my chicken. Ever so slowly, he poured directly along the crevice I'd cut.

The jug was then set down, but he wasn't done. He dragged his finger through the cream as he gradually leaned back over the table to sit down.

Don't look, don't look, don't—

The sound of him sucking his finger lured my eyes like fire to kindling.

My cheeks flushed even more, and I unhooked my hair from behind my ear in an effort to hide it.

Hiding anything was futile. Our scents, as Phineus had said, and our behavior gave our arousal and this perilous game away.

Regardless, I ate. I knew I needed to in order to survive whatever plan the devious prince had in mind.

Atakan broke the taut quiet. "As I mentioned earlier, the princess has garnered some important information for us," he said smoothly. "Hence why I've permitted her release from the dungeon."

Cordenya paused in brushing something from her apricot bodice. "Yes, of course." She straightened. "Let's hear it, then."

But I hadn't the ability to tell them what I'd intended to tell Atakan. I could scarcely remember what it was, or why I'd even needed to.

But then Phineus reminded me. "I was very sorry to hear about your father and stepmother, Princess." He paused. "Well, not so much the latter."

Pholly said, "Unnecessary, don't you think?"

Phineus just shrugged.

He'd seemed sincere, yet I couldn't look at him as grief tried to weave through the curse of intense arousal. It pricked like tiny needles, bursting the heavy beat of my heart.

It strengthened enough for me to steel my spine and ask, "Where is Lord Stone?"

Silence reigned.

Then Cordenya said carefully, "He fled shortly after Atakan took you, as the Unseelie court believes it was he who vanished you beyond the wards."

I looked at her. "Why would they think it was him?"

"Because…" She slid a wary glance at Atakan. "He knows where some of the fractures are."

And very few others likely did.

"They'll kill him," I whispered, imagining those jeweled hands streaked crimson with his own blood.

Cordenya earned my attention again. "Not if this ends before it goes too far." Before I could tell her they stood no chance at defeating Vane's armies, she propped her hands beneath her chin and said, "Tell us what you know, Mildred."

So I did.

I told them about the pytherions, the warriors training to ride them into battle, the eggs they'd been hiding to lure the enraged beasts right to this castle and the city…

And I felt not a shred of guilt.

Satisfaction lifted my chin, even as my body screamed that it wasn't satisfied at all. Arousal still burned, bittersweet. Yet it was easier to breathe when I thought of what Vane had done to my family. To me. And what he intended to do to our kingdoms.

As I finished speaking and Phineus asked me about the warriors, Pholly taking out her parchment and drawing something, Atakan remained quiet. He studied me with low brows and a fixed jaw that barely moved to chew.

"Thirty pytherions," Cordenya breathed and glanced at Atakan.

He ripped his bread in half and continued to stare at me.

"Nearly," I reiterated as if it mattered.

"We need to find those eggs," Pholly said to her parchment, hand moving furiously. "Or this castle will be reduced to cinders as soon as they arrive."

Phineus concurred, and they made plans to begin searching tomorrow.

Atakan interrupted them. "The city first." It was more of a grunt, his gaze still firmly stuck to me as I ate.

"There's one egg somewhere in the center," I said, reaching for water. "That's all I know about the location." I sipped, but it failed to quench my thirst.

"I don't suppose you know how much time we might have?" Phineus asked.

I shook my head. "They were ensuring they'd be ready to strike as soon as the wards fell, but being that they've only fractured…" I shrugged.

Cordenya determined, "They'll need to find gaps big enough for their army of flying serpents first."

Atakan's hum was too throaty. Too damned deep.

That ache morphed into agony. I withered in the chair, the fork falling from my slack fingers.

Beside me, Phineus sighed. "For skies' sake." Then his chair creaked as he stood. He collected what remained of his dinner, presumably to eat elsewhere. "You truly are heartless, Atakan."

The prince licked a smear of cream from his upper lip, then grinned wide and wolfishly.

I wanted to follow Phineus, then Pholly when she left a moment after her brother, her laughter tinkling from out in the hall.

But I couldn't surrender. Not when I'd made it this far.

Not when the prince stared at me while he leisurely drank his wine, and I stared back while I ate, and the tension grew taut enough to make Cordenya leave us.

She paused behind Atakan's chair, a hand poised to land on his rigid shoulder. Then she sniffed and thought better of whatever she'd been about to say. Her gown's small train of blue butterflies whispered across the floor in her wake.

My hand trembled as I clasped my water.

Atakan leaned back in his chair, his gaze wholly green. He watched me drink while further loosening the neck ties of his cream tunic. "You look like you've barely had your fill."

The word fill was a stone falling through my body, landing with bruising impact at my swollen core. I shifted in my chair. "You look like you tricked me, yet still so very…" I trailed my finger through the condensation on the crystal goblet. "Unsatisfied."

He reached beneath the table, and I didn't need to see to know that he was palming himself over his pants. "That's where you're wrong."

Tempted to leap across the table and maul him, I raised a brow. "Oh?"

"You should know by now that watching you squirm pleases me beyond measure."

"I thought making me surrender into quivering pieces did that?"

A dangerous question, but one I hoped would lead to an end of this suffering. "Or am I imagining someone else?"

I didn't care who he was.

I didn't even care about what he'd done. All I wanted, all I could think about, was having him inside and all over my needy body.

It worked.

His upper lip curled. A low growl that induced a shiver rolled through the dining room. Between gritted teeth, he warned, "Better run, dread. If I reach you before you make it to my chambers, I'll take your surrender wherever I find you."

I didn't ask any questions nor linger. Victorious, I smiled as I stood.

And then I ran.

Twenty-Seven

I MADE IT TO THE TOP OF THE TOWER STAIRS BEFORE REALIZING he wasn't running.

A hunter who'd cornered his prey, his steps were slow and sure. Each one made my heart jump higher as I fumbled with the brass handle and pushed open the door.

As soon as his shadow filled the doorway, I asked, "What did you do to me, Atakan?"

"We made a blood-binding deal." He closed the door. "Now, remove the gown."

Intentionally, I retreated toward the bed. "Remove your pants."

He kicked off his boots, then leaned against the door. He simply waited, oozing control although his erection bulged his tight black pants.

I stood before the bed. With the exception of my chest rising and rising, neither of us moved.

The meager light from the sconces on either side of the bed cast half of his divine features in shadow, the other half in a stark glow that illuminated the changing hue of his eyes.

Energy gathered as if a storm crept into the bedchamber, and when I lifted the gown over my body, letting it fall through my fingers to the floor, it cracked.

Atakan was on me before I could see him move. Over me before I could reclaim the breath robbed from my lungs.

He pulled me up the bed with ease while I fought the urge to snatch his face and kiss every cruel inch of it. A low sound rumbled within his chest, drawing my eyes to the glimpse of it through his loosened tunic ties.

I wanted that sound against my mouth. Wanted it drowning out the ringing pulse in my ears as he took me. My legs curled around his back. His eyes met mine, a warning within.

Smiling, I ignored him. He'd done this to me. Now, he could damned well fix me.

I pushed my feet against his ass.

Of course, he was far stronger than me. But he allowed it, and lowered his body between my thighs. He rolled his hips into me and hissed. "Fuck."

Though he was fully clothed, the press of him against my core engulfed me in torrential flames.

The need to rut, to have him fill me, was so acute that I couldn't help it—I pleaded, "I don't know what tricks you've pulled this time, but I need you." Desperate, I groaned, "Right now."

"Say that again, and I'll give you what you need."

I fisted his tunic, drawing us nose to nose, and nipped his upper lip. "I fucking need you."

His tunic ripped as he quickly rose to tear it off before shoving down his pants. They made it over his ass only, and then he was pushing into my body.

My back arched.

We both groaned in relief as he breached my opening. Then slowly, his entire cock invaded me. He collapsed over top of me, face buried in my neck.

Breath escaped us in wild bursts as we just lay there, delirious and relieved.

"Prince." I twined my legs around him again. The question came airless—choked. "What in the skies have you done?"

"You did this." He grunted, then trembled when my fingernails dug into his smooth back. "And there's no changing it. Believe me, I've tried."

He didn't give me the chance to ask what he'd meant. To speak at all.

And I was beyond caring when he rocked his hips. Every lazy thrust created an overflow of sensation. Pleasure careened through me. Too fast. Bubbling over.

Rapidly and violently, I came undone, fingers scraping down the back of his arms.

Snarling softly, Atakan pushed onto his forearms. Blazing green eyes watched me twist beneath him. Arch into him. Then he tipped his head back and groaned. Veins corded in his neck and along his upper arms as he stilled and shook and emptied inside me.

But whatever spell had trapped us wasn't broken yet.

I could have wept as the prince began anew.

He pushed his hand over my stomach, between my breasts. "These fucking tits." Eyes stuck to them, he leaned over me and deepened his thrusts until they rose toward his mouth with my curling back.

His teeth stole my nipple. Biting and pulling, he rumbled his approval when my fingers sank into his soft hair.

He drew away as his thrusts gained speed, his teeth bared. Over and over, his muscles straining and his nostrils flaring, he pounded into me relentlessly until climax claimed us again.

I'd have thought it a wild dream if it weren't for the overwhelming pleasure that seemed to never end.

We refused to let it.

After removing his pants, Atakan lifted me onto my shaking hands and knees, my hair gathered in his fist. Looming behind me, he tugged until he could lick my jaw while he fucked me so deeply, his arm banded around my waist to hold me up.

But when our next climax struck, we both fell. He ended up on his side, leaving me tangled beneath him.

Crawling free, just enough to turn over, I wrapped my hand around his wet and half-erect cock. It hardened fully, and not a ruptured breath later, he climbed between my legs.

He leaned on an elbow to watch as I urged him back inside my body. When his gaze met mine, something passed through the changing hues of his eyes. He lowered, and I thought he might finally kiss me.

"I can't stand it," he said, voice hoarse. "Can't stand how fucking good you feel." Forearms braced beside my head, he bit my lower lip, then lapped at it so tenderly, I climaxed again. He shivered with me, licking my mouth while I mewled and writhed into every slow thrust. "Can't stand how making you come feels like the only victory I'll ever need."

I hadn't enough sense to be irritated by those words.

He'd created an ache that only he could quell, and by the skies, all I wanted was more. More aching and more satiating. More of the sounds of our coupling and heavy breathing and thunderous heartbeats.

Pain mingled with infinite pleasure when his teeth sank into my throat, and he drew blood. Yet I tilted my head to give him better access.

Only for him to stop fucking me.

I was about to beg him to move or push him to his back to take what I needed, but he captured my face in his hands.

He held me trapped as his blood-covered tongue dragged over the center of my throat to my chin. He nipped it, tilting it down, then licked my upper lip. My lower lip was next—my entire mouth painted in my blood by his tongue.

My fingers clasped his face to push him away, to return more air to my lungs. Instead, they roamed the skull-sharp crests of his cheeks, prodded the exact spot where his dimple hid.

Atakan froze, and I expected he'd put an end to my exploration as I traced the perfect bow of his lips.

He didn't. But he bit my finger, earning a smile that quickly fell when he slowly moved. He withdrew his cock from my body, then struck deep and precise.

My fingers slid from his face.

He growled, disapproval furrowing his brows.

So I put them back but moved one hand down his neck to touch his Adam's apple. It bobbed when he swallowed, and when his pace increased, I felt his rumbled groan vibrate against my fingers. Then, pulling him closer, against my mouth and tongue.

He nudged me away, ordering, "Let me see." As if thinking I

would defy him, he took my cheek to hold me still as rapture swept through me in another mind-emptying rush. "I need to see what I've reduced you to."

His fingers crept to my mouth, then inside it.

Feral delight shone in his eyes. Twin emerald jewels. They held me hostage as he pounded into me. As he pried my mouth open with his fingers and growled into it, "Mine."

He sucked my tongue between his teeth before I could question what he'd said.

I wouldn't have been able to anyway.

Yet again, I came undone, all breath and thought and strength drained from me. The room twirled as if I were on the cusp of vanishing, fire-touched darkness flickering.

Fingers squeezed my chin. "Breathe for me, dread." Atakan exhaled into my mouth. His pace turned frenzied, the bed frame protesting. "Only for me." Then he tensed.

A strangled and gasped sound left him. It entered my mouth as he jerked into me. He kept it open and covered by his, my body trapped beneath his, and stole each breath until I wasn't sure why I needed them. Why I needed anything more than this.

Than this horrid and addictive creature.

As he trembled and twitched, I drowned beneath him. I was brought back to the surface by the ridges of muscle under my roaming fingers at his back, the way each touch made him tremble more.

Then cold washed over me, and I blinked up at the dark canopy of the bed. Had I the energy, I feared I would have mewled in dismay when he left me. But he didn't entirely.

On his stomach between them, fingers gripping my flesh, he opened my thighs wide.

He looked up at me, at the blood on my swollen lips that trailed toward my breasts, then back between my legs. "Never have I seen a better sight."

He turned me onto my stomach. Strong hands kneaded my ass. Bruising fingers squeezed it, and I moaned. He released one cheek.

Teeth sank into it at the same time two fingers slid inside me from behind.

Gasping into the twisted bedding, I began to shake.

His teeth left my ass, but his fingers didn't. "Push up onto your hands." He dug those fingers into my flesh, keeping me from rising onto all fours. "I'm going to fist my cock, and you're going to stay right there, seated on my fingers until you make yourself come."

I moved my hips until his fingers were rubbing against perilously swollen tissue. Unable to rise too high, I rocked over them. I circled my hips and tilted back and forth.

He curled them and stroked exactly where I needed. Over and over, he petted me like a good little pet until I was rendered useless, awaiting the crest of release and breathing noisily through gnashed teeth.

A knock pounded on the door. Urgent.

"Ignore it," Atakan whispered. "And don't make a fucking sound."

I needed more. "I want you," I whispered, rocking faster, getting so close yet not nearly satisfied. "Atakan, please."

He cursed and removed his fingers.

Before I could turn my head, he'd lifted my hips and impaled me from behind once again.

He kept me from falling forward by snaking his arm over my chest to cover my mouth. His own warmed my shoulder blade. Teeth pinched my skin hard enough to draw more blood. Leisurely, he lapped at the droplets while he circled his hips.

I clenched, muscle seizing.

He failed to trap his groan, and his attempt created a low rumble that pushed me over the precipice.

My knees weakened.

He held me against him. His fingers grasped my face and his arm braced around my breasts. It caused his cock to slip from my body. He jerked, spilling his seed onto the bed between my thighs as he smothered my cries with his mouth.

But whoever knocked earlier had returned.

The fingers at my cheek and chin loosened when another knock came. Followed by another and another.

Atakan licked the roof of my mouth and my cheek before his hooded eyes absorbed my dazed state. Then he eased me down onto the bed.

Reality was too slow to return.

As it did with the sound of Atakan pulling on his pants, I blinked at the soiled bedding. Feathers floated from a torn pillow, and scratches decorated the prince's broad back.

The faerie in me purred at the sight of them, disgustingly pleased, and my suspicions became an alarming and undeniable knowing.

"Atakan." My voice croaked. "Tell me what really happened."

He halted before the door.

Without looking at me, he dragged his hand through his hair, pushing it back over his head as he exhaled roughly. "We mated."

Twenty-Eight

MATED.

The word and the memories of what I'd done became a ghost that distracted even hours after the intense claiming.

Atakan had been gone since we were forced to cease fucking the previous evening. I'd spent more time than necessary wondering when we might have stopped if we hadn't been interrupted. For although I was uncomfortably tender, it was still there, a simmering need for more.

Pride, mostly, kept me from asking for the prince's whereabouts. Pride and a boatload of fury. So much so that after I'd woken well past midday, I'd paced Atakan's rooms, imagining the vitriol I would spew at him as soon as he returned.

But he hadn't. I'd been collected by Pholly after dinner, who'd sniffed and said, "Quicker than I expected."

I'd frowned. "Excuse me?"

She'd given me an amused look. "No need to be offended. Atakan might have met his match in you, but he's been swindling his way through life since he learned how to walk."

We'd vanished before I could wholly realize she'd been talking about accepting the bond forced upon me.

A bond breakable only in death.

The royal city of Cloudfall was a tidy maze of streets crafted from emerald hedges and towering wood and stone structures.

Pholly had vanished us to the business district where we'd meet Phineus and Elion. To avoid detection from any loiterers, we arrived a few streets away from the heart of the city.

Though as I peered into the shadows, I wasn't sure we'd be successful. Without the protective wards of Cloud Castle, even if we escaped the notice of those out and about at the late hour, I wasn't sure Vane wouldn't discover what we were up to.

I cast the worry aside as I imagined the horror he would bring to this beautiful city, and all those who dwelled within it. He could learn that we were hunting his pytherion eggs, but there was little he could do to me, little he could do to stop us, until he enacted his monstrous plan.

More stone than wood made up the buildings lining the cobbled streets. It gave no solace. The amount of fire unleashed by just one pytherion was enough to spread throughout half of this city before it could be contained.

Iridescent plumes dispersed into tendrils that spiraled around Phineus and Elion as they vanished onto the street.

The latter immediately swallowed me in a hug that took me by surprise. He laughed when I tensed and failed to hug him back.

Clasping my cheeks, he said, "You are more clever than anyone could have anticipated. Merely *rupturing* the wards…" He grinned as bright as the moon above. "Genius."

I frowned, feeling more confused than clever.

Phineus tugged him away. "You're frightening her."

"I am not." Elion's deep-blue hair shone beneath the lamplight before he hid it with the hood of his cloak. He then surveyed me, brows furrowed. "Did I frighten you?"

I smiled. "Merely surprised me."

Phineus chuckled. "Well, you've certainly surprised all of us, Princess."

"Less muttering, more walking," Pholly hissed from down the street.

We all hurried to catch up.

Phineus, hands tucked in the pockets of his mustard cloak, kept his head low. All of us followed suit, though I wished to look closer at the colored windows and the carvings in wooden doors we passed. Looking at the damp and mossy stones of the street did nothing to curb the riot of feelings within.

I wanted to find this egg and smack the prince in his pretty face with it. I wanted to find it, then find him, and impale myself on his cock while I took my anger out on his perfect lips.

I supposed I'd known. Perhaps I hadn't known what it was, but I'd always known that my attraction to him wasn't mere obsession for something too lovely and lethal for my own good. The games we'd played, the punishments we'd served, and the years pushed between us as buffers…

I never was quite certain I should have survived it.

Now, I couldn't help but wonder if my defiance would have been tolerated had I not been destined for him. Then I wondered how long he'd known that I was, and why he'd never so much as hinted at it, let alone said anything.

I looked up as we walked by a glowing shopfront. A butcher. Within, a golden-haired male in a streaked apron was cleaning. His soil-dark eyes narrowed at the window just as we moved on.

Murals colored any large expanse of blank stone, wood, and even countless doors—sun-drenched fields of wildflowers, faerie hovels within mountain foothills, and many depictions of the sky goddess. In every one, Etheria's hair was a rainbow and her clothing rays of sunshine or fluffy pink clouds.

Studying the buildings helped keep my thoughts from straying and circling repetitively around the prince. But as always, nothing ever kept him away for long.

A boisterous laugh leaked onto the street from a tavern we'd passed.

As soon as we turned onto another street, Phineus disobeyed his sister and said, thick with amusement, "Anyone else unable to ignore how different the princess smells?"

Elion nudged him.

"I'm right here," I needlessly drawled.

"*You* can't smell it." Phineus said to the others, "You must admit the way it screams is distracting."

That was true. I failed to notice anything different about my scent.

Beside me, Pholly sighed, kicking at a cream rock. It skittered over the cobblestone into the shadowy doorstep of a jeweler. "Only males get a rise out of such archaic nonsense."

"Don't worry, Phol." Elion's smirk was bright in the dark. "You'll eventually find a mate who can put up with your gloomy ways."

"You don't know anything," Pholly said.

"We know plenty," Phineus sang, walking backward and winking at his sister. "And when these wars stop, all of us might just claim our own blessings."

Pholly sneered. "You're so hopeful, it's honestly revolting."

The sloping street widened into a flat and empty market square.

"Can't get more center than the heart of the city itself." Phineus rubbed his hands together.

The thick pillars rising toward the star-splattered sky slowed my feet. A temple. Open to the elements, pink and blue flowering vines delicately choked the cracked stone. As if crafted from both sun and moonlight, the stone was a cream so clean, it seemed to shimmer.

When I caught up with Pholly at the temple, Phineus and Elion were gone. "Are they searching the rear?" I asked.

She laughed. "Possibly."

Understanding her meaning, I laughed too.

Then I peered into the dark beyond the hedges and fissured stone steps. Only more darkness loomed on the other side, and given how open the temple was, I surmised a pytherion egg wouldn't be hidden within.

"They don't get much privacy in the castle."

I remembered the way Elion had looked at Phineus during my welcoming ball. Perhaps it had been more than jealousy. Perhaps it had been longing. "Why?"

"Phineus's future belongs to Garran," she said.

"Do you mean marriage?"

"Yes."

We turned upon the wide street, studying the long building with pink-stained windows opposite the temple. White paint peeled from a pipe that leaked into a drain at the corner. No gardens. None surrounded the building aside the temple either.

"But he is hardly a prince," I whispered.

Pholly snorted. "Don't tell Phineus that." Her voice lowered. "Garran ordered them to cease their relationship while he tends to negotiations. But those negotiations were halted before the wards on the Unseelie realm were instated."

I failed to make sense of that. "But then there's no need. He's tormenting them, surely."

Pholly said, "And if we wish to call Cloud Castle home, we are beholden to Garran and his arrogant whims."

"You don't wish to live elsewhere?"

"Where else is there for nobility without wealth or other lodgings?" Before I could ask more, she said, "My father disappeared fifteen years ago. We don't know what happened. He left us to meet with Garran two weeks prior to the Spring Ball, and he never returned."

I looked at her, noting the hard set of her delicate jaw as she stared at the night sky. She wrapped herself tight in her gray cloak. "It's all very boring, really."

"It's disturbing, Pholly. Did Garran take you in after that?"

She nodded. "A week after our father left, Garran and his entourage arrived at our estate with wagons to transport any belongings we wished to keep. Five or so years ago, I found our father's will while searching for clean parchment in Garran's study. It'd been hidden within an old pad of parchment."

"He took your fortune," I surmised.

"The Ethermore's are our only living relatives, so in the event of our father's death, we were to become Garran's wards. In exchange for his protection and accommodation, he was entitled to access our fortune." She drew a breath and almost snarled, "Permitted to use it as he saw fit, and it just so happens that his coffers were nearly drained by a certain someone not long before our father's disappearance."

We both knew disappearance meant death.

I whispered, "The Seelie king had no coin to feed his armies." And at a time when the Unseelie attacks had been worsening.

So much so, Garran had eventually sought help from mortals in the years that followed. From my father.

"Barely enough to feed those in the castle," she said, uncaring for her volume. "Now, he holds the strings to our fates, and because of the crown he doesn't deserve to wear, there's no changing that."

Garran had taken Pholly and Phineus as his wards to fund the war against the Unseelie. But he'd stood no chance at defeating them. No Seelie army could defeat an army containing faeries who could shift into a myriad of monsters.

So he'd collected as much strength as possible by forging the alliance with my father, and forced their retreat to pen them behind wards. For even with the alliance, I understood now that the Unseelie would not be defeated.

Phineus's laughter echoed from a distant street, and Pholly's lips curved into a reluctant smile.

Sensing she was done talking, I said, "If there's something I can do, let me know." Although there likely wasn't much to be done about their stolen inheritance, I shrugged. "I don't mind a tough game."

Her smirk brought some shine back to her eyes. "Egg hunt first. Treason later."

Withholding a laugh, I turned to the hedges lining the temple. "Suppose we start with the gardens."

"Seems foolish when they'd be quite large." Pholly studied them, too. "Hiding one in there would be difficult unless it was half buried in the soil."

"Other than atop the surrounding buildings, there's nowhere else it could be." I surveyed the square again. "Vane personally saw to hiding the eggs near the castle, so I assume he did the same here." Needlessly, I said, "And he can fly." Though I kept from mentioning his fear of heights. Just another lie to endear me to him, most likely.

Pholly sighed. "Well, we certainly can't."

"Gardens it is."

We began our search at the farthest ends of the hedges, slowly making our way toward the temple entrance. Beetles scurried and thorns tried to prick, but although it seemed impossible, I looked for any unusual disturbance in the soil.

Night birds sang soft tunes from atop the temple, as if discussing what we might be doing.

Pholly reached the hedges closest to the steps first, near enough to hear me. "Thank you for freeing me." I brushed a spider from my finger, adding when she said nothing, "From the dungeon."

Her quick laugh was mischievous. "I didn't even know you were in there until Atakan told me when to let you out. I suspect the dramatics were to keep Garran from discovering your return before he left to meet with our military."

I must have looked as stunned as I felt because Pholly eventually straightened from the hedge. "My skies, are you about to vomit?"

An owl hooted as it soared overhead.

I swept a hand through my hair, knocking the hood of my cloak back. "I'm not sure."

"Well, do keep your distance. This cloak belonged to my mother."

A comfortable silence settled, interrupted only by the birds and the crunch of our boots shifting over the cobblestones. "What did Phineus mean before?" I asked. "About the war ending and mates?"

"You shouldn't listen to him. Hope is contagious and deadly."

"Simply curious."

"Curiosity is just as bad, you know."

I couldn't exactly refute that, but I said, "Humor me."

After a handful of moments, Pholly finally did. "It's become rare these past decades," she said. "As if the twins have decided that we aren't to be blessed with such a connection due to our violent antics."

"How can they abhor violence when they enjoy chaos?"

"The goddesses crave the balance they upset. Death must be met with life. Hatred must be matched by love. All things need balance, or all things will perish."

A thorn sliced my finger while I failed to snuff the urge to ask more. "Do you know what happens when a bond is formed?" Believing it would never concern me, I'd never much cared to learn.

Peering within one of two large potted shrubs on the steps, Pholly paused. "The intensity is the same for all. An attraction that can be fatal if ignored or a mate is rejected."

"Because it hurts?"

"No." She snorted. "Because too often someone is already with another, and that other is too often killed."

My eyes widened. "Oh."

She laughed, then swiped dirt from her hands as she leaned against the ribbed column of the temple. "For some, I've heard that when separated, they can share thoughts. But only if those thoughts pertain to one another—to the connection."

The voice I'd heard when the wards had fractured. Atakan's voice.

My stomach dropped.

As if she sensed it, or noticed the paling of my face, Pholly smirked. "Dreams, too," she whispered, her eyes dancing. "If one from the pairing is not nearby but they're awake and thinking of them, then the dreamer can glimpse what they're doing."

The dreams of Atakan prowling into the dungeon and down the hall in Cloud Castle struck through me like a spear.

"Supposedly, it's as if you're truly a part of them in those dreams," Pholly continued. "Privy to what they're feeling, seeing…" She shrugged. "Hearing."

An unsuitable warmth filled my chest as I recalled the silk scarf in Atakan's pocket during the dungeon dream. But cold dread replaced it when I thought of him glimpsing what I might have been doing when he'd been asleep.

For I'd thought of him many times when I shouldn't have. Even when Vane had kissed me.

"Over time, as the bond intensifies, these abilities can manifest. Magical, yes," Pholly said a touch wistfully. She then straightened with a forced sigh, and her tone turned mocking. "Also a massive invasion of privacy, if you ask me."

I laughed, but the sound was brief and roughened by lingering shock.

Attempting to hide how unsettled I was, I cleared my throat and continued searching the hedge. "I didn't think halflings could find a mate."

"I've only heard of two." She paused before saying, "It makes so much sense now. Atakan searched high and low for you for days, believing you'd somehow fled. He didn't stop until we learned the Unseelie king had you, then…" Her voice quietened. "He just disappeared."

I shouldn't have cared enough to ask, but I did. "For how long?"

Pholly shrugged. "He'd return every few days and leave almost instantly. It didn't cease until he brought you back."

Heart beating hard, I stared at the hedge, lost to wonderings of what Atakan might have been doing. Had he been searching for a way to retrieve me from Vane? Hunting remaining Unseelie warriors and sympathizers who'd been attacking the Seelie?

The cut on my finger left beads of blood on the shivering leaves. I sucked it clean, then stepped back when I realized the leaves weren't shaking from the breeze.

The beads of blood rose from the leaves.

They formed a small and translucent bubble. It bobbed before me, as if making sure it had my complete attention, then floated away.

I turned to Pholly to ask if she knew what was happening, only to find she'd moved inside the temple.

I looked back at the crimson orb drifting toward the building across the street from the temple. I followed, hoping it wasn't another faerie's magic luring me someplace to snatch me.

But it couldn't be. It was my own blood.

The bubble dropped to the moss-laden drain at the corner of the building.

And popped.

Bunching my cloak and skirts, I crouched and listened closely for any creatures within the drain. Then I lowered to my knees and wedged my fingers in the grate. I pulled, surprised to find it lifted with ease.

Perhaps because someone had recently opened it to hide a pytherion egg.

For seconds that might have made minutes, I just stared into the dark drain. Black scales blended among the muck and gloom. A shard of moonlight slicing over my shoulder illuminated the sharp crest of the egg.

A second later, the shine vanished as if the scales had absorbed the light to feed the babe within.

Softly, Pholly called my name.

Fear became a pattering beat in my chest and ears as I reached into the drain. Carefully, I touched the scales, and the cut on my finger seemed to warm when I pried the egg free of the puddle of muck.

It was heavier than I'd expected. Though I should have expected it, being that Vane had selected eggs that had already been incubated in pytherion nests.

We want to use them, yes, but not risk them.

The beastly babe was likely due to hatch soon.

Pholly's steps sounded right as I set the grate back over the drain. Holding the egg in my lap, I turned onto my ass and smiled up at her. "Look what I've found."

Her eyes widened as she reached me, then narrowed as they met mine. "What beneath the skies possessed you to even *think* to look in there?"

"It's the perfect spot, really."

Phineus and Elion returned, the former laughing before he whistled to us and said, "I think that king was feeding you false information to earn your trust, Princess."

Pholly was still staring at me—assessing me as if trying to piece a puzzle together.

Uncomfortable, and not because I was sitting on a dirty street, I swiped some wet grit from one of the scales and extended my hand for Pholly to help me up.

Phineus slowed when they neared us, and he spied the dark egg held tight to my chest.

"Brightest fucking skies," Elion breathed, fingers fluttering to his kiss-swollen mouth.

Phineus asked, "Where was it?" He took a step closer to touch the egg.

"Mildred found it in the drain." Peering around the empty square, Pholly said, "We should go." She took Elion's hands to vanish back to Cloud Castle.

As Phineus aligned my back to his chest to do the same, he whispered, "How did you know it was in there?"

I stared at the drain, unsure if I could form the words to describe it. As the night grew darker and a tunnel of wind sucked us from the city street, I decided on, "There are few other places it could've been."

Tension seared before the air around us settled and our bodies ceased swaying in the foyer.

A tension that shouldn't be in a slumbering castle.

Phineus cursed. "He's back." He released me before I could confirm he'd meant Atakan. Leaping onto the stairs, he then spun back. "Take it to your tower and stay there, all right?"

I nodded, following him up the stairs. He disappeared in two heartbeats, his hurried steps in three.

I should have pondered what had him so on edge, but the egg's weight and what I'd done to find it became all I could think about.

My arms protested, but I continued up the tower stairs to Atakan's rooms without pause. I wouldn't set it down until I found somewhere safe for it. Pholly had promised the eggs wouldn't be destroyed. Rather, they would be vanished into dense woodland near the warded borders of The Bonelands.

I sensed someone beyond the door and wondered where Phineus had run off to if Atakan was here in his chambers.

But it wasn't Atakan who'd returned.

The door closed behind me like an echoing drumbeat.

King Garran turned from the open doors of the balcony. The scarf stained with my innocence slithered between his fingers as he smiled warmly. "Welcome back to Ethermore, Mildred."

Twenty-Nine

MOONLIGHT GLINTED ON THE ARMOR COVERING THE Seelie king's chest, and illuminated a long streak of dried blood on his tunic sleeve.

What Pholly said earlier screamed through my mind like a howling wind. Atakan had kept me in the dungeon because of his father.

And I was now alone with him.

I hadn't needed to question why Atakan wished to keep me from him, and my assumptions were confirmed as that warm smile waned.

"I find it interesting…" Garran gazed down at the silk in his hands. "That no one thought to inform me of your return. I learned of it from a beast we captured at a gap in the wards."

I swallowed, hoping he didn't hear it or the uneven rhythm of my heartbeat.

He looked up. "You've done something rather unfortunate, Mildred, as I'm sure you're aware."

I remained quiet, though that part of me inwardly roared—the part that insisted on survival over all else. Flicking my eyes to the rumpled bedding, I purposely thought of Atakan.

King Garran released a weary exhale, then finally seemed to notice the egg I still clutched. His head cocked, arms falling to his sides. "Why are you holding a monstrous egg?"

I found my voice then. "It's a pytherion egg."

What's happening? Atakan's voice startled, although summoned intentionally.

But every inch of me was now absorbed in Garran's slow steps toward me.

Your father, was all I could manage.

The wood floor creaked as Garran stopped and rubbed at his beard. His hazel eyes remained trained on the egg. "Dare I ask what you're doing with it?" His gaze rose, aglow with accusation. "Do you intend to lure the fire-breathing beasts to this castle?"

Drivel on about the fucking eggs. Tell him how and why and who. Atakan's voice was sharp, like claws scraping over my mind. *Just don't stop talking. I'm coming.*

"No," I said to the king and lifted my chin. "Quite the opposite. We found it in the city this evening, and we'll be taking it elsewhere as soon as possible."

His heavy brows jumped. "We?"

I wouldn't name who'd accompanied me. I simply said, "While I was in The Bonelands, I heard their plans to bring an army of pytherions to this castle and the royal city."

"You just heard it, did you?" Another smile curled his lips, and they twitched before he sighed. "Did you also hear that the wards entrapping them have ruptured?"

I nodded.

He nodded, too. "You ruined them, Mildred. You broke a curse that cannot be broken, yet somehow..." He threw his hands out, the silk falling from his fingers to land in a gentle heap. "Here we are."

"It isn't my fault you believed your son to be heartless." I refused to step back, to cower, as Garran reached behind him, and I heard the whispering ring of an unsheathing blade. "And it isn't my fault he brought me back here."

At that, he tensed. As if I'd confirmed his suspicions, his features scrunched.

He inhaled deeply. "But it is your fault." Exhaling a quiet and rasped laugh, he shook his head. "Any hot-blooded male can recognize that scent." His chin rose, eyes sparking as he stared me down. "The scent of a freshly forged mating bond."

I gave that no response.

He belted out another laugh, gesturing to the soiled bed. "Not to mention the fucking reek of it all over this chamber."

Heat crept up my neck. For once, I didn't care. I let it—let it infuse my cheeks. Intentionally, I stared at his boots and stumbled on my words, "I didn't know he was my mate."

"But he knew you were his."

That made me look up at him, and I pretended I had no inkling of his intentions. Pretended to be the besotted half faerie who never thought she'd win the nonexistent heart of Prince Atakan. "Since when?"

King Garran waved his finger. "I see what you're doing, Princess, but I'm afraid even if you were more believable, your time here has now come to an end."

"Why?"

He sent me a flat look. "You know why, Mildred."

"But where shall I go?" I blinked furiously—as if to fight back panicked tears. "Home to Bernie?"

"Your body, yes, along with a sorrowful apology for failing to save you from the Unseelie king's invading forces."

He was serious. Of course he was.

As torrential fear tried to make me lose my perilous footing, I scrambled for something to say. Anything to say. "Killing me would be unwise, King. Not only will you then need to contend with my sister, who will see through your lies, but also your son."

"Atakan understands that your very presence is a threat we can no longer tolerate. Hence why he snatched you from The Bonelands before you could further damage those wards or make them fall entirely."

He was lying. We both knew that wasn't why Atakan had come for me. But as the dagger moved from behind his back to hang at his side, it didn't matter.

And there was nothing I could say that would matter.

Atakan said he was coming and to stall his father. But there wasn't anything left to do but set the egg down and find a way to defend myself. Garran was all of four steps away, so I said, "Give me a moment," and headed to the bed.

As soon as I set the egg on the bedding, the king was at my back. The tip of the blade poked through my cloak to nick at my side.

"We can make this painless, Princess."

I didn't want to do it, but I trusted the scales were as strong as any metal. Quickly, I heaved the egg over my shoulder. Garran grunted as it met his face.

Stumbling back, he clutched his nose.

Then he growled and moved faster than I could have anticipated, taking me down onto the bed.

The egg rolled toward the pillows, the wind knocked from me as Garran landed atop me with the blade poised at my jugular. Blood dripped from his nostril to my cheek as he grinned. "Painful it is."

A different growl came from the balcony. But I couldn't spare a glance at the beast who'd alighted upon it.

Garran did, though, and it cost him.

I shoved the blade from my throat before I lifted my knee to his groin. He grunted but barely moved. Not until Meadow snarled in warning as she entered the prince's rooms.

He rose then, dagger in hand. It clattered to the floor when the felynx leaped at him.

I screamed, the sound covering Garran's howl of pain.

She might have been strong, but she was not yet fully grown, which showed as Garran tossed her off his arm.

Meadow slipped over the wood floor. Blood dripped from her maw. Garran's.

It soaked the sleeve of his tunic. He kept his eyes on the felynx as he reclaimed his dagger. She bared her teeth, hunching to strike again.

I ran.

The king whirled before I reached him and grabbed me by the throat. I kicked and clawed at his wrists, but it was futile. He walked me backward, the blade raised at Meadow when she growled.

The king threw me down onto the bed once more.

As the dagger returned to my throat, his other hand twisted behind him. Meadow released a rasped mewl, her advance halted.

The king's eyes stayed fastened to me. His jaw tightened, and the hand holding the dagger trembled slightly. Energy gathered like wind, bursting in a flare of warmth when my felynx slumped to the floor.

Tears welled. He'd used his air magic on her lungs.

Satisfied, the king gave his entire attention to me. "Now, be a good little halfling, and I promise I won't kill your pet after I finish with you."

I sneered, "Your promises don't mean—"

"Hush." I feared even swallowing as he pressed the blade into my skin. "This has already taken far longer than—"

The door crashed open.

Atakan's scent was a cloying cloud providing instant relief, and his venomous tone a sweet song. "Unless you wish to wear your entrails as a crown when I chain you in iron and bury you alive, remove yourself from my bed and my mate."

But Garran didn't move. His eyes stuck to mine. The blade shook at my neck.

He wasn't going to back down. I knew it within my quaking bones. He was a king. A king willing to do whatever it took to hold on to victory.

A king enraged.

He roared, forced away from me by the armor covering his torso, and was tossed to the floor. He rose onto an elbow, glaring at his son and seething between clenched teeth, "You know what needs to be done. If you won't let me, you must handle this problem yourself."

I sat up, chest heaving.

Atakan, dressed head to toe in tight black, didn't remove his gaze from the king. "I'm well aware of what we need." He jerked his head to the open door. "A word first, Father." Not a request but a cold command.

He turned on his heel, apparently confident the king wouldn't attempt to kill me while his back was turned.

My hand came away dotted with blood when I touched my neck. Garran had barely broken the skin.

The Seelie king finally tore his furious gaze from me and peeled himself off the floor, lacking the graceful fluidity of his son. He whispered tauntingly, "If you wish to give us something new to hunt, now is the time to flee, Princess."

The door slammed behind him.

I hurried to Meadow, brushing my hand over her fluffy cheek. She was breathing. Shallow, but breathing.

"You've gone too far." Garran's voice floated through and beneath the door.

So I sat against it, listening as I watched Meadow and determined they stood on the stairs to Atakan's rooms.

"Why would you accept a bond with the creature who can undo everything we've worked so hard to achieve? Are you as fucking mad as they all say?"

"Far worse, I'm afraid," Atakan drawled. "I intend to marry her." Silence stunned like a blade slowly arcing through the air. "Tomorrow."

My heart stopped.

Garran laughed—an avalanche of humorless disbelief. "What beneath the skies are you playing at?"

If Atakan answered, I failed to hear it.

"Why?" Garran seethed so quietly that I almost missed it. Then each word became louder, growled in growing rage. "Why would you marry a halfling? A creature you've incessantly claimed to loathe?"

Atakan's tone remained aloof. "Call it insurance for the kingdom. Bloodshed will drown these lands any day now, and we need to ensure our longevity."

Garran shouted, "Since *when* do you care about this fucking kingdom?"

"Since I'm the new king."

Not a moment after those chilling words, a thud echoed up the stairs.

I barely breathed in the eerie silence that followed, staring wide-eyed at a pair of Atakan's suede boots.

He couldn't have, surely. But I knew before I rose on trembling legs and opened the door.

When I peered over the railing, I knew I would find Garran sprawled beneath the spiraling wooden stairs.

What I didn't expect was the dark hole in his armored chest.

Atakan didn't move from where he leaned against the railing a few steps below me. Staring at his hand, he murmured with a calm that shouldn't exist. "Go and bathe, dread."

But I couldn't remove my eyes from his crimson hand—from the heart he held within it. Couldn't keep from wondering how in the darkest skies he'd pried it from a chest, and one covered in armor.

"Mildred," he said too softly.

And too close.

The use of my name delivered my eyes to his. There was nothing there. No remorse. No fear. Nothing. Just bronze burning in the dim of the tower's innards.

On the step beneath me, our noses nearly perfectly aligned, he observed me with a faraway look in those ever-changing eyes. They turned a hypnotic green as he ran his finger over the organ in his hand and lifted it to my mouth.

I should have, yet I didn't recoil as he pressed that bloodstained finger to my lips. "Let this be our little secret."

My eyes closed. My heart slowed.

His finger slid over my mouth, replaced by his whispering lips. "He'll never touch you now." He kissed me, then licked Garran's blood from my lips. "So go bathe while I tend to this unfortunate mess."

Even if I had the desire to argue with him, I knew it wasn't the time. I opened my eyes and stared into his, then nodded and slipped soundlessly back into his rooms.

Nearly tripping on the way to the bathing room, I gripped the bedpost. I blinked over at Meadow, then at the bed where I'd almost died three times.

Twice from a blade and once from an hours-long mating frenzy.

Immersed in the warming water, I withheld a crazed laugh when I thought of the latter. The extremes that had befallen me within a matter of hours. I laughed before I could cry. I laughed until the sound grew hoarse, then I turned off the faucet with my toes.

I was stirred awake by hands slipping beneath my water-wrinkled body. Instinctively, I clung to Atakan's neck.

"I said bathe, not sleep," he muttered.

"Tired," I mumbled, and tucked my nose into his neck.

"Obviously."

I inhaled him deep into my lungs and felt something within both awaken and settle.

He set me upon the towel he'd lain over the bed. "I never gave you your own," he whispered, patting me dry with another. "I couldn't, of course, and I also wanted you to smell like me."

Those words roused me.

The memory of Garran returned with his scent that had yet to fade from his son's bedchamber. What he'd tried to do. That he'd intended to kill me. And what Atakan had done.

He'd murdered his own father. The Seelie king was dead.

Atakan was now the uncrowned king of Ethermore.

I gazed up at him, his features still blurry, as I rasped, "How did you do that?"

"By refusing to put another towel in the bathing room," he said dryly. Pieces of blond hair fell over his brow as he took his time rubbing water from my stomach and breasts.

"Not that." I placed my hand over his at my chest, then pushed my elbow beneath me to rise. "Your father."

We were so close, I could feel the warmth of his breath on my lips. I could lean forward and kiss him. Bite him.

Vow to punish him forevermore for bonding me to him without my permission.

But loathing him for the mating bond was pointless when I'd asked him to marry me to fix the alliance between our kingdoms—and when I remembered the strange things he'd done. Such as locking me in the dungeon to keep word of my return from reaching his father.

As if waiting for my vitriol, his lips wriggled.

I scowled.

He whispered against my mouth, "I think you're far more interesting when you talk in your sleep." Then he gently pushed my shoulder.

I fell back onto the bed, but snatched his wrist before he could leave. "Liar."

He glared at my hand, then at my face.

"You killed him, Atakan."

Exasperated, he swiped his other hand through his hair. "And?"

Those strands stayed right where he'd put them, and I observed the shadows gathering beneath his luminescent eyes. "We both know it wasn't to save me."

He stared down at me, expressionless yet again.

He remained that way, eventually saying, "I assume you know why the Unseelie began to attack us before we formed the alliance with your father."

"Yes."

Atakan waited.

I frowned, but said, "Queen Kalista fled from the Unseelie king and fell in love with your father." I stroked his wrist. "Who claimed he'd rather see her dead than suffer a marriage of torture. So when she tried to return to her homeland to stop her husband's violent hunts for her, Garran killed her."

"Somewhat true." He peered down at my roaming finger. "Kalista's husband indeed hunted and caused ruin for years, not knowing the creature providing his wife refuge was my father."

"How did he never discover she was in this castle?" He knew just as well as I did that secrets danced through castle halls.

"She was tucked away in a cottage deep within the woods surrounding this castle. My father's love for a queen that was not his to keep made him a blight on this realm." His laugh was brief and absent of humor. "A curse worse than any other."

"Because he killed her?"

"Because he should have. Instead, he eventually sparked the rumor of Kalista's death and gave her the means to flee." He stared at the ceiling, his whispered words riddled with scorn. "Not only from her Unseelie husband, who vowed to ravage these lands until he drew his last breath, but also from this continent."

Stunned, I watched his throat bob and those long lashes flutter toward his sharp cheeks. The drained coffers Pholly had mentioned when she'd told me how she and Phineus had ended up at Cloud Castle…

Breathless, I said, "Queen Kalista lives?"

"Yes, though only the goddesses know where." Atakan rose from the bed. "In return for her freedom, she had to agree to leave me behind." As he vanished from the chamber, he said, "My mother left and never once looked back."

Thirty

"The staff are positively flummoxed," Elion said the following morning.

It was far too soon to be awake after getting so little sleep. But the steward had entered after knocking once, declaring there was no time to waste and that he expected me fed and ready to be wed as soon as he returned with his supplies.

I was getting married. Not to a prince. To a king.

Our little secret.

How long Atakan intended to keep a secret that was anything but little was beyond me. I'd been unable to escape the memory of his father's heart in his hand, and though I itched to pepper him with questions, I hadn't seen him since he'd vanished from his chambers last night.

Since he'd told me that Queen Kalista was his mother.

"Why?" I asked Elion, my fingers continuously rubbing over the silk ties of my robe.

The steward pinned another tiny braid into the nest encircling my head, then walked in front of me to inspect his work. "Because…" He laughed and made a face that said it should be obvious. "It's happening. No one believed Atakan the heartless would actually marry you."

Few things were obvious in the faerie realms, but I kept my mouth shut.

Elion dabbed a finger into a pot of pink powder selected from the tray of supplies on Atakan's nightstand.

He then crouched before me to brush it over the crest of my cheek. "And the bond," he whispered, dusting my other cheek. "Rumors gather force like a storm since Syndrid collected the soiled bedding this morning."

The ruby-haired faerie who'd arrived with breakfast after Elion had woken me. When I'd returned from the bathing room, she was gone. The bedding too, and in the doorway of the dressing chamber, a sleeveless gown had been hung. An array of dried flowers decorated the lilac gossamer overlaying the ivory silk skirts.

I refrained from looking at the gown or the bare mattress. The small dark-red stains that had seeped through the sheet.

"No one thought he'd do *that*." Elion scoffed. "Honestly, I've always known he isn't as heartless as he seems, but I still never thought he'd accept a mate."

Quietly, I confessed, "I didn't know."

Elion went back to the tray. "Then he has indeed kept all trace of being fated to you well-hidden."

It didn't take much thought to understand why Atakan had done that. "Because I'm a halfling, and he loathes me."

A tiny brush and another pot in hand, he returned. "Does he, though?"

I was rescued from answering when he combed kohl onto my lashes and asked me to open and close my eyes.

He stepped back, surveying me and smiling. "Beautiful."

I returned his smile, but it fell when he held up a golden-framed oval mirror. A faint and glittering pink tinged my cheeks. Half of my yellow hair had been piled into a braided crown atop my head. My green eyes were brightened by the dark weight of my lashes.

And you have the darkest green eyes I've ever seen, but I don't call you seaweed.

As if summoned by the memory, Meadow scratched at the balcony doors. Elion let her in, then collected his tray and bowed. "I'll have your slippers waiting for you beneath the stairs, Princess."

I thanked him, absently stroking the felynx's ears.

Mercifully just fine, she'd let herself out with the arrival of breakfast. I opened the balcony doors so that she wasn't trapped, allowing the crisp spring breeze to kiss my cheeks and wash away unwanted thoughts of Vane.

Yet as I struggled into the ivory and lilac gown, I couldn't resist wondering where he was and what he was doing. If he was furious—with me or just with my absence—and how long we had until that fury darkened our skies.

Guilt poked, irritating because I hadn't done anything to warrant the feeling. Nothing except demand that the prince marry me to keep our kingdoms united. I refused to acknowledge the part of me that had done it from a place of hurt—from a place hungering for vengeance.

There was no room for guilt in games of life and death.

The gown was almost too ginormous for the tower stairs. I did my best to lift and gather the skirts, but the heavy mixture of silk and shimmering gossamer still brushed against the railings and snuck beneath my feet.

At the bottom, I stepped into the lilac slippers and dropped the skirts. I lifted my long hair to fall over the matching lilac bodice strangling my chest, then drew in a breath and opened the door.

The halls beyond were quiet and coated in the glow of midmorning. No clouds drifted through a sky so blue, it resembled the soft purple of my gown.

Only a handful of people waited in the throne room.

Pholly and Phineus stood with Cordenya among a smattering of faeries who carried the air and telltale signs of wealth. Nobility, maybe, here to bear witness. I supposed there hadn't been enough time for every influential faerie to attend.

I also supposed that had been intentional.

Entering through the doors farthest from the throne, I stopped and inspected the cavernous space. Nervous energy muddied my thoughts, rendering me unsure what to do. Where to tread next.

A mural of rainbow-forming butterflies dancing amid clouds in an endlessly blue sky spanned the ceiling. All four of the chandeliers were aglow. Candles flickered within crystal spheres floating upon the curving, branch-reminiscent brass.

As if he was the sun missing from the painted sky above, warmth tapped along my skin, and his energy drew my eyes.

Atakan stood before the throne in a soft gray dress coat with a high collar that tried to touch his hewn jaw.

His back was turned to the people in the room, black-booted feet braced apart and his hands clasped behind him. He appeared to be gazing through the row of arched windows lining the far end of the throne room, lost in thought.

But I knew he wasn't lost at all.

The calm violence of last evening, the way he'd casually lured his own father from his rooms to his death, made me wonder if it had been thoroughly thought out.

And if Atakan Ethermore did anything that wasn't premeditated.

He'd *wanted* his father dead. That much he'd admitted. He'd even told me why. Yet I'd known him long enough to know there was more.

As much as I wished I was as cunning as he, this marriage wouldn't be happening if he didn't also want it.

A priestess with hair that was half-silver, the other half dark brown, walked toward the prince. Her lacy sky-blue robes draped from her thin shoulders and arms, and trailed behind her over the worn floor.

Eyes of deep orange found me as she stood beside Atakan. Her dark-red lips parted in a slight smile.

Atakan turned then, speaking low to the faerie priestess.

Behind them, upon the seat of the throne, perched two black goblets, the rims inlaid with sapphires and rubies. As I waded across the room, I saw the slim knife glinting between them.

I'd known faerie customs were far more dramatic than what I'd grown up with in the mortal realm. I still looked from that knife to Atakan with a brow raised.

Only to find him glowering at me.

Not me, I realized as he and the priestess took their places before the throne and I stood before him, but my gown.

Quiet settled over the room.

The priestess began to chant, and Atakan's hands clenched with his jaw. His eyes slowly rose over my body, and when they collided with mine, that glower turned blistering.

Our blood was drawn from the lifelines in our palms, collected by those awaiting goblets. Atakan was to recite the oath first.

He dipped his finger into his goblet, then painted my lips in his blood. "We've done this already," he said, teeth flashing.

The priestess, hands pressed together beneath her pointed chin, cleared her throat. "Please say the oath, Your Highness."

But Atakan gathered more blood from his goblet first. Delight brightened his eyes as he took his time decorating my lips. "Mothers above, witness and bless my love, as I bind myself to thee."

The word love sucked the air from my lungs and threatened to send heat climbing up my neck.

I fought it, and smiled to feign nonchalance, as I dipped my finger into the goblet of my blood and painted his lips. "Mothers above, witness and bless my love, as I bind myself to thee."

"Seal it," the priestess instructed.

Against my mouth, Atakan whispered, "You have no right making that monstrosity of a dress look good."

"Oh." I kissed him, then whispered, "Did you intend to embarrass me by making me wear this beautiful gown?" I kissed him again. "I'm afraid you've failed."

A growl rumbled from his chest. But he didn't let it pass his blood-stained lips.

As we stepped back for the priestess to weave between us with her cloying pink smoke, I held his furious gaze. I relished the tic of his jaw.

And I smiled.

His eyes narrowed.

We were then forced together, his arms tight at my waist and mine at his neck, as she danced around us to a round of raucous applause from our few guests.

I pushed away first, but not without whispering, "I might need assistance to remove this monstrosity."

His hands squeezed my waist, mouth skimming my temple. "I might be able to assist you."

I battled another smile as Phineus stepped between us, clapping and grinning. "Pholly owes me two gold coins."

The priestess scowled at Phineus, and I noted his dress shirt was a similar shade of blue to a certain steward's hair before a familiar scent stiffened my spine.

I whirled, my skirts swooshing, and beamed. "Royce."

My sister's husband bowed, although he was now a king, and smoothed the brown lapels of his dress coat as he straightened. He offered his arm.

I took it, and we walked along the wall adorned with tapestries of the Ethermore royal crest to the opposite end of the room for privacy.

"The prince notified us of your nuptials, and that he'd send for someone to bear witness. Of course, your sister is in no state to be vanished by a faerie, so I thought I'd provide her some relief and come myself." He patted my hand. "I must admit, I too am relieved to see you."

I stopped us near the doors. "How is she?"

His smile comforted. "Good, though her feet are forever swollen, and she hates not wearing shoes."

I laughed, taking his hands and squeezing them. "How long now?"

"A few weeks, they say." He swallowed, peering over my shoulder. When he looked back at me, his brown eyes hardened. "The prince informed us about the assassination."

Between that, the looming war, and this wedding, Atakan's disappearances were beginning to make more sense. Not to mention getting rid of his father's corpse and any evidence.

Though Royce certainly wasn't referring to Garran's demise, I still hesitated before nodding. "I overheard the truth during my time in The Bonelands. Ethermore indeed had no part in it."

"We suspected as much, which is why I'm witnessing this marriage rather than demanding your immediate return to Nephryn," he whispered, then exhaled heavily. "Their deaths were too much of a statement, much too…" He didn't say more, and he didn't need to.

He'd seen it, then.

"We did demand your safe return, by the way," he said, and my heart swelled. "Numerous times. Your father intended to collect you himself."

Sorrow cinched tight around my throat, rasping my words. But if I missed my father, even after all he'd planned for me, then poor Bernie… "How is she?" I asked again. "Really?"

Royce swallowed. His gaze drifted to the brown laces of his pointed dress shoes. "She rises with purpose to see to what must be done, but I'm afraid the evenings are spent far differently." My concern must have shown, for he smiled sadly. "She grieves, Mildred, and as she should. She grieves her parents and also the life she lost. But she was raised for this moment." He nodded, as if to reassure himself, too. "She's managing."

There were so many things I wanted to ask.

But the look Royce gave me reminded me that now was not the time. He sighed, then opened his arms. I stepped into them, tears pressing at my eyes.

A thin piece of parchment was slipped between my fingers.

"Come home whenever you like," he whispered in my ear. "We're willing to deal with any repercussions. If no one else will, then the guard with no hair and violet eyes will vanish you."

Somehow, it seemed Bernie had a faerie spy under her employ. Perhaps the male I didn't dare seek out had worked for my father. I didn't know. But I was grateful when Phineus arrived to take Royce back to Nephryn, and I unfolded the parchment to find Bernie's perfect handwriting.

Butter, you are loved.

Closing my eyes, I bit my lip so hard it bled as my shoulders quaked. When I opened them and brushed an errant tear from my cheek, I found Atakan frowning at me from across the room.

He stood alone against the side wall. He had a perfect view of everyone in the throne room, yet he stared at me for an unnecessarily long time.

So long, I took a step toward him.

Then Pholly hooked her arm through mine and dragged me toward the arched windows beyond the throne.

She released me and pointed at two stools that hadn't been there before we'd been married. "Stand completely still or sit."

Though skintight, her black pearl-lined gown folded easily with her as she bent before the banquet table lining the wall between the entrances.

A giant piece of parchment in hand, she stood.

I balked. "We have no time for portraits." I glanced around, then hissed, "We need to find the eggs." It wasn't merely an excuse.

Elion had informed me that they intended to look for those near the castle right after the ceremony. He hadn't told me I'd needed to accompany them. But even without the odd trick that'd already led me to one, I would want to.

"You won't do this again, should you be so lucky." Taking a seat upon the wood floor, Pholly glared at the throne.

At Atakan, who now leaned against the arm made of thinly twined branches.

"Please," she drawled. "Take all fucking morning."

I thought he'd ignore her—ignore me too—now that we'd said our oaths and it was done.

I was his wife, and he was my husband.

The weight of that sagged within me when he straightened and stalked toward us. "You have thirty minutes," he told his cousin, then seized my hand.

I was tugged in front of him. His hand splayed across my stomach and the other curled over my shoulder.

An unmistakable display of possession.

Pholly's gaze widened comically. Then she blinked and nodded, fumbling with her charcoal. "Right, very uh…" Her tiny nose crinkled. "That will do."

I should have shoved his hands away and sweetened the pose, but when his fingers spread over my stomach, I leaned back into him instead. He hummed in approval, lips stirring my hair, and opened and closed those fingers.

"Where's the egg?" I whispered. It hadn't been on his bed when I'd woken, which led me to believe he'd returned before then and taken it.

"Safe," was all he said. His hand at my shoulder became

firmer—heavier—when I shifted. He tsked. "You were told to stay still, *wife*."

I swallowed, trying to determine whether this was the worst kind of torment he'd handed me thus far as that hand at my stomach dipped lower. As those fingers continuously opened and closed.

And as I became so aroused, I nearly wept in relief when Pholly had formed an outline of us that would certainly be enough for her to complete later.

But before I could leave, a male came forward from the small crowd, dripping in gold with blue tassels hanging from his waistcoat.

Atakan's sigh warmed my ear. "Lord Nibbledon." An introduction for me more than it was a greeting to the male.

The lord bowed, pushing long strands of his fuzzy golden hair back as he straightened. "Congratulations, Prince." His dark brown gaze slid to me, his mouth curling slyly. "Princess."

I smiled thinly, almost grateful for Atakan's possessive hold as the lord took his time to remove his knowing eyes from me. Instinctively, I knew this was a male to avoid—one with the ego of a king.

To Atakan, he said, "Where might your father be?" The lord made an unnecessary show of peering around the throne room. "I've yet to see our dear king at all."

I tensed but kept my features neutral, though he wasn't looking at me.

Feeling it, Atakan squeezed my shoulder. Apathy oozed from his tone, as if each word required a horrid amount of effort. "He has more important matters to tend to, as I'm sure you are abundantly aware."

"Of course," Nibbledon said. He shifted, and I thought perhaps he'd take the hint and leave. But he tapped his chin and huffed a brief laugh. "Though I just can't help but find it a bit strange. The king would never miss such a history-making milestone."

But I knew exactly what the lord really meant. As did my new husband. That Garran wouldn't have gone through with marrying his son to a half-mortal.

"What I find a bit strange is your interest," Atakan said crisply. "When it is a privilege for you to witness such a history-making milestone."

The lord's bushy brows nearly met above his long nose. "I am aware of the incredible honor, my prince, I'm merely—"

"Then kindly breathe elsewhere or cease doing so."

I trapped a shocked laugh behind tight teeth and averted my gaze when fury reddened the lord's face. But beneath his apricot and whiskey-like scent, a sour aroma wafted.

Fear.

I didn't need to look to know Atakan was delivering the lord a withering glare. I felt his impatience in the curling of his fingers at my stomach, and in the flaring of his own scent.

Finally, the lord left.

Pholly smirked at her parchment. It made me wonder if she knew what Atakan had done, or if she was just amused by the awkward exchange.

As some less audacious guests dared to offer quick congratulations, I then wondered if I was the only one who knew what had befallen Garran. And if those who might assume correctly were simply too afraid or indifferent to say something.

"Still so tense," Atakan murmured quiet enough that only I would hear. "Are you not pleased, dread?"

"Are you?"

He took his time responding, as if knowing I longed to leave the watchful eyes in the room, and that I longed to hear what he'd say. "Pleased doesn't begin to describe it." He placed his mouth over the crest of my cheek. "Victorious is what I feel."

The crooned words struck like a dull blade.

His low chuckle stalked as I hurried through the doors and haunted long after I'd locked myself in his chambers.

THIRTY-ONE

My little trick with the blood was far less impressive when facing an area so vast, I'd had no idea where to start.

So as Pholly and I trudged through the brush, I continuously cut my palms with my fingernails. We'd both changed out of our gowns. In knee-high boots, fitted brown tunics and pants, we searched the western woods while Phineus and Elion searched the east.

We'd surmised the eggs would be as close to the castle as Vane could have managed without detection, but after hours of searching, I'd been led to only one.

Pholly's steps crunched in the distance behind me. As the blood bubble bobbed toward the crystal-cobwebs lacing an overgrown path ahead, I tensed, waiting for her to notice.

Since we'd begun the search, I'd pondered how I might explain something I couldn't.

But it wasn't Pholly who spoke when I retrieved the egg.

"Must you disappoint me on my wedding day?" Atakan's voice froze my feet. "You managed to remove your gown without any help at all."

"You were too busy gloating over your perceived victory."

"Perceived," he repeated, as if tasting the word and deciding he didn't like it.

There was no sign of Pholly anywhere, and when I turned to Atakan, who leaned against the trunk of a tree, he explained, "She's gone to find Phineus." He flicked the apple in his hand toward the foliage surrounding us. "Who has mysteriously disappeared."

I rolled my eyes. "He doesn't wish to be found."

"He always has been mostly useless," he said, yet he didn't seem bothered.

I snorted, but then spied what stood behind his boots.

He too had changed out of his wedding attire. He now wore a thin cream tunic that gaped at his forearms and neck. It was half tucked into his deep brown britches. Which matched his clunky military boots, and behind them…

An egg.

I hurried to him. "Where did you find it?"

"I suspect this one was hidden in a hurry, or the unseemly king is merely lazy." He tapped it with the side of his boot, and I nearly winced. "Found it perched against a boulder just beyond the tree line." He bit into his apple.

The crunch drew my eyes to his mouth. "The guards never noticed it?"

"Perhaps they thought it was a rock." He chewed, staring down at the burnished scales. "It does sort of resemble one, don't you think?"

I tilted my head, unsure I agreed but unwilling to waste more time. Daylight was fading. I set the egg I'd found upon the ground next to his, and gave the gray-and-black scales a gentle pat.

Atakan huffed.

"What?"

He shook his head, then tossed his apple over his shoulder. It crashed into the brush downhill. "You said there are more, so let's get on with it." I made to collect the eggs, but he said, "Leave them. They'll only slow us down."

I didn't argue, though I wished to—merely to poke at him.

He walked ahead, and I gave up on trying to take any type of lead. As well as the thought of putting distance between us. He'd already scented it. "You've been bleeding."

I wasn't sure I should speak of it. I wasn't sure why I shouldn't either.

"I can hear the cogs turning in your mind, dread."

I glared at his broad back, and ignored the odd feeling in my chest when he held back a sharp branch. I took it, releasing it as I followed him down a damp and rocky ridge. "The egg in the city," I started, then squeaked as I slipped.

He turned, stopping my descent with his hands on my hips. Green flickered in his eyes. "Careful," he taunted, that gaze falling to my breasts, then lower to my pants. "Perhaps you should walk ahead."

"So that you can stare at my ass?"

Atakan grinned.

But I gave him what he wanted, mostly to keep from rising onto my toes to kiss that smile from his sinisterly handsome face.

"You found the egg with your blood," he said a tense minute later. "I saw it."

Halting next to a giant oak, I turned to him. "And how can you be so sure that's what you saw?"

"You have Unseelie blood, and pytherions are native to The Bonelands." He lifted a shoulder, the breeze swaying strands of his near-white hair across his forehead. "Blood binds all."

I didn't know that I agreed, but I continued walking until the blood on my hand stirred again.

"Go on," Atakan dared, jerking his head.

He stood fascinatingly still as we watched the bubble float toward a ravine. We followed it across a shallow creek. The trees lining it were thin enough that I could see the rear gardens of Cloud Castle in the distance.

The location close enough to draw Vane's pytherion army over the grounds.

Relief never came. A slow-moving sludge filled my stomach as I stared at the mottled gray egg. "What if we don't find them all in time?" I gnawed at my lip. "Maybe we should've enlisted help from—"

"You seem awfully worried for a creature who cared little for this castle and its occupants a few moons ago." Atakan stepped beside me.

"And you seem hardly worried at all."

He said nothing.

Fear spiked my irritation further when I recalled the size of Surella. The foot that'd threatened to destroy the steel her claws had curled over. "I saw them, Atakan."

"The pytherions," he said.

"Yes."

"Our armies are ready."

"You don't understand. They're so big, so hostile…" Memories swirled. "Incredible but deadly. We truly don't stand a chance."

The prince—secret king now—remained silent, and I turned to discover his lips wriggling.

"You think certain death is amusing?" But then I searched those cruelly beautiful features and scoffed. "You certainly would." With vivid clarity, I remembered what he'd done to his own father.

"But of course." As if he knew exactly where my thoughts had gone, all traces of humor left his face. His eyes flared a burning bronze. "Atakan the heartless." Noting the way my mouth slackened, he smirked, reaching for me. "You think I don't know what everyone calls me?" He skimmed his knuckles over my cheek. "Dread, I practically begged them to."

The gentle touch frightened more than the memories of fire-breathing beasts. So I turned back to the egg.

"You're the only one to never ask me about it, you know," he said.

Crouching, I carefully brushed some leaves from the egg. "Only what?"

"Lover, I suppose."

The simple mention of his past lovers rankled. I blamed the bond. Blamed the heat of his gaze searing into my back as I pretended to fuss with the egg. "I'm not your lover."

"Fated foe, then."

At that, I looked up to find him grinning wolfishly.

I glared.

His grin only became more devastating until he said, "You're right. You're not my lover. You're now my wife, yet that doesn't seem quite enough either." I nearly swayed when I rose, and he went on. "What do you call the only creature you want to watch and touch endlessly?"

I couldn't meet his gaze. "I wouldn't know," I lied and braced for what I knew he'd say next.

It still raked claws over my chest. "A mate?"

Unsure why he was goading me this way, and even more unsure of what to make of it, my frayed nerves got the better of me. "Are we going to talk about how you tricked me, then?"

"Oh, you mean how you knew exactly what was happening but went along with it anyway?"

That sent my gaze straight to his, and I scowled.

But he was right. It was something else that made it impossible to accept I'd willingly thrown myself into a trap I hadn't wanted to avoid. Belated self-preservation, maybe. I didn't know.

His eyes shone, green and bronze and knowing, and that devious mouth curled.

Forcing a smirk of my own, I retaliated with, "Perhaps once we've found the rest of these eggs, I'll consider indulging such fabrications."

He didn't try to refute it. We both knew I was the one lying. Instead, he dragged his thumb over his lower lip, and his eyes over my tightly clothed body. "Is that a promise?"

I said nothing, knowing that if I did, I'd betray myself more than I already had, or I'd surrender to the desire to climb him like a tree in these woods.

He sighed, then said, "Fine. Make your way to the eastern woods." He stared through the trees to the mountains on the other side of the castle. "I'll inform the others that they've been no help at all and they may as well head inside." He added curtly, "If they haven't already."

He vanished, and I looked at the egg, deciding to take it to the two we'd found to collect later.

No guards were patrolling.

Atakan had likely sent them elsewhere, I surmised, unable to keep from staring at the garden shed while crossing the grounds.

By the time he found me, twilight had tentatively darkened the forest floor. During his absence, I'd been led to one egg, and it waited in a ditch by the tree line.

"Pholly found one," Atakan said by way of greeting. He tossed it from hand to hand as if it weren't twice the size of his pretty head and covered in scales with edges sharper than his cheeks. Noting my expression, he looked from me to the egg. "This one is dead."

My eyes widened.

"That's what they get for playing war games with their precious army's young." He set the egg on the ground, explaining, "I sensed no heartbeat."

I hurried to it, lowering to my knees and carefully pressing my ear to the scales. "You're right."

"What do I gain from lying?"

"Maybe you can prove this is pointless and that I'm stupid if they're all dead."

"The beasts won't care. If anything, sensing a dead babe will only enrage them more." He eyed me for a moment, curiously. "Why would I want my own castle to burn?"

"*Your* castle?"

His smile was maddening. "That's what I said, and that's what it is."

"And when do you plan on telling your loyal court what you've done?"

"That I saved my mate?" He lifted his hand when I glared, amending, "Apologies, my *wife*, from being murdered?" He turned on his heel. "I'll go spread the good word right now if it will appease your conscience."

I seized the back of his tunic.

He whirled and hauled me against him with a hand at my lower back. As it crept to the base of my neck, he walked me deeper into the trees. "You might not like what I did," he said, voice distractingly deep. "But it had to be done."

When I failed to answer, he stopped walking and took my chin.

"Quite the contrary," I said with sweet venom and hurled the truth at him. "What I don't like is how much I like it."

His head tilted. He studied me, determining whether I'd spoken true.

Then his laughter transformed his ethereal beauty into something so inviting that I itched to touch his face. Instead, I just stared, helpless and enraptured.

Atakan smiled down at me. "I'll keep your secret, dread." His eyes glinted, then narrowed. "On one condition."

"Do I even want to know what that might be?" I asked, enticed by the challenge in his husked voice. I didn't care if he spilled my secret.

His hooding eyes said he knew it. "Oh, you'll be glad to know."

"Then do cease making me perish from anticipation."

Humor faded from his eyes, and if I wasn't mistaken, a tinge of vulnerability ripened his tone. "You must put your mouth on mine and kiss me until I tell you to stop."

My foolish heart skipped. Still, I taunted, "But what if you never do?"

"Trust me." He dropped his forehead to mine. "I never fucking will."

Relieved and desperate, I kissed him. Wanting to feel the softness of his lips, needing to taste his poison, I seized his face and lavished his mouth in adoration he certainly didn't deserve.

But I didn't care. I deserved it.

I deserved to take what I wanted, and I more than wanted him. I needed him in ways that would doom me, but when he looked at me, touched me, I welcomed my fate.

For years, Atakan had made sure the only thing I cared about was him. Since the moment I'd met him, he'd poked holes into my mind, recolored my heart, and snatched my soul.

He'd made sure the only thing I craved was the one thing I shouldn't want.

I wrapped my legs around his waist when he picked me up. He navigated the dark forest with ease while I devoured his mouth with fervor that made him groan.

My legs refused to uncoil from his waist as he laid me down upon a pile of cool leaves. He took his mouth from mine to kiss my neck, teeth grazing as he ground his erection against my core.

My head tilted back. My body heated.

"I can smell you so much easier," he said, hoarse and licking my fluttering pulse. "Never again will you be able to hide how much you truly loathe me."

"You really do gloat too much."

"Tell me I'm lying, then." He moved away to remove my boots. "Or better yet…" He tore my pants from my legs. "Show me."

They opened instantly, cool air brushing over my thighs.

But he didn't look. No, he touched the scars on my ankle, given to me by the two-headed serpent. Almost reverently, he stroked them. "When you touch them, do you think of me?"

The velvet question should have been a statement. He knew I did. Even so, I said, "I forget they're there at all."

"Liar." His gaze moved to my core. "Open that lovely cunt for me." Daringly, he ordered, "Show me the truth."

Intentionally, I hesitated—just to earn that delicious look of disapproval when his eyes swept up my body to mine. I smiled, then bit my lip. My fingers parted my sex slowly, and my eyes absorbed his slackening features.

His lips, reddened from my kisses, parted. His lashes drooped. His nostrils flared as his chest heaved.

Then he was between my thighs.

He groaned as he gripped them and swiped his tongue over me. Through me.

My back arched, and I moaned to the canopy of towering trees above.

He began slow, as if savoring the taste of what he did to me. Long laps of his tongue that made me pant. Every inch of me, even the sensitive skin of my inner thighs, was tasted and licked clean, only for his ministrations to render me even more wet.

Then he feasted.

His fingers dug into my thighs, and his tongue into my body. The sound of his swallow and his hum of approval had me reaching for his hair.

I clenched it, and failed to keep from rocking into his face as he sucked my clit, then tormented it with fast flicks of his tongue. Just before I unraveled, he pushed a finger inside me.

All of me tensed, then liquefied in spasms as I moaned at the stars.

I sensed him above me before I opened my bleary eyes. He curled his finger inside me, and I flinched.

He tutted when I tried to reach for his hand and bit the tip of my nose. "I don't leave until you stop clenching." He kissed me, barely-there touches that tortured even more, eyes open and blazing green. As my body finally calmed, he crooned, "There we are."

After another kiss, he withdrew and rolled onto the leaves next to me.

I blinked over at him.

He kicked off his boots and his pants, then sat up and hauled me onto his lap. Sliding his hands over my hips, he pushed my tunic until it sat rolled above my breasts.

Hoarseness lowered his voice. "Tilt back for me, dread."

When I did, my half-bound hair brushed his legs, and his mouth latched onto my breast. He held me around the waist as he sucked and cupped and squeezed each globe.

Breathlessly, as he flicked my nipple with his tongue, I said, "We really shouldn't consummate our marriage in the woods."

The challenge did as intended, and he straightened my back by sweeping his hand up my spine to my neck. "It would be incredibly indecent."

I laughed, and worsened the glazed look on his face by gripping his cock. Squeezing it gently, I took his chin to tip his head back. His eyes remained open, piercing as I ran my hand up and down his length and licked the taste of myself from his lips.

He shuddered.

He was so soft yet so very hard, and I wondered what he might do if I decided to learn how each vein felt against my tongue.

Swallowing, he blinked drowsily. "Have I ever told you that you're beautiful?"

Stunned, my hand stilled.

Another game, I determined. So I rubbed him again and smiled against his lips. "You would never."

"You are," he said, voice thick. "Everything about you, even your tiny hand fluttering over my cock, is maddeningly perfect."

I stopped again, frowning at him.

He smirked.

Then he kissed me, firmly before taking my lip between his teeth. He released it, eyes vibrant and daring in the dark. "Put me where I belong." He angled his head and brushed his mouth and tongue across mine. "One inch at a time."

Still reeling from what he'd said, I rose onto my knees. "Just an inch?" I held him at my entrance, unsure.

His throat dipped. "Yes."

Gripping his shoulders, I lowered over him, gradually taking him into my body until he seized my hips and hissed, "Stop." He looked down, then up at me with eyes of pure green. "Now a little more."

My fingers dug into the grooves in his shoulders as I did.

"Good," he groaned. "So fucking good."

I wanted more, but this position made it hard to believe I could take all of him without it hurting.

His hands clenched my hips, and he pushed me down farther.

I tensed.

He whispered in my ear, "You can take it, dread." He pulled me down again, pressing so deep, I whimpered. "You were made to handle me." He placed a single kiss at my jaw. "To take me."

His mouth smothered my airless cry. He remained still as I adjusted. He kissed me until I relaxed, then laughed scathingly soft when a howl echoed from deep within the woods and I tensed again.

He smoothed his hand up my back. "I'll protect you."

I stared down at him, a brow raised. "You once said that you were the one I'd need to be protected from."

"You remember."

The admission left me before I could think it through. "How does someone forget words that made them who they are?"

Atakan blinked, but rather than show an inkling of remorse, the monster I'd married just grinned. "Made for me indeed."

My heart careened to a halt and swelled. Still, I scowled. "That wasn't a compliment." I bit his nose.

He snarled and claimed my mouth. Then every breath I failed to properly take as he gripped my hips to grind my body against his until it trembled.

My mouth slid from his, useless. He didn't seem to mind, his spread lips gliding over my jaw and my galloping pulse. My hips rocked. Pleasure unfurled, and I chased it with mindless abandon.

He took control when it raced through me, sharp and seizing.

My head flopped to his neck. I clutched it as he used my body to milk his cock. I licked his throat, wishing I could taste the deliciously rumbled sounds he made.

"Fuck," he groaned, holding me so tight, I moaned again as he shook beneath me. His hand crawled up my back and into my tangled hair.

My eyes closed.

Birdsong and the scuttling of creatures quietened, as if we'd sent them scattering.

Slumped over him, it took too long to realize what he was doing. His fingers combed through my hair over my back. He toyed with the strands while his other arm banded around my waist, trapping me against him.

I wanted to stay there.

I could get far too accustomed to holding him. To being held by him. To feeling the overwhelming heat of his skin against my nose as I nuzzled his neck. To hearing the beat of his heart slowing alongside mine within our touching chests.

But such a mistake could prove fatal.

Leaves rustled as I rolled off him and sprawled over them to stare up at the night sky.

Atakan watched me for a moment before lying down, too.

The moon, full and bright, flashed between the swaying branches above.

We should have left. I should have left. Yet I couldn't bring myself to reach for my pants or even roll my tunic down. "Someone will probably come searching for us soon."

"Unlikely," Atakan rasped. "Most know we're together."

The way he said together was a blade grazing vital organs. Perhaps because I shouldn't have liked the way it sounded even though it wasn't what he'd meant.

"Mated," he said, as if knowing what I'd been thinking. But he couldn't hear any of my thoughts when we were in close proximity. "And freshly wed."

I shouldn't have given that a response. But I'd never been able to back down from him, and he was evidently not done provoking me. "You speak as if those things mean much at all."

Silence, far too heavy for the forest, invaded. I could feel his attention like a kiss from the sun.

But I kept staring at the moon.

Even as he murmured, "You speak as if they don't mean anything to you." He shifted onto his side. "When you know that I know you, dread, and I always know when you're bluffing."

I looked over at him.

His arm was bent beneath his head. He ran his hand through his sweat-misted hair, pushing the strands back to worsen the beauty a creature so cruel and untrustworthy shouldn't have.

But there was honesty in cruelty.

Maybe, especially now that I'd learned what gentle males could do, Atakan wasn't as untrustworthy as he seemed.

At least, not to me.

I rolled onto my side. "I know when you're bluffing, too."

His teeth flashed with his half smile. "Are you sure?"

Nodding, I moved my arm to cushion my head.

Minutes might have passed, but neither of us moved nor spoke.

We just stared. I told myself that I was waiting for a glimpse of his next move. When really, I was simply too content to study him.

But his next move was one I never would have anticipated. "You cannot love him."

A shocked laugh left me. "Why? Because you're my mate and I must love you?"

He didn't answer. He didn't smirk. He watched me with a hardness to his features I'd never seen before. An intensity that hinted at uncertainty—perhaps even nervousness.

But that couldn't be true.

Atakan didn't get nervous or anxious. His malice and arrogance would snuff anything that made him feel that way before it got the better of him.

Yet he seemed at such a loss for words, I almost laughed and rolled into him to kiss him. Almost opened my mouth to say something. Anything.

Instead, instinct propelled me to touch his sharp cheekbone. The pad of my finger glossed over it, then dropped to his jaw.

As I traced the bladed edge, it unclenched.

His eyes closed. "I want your unyielding defiance, your mischievous curiosity, your ceaseless muttering in your sleep." His eyes opened. "Your buttery hair in my hands."

I wasn't sure I breathed. Wasn't sure that if I looked away from him, I would believe this wasn't a game.

The conviction roughening and firming his voice held me utterly still. "I want you, Mildred. Always and incessantly, I've fucking wanted you."

I might have been dazed, but I heard what he truly meant. I heard it, and I saw it in those eyes. Though I could hardly believe it, I did. He wanted me at his mercy.

He did want my love.

I didn't say that. I couldn't. But wanting to say something, I shifted closer and whispered, "And if I cease being defiant?"

His large hand covered my cheek, his eyes searched mine. He

leaned in to rasp against my mouth, "Then I will assume I've failed in holding your attention, and I'll be sure to remedy that."

It was the closest thing to a promise that I would get from a creature I'd never expected to tame. Whether it was enough…

I hadn't the ability to care when he moved atop me, and I was forced to my back. He smoothed a fallen braid away from my face. My body rewarmed instantly, matching the heat swelling the organ in my chest.

He kissed me once, lingering and soft.

As I reached for him, for more, he lifted his head. "Mildred, when they arrive, you must head underground to the dungeon and stay there until I return."

Almost forgetting how we'd ended up in this forest in the first place, it took me a moment to grasp that he was talking about the Unseelie warriors and their pytherion mounts. "But once we find all the eggs, the castle should be—"

"Argue with me about anything you fucking like, but not this."

I frowned. "Atakan—"

"Please."

Beyond shocked, I laughed. "I don't believe I've *ever* heard you say that word."

He grumbled, "Now you have."

I wasn't about to refute his request. I had no desire to be anywhere near those beasts when they descended upon these mountains. But as he glanced up at the trees, I noted the way his shoulders tensed.

I felt the energy around us begin to quake, and I said, "You know something."

His glowing eyes dropped back to mine, and I realized it wasn't the energy of the forest. As it kissed my skin in a whisper-soft caress that hummed as it increased, I recognized it. My own energy recognized it.

It was Atakan.

"Sense something," he said in a voice so cold. A tone unlike any I'd heard from him before.

Though he'd yet to be formally crowned, Atakan was the Seelie king. It was said a ruler's connection to their realm heightened their abilities. Now, he could likely sense a great deal of things the rest of his kin could not, and the forest…

It had been so unnaturally quiet for skies knew how long.

He leaped to his feet.

"Something comes." Fear threaded into my voice. "They're here, aren't they?"

He snatched my arm to pull me up. After handing me my pants, he pressed his mouth to my forehead, and ordered, "Dungeon."

I stepped into my pants on wobbling legs. Pulling down my tunic, I looked up to find Atakan walking backward into the trees. He said nothing. He just watched me.

Confused, I called, "Where are you going?"

He didn't answer. Features void, he stared at me for breathless seconds.

Then he vanished, mist curling over the greenery in his wake.

I'd reached the gardens before the first roar came. Almost stumbling into the bed of tulips, I turned back and looked up.

To a sky emptying of stars—because of the mass of darkness sweeping across it.

Thirty-Two

Pholly found me as soon as I entered the foyer. "What took you so long?"

"I was in the forest." I stopped to gather my breath. My heart sank. "Oh, skies. The eggs, Pholly." I turned back. "They're still there."

She caught my arm before I could leave. "What would you do with them anyway?" I noticed she was also still wearing her tunic and pants. "Toss them into the river and hope it carries them far enough downstream?"

As if to punctuate her stern words, a screeched roar made us both tense.

"We can't leave them there."

Her features fell lax. "They're not there anymore. Come."

I was dragged upstairs before I could protest. "Where are they, then?" Remembering, I said, "We need to get everyone beneath ground. The dungeon."

The roaring became thunder. A rumble that seemed to shake the earth and everything atop it.

Her steps quickened until we were almost running down the hall. "Already done. We'll join them in a minute."

We reached the third-floor balcony, and Pholly jerked to a halt when I stopped and demanded, "What are you doing?"

"I was told to tell you." She released me and walked to the railing. "But it's easier to show you rather than explain it all."

Stepping forward, I gripped the wooden railing and searched the dark below until my eyes caught on glinting objects.

Pytherion eggs.

Every egg we'd found had been placed just beyond the castle gates. More than what we'd found. I counted ten before turning to Pholly. "Who put them there? We need—"

She hushed me and pointed at the drive right as a tall figure emerged from the darkness.

Atakan.

Unhurriedly, my mate and husband walked down the drive, stark naked.

No guards stood at the gates he opened and closed. I would have thought him mad, would have screamed his name, were it not for his casual pace and the way he stopped and appeared to stare up at the night sky.

And were it not for the mist coalescing around his legs in a whirlwind that spiraled higher until it had swallowed him from view entirely.

The mist proliferated like a storm cloud, widening and darkening until it blended into the giant scales and wings of the form revealed beneath.

A pytherion.

Larger than any I'd seen in The Bonelands, and coated in bronze-tipped scales of impenetrable black. Wings spread, each one wider than the castle gates. A long neck curled, giant head tipping back. Bronzed spikes glinted as the monster released a mighty roar.

My clammy hands clenched the railing.

"He's summoned them," Pholly said, breathless beside me.

I couldn't spare her a glance as the dark mass covering the stars neared the castle, and answering roars rattled my bones.

"The warriors will try to make them fight it," she said. "But by the time they realize what's happened, it will be too late."

Although I didn't understand, she spoke as if she'd anticipated this moment.

Finally, I tore my attention from the beast I didn't recognize. "He's…" My throat constricted. "Atakan's a shifter."

"Not merely a shifter." Pholly's dreary blue eyes met mine, a wet sheen coating them. "His mother was the Unseelie queen, and her grandfather the last pytherion king to grace these lands." She frowned. "You didn't know about Kalista?"

"He told me she was his mother." I shook my head. "*Is* his mother, but…" I looked back down at the drive. "Nothing more."

"He couldn't."

I begged to differ, but now was not the time to argue about it. Atakan nudged an egg with his snout, and it rolled downhill toward the river.

My stomach churned. My thoughts crystallized.

Atakan had known I'd find the eggs because I was mated to him. I was blood-bound to a pytherion.

"Besides Cordenya, I was the only one who knew," Pholly said. "And that's merely because I was drawing in the woods at the wrong time." As if remembering vividly, she laughed. "He was naked and covered in blood, hunting for his clothes. He could feign taking his ruthlessness to a very bizarre level or admit the obvious—that he was a shifter."

"Cordenya?" I questioned, disbelieving.

"Well, she did practically raise him."

That stumped me, but only momentarily. "What about your brother? Does he know now?"

"He'll find out when everyone else does. He's always known something isn't right about Atakan, but he never questioned him. Phineus is an observer who sticks his nose in other people's business only when it suits him."

She ceased talking when Atakan rose onto his legs. He spread his wings impossibly wide, and roared again—welcoming the advance of the pytherion army sent to destroy his home.

But it wasn't his home.

Although younger than Vane, Atakan was a pytherion shifter—the true Unseelie heir who'd spent his whole life masquerading as a Seelie prince.

Part Seelie, part Unseelie. He didn't have mortal blood, but he was still a halfling. Just like me.

Anger burned through my shock and awe, warming my cold blood.

As if sensing our attention, the beast turned. Smoke plumed from his snout, steaming the crisp spring air.

"We should head in," Pholly said. "He's a different evil entirely in that form, but he still knows we shouldn't be here."

Not a second after we entered the doors, a mighty whoosh caused them to slam. A screech, ear-piercing and sickening, followed. The castle walls shook as though part of it had collapsed over the drive.

It wasn't the castle.

I turned back to the doors, reaching for the glass.

Dirt settled, revealing a brown-and-black pytherion twitching upon the drive. The warrior strapped to the beast's back lay unmoving beneath the scaled bulk.

Atakan landed beside it.

A silver-scaled pytherion soared toward him. He dodged it. His serpentine body left the ground with ease, and he roared low and deep—as if warning it.

"Mildred," Pholly called.

"Coming," I said, but it was more of a whisper as my hand slid down the glass and my eyes refused to part with the swarm of deadly beasts colliding in the sky.

The silver-scaled pytherion descended to the ground, then lowered—seemed to bow its head. The warrior atop its back couldn't be seen due to the distance, save for the glint of their weapon.

The floor became mush beneath my unfeeling feet as I drifted down the hall to the sound of endless screeches and growling. Portraits rattled upon the walls. One of the stained windows cracked.

Yet all I could hear were my racing thoughts.

Out of all the dangers awaiting you in my court, I'm the one you'll need to be protected from.

Memories turned through my mind like a pinwheel, each more vivid than the last.

And here we all are, believing our united forces have herded the monsters into their spelled cage.

They missed one.

At the bottom of the stairs, I looked up at the portrait of the late king in the foyer.

You truly are a monster.

You have no idea.

Had Garran never known what his son was?

Reaching the back hall that led to the dungeon stairwell, I stopped. Tangled emotions sailed from me in a quaked exhale when I beheld the Unseelie king standing in the rear courtyard.

With my felynx in his arms.

Thirty-Three

"I told you I didn't want a pet," I said by way of greeting. "This is the second time she's been used to lure me into danger, but you insisted."

Vane drawled, "Marrying monstrous males is dangerous indeed." Yet there was no humor in those blue eyes. Not so much as a twitch of his mouth.

He hadn't moved from the black diamond paver he stood on, which led me to believe the wards on the castle began there.

"I do hope you haven't harmed her." I remained before the doors and crossed my arms. "I don't know if I can ever forgive the crimes you've already committed." That ache resurfaced and softened my voice. "Don't make it worse, Vane."

"I don't want your forgiveness, Mildred." Every word was gritted, almost pushed between his teeth. "I just need your husband to die."

Although his tone made me more than uneasy, I still tried to delay whatever his plan might be. "Have you seen him?" I gestured lazily toward the thunderous noise coming from the other side of the castle. "I don't like your chances."

He dropped Meadow, and she yelped before darting behind me into the castle.

Now, all I needed to do was step back inside and close—

"Mildred?" Phineus called.

Fuck.

Vane cocked his brow, then held out his hand. "I will get to him, and I won't hesitate to slit his throat and use him instead."

I looked at that hand. "What do you want from me, Vane?"

"He's almost here." He jerked his chin behind me, a crooked smile revealing a glimpse of his clenched teeth. "More of your friends accompany him."

Their steps were hard to hear over the pytherions in the valley. But they were indeed headed this way.

I didn't even make it to the paver he stood on. He reached out and snatched my hand. He was too strong for me to fight, and fighting was useless when I'd made my choice.

Between one failed breath and the next, we vanished.

Darkness dispersed slowly, unveiling the star-flecked sky and a series of cottages.

A village.

Two armed warriors stood beneath the broken awning of the home Vane tugged me toward.

Hurried steps over the grass gave my attention to another warrior, who slowed as he neared and rushed out, "Jex just returned with a report, Sire."

Vane halted. He grunted, "Speak," as if he already knew what he would say and didn't wish to hear it.

"They've turned."

His question was flat. "All of them?"

"Nearly." Fear shone in the male's brown eyes. "Nineteen. Two are deceased."

"Then use what remains to take them down," Vane ordered. "Ready the iron bolts."

"Sire." A female approached. A warrior, blood streaking her cheek and gleaming on her armor. "The years we've dedicated, the bonds they've made with them…"

"What good is a bond with a murderous beast you can no longer control, Saraiya?" Vane growled.

She flinched and stopped a safe distance from the king.

Looking at the male who'd given him the report, Vane said, "Have Jex deliver the order at once."

The male dipped his head, then ran toward a field beyond the cottages. Lanterns glowed within two tents erected in the long grass.

Vane heaved a rumbled breath and moved his hand down my arm to my wrist, pulling me to the entrance of the cottage ahead. There was no door, and the moonlight barely glazed the steep stairwell beyond the threshold.

Vane yanked me upright before I slipped down the soil-packed steps.

Though shocked he'd bothered, I refused to show gratitude.

A tunnel opened to the right. A torch, thrust into the soil wall at the bottom of the stairs, provided little light to guide the way through the long passage. At the end, two more torches revealed another tunnel. We veered right, encountering poorly crafted cells that stretched beyond view into the torch-lit gloom.

All were empty.

Vane opened the steel door to the first cell and released me once I'd stepped inside. But I wasn't left alone.

With a whine, the door slammed behind him.

I didn't believe I'd get an answer, but I still asked, "Where are we?"

Surprisingly, he said, "Hours south. He won't find you until we're ready for him to."

I felt the need to point out, "He didn't see you take me."

Vane stood before the door, arms crossed. "But you're *mates*," he said, lethally quiet. "Eventually, he'll slip into your thoughts, and you'll tell him you're at an outpost in the war-ruined village of Venellah."

Stunned that he knew, though I shouldn't have been, I could only say, "Then I'm afraid this plan is futile, for I have no idea what you're talking about."

"You reek of him," Vane seethed, eyes raking over me with intentional slowness. His lip peeled back before he tamed his ire. "And not just in the usual post-coital way one does after being thoroughly fucked."

"Getting thoroughly fucked by royal males seems all too common for me." I licked my teeth, then smiled. "Except when *you* did so, there was not an ounce of pleasure involved."

He was on me in an instant, and I stumbled back against the

wall—trapped as he drew a knife and pressed it to my throat. He snarled, "I should kill you."

Foolishly, I glared up at him and hissed between my teeth, "Then why haven't you, King?"

The blade dug into my skin, blood drawn and trickling. My eyes held his, even as the sting delivered traitorous tears. Even as fear began to overpower my belief that he wouldn't kill me.

Tension frayed.

Then snapped as he growled so loud, it was almost a roar, and stepped away.

I closed my eyes. The sheathing of the blade opened them. Breath heaved from me as I placed my hands against the soil wall.

Vane paced the short length of the cell. "Why would you bond to him, Mildred?" He dragged a hand through his crimson hair. "*Marry* him? Even before he revealed his true self, he's proven to be nothing but a monster."

I could play this game as long as he wished. "Is Morona really an *old* lover?"

He ceased pacing.

His hand fell to his side, and the anger that had harshened his features vanished. "Did Stone tell you about her, too?"

"Stone told me nothing. I heard you talking that night in the city when you thought I was asleep. You gave yourself away." I had no interest in defending the lord in hiding, but it was true. "And again just now by confirming what I've suspected about Morona since that night."

Vane stared at the ground, rubbing the scruff around his mouth. "I wasn't with her when we—"

"I don't care," I lied. "You killed my father, my stepmother, and their associates." The wound he'd given me yawned open, thickening my voice. "You made me believe otherwise while using me to free your people, and now you've dragged me here as bait, and you speak to me as if *I'm* the traitor? As if what I've done deserves *your* ire?" My low laughter faded quickly. "Even if I never knew Atakan, you've lost all chance of getting rid of those wards, Vane, and you've only yourself to blame."

"Mildred." His tone softened, his gaze lifting to my bloodied neck. It stayed there until he said, "Fuck." He paced again. "What a rotten fucking mess."

"I'll say."

For a while, his crunching steps were the only sound. Then he asked, "How long have you known about him?"

I slid down the wall and draped my arms over my bent knees. "That Atakan's a pytherion shifter?" I loathed admitting it—and how my weakened tone gave away the betrayal I felt. "I had no idea until tonight."

"None?"

"No one did," I snapped, withholding a wince at my defensiveness.

He stared at me for a moment, assessing. Then he laughed, a broken sound that lacked humor. "Of course. If anyone knew, then…"

"He'd never inherit the Seelie throne," I realized out loud.

Vane kept quiet as he took three strides across the cage he'd penned us in, over and over. I counted twenty-one before he stopped. "With my death, he stands to inherit my throne."

Although I knew nothing about Atakan's intentions, I still shook my head. "I don't see him doing that."

"Then you're as naive as you are reckless."

"I prefer bold." I dropped my chin atop my arm at my knee. "Daring, even."

He huffed, then gave in and released a genuine laugh.

I hated the sound. Hated the way it pleased me to hear it. Hated that a part of me—the part that fractured the spell on his lands—still cared.

But not enough. Never enough to forget what he'd done to my family and to the fragile trust I'd given him.

"Princess," he said. "Believe me when I say that I detest what we did to you, and if I'd known that I would, then I wouldn't have done it."

I scoffed. "You said you don't want my forgiveness."

"Maybe I do."

"Well, you don't have it."

"Yet you'll forgive Atakan the heartless after everything he's done to you?" he asked, incredulous. "He trapped you in a fucking carriage with a two-headed serpent, Mildred."

"*Me*," I said, unable to resist smiling at the memory that shouldn't feel nostalgic. "Not someone I care about. What do you care anyway? You kept your love for another, and I gave you a morsel of mine to set your people free." I looked up at him. "Seems to me like you escaped unscathed."

He gazed down at me with an intensity that made my stomach squirm. A familiar look I'd seen countless times before. A weapon, that look. One he'd used to cut me open so I'd bleed for him. "Naive indeed."

I held his eyes and raised a brow, awaiting an explanation.

He gave none.

He turned to the door and scraped his fingers through his hair. "Do you know all of what Atakan is?"

"The true Unseelie heir." I flopped back against the wall, my legs dropping to the dirt. "A halfling just like me."

An amused hum accompanied the slight turn of his head. One of his blue eyes glinted at me briefly before he looked back at the bars caging us. "Then you know he's stealing the creatures we've spent years breeding and training."

My throat dried.

He continued. "Any faerie noble who can shift is not merely a faerie noble." Vane turned to me, ice dripping from his deep voice. "They're an alpha of that species."

"He knew," I rasped. "Atakan knew you were breeding pytherions."

The pytherion who'd appeared to bow to Atakan and the warrior's report...

He would turn Vane's power against him—use the pytherions to hunt them all. Every warrior. Atakan had become so much more than the king of the Seelie Fae.

He'd become utterly untouchable.

"I've had my suspicions about who his mother was since discovering his blood was used to make the wards, but it didn't matter," he said. "Until now."

As silence reigned, I gave up on finding words. Murmurs crawled down the tunnel, unintelligible. I gazed unseeingly at a puddle in the corner of the cell.

Vane's attention scalded until footsteps padded over the dirt. "You need to help us end this, Mildred." He opened the door. "You need to help us end him, or we all lose this war."

Thirty-Four

Though I tried, I didn't sleep. I'd hoped I would so that I might catch a glimpse of what Atakan was doing in my dreams. Little effort was involved in keeping my thoughts revolving solely around him.

They'd always revolved around him.

So when his voice finally entered my mind, I was taken aback by how unprepared I was. *Where are you?*

There was so much I wanted to know. So much I wanted to say.

In the end, all I managed was a half-formed thought. *South. Underneath a ruined village that's now an outpost in Venellah.*

I heard nothing but my quietened breathing and straightened against the wall, adding, *They're counting on you coming for me.*

Good.

Atakan, they have something called iron bolts.

No response. Nothing but the incessant whirl of my own worries.

Atakan?

He was gone.

Finally, I slept.

I had no idea how long it lasted before the door opened and Vane entered. "He made contact."

Not a question.

I didn't respond. It took me a moment to remember where I was and what had transpired. I lifted my head off the wall, brushing dirt from it as I pushed away from the corner of the cell.

After a minute, he asked, "Do you need anything?"

I glared at him to find the severe features I'd almost fallen in love with now void of his earlier fury. Such sincerity had me withholding an incredulous bout of laughter, and I simply shook my head.

Though as he left, I could have wept for something to drink.

When Vane returned perhaps an hour later, he brought a bruised peach and a furry water flask. I wasn't certain they were safe to consume, so I croaked, "I don't want them."

He took a fleshy bite from the peach. Leather and armor creaked as he crouched in front of me and offered it. I stared at the missing chunk, then at him. When he swallowed, I snatched the fruit and immediately bit into it.

He chuckled, eyes narrowing on the juice that left my lower lip.

I swiped it away before he could dare, then almost choked as I swallowed, and a distant roar breached the underground tunnels.

Vane stilled.

Then he slowly rose. "Looks like your monstrous husband has arrived."

The fear cascading through me was illogical. Atakan was not merely a pytherion but a trained warrior. He'd likely vanished to somewhere nearby to assess the area before shifting into a form that was nearly impossible to kill.

Yet remembering the iron bolts Vane had mentioned made those things all too easy to forget.

A boom shook the ground above right as I climbed to my feet.

I stepped back against the trembling wall. Dirt rained, and the torchlight beyond the cell guttered. Shouts traveled from the other end of the tunnel, and another roar—this one closer—made my fingers dig into the peach I'd forgotten.

I dropped it, wiping my sticky fingers on my pants.

More dirt crumbled with another shudder. Closer this time. Almost directly over us, as if Atakan could sense where I was being held captive. Perhaps he very well could.

Vane stood frozen at the door I hadn't noticed he'd opened. "If he keeps stomping, we'll all be buried down here."

"So send me up." A useless suggestion. He wouldn't.

He smirked. Then he looked at the low-lying ceiling. "Soon," he stunned me by saying.

I frowned, stepping closer but keeping my hand on the wall when Atakan stomped again, and the soil beneath our booted feet bounced. A rock fell to my shoulder, pounding into the dirt.

I winced and shook soil from my hair. "Whatever you're planning won't work, Vane."

He arched a brow at me over his shoulder.

I said as gently as I could manage while the beast I'd married grumbled thunder above us. "You need to retreat."

"You need to do as I tell you, and I'll make sure you return to what remains of Cloud Castle."

My heart snarled in my chest.

"It still stands." I refused to believe otherwise. Not after all I'd done, after all I'd endured, and all it had come to mean to me because of it.

Vane's hard look softened as he beheld my features. "Mostly." He peered into the tunnel and cursed. "We need to move near an exit before we're trapped."

I wasn't given a choice, which was fine. Relief swam among dread in tightening circles around my bones as he seized my hand, and we headed to the fork in the tunnel.

We didn't need torchlight to see the mass of dirt that had caved in before the stairs, blocking the way we'd entered.

"He's given us only one way out," someone shouted from the gloom ahead.

Vane didn't respond.

I discovered they hadn't even been talking to him as we hurried down the tunnel.

Warriors huddled in more cells, the open doors revealing piles of weaponry and food supplies aside bedrolls. Another stomp made some of them flinch. One male leaned his forehead upon his sword pommel, eagle-like wings twitching as he muttered prayers to Asherlin.

A flame still flickered from a torch in the distance.

As we moved toward it, warriors converged into formation behind us. Muttered concerns buzzed like swarming insects. The scent of their fear was overwhelming.

Many of them, if not all of them, would die.

"Stop," I said to Vane. "Please, just…" I freed my hand from his and turned to his warriors.

The one nearest me glared.

I didn't care. "You can't do this. You'll—"

"It's much too late to attempt scaring them," Vane said behind me. "The plan is already unfolding."

Atakan released another mighty roar.

"What plan?" I almost shouted. "A plan to get every last one of you killed?"

"Victory will be had," the Unseelie king vowed.

"At what cost?" I asked them all.

No matter how much Vane believed it, I couldn't see how he'd succeed. As I looked upon the warriors filling the tunnel, all I could see was blood and death and heartbreak.

A cycle these courts had repeated for decades.

"At what fucking cost?" I asked again, shouting now. Then I turned back to Vane and shoved him.

He didn't move an inch, but shock widened his eyes.

"Even if you manage to kill Atakan, this won't end here." I stabbed a finger at his armored chest. "Whoever survives will only dance in more violent circles until *nothing* is left of either kingdom."

He just stood there and glared.

But he knew I was right. "You once said you never agreed with your father's methods, yet here you stand, willing to do whatever it takes to appease your ego in the name of retribution."

Someone snarled behind me.

Vane's gaze flicked above my head. "Mildred," he warned.

My resolve flattened when someone called out, "Sire, you cannot allow her to speak to—"

Vane's raised hand shut their mouth.

As he lowered it, he looked down at me, his stare granite. But I saw it in those blue eyes—the male he was beneath the weight of his dead father and his kingdom's expectations.

I saw how I might fix the unfixable.

And I stepped into him to whisper, "You told me I could have anything I wanted in exchange for breaking the wards." I peered down at his curling hands. "You made an oath."

His eyes closed when I met them. Through gritted teeth, he said, "Don't you fucking dare, Mildred."

Then he marched to the dirt-made steps, leaving me no choice but to follow or be pushed forward by the surge of warriors at my back.

But halfway up the stairs, Vane stopped.

Everyone stopped as something rolled down them, bouncing past his boots to land in the dirt before me.

Garran's head.

The rumbling and stomping above ground had ceased. All noise, save for muttered questions about the head and the holdup, had ceased.

Vane looked at the head for so long, I began to think he might not know what Garran had looked like. Then I realized he'd been absorbing the significance of what it meant.

Disbelief slackened his features. "You've been made queen," he said so softly, it was almost whispered.

I stepped close to the decapitated head. It appeared to have been severed long after Garran's death, the skin clean of blood when I crouched to unpin the note from the point of the late king's ear.

The rolled parchment contained one sentence.

Claim your victory and retreat.

Vane climbed down the steps to stand near me. Understanding what was happening without reading what Atakan had written, he barked to the warriors behind us, "Move away until we know what we're dealing with."

He knew what we were dealing with.

He also knew it was wise if no one else did. Though, I suspected some would still hear, as it was impossible to achieve privacy with so many cramped in the tunnel.

So I stepped over Garran's head and as close to the king as I was comfortable. "Retreat, Vane, and remind your people of all you have accomplished. The wards are—"

"Still not gone."

"But they are open. It will do." When he just sneered at the parchment, I flung it at his chest. "He's letting you claim victory. Take it and end this."

"Letting me," Vane seethed quietly, dragging a hand through his hair.

Then he kicked the head toward the awaiting warriors in the tunnel, and roared.

A roar from outside answered, the ground shaking from another stomp. More dirt crumbled atop us.

As Vane paced, I mulled over the repercussions of using the deal we'd made and allowing these stubborn warriors to take me outside toward certain death.

I didn't think Atakan would kill me.

I didn't think he'd hesitate to kill every last soul in this tunnel.

And I wasn't entirely certain that enforcing the bargain would even work with a will as strong as Vane's. Maybe he could withstand the pain that came with breaking a magic-made promise.

I was knocked from my thoughts when he clasped my upper arms. "What would you have picked?" Vane mistook my stupefied expression for confusion and said, "If you never knew what I did to your family, what would you have asked of me in return for breaking the curse?"

Why he wanted to know, especially right now, made me wonder if he was indeed preparing to die. The thought had me all the more reluctant to say it, and I wouldn't.

But it didn't need to be said. It lingered there between us, a warm energy that once burned.

"It no longer matters."

"It does," he said. His hands slid down my arms. His fingers touched mine.

I recoiled. "You know what I want now." I glanced up the stairs, then at the warriors. "This madness needs to cease once and for all."

He cupped my cheek, his sad smile failing to reach his eyes. "We don't always get what we want." He added, a barely-there whisper, "*Queen.*"

Then, with an order for his warriors to prepare, he walked up the stairs and took me with him.

The steel door above them hung open, painted an olive green to blend into the field it opened to. Cool air kissed my cheeks, but traveling on the breeze that welcomed us was the heavy scent of blood.

And smoke.

Fire encircled the entire field. Beyond the giant ring of flames, warriors shouted from the woodland in the distance. Arrow after arrow flew toward the monster perched patiently in the center of the field.

My husband.

Many arrows missed, while others hit his scales before snapping or simply falling to the grass. Bodies lay strewn around him.

What remained of them.

Warriors waited beneath the stairs in the tunnel. Bile climbed my throat when Vane pulled me aside the entrance, right next to a severed leg.

"It's a shame that we must meet this way." Vane's raised voice carried. "As it seems you're family."

On their fearful journey to the pytherion I'd married, my eyes caught on a pile of innards. Beyond horrified yet also concerned, I looked up at Atakan.

But his vibrant bronze eyes were focused on the king beside me.

On the hand holding mine.

He inhaled through slit nostrils, rumbling as he did, then exhaled through a monstrous maw.

Fire exploded across the field toward us.

Toward Vane.

It forced us to separate, carving straight through where we'd stood, and snapped me free from my shocked state.

"Atakan," I breathed, and dared to take a step forward.

But perhaps this creature was no longer him. Perhaps, as teeth longer than my arms glinted in the glow of firelight, he was nothing but a monster after all.

Unlike other pytherions I'd seen, no feathers adorned his head, nor the edges of his wings. His muscular legs were thicker than tree trunks. His scales weren't black, but familiar shades of bronze and darkened emerald that gleamed beneath the spray of the moon.

His serpentine body spread beyond my line of vision. Curved spikes similar to his teeth jutted unevenly from his back, growing larger and deadlier along his tail. His wings were tucked. Scales protected the leathery membrane and webbing of bones, arrows clanging against the spiked arches rising high above his back.

If he truly was a monster, then I shouldn't have thought him magnificent. I shouldn't have stepped closer. So close, Vane uttered a warning behind me. But he knew better than to provoke Atakan by reaching for me.

The beast rumbled his disapproval at the male, bright eyes unmoving from the Unseelie king.

I stopped far later than I should have, and stared up at his ginormous head. Spikes encircled it like thorns—like a mane—backed by thick scales that flared and morphed from deep to lighter green over his long snout.

He shifted, claws digging deep gouges into the earth, and finally tore his attention from Vane.

His long neck curled and lowered, and his exhale warmed the air around me. I froze. Fear tapped at my chest when those bronze eyes met mine.

Then I smiled, possessed by something that ridded me of rational thought as I reached out my hand.

The pytherion grumbled, turning his head as he exhaled another smoky plume. But he hadn't rejected my touch.

He'd avoided burning me.

That he was still sound of mind enough to know exactly who I was—even if it was the bond—emboldened me to say, "You need to leave."

He growled between gnashed rows of terrifying teeth.

I stumbled back, nearly stepping into a hole from his claws as he leaped forward.

An iron bolt, propelled by a bow that required two flying warriors, arced across the ring of flames. It landed behind me. Dirt sprayed and iron singed my eyes.

As the dust settled and I gaped at the burning bolt as big as me, the Unseelie warriors converged.

Their battle cries were lost beneath the violent rage of the pytherion, who welcomed their advance with fire and snapping teeth.

Carefully, I retreated. Not only to escape the carnage, but to give Atakan room to move without squashing me.

It seemed he'd waited for me to do just that, as he swung his tail toward five warriors advancing behind him. Four of them were instantly taken down. The fifth jumped onto Atakan's back, her sword raised.

I screamed, but Atakan rolled. The ground quaked. More dirt flew. Sickness roiled as Atakan climbed back to his feet and I beheld the warrior's remains.

Vane hollered, drawing my gaze from the meaty mess of steel and limbs. He ran toward me, slipping between Atakan's legs with skill that enraged him.

But Atakan couldn't remove his focus from the warriors still advancing from the underground tunnels. They were met with more fire and teeth and fatal sweeps of his head and tail.

But he quickly ceased caring about their attempts to kill him, even as another iron bolt soared across the field. Grass and dirt and rock rained as the bolt landed where he'd been just seconds ago.

Where he'd still be if he wasn't more interested in his half brother, who was closing in on me.

I stopped retreating.

Vane had no weapon. His crimson hair danced behind him. Determination tightened his features as he ran. "Mildred—" His eyes widened.

Due to the commotion, I didn't hear its approach. Pain burned through my side, and I folded over.

"Fuck," he hissed, reaching me as I stumbled forward and catching me as I fell.

Atakan roared viciously.

Bloodcurdling screams followed.

Vane knelt to the ground, lowering me to it with a hand behind my head. Gently, he pried my hand from my side, but there was no arrow. It lay upon the grass beside us, the sharp head coated in my blood.

Atakan unleashed a fire-filled roar. One that made it clear he'd been holding back. He'd given them all a chance. Even Vane.

And they'd squandered it.

Everywhere his head slowly turned, fire exploded—blaring brighter and growing taller than the ring shrouding the field—until another ring kept every warrior from reaching me.

And from reaching their king.

"You need to go," I rasped to Vane.

Each lumbering step Atakan took toward us was accompanied by smoky plumes from his nostrils. Unmistakable rage thinned his bronze eyes. His snarled warning trembled the grass and the beat of my heart.

"Vane," I whispered.

But he still held my head. Still leaned over me, inspecting the wound above my hip. "You need a healer."

I dared to take my eyes off Atakan.

I looked up at Vane. "In exchange for freeing your kingdom from the wards…" His eyes lifted, anger replacing concern as they locked on mine, and I said, "I want you to take your forces back to The Bonelands right now."

He bared his teeth.

His hand clenched my side, and I winced. But he hadn't done it to hurt me. He was trying to fight it. Although it was over, and there was little chance he and his remaining people would survive if they stayed, he still tried to fight the magic binding him to his promise.

Atakan's shuddering steps stopped, his giant form looming above us. But he couldn't harm the Unseelie king without harming me, and he conveyed his frustration with a shiver-inducing growl.

"I've asked you to go, Vane."

"And then what, Mildred?" Perspiration dotted his brow. His chest heaved.

"You live," I whispered. "Be free of this war that was never yours."

He swallowed. Muscle corded at his throat.

Shakily, I smiled. "Instead, fight against your fear of heights and use those lovely wings."

Vane huffed, sniffing as he held back a chuckle.

But then his eyes gleamed, his hands moved beneath my legs and back, and I knew what he would do. I'd known it was a possibility since he'd taken me to the tunnels, but I didn't protest.

He lifted me, and I waited.

Atakan sensed it and roared. Fire sliced past us, narrowly avoiding Vane's wings. I waited until true darkness wreathed, ready to vanish us to The Bonelands.

Then I pushed free of Vane's arms and rolled toward my beastly king.

THIRTY-FIVE

THE BALLROOM OVERFLOWED WITH FAERIES, MUSICIANS, and streamers in every shade of blue.

Piped cupcakes melted upon stands at lace-dressed banquet tables. Pholly made sure to eat one of each flavor while pointing out who to avoid and who wasn't so terrible and who deserved a sewing needle to the eye.

I laughed at that last one, sipping wine to hide how it ended too soon.

Though the sky was clear beyond the stained glass windows, it rumbled. A winged beast screeched as it soared across the castle grounds to meet and tangle with another over the woods.

For hours yesterday, I'd watched Sky Mountain's new residents from the window in Atakan's tower, entranced and torn after receiving word from Royce regarding Bernadette.

Any minute now, she would welcome her babe.

Pholly glanced at the pytherions before they vanished from view. She shivered and swallowed a large mouthful of wine. "That's going to take some getting used to."

Behind me, Phineus looped his arms around my waist. He whispered in my ear, "Your beast of a husband has returned."

"I don't care," I lied.

Since he'd delivered me to Cloud Castle the night before last, Atakan had been absent. He'd shifted back into his faerie form and, without a word, had vanished me straight to the healer's room near the kitchens beneath the castle.

Silently, he'd sat watch from the corner of the warm room until I was given a sleeping draught. When I'd woken long after dawn, the wound had almost healed, and he was gone.

I hadn't asked where he'd disappeared to.

There'd been no need when Elion had gone out of his way to

inform me of each meeting he'd been attending with Seelie nobility. Supposedly, Atakan sought their approval of a new treaty for the faerie realms. A treaty Pholly humorously believed he'd prepared many moons ago.

There was no time to waste if we wished to avoid more bloodshed, Elion had said.

I could only imagine what gaining their approval entailed. A single glacial glare was likely all Atakan needed to make them dip their quills into their inkpots.

Though I was glad measures were already being taken to avoid another war, I still hadn't been able to piece together what I needed in order to wholly understand what Atakan had done.

"Oh, come on." Phineus stepped before me and stole my wine. He took a hearty sip, then smacked his lips together. "He kept his secrets from me too, you know."

To all those in attendance, and in all of the realm, Atakan was the villain they'd needed. A savior they didn't want yet could not shun.

He was half Seelie, half Unseelie. A shifter.

An alpha pytherion.

But now that word had spread of Garran's death, he was also their new king, and there was not a lick of anything anyone could do to change that. Nor was there anything I could do to change my own fate.

A fate I'd asked for. One I'd brought upon myself.

"You're his cousin," Elion said, passing by with a tray containing wet rags. Scenting wine and frosting-tinged vomit, I winced, thankful when he disappeared to take care of it.

"Second cousin," Pholly said, adjusting the pearls strung tight at her slim throat.

Phineus scowled at her, then gasped. "You've got cake on your gown, clumsy thing."

"Get it off," she hissed and turned in a circle, although there wasn't so much as a speck on the black gossamer coiled around her body.

Smiling, I left them. I slipped easily between the guests who'd rather pretend I wasn't their new queen and out into the hall.

My thoughts clouded after I checked Atakan's rooms and found them empty. Slowing near the stairs on the third floor, I looked down the hall.

The entrance to what had once been Garran's tower was now sealed.

Most of the tower lay in ruins upon the castle grounds, as experts tried to devise a way to salvage the ancient tree that matched that of Atakan's tower. It'd been struck by a fallen pytherion—before Atakan had managed to gain complete submission from the army bred for retribution.

After all I'd discovered, I couldn't help but find it fitting. That Garran's rooms had been destroyed with him, leaving little trace of him behind.

It seemed Cordenya had been given new residence on the second floor, emerging from a grand room in a gown of stringy silver beads.

I stopped beneath the stairs to greet her, pondering how she must feel about the loss of her lover.

"Majesty." She curtsied as best she could in such tight attire. Straightening, she spread her crimson lips in a half smile. "Leaving the festivities when they've only just begun?"

They'd begun at nightfall, and she knew as much. But I tipped a shoulder. "Given the state of some of the guests, I'd say better now than later."

Her laughter sounded genuine, lighting her silver eyes as she stepped closer. Noting the way I tensed, she smiled again. "I mean you no harm, darling. In fact," she reached out to touch a curl that'd escaped my updo, "I am rather pleased by all that's transpired because of you."

I sensed there was more and waited.

"But I must advise against trying to get rid of me. There's a reason I was the only one who knew his secret, and why I put up with Garran after years of mistreatment." Cordenya's gaze sharpened. "Atakan might not have grown in my womb, but I will always be his mother."

Rather than tell her I had no interest in getting rid of anyone, except perhaps myself, I just nodded.

"Now, having said that…" Her lithe fingers stroked my cheek. "Give him all the trouble he deserves." Then she glided down the hall, her long wine-red hair covering the bare expanse of her back.

I continued my search downstairs. My heartbeat increased when I sensed his.

I hunted the sound, as well as his scent, into the throne room. Gently, I closed the doors behind me, then slouched against them when I caught sight of him.

Dressed for a ball he'd yet to attend, Atakan lounged in tailored black across the throne, legs draped over the branch-twined arm. In his hand, jewels glinted.

His father's crown—soon to be his—twirled around his pointer finger.

He watched the jewels throw colored orbs of light over the aged tapestries upon the wall. "If it isn't my darling wife."

"If it isn't my monstrous husband."

Finally, he looked at me, eyeing where I stood against the doors. "Afraid, Princess?" He hooked the crown upon one of the carved branches arching high above the throne's seat. "Apologies, I meant to say *queen*."

Taking three steps deeper into the room, I stopped within a strip of moonlight. Not because I was afraid of him, but because it was necessary. This bond only made the spell of his proximity all the more potent, and it reduced my mind to distracted mush.

"You tricked everyone, Atakan."

He dragged a finger beneath his lower lip. "This surprises you."

My whisper echoed across the long room. "You tricked *me*."

For five bruising heartbeats, he simply watched me with those eerily beautiful eyes. Then he smirked. "You're welcome, Mildred."

My fingers curled.

He noticed before I could unfurl them. "What truly upsets you?"

Arching a brow, he rose to his feet. "What I am?" He stepped down from the wooden dais. "What I've done?"

I didn't move as he took measured steps toward me. Each soft tap of his boots over the floor might as well have been bolts of lightning, as I struggled to keep still.

But he didn't try to touch me.

He circled me, slow and predatory. "Perhaps it's something else entirely."

"Were you going to kill him?" My quiet words seemed too loud in the silent throne room. "Take it all?"

His eyes gleamed as he walked in front of me. "If I had, would you have been heartbroken?"

At my silence, that mischief vacated his eyes. The green flecks flared, as did his energy.

"He wanted you to free his people." Halting beside me, his seethed whisper stirred the tendrils of hair at my cheek. "I made you the queen of mine."

"Answer my question, Atakan."

A throaty sound, almost a snarl, came from him as he continued to circle me.

Just when I began to think he wouldn't, he answered. "As much as ripping his head from his body would've satisfied me a great deal, alas…" He stopped before me. "Ruling both faerie kingdoms was never what I wanted."

"Then what was the point of this game?"

He exhaled a soft laugh. "Survival."

My eyes lifted from his chest. As they met molten bronze, some of my resolve melted. "Survival," I repeated.

He stared at my mouth for a moment. When our eyes locked once more, his lips curled. "You know a thing or two about that, don't you?"

Indeed. I almost laughed. "It was you I had to survive, Atakan."

"And did you?" His head tilted. "Did you survive me in the end, dread?"

We both knew I had, and as a result, that I hadn't survived him at all.

I didn't answer. Instead, I asked, "Why did you hide what you are when it could have been used to end this war?" I couldn't resist voicing my assumption. "Because you would have been used?"

He circled me again. "I've spent my entire life being a pawn for my father and his numerous mistakes. If I was going to cause immeasurable bloodshed, and risk my life and title, it would be when it suited me and no one else."

Though maybe they shouldn't have, those words stung. Even as I tried to imagine what it must have been like—hiding who he was for so long.

"No one knew I cared for you because for some years, I didn't. That changed when I felt what fate was doing. The bond," he said.

The question punched free of my chest, as if my heart demanded an answer. "When?"

"I first felt it when you poisoned me." His voice was soft, almost wistful, as he said, "The way you raised your wine to me when you should have been fleeing for your half-mortal life." He kept walking. "Not long after that ball, the plan to defeat the undefeatable was formed. I'd already heard murmurings of the Unseelie's intent to breed an army of pytherions."

"So you volunteered to help ward The Bonelands?"

"A curse ends the same way it begins." Cold words I'd heard before. "My mother's stolen heart began this war. I was to be used whether I liked it or not. I knew they'd need my blood to trap the Unseelie." His deep laugh lacked humor. "The plan was indestructible, as you cannot steal a heart from the heartless. So even as the bond with you became undeniable, I still made it a point to reject you time and again."

He went quiet for stretched moments, and his slow steps soon matched the pained beat of my heart.

"I hid it." His tone changed, lowered. "I loathed you while I loved you, as it was the only way to get what I needed. To be free, I needed my birthright." He gestured across the room. "This throne and the pytherion army."

Although what he'd confessed seared straight through my flesh to the core of who I was, I couldn't believe him. Although the proof glared in the broken wards surrounding the Unseelie kingdom, I refused to believe him.

"To steal them, you needed me to eradicate the wards." My eyes burned, but I didn't let them fill. "You needed me to fall in love with Vane."

And for that to happen, Atakan needed to make sure I didn't love him.

"Yes." He halted with his back to me. "I was supposed to let you go to him."

I frowned at his back. "That day in the woods…"

"I was watching you," he confirmed. "Waiting." His voice turned lethally silken. "Anticipating that you'd wander into enemy hands, just as I needed you to."

"But you stopped me."

Silence.

"You stopped me," I said again, harsher. "You took me into that garden shed, Atakan, and you—"

He whirled as he growled, "And accepted that I couldn't fucking do it." His chest rose and fell sharply. He dragged a hand through his hair, held it there as he gazed up at the muraled ceiling. "You were mine." His eyes returned to me, ablaze with the anger roughening his voice. "I knew then that I would rather remain trapped for eternity than let anyone think you're theirs."

I didn't want to believe that either, yet the heated memories were proof that he spoke true.

Casting his gaze to the throne room floor, he shook his head. "But then you made your own way there." He hummed. "Words cannot describe how it felt to discover that you hadn't simply fled, but that you'd ended up in the Unseelie realm after all."

Recalling what Pholly had told me that night in the city, how he'd reacted to my absence, I struggled to look at him.

Atakan stepped closer.

So close, I was given the mercy of looking at his clean-shaven chin and those ever-tempting lips. "Words cannot describe what I felt when I sensed the fractures in those wards—what it meant that I could finally reach you."

Guilt I shouldn't feel, for I'd asked for none of this, cinched tight around my chest.

"I expected to loathe you in earnest, but one look at you was all I needed..." His fingertips brushed my hand. "You're still mine, dread. Now, you will forever be just mine."

He was right. Even without the bindings of this bond and marriage, I was irrefutably his. No matter how much I'd tried to deny it, I was undeniably in love with him.

Perhaps I always had been.

But although it had failed to protect me, I couldn't simply drop the armor I'd worn for all these years. I couldn't just accept all he'd said, no matter how true it was. I couldn't surrender to this love after so many years of fighting it.

I didn't know how.

Gentle fingers clasped my chin. "Your heart is beating so fast." He lifted it to search my watery eyes. "Dreaded Mildred, don't you see?" His head lowered. "My entire life has been a game of survival, and now..." His finger stroked beneath my chin, tilting it until our noses skimmed and our lips nearly touched. "I win."

Something within me both healed and bled at the relief staining his voice.

I cupped his cheek and slid my thumb over it. "Congratulations." Our eyes met as I kissed him, a quick caress before murmuring, "King."

Then I left him with his crown and his throne.

Thirty-Six

"Your wolf-cat has stolen this evening's beef." Yawning, I sat up on the bed. "I told you she was clever."

"Yes, *clever*," Bernie emphasized. "Not a pain in everyone's ass."

"Spoken like a true queen."

"You can certainly talk."

I made a wide-eyed face at Millicent, who'd just woken from a nap on my bed, then looked over at her mother.

Bernie's flustered cheeks returned to their usual coloring as her annoyance ebbed. She leaned against my chest of drawers, a feeding cloth slung over her shoulder. "As much as having you where I can see you is magical for my stress levels, queens don't hide in other castles, butter."

"I'm not hiding." It was mostly true.

I was simply waiting. Also mostly true.

"Well, whatever it is you're doing, just make sure it doesn't lead to those dragon beasts descending upon our lands." She walked to the bed to collect her daughter. "I require at least five years of peace until this one is sleeping through the night."

Aghast, I asked, "You believe it will take her that long?"

"It took you four years, and she's stubborn." On her way out, she added pointedly, "Just like you."

I fell back onto the bed, inhaling the sweet scent of Millicent. As her presence did, it calmed the turmoil within me.

But only for so long.

My tea was soon delivered, and I stared at the heat rising from the white teacup. The pungent mint-like aroma was still too thick. So I waited and attempted to keep my thoughts from straying where they shouldn't as the effects of my last cup began to abate.

Though simply attempting conjured memories that summoned him.

As if he'd been waiting, he hissed into my mind, *Fucking finally*.

My body both tightened and loosened. I tried to think of adorable Millicent, but there was no forcing him out now.

His shared thought crooned, *I didn't take you for a coward, dread.*

My heart thrashed. A mere week had passed since I'd indeed fled from Cloud Castle like a coward. I'd made Pholly vanish me, knowing she wouldn't fear the repercussions.

Eyes closing, I swallowed. The ache was expected. It had been a constant since I'd returned to Nephryn. But the instant bite of yearning…

It drew blood.

Why are you blocking me from your mind? Atakan asked. *Better yet, why aren't you here, feeding me your sweet spite and taking my cock?*

He knew why I wasn't there.

So I reached over and sipped some tea, unable to resist the chance to prod him. *When did you turn into a pytherion for the first time?*

All I heard was my own wonderings over his whereabouts, and I almost believed the tea had taken effect. I swallowed another mouthful, set the teacup in the saucer, and flopped onto my bed.

I was almost ten years, he finally shared. *I followed a hare into the woods and killed it with a rock.*

My nose crinkled.

As if he knew, he sounded amused. *Perhaps it was the blood, or merely the thrill of the hunt, but night fell over me in the middle of the afternoon. It swallowed me whole.* There was a pause. *Tried to rip me apart with invisible teeth that yanked at my bones.*

Imagining the horror of such vast magic, I turned onto my side and toyed with a loose thread in the lilac comforter.

Cordenya, who'd been watching me play, searched the woods when she heard me. She found me writhing upon the ground, half of my body scales and claws and the other half skin. My fear had created too much resistance to change entirely.

My finger ceased moving. All of me tensed.

As I cried and pleaded for her to fix me, she coaxed me back into my skin by calming me. She said I didn't need fixing, but made me swear not to tell anyone, certainly not my father.

How did you keep it hidden?

A potion. Maybe four years later, I ceased taking it and shifted properly. I learned how to control it, and when I couldn't, I vanished so deep into the mountains, only other beasts would know a pytherion lurked there.

What he'd shared echoed through my mind, and again, I thought the tea had pushed him out.

But then I heard him. *Did you leave because I didn't tell you my beastly secret?*

I smiled at the teacup on my nightstand. *You know that's not why I left.*

More silence. Then, *Well, now that you've seen the fresh babe, you can come back.*

And she's beautiful, thank you for asking.

A soft snarl. *Come to me, and we'll discuss anything you like.*

Anything? I taunted.

The word was punctuated by a growl. *Anything.*

Why? Do you miss me, husband?

I miss playing with you.

I rolled my eyes and gave that no response.

I could have sworn he sighed. *Obviously, I do.* A moment passed, my heart failing to beat. *Miss you.*

My fingers drifted to my mouth, and that yearning birthed flames within my chest. I found the courage to ask, *You killed Vorx, didn't you?*

As a slow-moving warmth relaxed my limbs, I was answered by silence. The tea had taken effect.

But I didn't need an answer. Atakan might have carried wounds from his mother's abandonment, but he'd made sure Vorx had paid the price for them.

My hand squeezed harder and pumped faster as my thumb brushed the vein under my shaft.

Breath sawed between my teeth as I imagined her splayed beneath me. Soft yellow hair curled between those large breasts, tendrils kissing those rosy nipples. Perfect mouth bloodied and bruised by my own. Thighs spread, my seed oozing from that pretty little cunt…

Groaning low, I dropped my head back over the bathing tub's rim as my hips jerked.

My eyes flew open.

Night still shrouded my bedchamber, the white flowers painted upon the stone ceiling aglow in the dark.

Spying, dread?

You summoned me, and I do hope you're not laying in that water.

I'm saving it for my disobedient creature's return. She's going to lap at it while I fuck her from behind.

Though I had no interest in drinking bath water, I shivered and bit my lip.

Aroused, aren't you? His rasped laugh was menacing. *Glistening, I'll bet.*

I didn't confirm nor deny. *I was sleeping until you rudely entered my dreams by thinking of me while you pleasured yourself.*

Desperate times call for pleasurable measures. I'll do whatever it takes to get what I need.

I don't know if I believe you.

You've seen as much.

I have indeed.

Come here and taunt me. I promise not to punish you until you bleed, he lied with feigned sweetness. *I just want to push my cock inside you.*

And that's all?

And then I'll leave it there, so deep and still, while you clench around me and tug at the silk binding your wrists to the bedpost.

Atakan…

You'll say my name just like that while I bite your tits and make you come by tormenting your clit, over and over. Anger made each word more graveled. *You'll stay stuffed full of my cock and swollen from pleasure until you admit how foolish you were to run—*

You sound incredibly frustrated. Intense arousal flushed my skin from head to toe. But he couldn't see or scent it, and I refused to let him win when I'd gone this far. *Hasn't Ruelle returned yet?*

Silence.

I almost left the bed, fury halting my breathing and screaming through my mind as I imagined the worst.

Atakan chuckled.

I reached for the cold tea on my nightstand, drinking a large gulp when his voice entered my head again. *I never fucked her, dread. From the moment you first stepped foot in this castle, I never fucked anyone but you.*

I frowned. *First?*

Must I repeat myself?

Swiping my hand through my hair, I lowered on my side over the bed, grateful he couldn't witness my relief. *You can find pleasure without fucking.*

Indeed. From hearing my defiant mate say fucking. A throaty groan blistered my blood. *And from palming my cock to thoughts of ramming it down her delicate throat.*

I knew without asking that he was touching himself again.

Triumphant, I smiled until I remembered, *You spent the night in her room.* It shouldn't have mattered. We hadn't been mated. We hadn't been married.

We hadn't even liked one another.

Intentional, he informed smoothly. *To keep the loathing alive. Once she ceased pouting and fell asleep, I left.*

More silence.

Your jealousy is delicious.

I was merely curious.

If you're still curious, come and see for yourself that I'm all alone and immensely miserable.

I saw just fine.

Yet I see nothing. So fucking selfish, he purred silkily.

I turned onto my back, tempted to touch myself. Tempted to ask him to come and get me as I asked instead, *Are you truly miserable?*

I waited. Then waited some more before remembering I'd had some tea.

Though, not for the first time, I wished I hadn't. But games were no fun when you could easily share your thoughts of someone into their mind and risk them discovering your motives.

Perhaps even your cowardice.

This game was my last remaining shield. There were no more excuses and strategies to use as weapons. Atakan was no longer my enemy. He no longer needed me, and he never had. The unconquerable didn't need insurance.

He'd simply wanted to marry me.

In the days spent trapped in a home that felt nothing like it did within my memories, I hid from all that held me prisoner. The undeniable truths and the insurmountable fears.

And the desire to return to where I never expected to belong.

Thirty-Seven

Three weeks wasn't a long time for faeries. Yet waiting for Mildred to make her next move was a true taste of immortality.

A dull, aching, and maddening eternity.

I'd believed she'd left me in that throne room to return to the festivities, and that we would play-fight some more when she grew tired of suffering through the fanfare. Preferably with our bodies.

Only for Pholly to inform me that she'd vanished Mildred to Nephryn to visit her sister.

A visit shouldn't have taken three horrendous weeks. And someone who was merely visiting should have no issue with correspondence. Ceaselessly, I'd waited for thoughts of me so that I could share some of my own.

But I'd reached Mildred's mind only twice.

I might have been monstrously arrogant, but I wasn't wrong to believe that she would never stop thinking about me.

A concoction of thistle and hopeleaf, our healer had told me. It kept unwanted guests from prying into people's minds—popular many years ago among those with a mating bond they didn't want.

Ours was not a bond unwanted. So I'd then sent my troublesome Mildred a letter. Short, no-nonsense. *You have two choices—stop drinking that rotting tea or come back.*

No letter had been sent in return. No indication of her thoughts reopening to me.

And still no Mildred in my damned castle.

Pholly had vehemently warned against vanishing to the human lands to snatch her back. She'd said Mildred needed time, and I'd demanded to know what she knew and when they had spoken.

She'd claimed they hadn't, then rolled her eyes and said I was as obtuse as I was ruthless and to use my brain.

I'd told her to scrunch the parchment she'd been drawing on and shove it in her drivel-spouting mouth. But after more days of nothing, I'd reluctantly taken to pondering why Mildred wouldn't wish to be here.

Wouldn't wish to be with me.

And I'd determined it had nothing to do with the Unseelie king who'd taken two weeks to lick his wounds before signing the treaty I'd been preparing for the past year.

So here I was—staring at three guards. Two of whom looked ready to offer me their weapons rather than use them.

I poked the tip of the sword closest to me, and pushed it down. "Take me to your queen."

After gaping at me for wasteful seconds, they led me through the foyer and into halls that were far too bright. I refrained from hissing. It was fucking daylight, and every sconce had been lit.

Humans, I reminded myself.

Their senses must be abysmal indeed.

We reached a sitting room, and I was momentarily distracted by the terrace beyond the windows lining the hall. The same gardens where I'd taken my first look at the princess who would one day become my queen.

A guard entered first, announcing my arrival to the stunned human woman.

Her husband, Royce, was absent. A white musical table I vaguely recalled being referred to as a piano gleamed in the corner of the apricot and cream room. I pondered whether it was the one I'd seen in their ballroom the evening Mildred poisoned me.

"You have no wards," I said by way of greeting and flicked my fingers at the guards. They frowned but moved back toward the doors. "Anyone could just stroll on in here."

Bernadette set a squawking babe upon the settee behind her. "We don't often have faerie visitors this far east, King Atakan."

"There are faeries living in this realm." Though skies knew why.

"None with the ability to vanish into someone's home," she said pointedly.

I smiled with all of my teeth.

It fell when she picked up the babe and walked over to me. "What may we assist you with?"

"You know exactly why I'm here."

"Indeed." She struggled with the bodice of her gown while holding the babe. She didn't ask—she thrust the creature at me and demanded, "Hold her for a moment."

"Me?" I blinked.

"Unless you want my breasts to fall out of this hideous maternity gown due to your impeccable—"

I took the squirming creature before she could finish that sentence. Mostly because I didn't think Mildred would appreciate her mate seeing another female's breasts.

And a tiny bit because the hormones this queen exuded were a touch frightening.

Milk dribbled over the babe's chin as I held it suspended in the air before me. Ruffles decorated its sinisterly small form. A miniature nightgown of sorts, I concluded.

It made an odd sound and squeezed its eyes closed.

Royce arrived and halted in the doorway, breathing heavily as if he'd run through the halls to save his spawn and wife from my evil clutches.

"There." The human queen sighed and turned back to me. "Oh, my poor dear." She had a tinkering laugh. I didn't hate it, but it wasn't as nice as her sister's. "Hold her properly. She won't bite."

Her husband, reeking of fear, walked three steps into the room as he made an embarrassing attempt at a joke. "If she does, it won't hurt. She has no teeth."

His wife was kind enough to laugh.

I held the creature close, and dared to push the overabundant nest of lacy white material from its small mouth so that it could breathe. The creature cooed, a tiny hand punching toward my fingers.

As soon as they touched, I took them away, but I quickly gave them back when its lower lip bulged. "What is its name?"

"*Her* name," Bernadette said firmly. "We wanted to call her Mildred, but Mildred said she needed her own name, so we agreed on Millicent."

"Interesting," I lied, then lowered my head to take a better whiff of that smell. "Why does it smell so delicious?"

"Please don't eat her."

My eyes rose, thinning upon the male this land called their king. "Hilarious."

The babe stiffened, and I peered down at its reddening face. It twisted in my arms as if trying to break free. Before I could determine what it was trying to accomplish, a far less pleasant scent filled my nostrils.

The creature relaxed and gurgled, evidently relieved.

I held it away from me. "I do believe it just soiled itself."

The human king hurried over, taking the smelly babe from my outstretched hands without touching them.

I brushed them on my pants, then informed Bernadette, "I'm going to collect my wife."

"Uh, wait." She scrambled for words. "You cannot just *take* her, Atakan."

I huffed. "Believe me, I know." I walked on, wanting to escape the reek in the room. "We'll need to duel a little first."

She whispered, "Duel?" to her husband.

He mumbled, "How should I know what faeries do?"

Due to stepping out onto the terrace to breathe some untainted air, it took only a minute to find her.

Her scent reached me immediately, carried by the breeze and accompanied by the nudge that always warned when she was near. Since we'd accepted the bond, it was now more of a tremble.

One Mildred felt, too. She looked over from where she sat across the grounds against a tree.

The same tree we'd stood under when we'd first met.

I'd loathed her then.

Almost as much as I loved her now.

The felynx dozing upon the grass beside Mildred leaped to her feet when she heard my approach. Her lips peeled back, and she snarled.

"Adorable," I said dryly and walked right past the little beast.

Mildred petted her behind the ear.

The felynx huffed and sat, but her swishing tail and flattened ears conveyed her immense irritation as I stood beside Mildred.

I had hoped to be rid of the unfortunate consequence of Mildred's time in The Bonelands. Knowing she would never forgive me, I'd kept my claws and teeth to myself.

"If it isn't my monstrous husband," Mildred drawled, yet her eyes shimmered as she gazed up at me.

"If it isn't my misbehaving wife." I scowled at the book on the grass and lifted a brow at her. "Who's ignoring me for a book."

"I do believe I'm staring at you."

"I do believe you can do better after leaving me to rot for three weeks." I held out my hand.

She eyed it as if it were a trap but placed her hand in mine after a teasing moment. Just one touch made the restless beast within me settle, and I pulled her to her feet.

Our eyes clashed. A tremulous breath parted her lips, and her eyes dampened even as she poked, "Better?"

Relief softened my scathing tone. "Not nearly, dread."

Her gaze fell to my clenched jaw, then my throat when I struggled to swallow. Struggled to form words although I'd had so much I'd intended to say.

All of it became dust on the breeze with her hand in mine, her eyes eating their fill of my features, and her thudding heartbeat and addictive mouth so close.

Fuck, I wanted to kiss her. Needed to push her up against the tree and lift her skirts to see if she'd yearned for me, thought of me, dreamed of me as much as I had her.

Mildred sniffed, then smiled so brightly, I wondered if this might be easier than I'd thought. That is, until she said, "You met Millicent."

"I did."

"You held her," she said, almost accusatory as her eyes rounded. "I can smell it."

"I might have been forced to due to a situation I failed to foresee."

She frowned, then understood and laughed.

The felynx let out a whined grumble and trotted toward the woods beyond the gardens.

But I wasn't sure I breathed as the soft yet bird-like melody of that laughter seeped beneath my flesh and rib cage.

Mildred's smile waned as she squeezed my hand. "I'm assuming you didn't come here just to be accosted by a helpless babe."

"Certainly fucking not."

Another laugh. She stepped closer, tilting her head back as she saw right through me and goaded, "Then why?"

"I'm here to take you home." I grinned, then lied. "As it occurred to me that you have no means of vanishing, so therefore, you're stuck here."

"Stuck," she repeated.

I nodded once. "Of course, I did wonder if you were already on your way via carriage, but I thought it wise to check with your sister first."

Her eyes danced. "And if I had been on my way?"

"I would have found you based on when you'd left and perhaps even saved you from suffering the rest of the journey."

"Perhaps?" she asked.

"I suppose we'll never know."

"That would have been uncharacteristically gallant of you."

I no longer had any idea what we were talking about, let alone what I needed to say. "That's why I said perhaps."

"I see." She withheld another laugh but smiled.

And I wanted to lick all of those pretty teeth.

It was time to hurry this along, so I blurted the obvious, "I need you to come back, Mildred."

Her smile remained, though it ceased illuminating her eyes as she waited.

"I might not care for much of anything outside of my desires, but that doesn't mean I'm completely heartless." Her hand settled on my hip, and my clinical tone roughened. "That doesn't mean I cannot love you." I clasped her chin, my head lowering. "That doesn't mean I don't need you to be as obsessively in love with me as I am with you."

Birdsong joined our racing heartbeats in the quiet that followed.

Mildred blinked over the sheen coating her eyes and looked at the ground. "And what if I can't do that?"

"Then I wouldn't be standing here." I tilted her chin until she looked at me again. "Asking you to trust that you can."

My audacious creature curled her petal-perfect lips. "Is that what you're doing?"

"What I'm doing is collecting you, but I thought it necessary to make a sickly fool of myself first."

For torturous seconds, those big green eyes just searched mine. "Well…" Her smirk turned into a smile. "You've certainly taken your time."

Taken aback, I cocked my head. "You were waiting?"

This devious wife of mine didn't need to answer. She skimmed her teeth over that plush lower lip, and my hard cock twitched against the confines of my pants.

I scowled and almost growled, "Then why didn't you return my letter and tell me?" An incredulous laugh left me. "Or at least stop drinking that tea to let me access your thoughts?"

"Where's the fun in that, my king?"

Her taunting couldn't distract me. She might have been telling the truth—that she had indeed been playing with me from afar—but she'd omitted the reason.

Mildred was afraid. Not of me, I knew. She simply didn't know what to do now that she no longer needed to survive. Now that she needed to live.

Now that she was free to love instead of loathe.

My ire was replaced by an overwhelming heat that expanded the organ in my chest.

Knowing exactly what she needed now, I glowered at her until she shifted closer, uncertainty furrowing her golden brows.

Then I slid my fingers into her hair, my other hand over her back, and I hauled her to me. I kissed her, once and bruising, and bit her lip. "Here I was…" Against her mouth, I whispered, "Thinking the games had ended."

Her soft hand cupped my cheek. The breeze stirred her long hair over her shoulder, allowing a better view of the confidence coloring her cheeks. "I hope they never do."

"Never?" I challenged.

Her arms coiled around my neck, and when she rose onto her toes and breathed, "Never," I caught her lovely ass and lifted her.

"A dangerously long time," I warned.

She wrapped her legs around me. "It had better be."

Holding her against the same tree we'd stood under when I'd loathed her, I placed my forehead on hers and promised, "Then far be it from me to disappoint the queen who loves me."

She laughed.

Relieved I'd broken through that fear, I whispered daringly, "Tell me, dread."

"Tell you what, monster?"

I snarled, then bit the tip of her nose, which earned me another luminescent laugh.

But she sobered when she found me waiting, impatient and likely looking as desperate as I felt. I failed to care. She was the only thing I truly cared about.

And as her smile faded while she touched my cheeks with the pads of her fingers, I knew I would do anything to ensure she always looked at me like that. With a wonder that let me believe I was the only thing she wanted to adore for the rest of her days.

"If I do, what do I get in return?" she asked, yet the fear hidden from her playful tone crept into her eyes.

It wouldn't deter me. "Tell me, and you'll find out."

"Fine." Taking my cheeks, she pressed her nose to mine and said in a rush, "I love you, Atakan."

My chuckle made her face redden, but I kissed her before she could retreat and crooned, "Very good. Now, are you ready for your reward?"

She nodded, waiting.

"Here it comes…" I cleared my throat far more dramatically than necessary and declared, "I love you, too."

Her eyes narrowed as I grinned in victory.

But her feigned displeasure couldn't fool me. Nor could it win against the joy spreading from her pounding heart to her eyes and curling mouth.

Still, I taunted, "Disappointed?"

"I've yet to decide." She repeated words I'd once said to her. "Perhaps you should take me home so I can properly ascertain how I feel."

The beast within me roared as I stared into those green eyes.

Then I kissed her, and I didn't stop until she was stripping free of her gown back in our tower, her felynx sadly left behind.

'Epilogue

TWENTY YEARS LATER

In the far north of Sky Mountains, pytherions flocked atop cliffsides and soared over the Moss Sea.

Upon a hillside overlooking a small valley of wildflowers, we watched them and the setting sun. The latter melted into the edge of the ocean and gilded Surella's dark green scales.

From where she'd perched at the opposite side of the valley, she eyed the beast I leaned against, always curious and close whenever we visited.

Atakan's tail curled before me on the grass. The spiked tip shifted, squashing the wildflowers our daughter insisted on feeding him every time we brought her with us.

He'd wake bemoaning the state of his stomach tomorrow, yet he ate every one without complaint.

Lumina giggled and clapped her tiny hands, then trudged over the grass to collect more.

Her father didn't take his bronze eyes from her, although the beasts in these mountains would never dare harm either of us, and I petted his scales.

He huffed, the steam from his nostrils dissipating before Lumina returned. The wind spun her creamy blond hair around her face, buying her father some time as she lost her flowers while trying to free herself from the tangled curls.

Smiling, I gave my attention back to my book—another recommendation from Daylia.

When the first had arrived six months after the treaty was signed, with notes tucked into her favorite chapters, I'd known what it was.

I'd accepted the olive branch by reading and returning the

book with my own notes. Ever since, when we read something we loved, we shared it.

Atakan munched on more wildflowers, making a show of it to make Lumina laugh from her stomach and swipe at her eyes. She touched his snout, saying, "Good beasty," then hurried to fetch him more.

The grass swayed as the ocean breeze gathered force, revealing something dark within the valley's bright reds, golds, and greens.

A shadow.

Not a threat. Rather, a greeting of sorts.

I smiled warmly at the dark tendril and lifted my book slightly from my knees. The shadow wobbled, appearing to grow with the information it absorbed. Then it vanished, presumably to pass on my greeting and well-being to its king.

It wasn't the first time I'd glimpsed one, and I hoped it wouldn't be the last.

I hadn't seen Vane since the end of the war between our realms, but I assumed he was well. I trusted Daylia would let it be known in her notes otherwise, though it was none of my business. While that might have been true, I sometimes wondered if he was happy. For I was, and despite all he'd done, I wanted that for him.

The wards surrounding the Unseelie kingdom remained.

Many were sure they would never be removed. But over the years, witches and magic wielders had found ways to widen the gaps. This gave hope that there would come a day when the wards did not exist.

The pytherions continued to breed.

A handful of hatchlings arrived in the wake of each spring. The pytherions could roam wherever they wished, but Atakan said they would never roam far from where he dwelled.

He was their alpha.

Everything he'd done had been to free himself from his deadly secret—until that secret could become his greatest weapon.

A guardian against war between the realms. An Unseelie and

Seelie king who could not be challenged. Instead, he was as feared as he was revered.

A monster, most certainly.

Atakan ruled with the ruthlessness and cold apathy that made him untouchable regardless of the form he took. He included me in any issues this kingdom faced that might satiate my hungry survival instincts, and I sparred with him to satiate his bloodlust during dull lulls in politics.

Atakan was more than my mate—he was the edge I sharpened my armor upon and the safety I surrendered my softness to.

I'd survived him because he'd allowed it.

But I truly lived because I'd allowed him to prove he wasn't heartless.

We'd been blessed with a daughter who'd slept through the night since she'd arrived screaming into this world four years ago—but only if she slept in our rooms.

As soon as Lumina learned how to walk, she crept into our bed, forcing us to get more creative with how we found time alone.

Though Pholly, Elion, and I had spent weeks decorating Lumina's rooms on the third floor, Atakan hadn't the heart to make her use them. Often, I'd lay awake after reading late into the night, Meadow snoring upon the cushions at the foot of the bed, watching them sleep. Lumina's little body always ended up sprawled over Atakan's, her long curls smothering his mouth.

While awake, Lumina was just as cunning and cutthroat as her father, and while asleep, just as secretly and intensely adoring too.

Atakan found me mere minutes after I'd hidden from him.

He ensured the throne room doors latched behind him. "Again," he said.

So perhaps it wasn't all that creative. But it was my favorite.

With a sly smile, I uncrossed my legs slowly, lifting them as I did. I tapped my nails on the arms of the throne and said, "Would you rather I play a prisoner in the dungeon again?"

It had become a second favorite of mine since we'd put a torture table down there. Although we seldom had real prisoners, Atakan had warned that it was not to be used by anyone but him.

I was certain the entire castle knew what that table was used for, and I liked being used on it so much that I didn't care.

Atakan removed his shirt. Each step was intentionally unhurried as he tossed the creamy froth onto the floor and dragged his thumb across his lower lip. Though I wasn't seated on the throne he'd had made for me two decades ago, but on his, he still said, "I like you right where you are."

I arched a brow. "I'm not sure I believe you."

He tried to turn the tables. "Would you like me to show you just how much I like it?"

"I think I would," I whispered while bunching my nightgown.

He unfastened his black pants, and my eyes rose from the smattering of golden hair leading inside them. They took their time roaming his defined abdominals and broad chest.

As he climbed onto the dais, I met his hooding gaze and smiled. Before he could make his next move, I stopped tapping my nails, spread my legs, and said, "Kneel."

Atakan stilled.

His hands fell lax at his sides. His eyes gleamed wholly green, every inch of him defying the challenge.

But he wouldn't.

"It would be my pleasure." He dropped to his knees before his throne, slid his hands over my inner thighs toward my sex, and looked up at me with sinister intent.

I ran my fingers through his hair, the combed-back strands falling into a hypnotic mess. "Something as pretty as you is bound to lie."

"Then by all means"—he gripped my thighs—"allow me to tell you the truth."

I laughed as he tugged me forward to the edge of the throne. But it turned into a moan when his tongue met my core.

He stopped. "Need I remind you how much this room echoes?"

Though I desperately wanted him to resume, I taunted, "I think you should."

He bit the inside of my thigh.

I squeaked and laughed, the sounds indeed bouncing off the tapestry-bedecked walls. "Fine," I panted. "I'll behave."

His fingers crawled over my stomach, gathering my nightgown over my breasts. When they reached my mouth, he ordered, "Suck."

I did, and he groaned, eyes stuck to my lips as they wrapped around the two digits. His nostrils flared. Still staring, he rasped, "If you keep them there like a good little queen, maybe I'll put them inside you."

I flicked his fingers with my tongue, smiling around them.

He gave me a crooked grin, then pulled my body up to his mouth until I relied on him to keep from sliding off the wooden chair. One leg draped over his shoulder while he held the other wide. He feasted languidly at first, like always, savoring every morsel of the excitement exuded from his exquisite torture.

As my breaths grew noisy, his fingers pressed against my tongue and bottom teeth. Rapture crested, and I bit down on them, rocking into his mouth.

Atakan groaned and withdrew his fingers from my mouth.

Then he plunged them into my body. His mouth latched onto my clit, tongue flicking.

I dissolved so thoroughly and moaned so loud that he pulled his fingers from my body and caught me in his lap. His mouth captured mine. He smothered my next moan by covering my lips entirely with his, and reached between us to free himself from his pants. He tore away to say, "Sit."

I clenched around him as I did. He let out a ragged sigh before he stole my mewl with his tongue. It swept into my mouth, forcing me to taste myself, and then he seized my legs.

He rose and held me tight until he was seated upon his throne.

Then his hand glided up my back, collecting my silk nightgown over my head. He tossed it to the floor. My knees pressed into the cushioned seat as I shifted over him.

Slouched on his throne, he drew lazy circles around my nipples. Although my breasts had changed since having Lumina, he'd only grown more obsessed with them. After lifting the heavy globes and squeezing, he dropped them and looked up, waiting.

Knowing what he wanted, I tipped his chin to put my lips on his.

His eyes stayed closed, but he twitched inside me when I laid my forehead against his. He inhaled deeply, and a rumble climbed his throat as he exhaled. His hands rubbed my back. One tangled in my hair at my nape, and the other grasped my hip.

Then he straightened.

He tilted my head back by my hair and sank his teeth into the curve of my neck—at the same time, his other hand hooked over my shoulder and pulled my body down.

My back arched.

He licked my throat as I struggled to draw breath, laughing low. "For making me kneel."

I squirmed. He bit me again. This time, on my collarbone. As he loosened his hold, I pushed my hands against his chest and grinned at him. "You could have denied me."

He scowled as if I'd struck him.

Still smiling, I traced his bladed jaw until it relaxed. Then I kissed the tip of his nose. "Don't pout."

"Don't say asinine things."

I laughed and watched his annoyance fade even more.

He collected my hair behind my shoulders. "For you, I would stay on my knees until they bled your name."

Breath feathered past my lips. I laid them over his and whispered, "I've tamed you so well."

His laughter was deep and rasped as he gripped my nape. "My dreadful, daring, devastating creature…" He kissed me so softly, the truth he unleashed was irrefutable as I melted atop him. "I've tamed you."

If you enjoyed Amid Clouds and Bones, you might also enjoy another enemies to lovers standalone…

The king of wolves was more beast than man, more tyrant than king, and so much more than he seemed.

Raised to avenge his murdered parents, he'd been trained and conditioned until nothing but violence and hatred lined the walls of his dead heart.

For nearly four years, I'd done all I could to help my kingdom as we faced the wolf king's unconquerable evil—hardly anything at all. As the only heir to the Gracewood line, I'd been relegated to menial tasks that would keep me and my secrets safe.

A chance to do more than fret behind our castle walls arrived when I breached them after overhearing my parents' plans for my future. Fleeing, I unknowingly raced into a fate we'd all desperately hoped to avoid.

By the time I saw him coming, it was far too late.
For my family. For my kingdom.
For my heart.

Before I could staunch the bleeding, the king had me under his giant paw, and one wrong move after another caused those razor-sharp claws to sink deeper and deeper beneath my bruised skin.

I might have been trapped, naive, and furious, but I still had a kingdom to save—and a plan.

Yet when we collided, the bloodshed, the fear, his atrocities… all of it dissolved like stardust upon the night sea.

The stars had mapped out our destiny, but it didn't matter what they or my heart wanted.

I refused to see the enigmatic male, the heartless lost boy with a soul beneath the flesh of a monster.

The savage king who'd destroyed everything I loved would fall—even if my heart fell with him.

The Savage and the Swan is available now.

MORE FANTASY ROMANCE BY ELLA

The Deadly Divine Duet
The Royals Duet
The Savage and the Swan
The Wolf and the Wildflower
Kingdom of Villains

NEVER MISS A THING!

Follow on Instagram
www.instagram.com/ellafieldsauthor

Website
www.ellafields.net

Printed in Dunstable, United Kingdom